"Tells us more about Libbie's romance and adventures with George Armstrong Custer than readers are likely to find in a dozen histories."
—Dee Brown, author of *Bury My Heart at Wounded Knee*

"*Libbie* is probably the book Mrs. Custer would have written had she not been determined to protect her husband's name. It offers a new slant on the Custer story."
—Elmer Kelton, author of *The Far Canyon*

"Judy Alter paints a vivid portrait of Libbie Custer. . . . Alter is such a talented storyteller that . . . readers will find themselves developing a kinship with Libbie."
—*The Oakland Press*

"An entertaining novel."
—*Booklist*

"Vivid and exciting . . . Ms. Alter has done an outstanding job of making Mrs. George Armstrong Custer come alive. All in all, *Libbie* is brilliant in its reconstruction of the times, the people, and the American dream as it was lived during the days of Manifest Destiny."
—James Ward Lee, director, Center for Texas Studies

"A fine work of the imagination applied to known historical facts. Judy Alter has written a keen and perceptive novel."
—Larry L. King, author of
The Best Little Whorehouse in Texas

"A wondrous, intimate story of an unsung heroine of the West."
—*Romantic Times*

"A candid portrait of an American legend. *Libbie* brings to life a personality and a period of history in a way only a good storyteller can. . . . One comes away from this tale with a hearty respect for the loyalty and love Libbie bore her famous husband."

—Clay Reynolds, author of *Franklin's Crossing*

"Rings . . . authentically true. . . . Brilliant and memorable. Kudos to Ms. Alter for a refreshingly unique story."

—*Affaire de Coeur*

"Between hard covers and soft, on the screen and on the tube, we have studied Custer to extinction. Judy Alter surprises us, however: she looks into his heart through the heart of Libbie Custer, the wife he loved who loved him, and what she finds is new. I congratulate her. I recommend *Libbie*."

—Glendon Swarthout, author of *The Shootist*

"Finely written."

—*San Jose Mercury News*

"A marvelous novel . . . more readable than any history book. It will entertain as well as give the reader new insight into a familiar figure in U.S. history."

—*Rendezvous*

"Superb historical re-creation . . . a haunting, touching, beautifully written tale."

—*Spotlight*

LIBBIE

Also by Judy Alter

A BALLAD FOR SALLIE

MATTIE

LIBBIE

Judy Alter

BANTAM

New York   Toronto   London   Sydney   Auckland

LIBBIE

A Bantam Book

PUBLISHING HISTORY
Bantam trade paperback edition published March 1994
Bantam mass market edition/May 1995

ISBN 0-553-56950-3

Published simultaneously in the United States and Canada

Bantam Books are published by Bantam Books, a division of Bantam
Doubleday Dell Publishing Group, Inc. Its trademark, consisting of the
words "Bantam Books" and the portrayal of a rooster, is Registered in
U.S. Patent and Trademark Office and in other countries. Marca
Registrada. Bantam Books, 1540 Broadway, New York, New York 10036.

PRINTED IN THE UNITED STATES OF AMERICA
RAD   0 9 8 7 6 5 4 3 2 1

For Colin, Megan,
Jamie & Jordan
with love and thanks

SUPER CROWN #572

04/14/95   12:36   F   24   14688
REFUNDS WITHIN 30 DAYS WITH RECEIPT ONLY
           MAGAZINE SALES FINAL

PUBLISHER PRICE	CROWN SAVINGS	CROWN PRICE
GENTLEMANS DAUGHTER		
1@ 3.99 0821749463	10%	3.59
WOLFE WAGER		
1@ 3.99 0821749455	10%	3.59
LIBBIE A NOVEL OF ELIZA		
1@ 5.99 0553569503	10%	5.39
INNOCENT IMPOSTER		
1@ 4.50 0821749447	10%	4.05
STAR WARS: COURTSHIP OF		
1@ 5.99 0553569376	10%	5.39
SUBTOTAL	$	22.01
SALES TAX @ 8.25%	$	1.82
TOTAL	$	23.83
TENDERED Check	$	23.83

YOUR SAVINGS AT CROWN... $ 2.45

PUBLISHER	CROWN	CROWN
PRICE	SAVINGS	PRICE
GENTLEMANE DAUGHTER		
19 3.99 0821749463	10%	3.59
WOLFE MAGER		
19 3.99 0821749453	10%	3.59
LIBBIE A NOVEL OF ELIZA		
19 5.99 0553569503	10%	5.35
INNOCENT IMPOSTER		
19 4.50 0821749547	10%	4.05
STAR WARS: COURTSHIP OF		
19 5.99 0553569376	10%	5.39
SUBTOTAL	$	22.38
SALES TAX @ 8.25%	$	1.82
TOTAL	$	23.83
TENDERED Check	$	23.83

YOUR SAVINGS AT CROWN... $ 2.45

Author's Note

Elizabeth Bacon Custer left very public records of her life with General George Armstrong Custer. Her three books—*Tenting on the Plains, Boots and Saddles,* and *Following the Guidon*—might fairly be called propaganda pieces, designed to glorify the reputation of the late General Custer. Similarly, biographies of Libbie tend toward idealization, describing her as always good-natured, self-sacrificing, devoted to Custer. Only occasionally—in books about Custer, in some surviving correspondence—do hints surface of conflict in the marriage, of Autie's wandering eye, of perhaps even a glance or two in another direction taken by Libbie herself. What, one wonders, was life really like with the brilliant and erratic boy-general? What kind of woman married him—and then remained so selflessly devoted to him?

This novel will not answer those questions definitively. It is but one attempt to see inside the life of Libbie Custer, and it is, above all, fiction—an attempt to tell a story about life on the frontier and one particular woman there. So, dear reader, read and enjoy, but do not hold the storyteller accountable for some slight deviations from history. The truth of history forms a foundation upon which I've tried to build a novel.

COURTSHIP
AND
MARRIAGE

Chapter One

 I KNEW THAT HISTORY WOULD MAKE A PLAYTHING OF Autie, and when that happened, all my battles would be lost again. Autie rarely lost a battle—save that last big one—and his fights were always glorious, painted on a broad screen by the clamoring newsmen if not by himself. My battles were small and silent and private, but oh! they were important to me, and I had managed to hold the line. I would not see it all wiped away with the muckraking cry that Autie's overweening ambition had led him to disaster at Little Bighorn. I would make sure that the world saw the George Armstrong Custer I wanted seen. Only this private journal—to be burned upon my death—records my own wars.

Twelve years is not very long in a lifetime, yet it seemed my whole life was lived in those brief years of marriage. I had fought battles of my own, hard battles, to marry Autie, and once married, I thought myself the happiest and luckiest of women—married to the great boy-general, the hero of the

Civil War. We would, I knew, grow old together, savoring the best of life, the last for which the first was made, so the poet wrote. I'm not sure when, exactly, that I knew that dream was not to be, that a love as intense as ours could not survive, that two people as willful as we could not be bound so tightly together. And yet, when all was said and done, I would not have traded those twelve years for anything on earth. Were they worth a lifetime? There is no answer, but even to think about it, I must begin earlier, back in Monroe. . . . I remember yet one snowy night when I was but sixteen years old.

Voices woke me—distant, yet loud. For just a moment I froze in fear, and then, shivering, I crept out of bed. There had been an early November snow in Monroe the night before, and the wind off Lake Erie was strong and cold, sneaking in through cracks around the windows. Papa had let the fires die down for the night, and the house had its winter chill. I pulled on my robe and padded to the window, pulling back the lace curtain liner so that I could look out on the street.

At first it seemed empty, with nothing but the moon shining on the snow and glistening off the ruts made during the day by carriages. The street lamp in front of our house gave off a sort of dull glow, as though hopeless against the dark of winter.

Then two men staggered into sight, their arms locked around each other, their voices raised in some kind of unrecognizable song. It was the sound that had wakened me. I watched curiously as they drew into the dim circle of light directly outside our gate. For a moment their very momentum propelled them apart, and laughing and calling loudly, they held their arms out to each other. Then, wobbling, they made their way together again and blundered off down the street, out of the light. I could tell little or nothing about them except that one of them was tall and thin and had extraordinary long blond curls.

When they were gone, I went quietly back to my bed, just in time to hear my father plod up the stairs in his bedroom slippers. "Drunken louts," he muttered, and I could

picture the look of disapproval on his stern face. He would, I
knew, be wearing his long nightshirt, which hung ridiculously
about his knees, and carrying a candle in the brass holder my
mother had once given him. My stepmother, waiting in the
hall outside my door, breathed the question on my mind.

"Who were they?"

"That Custer boy was one of them," Papa said in tones
of disgust. "I didn't know the other one. Come, let's go back
to bed, now that the night is quiet again."

Neither knew that I was awake and had seen the tab-
leau, nor did I ever tell them. I knew "the Custer boy," from
two brief but important encounters in my childhood, but I
had not seen him in several years. Talk in town was that he
was freshly graduated from West Point, an officer in the army
—younger by far than most officers, they said—and he'd
come to Monroe to stay with his sister, Mrs. Reed, while he
was on sick leave. But the Reeds were Methodists, and we
Bacons were Presbyterians, so we never met at church and
seldom anywhere else. If he'd cut off those blond curls, I
wouldn't have known George Armstrong Custer if I'd run
full into him in the street. But ever after that evening there
was a wildness about him that caught my imagination.

Next morning at breakfast Papa asked if I slept well, and
I, thinking he would not talk to me of the scene I'd wit-
nessed, said mischievously, "Something woke me in the
night. Some commotion in the street."

"Young men who'd indulged in whiskey," he said scornfully from behind his newspaper. Papa was a judge, and
somehow he often seemed to sit in judgment on people, even
outside his court. This morning, as usual, he wore his dark-
gray suit with a gold watch chain stretched across his large
middle. His jowls had sunk, as they will in middle-aged men,
and his chin had the look of turkey wattles. My father had
not been a young man even when I was born, and he was
now well into middle age. His voice was stern as he warned
me, "See that you stay away from such kind."

"Yes, Papa," I said, while my imagination was even then
caught by the blond curls. "Do you know who they were?"

"Yes," he said, and stopped cold, making it clear he wouldn't tell me.

"Daughter, you might meet them at some party," my stepmother said, hovering over me, "and we wouldn't want you to be prejudiced against these young men. Surely it was an indiscretion not to be repeated."

No need to tell them that I knew perfectly well who one of the young men was, and that he held a special place in my heart. They knew of neither of my previous encounters with him.

Mama, as I called her, sat opposite Papa at the table, wearing a practical linsey-woolsey wrapper against the cold. But her hair was perfectly groomed, and she had dusted her face with powder. Mama never disagreed with Papa, and sometimes I wanted to demand, "Don't you have a thought of your own? Why do you echo everything Papa says?" She had made Papa happy in the two years since their marriage, but I still burned with resentment that he had not given me a chance to make him happy, that he had taken a second wife after the death of my mother.

We sat, very formally even at breakfast, in the dining room of our large house at the corner of Second and Monroe streets. Behind me, a sideboard held dishes of eggs and bacon and potatoes. Pots of sweet cream butter and apple butter sat before us on the table. Mama rang the tiny bell on the table, and Betsy, the hired girl, bustled in with fresh, hot rolls.

I buttered my roll and let my imagination dwell on those blond curls.

Monroe was a grand town in which to grow up. It was on the Michigan side of Lake Erie, in a country of thick forests, cold winters, and cool summers. It was not a new town, even in the 1850s when I was growing up, and its streets were lined with tall trees, its houses solid and comfortable. Our house had cleanly painted white siding, with bottle-green shutters and a white picket fence that Papa always kept in good repair and fresh paint. In front a neat lawn was surrounded by elm trees, and in the back there were cherry, apple, and pear trees, along with a swing built for me when I was ten.

Monroe had farmers as well as the bankers and merchants who lived in the big houses, and somewhere, off on one edge of town where I never went, people like Betsy lived in one-story wooden houses, gray from weathering without paint, and worked for the people in the big, clean houses on Monroe Street.

The Reeds were among the farmers, and Armstrong, whose parents lived in Ohio, spent summers working for his brother-in-law, David Reed, from the time he was quite young. When he was fourteen, he moved to Monroe to stay with the Reeds and attend the Stebbins Academy for Boys—even then everyone was looking out for Autie's education, though I suspect it was because they hoped he'd be a preacher. Vain hope that! I later heard that he used to hide wicked novels behind his geography book, reading them with relish while he appeared to be studying.

Monroe valued its lakeside setting. You could travel by steamship from Monroe to Buffalo, New York, making the trip much more pleasant than the previous long-way-about over land. Steamships brought their loads of grain and wood and furniture and all manner of things to the wharves on the lakefront. I loved to visit the wharves with Papa—the air blowing off the lake smelled of water and fish and freshness, and the steamships sounded loud horns as they approached. When they were unloaded, the scene was one of confusion—men running everywhere, ship owners shouting at the men who did the unloading, store owners trying to watch out for the goods they had ordered to see that they were handled carefully. Papa once told me the whole process was without order, as though he would have imposed some order on it if he could. I loved the noise, but I never told Papa that.

The railroad came to Monroe, too, so we considered ourselves a major and important town. It reached Monroe in the late 1840s and made us very up-to-date—not all towns in Michigan had trains. Once, when I was about five, Papa took Mother and me on a trip just to the next station, and back on the return train, so we would know what train travel was like. I remembered the noise and cinders, but even more I remembered the sensation of watching trees fly by the window.

Monroe was built around mills—it had flour mills, a woolen mill, and a sawmill. But by the time I was a child, it also had an iron foundry and a tannery, three banks, two mercantile stores, a daily newspaper (which was small but, as Papa said, "informative"), three lawyers and two doctors—a strange proportion—a few other businesses, and six churches. We attended the Presbyterian Church, where the Anglo formality suited Papa perfectly, and at home we prayed together as a family every day. I grew up thinking most folks, at least in Monroe, were that devout and that I was probably the only wayward child whose mind wandered while her father implored the Lord to teach us humility and thanked him for the too-generous bounty he bestowed upon us.

Everyone in town knew the Bacon family, especially Papa, whom they called "the Judge," as though there were no other judge in the world. I was petted and spoiled by the whole town. Everyone fussed over me because I was the Judge's daughter, and then, later, they worried over me because my mother died suddenly the summer I was twelve.

I remember her as bright and laughing and pretty, with dark hair and dark, gentle eyes. When I was little, she sang with me—later when I thought of my mother, the words and melody of "All Through the Night" played over and over in my mind, and I saw her sitting at the edge of my bed, singing softly until I slept. But she stopped singing one day, and a few days later my father came to me, more stern than ever, to tell me that Mother had gone to live with angels.

"Do they sing?" I asked.

"Who?" He was startled.

"Angels," I replied. "Mother won't like it there if they don't sing."

He patted my shoulder awkwardly and wandered away, lost in sadness.

For three days my mother lay in our parlor, wearing her best gray silk, a dress she had dearly loved. I wasn't allowed to see her—Papa thought it would upset me—but her sister, Aunt Harriet Page from Grand Rapids, told me how lovely she looked. Those were her very words, and I tried to smile in appreciation, but I couldn't imagine Mother looking lovely without her smile or her voice.

I wasn't so young and naive that I didn't know about death. I knew that, contrary to singing with angels, Mother was in a coffin—hadn't that very coffin been in our parlor for three days?—and that she would be buried in the earth and that I would never, ever see her again. But no one talked to me about that or even about her—they just fussed over me as though I were five or six. I never asked uncomfortable questions about the grave and eternity, because I knew that Papa would not answer them. But in the night, by myself, I sobbed, brokenhearted, for my mother.

Just as he kept me out of the parlor, Papa didn't allow me to go to Mother's funeral. "It might upset her," I heard him tell the minister. And so three days after he'd told me about Mother and the angels, I found myself alone in that big house with Betsy, who patted me on the head and murmured, "Poor, poor dear" every time she walked by me. I sat in the window seat watching for the people to come back from the graveyard until, frustrated, I slammed out the front door.

"Elizabeth Bacon, you come back in here this minute," Betsy called. "It isn't fitting for you to be outside, them burying your poor dear mother and all."

I ignored her and went to swing on the gate, an activity strictly forbidden by Papa because he said it would pull the gate off its hinges.

"Libbie!" Betsy called again, and again I ignored her.

A young boy, obviously a farmer from his clothes and heavy boots, came sauntering down the street, walking as if he owned it. I recognized him as Armstrong Custer because all the girls at school had twittered over his long blond curls.

"Hey, you Custer boy!" I called, and he turned toward me, smiling. But then his smile faded.

"You're Libbie Bacon, aren't you?"

"Yes," I said.

"Your mother just died, didn't she?"

I swung furiously on the gate. "Yes."

Real tenderness crept into his voice. "I'm sorry," he said. "It must be awful hard on you. Are you all right?"

He was the first person who'd done anything but pat me on the head. I had to bite my lip hard to keep from bursting into sobs. "I'm . . . fine, thank you," I managed to utter.

"No, you're not," he said perceptively. "But you will be. You're strong, I can tell."

No one had ever called me strong—in fact, Papa constantly hinted that I was frail and must take care of myself. Yet here was this strange boy telling me I was strong. Tears streaming down my face, I turned and ran into the house, flying past an openmouthed Betsy to end sobbing into the pillow on my bed.

By the time everyone returned from the cemetery, my tears were dried and the red was gone from my eyes. I wandered through the house letting people pat me on the head and call me "poor, poor dear." But inside I said to myself, *I'm strong.*

Two days after the funeral, Aunt Harriet took me to the cemetery. Papa was shut in his bedroom, where he was to remain for weeks, and I doubt she even told him where she intended taking me.

"It's a nice spot," she said to me, "under a maple, with a cool breeze. It's a place your mother would like."

I wasn't at all convinced of this, but Aunt Harriet meant well, and I went along quietly. The cemetery was pretty, if those places ever can be. It sat on a hillside, ringed on two sides by thick Michigan forests, and in the distance you could see the shining waters of Lake Erie. Mama's gravesite was indeed the kind of place she would have liked—if she were alive and could picnic there. Dead and in the grave, she might not, I thought, be as enthusiastic about it.

I was overcome with sadness, sitting there beside that newly mounded grave with its brave floral pieces and the marked-off space of a headstone yet to come. I had loved my mother a great deal, and I would miss her, but more than that, I was fearful of life without her. I respected Papa, even feared him some, for he was much the disciplinarian in the family, but I was sure that he didn't understand me and that he could never, ever make up for the loss of my mother. Life loomed bleakly before me, and I tried to remember what Armstrong Custer had told me. I hoped he was right.

"Libbie, you're to come to Grand Rapids with me for a few weeks," Aunt Harriet said, busily pulling my clothes out of a wardrobe and sorting them, packing some into a large suitcase. "Let's see, you'll need a warm shawl for evening, and some cotton wrappers will do for daytime. . . . Your mother did have such taste in clothes!" She fingered a flowered cotton wrapper that Mother had had the seamstress make, then put it back in the wardrobe, murmuring, "You can't wear it now. We'll have to get you some black dresses."

The dressmaker was even then at work on several suitable mourning garments for me. The lavender calico, my newest dress, would have to sit in the closet.

"Won't Papa need me?" I asked.

"No, dear," she said. "He's best left alone to deal with his grief."

"And me?"

"You need to have loving family around you," Aunt Harriet said in a wise tone that settled it all.

I wished someone would ask me. I wished for my Papa —to take his arm, tell him I loved him, to listen to him tell me what was right and wrong. I wished most of all for my mother to sing.

I pulled out a heavy woolen shawl and then, defiantly, a flowered silk apron. I might not be able to wear it, but it would comfort me to have something bright with me. Chambray wrappers and muslin short gowns and petticoats followed, and an enormous pile began to accumulate. "How long am I to stay?"

"Several weeks. Until your father is able to arrange things."

Arrange things? Our lives were arranged, I thought. The house would be empty without Mother, but life would go on. "I'll miss the opening of school," I protested.

"You'll begin in Grand Rapids. And then when you get back to . . . when you get back to Monroe, you can catch up on what you've missed. You're a good student, Libbie, aren't you?"

I was a so-so student, and she knew it.

Papa saw us to the train station, full of stern advice against talking to strangers and warnings not to eat the food in the stations when we stopped. "Betsy has packed you enough to last," he said. "Best not to try anything else."

The train was better than I remembered it, though in late August the trip was inevitably hot, and cinders and sparks still blew in the open windows. Aunt Harriet got a cinder hole in the blue chintz she had chosen for traveling and muttered over it for miles. I watched the scenery, slept when I could, and arrived in Grand Rapids feeling tired and dirty.

I remember little of my stay in Grand Rapids, though my several cousins there tried to cheer me, and Aunt Harriet hovered over me so that I was most relieved when it was time to return to Monroe. Papa met me at the train.

Once settled in the carriage, we headed not for Monroe Street but across town in the opposite direction. "Papa? Where are you going?"

"The seminary," he replied, his voice distant. The seminary was Monroe Female Seminary, where all the proper girls went.

"The seminary? Papa, I cannot go to school straight from the train. I'll enroll tomorrow. I've already missed three weeks of school. One more day won't matter." I was baffled by his behavior.

Reluctantly, slowly, he said, "You're going to be a boarding student this year, Elizabeth. I've closed the house, and I'm living at Humphrey House." Papa never looked at me when he said this.

"Humphrey House? A hotel? Papa, you can't!" Had it been anyone else but my papa, I would have suspected a grand joke, some high jinks designed to fool me, especially since Humphrey House was owned by the father of my best friend, Nettie Humphrey, and she and her family lived there. But close the house? Of course that was impossible. We would live on Monroe Street, and I would climb the stairs each night to my bedroom with its poster bed and flowered wallpaper and organdy curtains, and Betsy would cook and clean and care for us, and Papa would read his paper at the breakfast table and study his law books late into the night, seated at the round oak dining table.

"It's for the best," he said without emotion.

By now we were in front of the three-story brick building that housed the Monroe Female Seminary. I'd gone to school there as a day student for several years and always felt twinges of sympathy for the boarding students, who, I thought, lived a bleak existence. Now as I stared at the square and formidable building with the long veranda across one end, its rows of windows, all with identical chambray curtains, seemed to mock me. I made no move to alight from the carriage.

"This is for the best," Papa repeated, shaking his bald head as though in despair. "I can't care for you now. Come, let's go in."

"I will not get out of this carriage," I said firmly. "We need to go home."

"Daughter," he said in a weary tone, "we cannot go home. Don't make this any more difficult than it must be."

I looked at him, saw the grief in his face, and realized that I was defeated. Papa, so lost in his own sadness, had no sense of my grief, my need for the house on Monroe Street. Feeling both angry and betrayed, I ignored his offered hand and alighted from the carriage. We both knew that I often jumped from the carriage almost before it stopped, so anxious was I to get to school and see my friends. But not this day.

Inside I was greeted enthusiastically by teachers who hugged me and muttered, "You poor, dear thing"—that, again!—and by students who eyed me uncertainly. What, they were wondering, do you say to someone whose mother has died? I swept by them without a word, even turning a cold shoulder to Nettie Humphrey. When Mr. Boyd, the headmaster, reached out a comforting arm, I shook it off and asked, "Where am I to stay?" I knew they all thought me rude, but I was trying desperately to keep from crying. And I never looked at Papa again that afternoon, even when he left, saying, "I'll be back tomorrow to see you."

Once alone in my room, one in a corner of the building with windows on two sides, I threw myself on the bed and sobbed bitterly, sobbing for my dead mother and for myself, for all the joy that had gone out of my life. Vaguely I remembered Armstrong Custer again. Was I really strong?

My black mood passed quickly, as such moods will with young people. But no one else recognized my need for warmth and comfort and—yes, even laughter. Instead, during my first few months back at the seminary, everyone, teachers and students alike, treated me as though I were made of fragile porcelain, liable to break at any moment. They expected me to be somber and silent. I couldn't see that prayers or quiet meditation or a long face would bring my mother back, or move my father out of Humphrey House, and I longed for brightness in my life.

On the other hand, I traded unmercifully on the special attention given me. "Mr. Boyd," I would say in a tremulous voice, "I wasn't able to finish my French exercises," or "Miss Taylor, I'm afraid I'm not feeling well at all today. May I miss the nature walk?" Dear things that they were, the teachers allowed me to get away with this outrageous behavior. I longed for someone to shake me by the ears and tell me to behave, as Mother used to, but all Papa said was, "You must try to do better, my dear." At night I often cried myself to sleep, for I was lonely and miserable.

My misery peaked at Christmas, when all the girls packed to go home for the holidays. Nettie had asked if I could not come to Humphrey House to stay with her, but for reasons I did not understand, Papa decreed that I was to stay at the seminary, where the Boyds would be my only companions.

Christmas Day dawned cold and gray, matching my disposition. Papa was to come take me to Christmas dinner at Humphrey House later in the day, and we would exchange presents then, but a long, empty day stretched before me, and I could not help but recall the joy of previous Christmases, when Mother had decorated the house with pine garlands and gilded pine cones and had filled the air with the aromas of fresh baking.

Suddenly I knew what I had to do, where I had to be. I bundled up in a warm shawl, with boots on my feet, heavy gloves, and a wool bonnet. Then, quietly and carefully, I crept down the stairs from my third-floor room. Nothing but quiet came from the Boyds' apartment, which was, purposefully I suppose, right next to the door. I eased the heavy oak door open, squeezed out, and pulled it gently to behind me. Then, heart pounding, I began to run.

The streets of Monroe were empty—each family was celebrating Christmas, I thought bitterly—so no one saw me pass. By the time I reached Monroe Street, I was cold to the bone, but the sure knowledge that I would soon be in my own home cheered me. I fairly bounded through that gate, still tight on its hinges in spite of my swinging, and up the stairs. The door was locked, of course, an obstacle I should have anticipated. I tried the side door on the veranda, found it locked, and went dispiritedly to the back and the kitchen door. To my surprise, it gave when I pushed, and I entered a stone-cold, silent kitchen. Had I expected Betsy to be bustling around fixing Christmas dinner?

I hadn't been prepared for the house to be as empty as it was, nor as cold. I wandered into the parlor, where I found all the furniture covered with sheets, creating ghostlike shapes in the dim darkness. The only familiar thing I saw still uncovered was Papa's prize picture of General Winfield Scott. When I was very little, during the Mexican-American War, I'd heard much talk about soldiers and bravery and fighting for one's country, and the talk had always come back to Scott and that picture of him, which Papa prized so. General Winfield Scott became my childhood hero, the epitome of a brave soldier. The general at that moment seemed to be frowning at me.

I was cold and hungry, but I found nothing to eat in the kitchen save some preserves, which didn't appeal at all. Fleetingly I thought of Mother's Christmas dinners, with roasted duck and cranberry relish and mince pies. At least I could do something about the cold, for I'd watched Betsy start a fire often enough to manage it. And there were kindling and coal in the scuttles next to the parlor grate.

It took me ten or fifteen minutes, and cost me tears of frustration, to get that fire going, but at last a small flame flickered to life, and soon I had enough of a fire that I could warm my frozen hands and then toast my feet. I pulled one of Mother's knit afghans out from under the sheet that covered the couch and wrapped myself in it, growing drowsy as I grew warmer. At last I slept.

A knocking on the front door woke me with a start, and it took me just a moment to remember where I was. The sheet-covered furniture brought me back to reality, and the knocking reminded me that I'd run away and someone would no doubt be looking for me. I crept to the bay window, where, if I was careful, I could look out without being seen. If it was Papa, I was not going to answer the door.

Armstrong Custer stood at the door, cupping his hands to peer through the glass panels. A part of me wanted to ignore his knock and be alone with my misery, but a greater part of me was lonely and afraid. I opened the door.

"I thought it was you," he said matter-of-factly, pushing past me into the parlor.

I closed the door behind him. "How did you know I was here?"

"Saw the firelight flickering and knew the house was supposed to be empty."

"Did my papa send you?"

"Your papa?" He was genuinely startled. "I don't know your papa. Why would he send me?"

"I suppose," I said dramatically, "everyone's looking for me. I've run away."

"Run to a pretty obvious place, I'd say. How long you plan to stay?"

My foot traced the flowers in the Axminster carpet, and

my eyes followed it, avoiding looking at Custer. "I don't know. . . . I haven't thought. . . ."

"Seems to me you ought to have a plan if you're going to run away," he said seriously. I looked quickly to make sure he was not making fun of me. "Course," he went on, "I thought you'd do better than that. I thought you'd stay at that school. I heard you were a boarding student."

"How did you hear that?" I asked, genuinely curious why this farm boy should know anything about my life.

"Everyone knows what the Bacons do," he said, "and besides, I have a particular interest in you after that day I found you swinging on the gate. How is school?"

"I hate it!" I said fiercely.

"No doubt you do. I hate Stebbins, too, but I aim to be something one day, and I figure sitting through things I hate is the only way to do it."

"What do you aim to be?" I asked curiously, unconsciously mimicking his speech.

He smiled, and his blue eyes twinkled. "A famous general in the army. I'm going to West Point."

"You can't get an appointment," I said without thinking. "They only go to rich boys and . . ." Embarrassed, I let my voice trail off.

He had seated himself before the fire and was poking at it now with the fireplace iron, stirring the cinders into life. "And I'm not rich," he finished. "No, but I'll get there one day, you wait and see. What do you want to be?"

What did I want to be? I'd never given it a thought. All I wanted was to have my mother back and to live in the house on Monroe Street. "I don't know," I said hesitantly, seating myself beside him. "I guess someday I'll be married and have children."

"Maybe," he said mischievously, "you'll be a general's wife."

I laughed at him.

"Come on, it's time for you to go back now." He stood up and held out a hand to help me. "Before everyone starts a row looking for you."

"Let them," I said petulantly, refusing to get up. "I'm not going back."

"Sure you are. Before anyone knows you gave in and ran away. You're going back and show yourself how strong you are. Besides, I'll take you on my sled."

"You will?" For a moment I was tempted. Then I shook my head. "No, I'm not interested in being strong. I hate that school!"

"You'll never get beyond it if you let it beat you. You'll never be a general's wife or anything else interesting. What would you do? Run from school all your life. Sounds like a poor living to me."

He was right, and in the end, after much more persuasion by him, I let him take me back to school. In spite of my nap, I hadn't been gone more than two hours, and no one had missed me. Armstrong pulled me on the sled, running to give it speed, and delivered me to the front door of the seminary.

Mrs. Boyd was at the door in an instant. "Libbie! I thought you were upstairs! Where have you been?"

"Oh, I just took her for a Christmas ride," Armstrong answered for me. "Hope you don't mind."

"No," she said, "but your father will be here any minute, Libbie. You best dress for dinner."

"Yes, ma'am," I said meekly. Then to Armstrong, "Will I see you again?" Quite the coquette I was, even at thirteen.

"I'll be by to see that you're working on being a general's wife," he said, smiling. Then, in an affectionate gesture, he reached down and cuffed me gently on the nose. "Take care, Miss Libbie Bacon." And he was gone.

Papa tried hard to make our Christmas dinner festive, but he would have been horrified if he knew why I was in such bright spirits.

The winter of my third year in high school, the monotony of life at the seminary was broken by two fires, both of which nearly touched me closely and did scare me more than a little.

The first happened while we attended Sunday services, as a class. As Methodist ministers were wont to do, Mr. Smythers was preaching at length, and we girls were trying hard to pay attention, knowing that any wandering of the mind would bring a severe look from Headmaster Boyd. Just as Mr. Smythers reached the point where he pounded on the pulpit to remind us that God saw every little thing we did, a cry erupted outside the church.

"Fire! Fire!"

In the distance, we could hear the fire bell ringing, and the shouting as volunteers ran to their posts. Several men in the congregation jumped up immediately and headed outside, no doubt to do their part in fighting the fire. But Mr. Boyd remained in deep concentration, staring at Mr. Smythers, who continued as though nothing had happened. One look from Mr. Boyd told us that we were expected to do the same.

Then the cry outside came more clearly: "The seminary's on fire!" Mr. Boyd bolted, followed by a whispering, worried flock of girls. Behind us, I could hear Mr. Smythers's voice falter.

We ran the two blocks to the seminary, holding our skirts up just enough to allow us some speed but never enough to compromise propriety. When we stood, panting, in front of the building, we could see flames coming out three or four windows on the top floor.

"It's close to your room," Laura Noble said, hand over her mouth in horror, and I stood paralyzed, watching the flames move across the front of the building toward the corner where my bedroom was located. "What," I asked myself, "if they do burn? What am I losing?" The answer became clear—I was losing a wardrobe full of clothes that I loved.

I'd worn black mourning for one long year, then spent several months in half mourning, which meant black and white ribbons instead of all black, white or pale dresses on occasion, but still no flowers. At long last I'd emerged from that period and was able to order my wardrobe again, but now with a much more specific taste than I'd had as a twelve-year-old. The lavender calico, which I'd so lovingly put away, no longer fit—it was made for a slightly chubby and much shorter person; at sixteen I'd grown taller and, to my pleasure, much thinner, though Papa worried constantly that I was not eating enough to keep a bird alive.

The calico had been replaced, though, by plaid silks, flowered cambrics, light pastel short gowns to match striped heavy skirts, all manner of pretty gowns, and none of those awful homespuns I'd worn as a young girl. I secretly prided myself on having the finest wardrobe in the school, mostly because I had no mother to oversee my clothes, and my father allowed me to order as I wished from the dressmaker. Strict as he was, that was one area of my life that baffled him.

Of course, I was careful. There was a girl at the school named Fanny Fifield whose dresses were always too bright, her plaids too loud, her ruffles too much. Even, as I whispered to Nettie Humphrey, still my best friend, the curls on her head were too tight. The result was, as Nettie once suggested, "ostentatious." I was so impressed by Nettie's big word that I looked it up in the dictionary and soon agreed with her—"ostentatious" was the word for Fanny Fifield. I, on the other hand, avoided ostentation, and yet I was still very proud of my clothes. And now they were about to burn up.

"We shall lose all the lessons," Mr. Boyd worried aloud behind me, wringing his hands. "How shall we ever make sense out of the school year if everything burns?"

"The lessons!" scoffed Miss Taylor. "We may lose the whole building!"

These grim possibilities hadn't occurred to me at all, and I watched with much more interest and some uncertain feeling while the volunteer fire fighters went about their work. I couldn't keep my mind from toying with the thought of a long, enforced vacation.

In the end the school was saved, though portions of it were badly damaged, notably the kitchen, where the fire had started, and a large portion of the sleeping quarters on the third floor, for the flames had shot right up a stairwell. It wasn't enough to keep us out of school, and Mr. Boyd found a way to make sense of the school year in spite of some scorched and water-damaged books.

But less than three weeks later Humphrey House burned, nearly to the ground, and Papa lost many of his belongings. Papa and I were not close in the sense of confiding in each other, but I always knew that his affection for me was as strong as his ever-present grief over my mother. He came regularly and dutifully to the seminary to visit me, bringing with him whatever small gift he thought might please me—fresh fruit in season, chocolate candies, a tiny porcelain figure for my dressing table. Papa was always, I later decided, trying to tell me how much he loved me, but he was too reserved to be able to say it. Armstrong taught me a whole new lesson about men who could express their feelings—but, then, those feelings were far different.

When the fire bell first rang and word went out that the hotel was on fire, I was in terror lest my father should be hurt or worse. Laura Noble and I were studying in the library —that infernal mathematics!—and I said breathlessly, "We must go, right away. I have to see that Papa is all right!"

Being somewhat of a goody-goody, Laura said, "We can't go, Libbie. Mr. Boyd would never allow that."

"Bother Mr. Boyd! I've got to see if my father is all right! Come with me if you want!"

She didn't, though she peered after me as though torn between friendship and fear. I flew out the door—luckily it was spring and I could go without a shawl—and ran the few blocks to downtown Monroe, where the hotel was located.

This time I was greeted by a much more fearsome sight —flames shooting out of every window, and roof timbers collapsing into the interior of the building. A large crowd had gathered, and I had no way of knowing where Papa was, except to push and struggle my way through the crowd.

"Excuse me . . . pardon me, please . . . have you seen Judge Bacon? . . . Papa?" People moved this way and that, paying no attention to one frantic young girl, until at last I saw Papa standing on the edge of the crowd, watching gravely as the hotel burned.

"Papa!" I threw myself into his open arms and hugged him tight. "I was so afraid for you."

He stroked my hair in a gesture uncharacteristic of him. "Shhh. It's all right, Elizabeth. I wasn't even in the hotel. I was at the courthouse. I'm afraid I've lost all my papers and books, but luckily no one has been hurt so far."

"Can you make sense of it?" I asked, thinking of Headmaster Boyd and his worry about making sense of the semester.

"Sense of what?"

"I don't know. The papers you've lost."

"Yes, I think I can. Things could be worse. And thank you, Elizabeth. It's good to have you worry over me."

I felt closer to him than I had since Mother died.

I guess Papa missed having someone worry over him more than I knew, for in my seventeenth year he married a Mrs. Rhoda Pitts, the widow of a minister from a nearby town. It was rather like Mother's funeral—Papa didn't tell me about the marriage until the ceremony had been performed. Then he came solemnly to the seminary, bringing with him my new stepmother.

She was not as pretty as Mother had been, heavier with a somewhat round face and faded blue eyes that looked at the world through wire-rimmed spectacles. Her hair was a soft color, sort of a light brown trying to turn gray.

"Child, this is your new mother," Papa said, with an amazing lack of tact.

Unable to say a word, I stared. She held out her arms and said, "I hope we'll be close." Unwillingly, but not knowing what else to do, I went into her embrace. She smelled of lavender.

I wanted to scream at Papa, demanding to know how he could let another woman take Mother's place. Instead, I asked, "What shall I call you?"

" 'Stepmother' doesn't sound very cordial, does it? Would 'Mother' make you uncomfortable? Or 'Mama'?"

We settled on "Mama," since I had called my own mother by the more formal term, "Mother."

"We've opened the house," he said. "It will naturally take some work since it's stood closed up so long, but we hope to be in it within a few weeks. It will be good to be in our house again."

I wanted to scream. It would always have been good to be in our house, and he didn't need a new wife to make that possible. I would have taken care of him, willingly, happily, though I guess I'd never thought to say that to him. Still, he made it sound as though opening the house again was possible only because he'd married. "I'll stay here until the end of the term," I said without emotion.

I moved back to the house on Monroe Street in the summer of my seventeenth year. Between my stepmother and me there was a frosty distance, made cool by my obstinate refusal to accept her. She tried everything, from baking my favorite chocolate cake to surprising me with new gowns, but I remained distant, unwilling to see someone else in my mother's role. I knew I hurt her feelings—sometimes I would catch her staring at me with a sadly pensive look—but I was selfishly uncaring. Neither she nor Papa had any idea how displaced I felt, like an intruder in my own home. When Mother lived, it had been my home, too, and it had been filled with singing. My stepmother never sang except hymns, off-key, in church.

By then I had begun to notice the young men of Monroe, and they me. There was one young man by the name of Murphy, a Southerner visiting relatives in Monroe, whom I thought particularly charming. When the crowd gathered at one house or another to sing and tell stories—Papa would not allow me to go where there was dancing—Lane Murphy was always among them, and he always had a special word for me.

"Miss Libbie, you're looking charming tonight."

My first reaction, being a practical Midwestern girl, was to say, "Oh, pshaw!" But I learned to say, with great delicacy,

"Why, thank you, Lane. It's such a pleasure to have you here."

"Libbie, I declare, Lane Murphy has a case on you," Nettie said one day as we sat in my bedroom, each of us hard at work fashioning ribbon trims for new dresses. Nettie, whose tallness, large frame, and pale coloring betrayed a Scandinavian ancestor somewhere, had no beaux, and I thought I detected a hint of jealousy in her tone.

"Nonsense, Nettie. He's just being polite. You know how those Southerners are." I laughed.

"No," she said, "how are they?"

"Well," I answered, "polite. That's how they are."

But I toyed with the idea of Lane Murphy having a crush on me, and let my imagination run until I saw myself as mistress of a fine Southern plantation, waited upon hand and foot by courteous and charming black slaves who were a vast improvement over Betsy and her sometimes caustic tongue.

Lane and I never managed a moment alone—Papa would not allow it—so our moments of tenderness were few. But he often greeted me by kissing my hand—a gesture far beyond the Monroe boys—and once he planted a gentle kiss upon my forehead, an act that sent a thrill through me. "You must come south with me," he would murmur, "and see how life is really lived." I was much impressed, until I learned after his departure that he said the same thing to every third female in Monroe.

There were other young men who intrigued me—Conway Noble, the brother of my friend Laura, for one. Conway was known for his daring—he'd once been in a fistfight in Ann Arbor, over a girl, or so I'd heard, and I thought it a terribly romantic story. And the summer I was eighteen, a new young minister came to the Methodist church, a Mr. Dutton, who paid serious attention to me until Papa forbade him to come to the house again. "He's far too old to be courting a girl your age," Papa said decisively, and though I had no particular interest in Mr. Dutton, I resented Papa making that decision. Besides, I knew that Papa frowned on a Methodist, since we were staunch Presbyterians. It made little difference to me.

In the spring of 1862 I finished school, at long last, with a great sigh of relief. But there it was. I was out of school, a young lady launched into the world with nary a thing to do with my time, except sew and paint and play the piano and sing in the church choir and, of course, go to parties. At first I reveled in my new life, treating each party as a once-in-a-lifetime chance.

We were at war by then. At first life seemed to go on as usual. I heard Papa talk about the war, of course, in tones of despair, and I knew that each day he walked to the telegraph office to read the list of wounded and dead. But few from Monroe were affected, and the ranks of young men seemed not diminished at all. But then we began to see soldiers on the streets, men in the proud uniform of the Michigan troops, and the wounded—young men who walked with crutches, or a young man who had lost a leg—I remember him yet. And the son of one of Papa's best colleagues was killed, his body sent home in a box. We all went solemnly to the funeral, and Papa was somber and quiet for days. I began to see that this war was going to reach out its tentacles of misery to all of us.

And I began also to hear bits of talk about Armstrong Custer. He had, as he promised, come to the seminary twice after my runaway escapade to check on me. But the Boyds frowned on his visits, and there was an awkward stiffness between us in that setting, so I wasn't surprised when I saw no more of him. The last thing he'd said to me was, "Remember about being a general's wife."

But now he was the talk of Monroe, the town's first officer in the regular army and the first to be under fire. The whole town knew that he had served with McClellan at Antietam and distinguished himself. The stories were probably exaggerated by the time they filtered down to the hometown folks, but it was said that McClellan had praised him for being always in the midst of the heaviest fighting and keeping a clear head. He was, so I'd heard, both reckless and gallant.

The town also buzzed with talk of his record at West Point—less than distinguished. He'd graduated at the very bottom of his class of thirty-four. I, who was not an outstanding student, could understand poor grades, but to be at the last of the class? It made me shudder. And there were the rumors of brushes with expulsion, especially close to graduation when he was supposed to have encouraged some kind of fight rather than stopped it, which was his duty. What kind of a man was this Custer?

I'd also heard that he was a ladies' man, most popular with all the girls, from the daughters of bankers and merchants to the farm girls.

"They say," Nettie told me one day, "that he's as brave as can be, charges right into every fight, almost not mortal."

"Pshaw!" I said. "Of course he's mortal. I imagine he puts his pants on one leg at a time, just like any other man."

Nettie was shocked.

Chapter Two

 "I BELIEVE YOUR PROMOTION HAS BEEN RAPID," I SAID, looking downward.

"I have been very fortunate," he answered. Then, under his breath, he muttered, "Custer's Luck."

It was Thanksgiving of 1862, he was home on leave, and we were introduced at a party given by Headmaster Boyd and his wife. Conway Noble had escorted me to the party, but then he'd said something silly that offended me—I think it was about my looking like my stepmother—and I'd walked away in a huff.

"Mrs. Boyd," I said, "who is that officer standing over there?" I knew perfectly well that it was Custer—he still had those long blond curls—but I doubted that he would know me, and I thought to fool him by being introduced.

"Libbie, dear, you've heard of our local hero, Captain Custer," she gushed. "Captain, Miss Libbie Bacon."

The man who stood in front of me looked neither heroic nor diabolic. He was fairly tall, well built, of solid stature, with strong features and deep, deep blue eyes, so intense they almost burned. And there it was, that long golden hair hanging to his shoulders and below in lovely curls. He wore the blue uniform of the Union and wore it proudly, his very presence giving off an electricity.

"A pleasure," he said formally, bowing low over my hand as Mrs. Boyd beamed. But those blue eyes, looking up at me, were laughing, and as soon as the headmaster's wife was out of earshot, he said softly, "I've been watching you. You survived school, didn't you?"

"Barely," I said lightly, "and now I'm a lady of leisure, trying to decide what to do. I see you're well on your way to becoming a general and a hero."

He just smiled enigmatically, as though he knew a secret.

"How nice," I said after an awkward moment, "that you could be home on leave. Will you stay throughout the holidays?"

"Probably," he said wryly. "They've seen fit to retire McClellan, so I'm waiting new orders. I was his aide."

"Your family must be grateful to have you home. . . . I don't believe I know them," I said.

"You wouldn't," he replied. "My parents have only recently moved to Monroe, to be near my sister and her family. They . . . well, they don't move in the same circles you do."

Were his eyes twinkling as he said that? I was sure I heard something veiled in his tone. "And what circles might that be?" I asked archly.

"Presbyterian," he replied firmly.

I smiled in spite of myself, but then said quickly, "I must find Conway Noble."

"Who's that? The fellow you were just talking to? He's over there by the punch bowl, pouting." He nodded his head toward the punch bowl, and his hair fell to one side as he did so. Offering me his arm, he escorted me formally to where Conway stood, then bowing slightly, backed away.

There was quite a crowd gathered in the reception area of the seminary, a fairly drab room that had been brightened with festooned ribbons to make it look gay enough for a party. Papa was talking seriously with Mayor Crenshaw, and Mama was in the midst of a group of older women. My crowd of friends stood around the punch bowl, which held only cider. Papa would never have allowed me to attend a party where alcohol was served, and the Boyds were too conscious of their image as schoolteachers to liven up their punch.

"There she is!" A deep voice boomed in my ear, and when I turned, I faced Walter Ashburn, a lawyer and contemporary of my father's. "Prettiest girl in Monroe," he boomed, to my everlasting embarrassment. "Give me a holiday kiss," and with that he put an arm around my shoulders and pulled me toward him. There may not have been alcohol in the punch, but Mr. Ashburn had found some somewhere —or drank it before he came to the party.

I pulled away, laughing to be polite, but seething inside. "Why, Mr. Ashburn," I protested, "what would your wife say?"

"She won't know," he said, now dropping his voice to a whisper.

"My papa is standing across the room, and he'll know," I said. But when I looked, Papa's back was turned.

Mr. Ashburn pulled me toward him again, and without hesitation I drove the heel of my shoe down hard on the top of his foot. I heard a soft "Aagh!" as I walked deliberately away from him.

Armstrong stood watching from one side of the room, his arms folded, a grin on his face. "Well done," he said. "I'd have come to your rescue if it had appeared I was needed. But you seem quite capable yourself."

"Thank you," I said wryly, and went in search of Papa to suggest that it was time to leave. I had little idea what impact that brief meeting with my childhood savior would have on my life nor the upheaval it would cause in the Bacon household.

The days from Thanksgiving to Christmas were filled with parties in Monroe. Mama hinted that it was time that I thought about marrying, and I wanted to assure her that I thought about it frequently but so far with no results. Papa occasionally frowned at me and said that my generation ought to be more conscious of the national crisis. But we were young and happy and the war was far away, though some of its officers often seemed close at hand.

Armstrong Custer appeared at almost every party I attended, and often I would find him at my elbow. "May I get you a glass of punch?" or "You're looking particularly lovely tonight, Miss Libbie." But then I'd see him offering Nettie punch or complimenting Laura or smiling down into the eyes of this girl and that.

The next time he told me how lovely I looked, I said archly, "Save your compliments for the others, Captain. I don't wish to be included in your admiring throngs."

"Oh, but Miss Libbie, you're the most important," he said, and those blue eyes looking into mine caused my heart to jump. The man was, I decided, devilishly attractive but unreliable.

Every year we looked forward to a party given by a family named Oldman. The Oldmans lived in a large house, much like our own, but farther out on Monroe Street. They were the parents of three unmarried daughters, and we used to joke that they hoped to marry off a daughter a year by giving their annual ball, but so far it had been unsuccessful—the two daughters who were older than I were still single. They were pleasant girls and not ugly, but they had no spark of personality, no liveliness, and I think by then they'd begun to lose confidence.

The night of the party was cold and snowy, and Papa bundled Mama and me under great thick robes for the short buggy ride from home. I protested that the heavy buffalo robe would crush my new dress of corded ottoman, but Papa responded that a crushed dress was better than pneumonia.

The Oldmans' house sparkled as we drove up to it, with candles in all the windows and gaslights burning in each room. The fireplace mantels in the dining room and parlor had been covered with pine branches—a fire hazard, Papa later grumbled—and the dining table boasted an array of fruitcakes and macaroons and divinity. A violinist played Christmas music in the dining room, though the crowd was so noisy that I doubt few appreciated the poor man's efforts. I recognized him, for he used to teach violin to a few unfortunate girls at the seminary.

The minute we were into the house, with our wraps safely stowed, and my dress fluffed out from its scrunching under the robe, I found Armstrong by my side. There he stayed the entire evening, never even smiling at another girl, until I was terribly self-conscious, especially since I saw Papa frowning at us from time to time.

When, at ten o'clock, Papa declared it was time for us to be headed home, Armstrong helped first Mama and then me into the carriage, while Papa stood solemnly by and managed a curt, "Thank you, Custer."

When we got home, I would have headed straight for my bedroom, but Papa stopped me.

"Daughter, that Custer boy was most attentive to you tonight," he said seriously.

"Yes," I replied as lightly as I could, "he was. He certainly is handsome, isn't he?"

"Takes more than that to make a man," he said. "I worry about him. I would not want you to get too involved."

"La, Papa, I have no intention of getting involved," I said, turning toward the staircase so that he wouldn't see that I was, unfortunately, telling a white lie.

"Your papa only wants what's best for you," Mama said, standing by Papa.

"Surely," I said as I headed up the stairs, "Captain Custer will be recalled to the army soon, and neither of you will have to worry."

But Armstrong was not recalled to the army. Christmas came and went, and still he was in Monroe, and still I saw him often. He had, as he later confessed, set seige, and it seemed whenever I stepped beyond our gate, I found him waiting. He appeared in church, not his natural habit, and was once caught by Conway Noble peeking through his hands at me during the prayer—according to Conway, both he and Armstrong had a good laugh about it. But Armstrong was there to walk me home from church, to escort me to a concert—he ended up taking Mama Bacon, too—to take me for a long walk in the snow.

"Bet you can't hit that tree with a snowball," he challenged one day as we trudged along through a new snow that had fallen the night before. The tree in question was a maple, fully twenty feet from where I stood.

"Of course I can," I laughed, and picked up a handful of snow, rounding it in my hands for a minute before taking aim. When I threw, my snowball came apart in the air before it ever hit the tree.

"Just like a girl," he laughed. "Can't even make a good snowball."

Another time we were walking home from church on a night that it had rained heavily. The crosswalk was muddy, and before I knew it, Armstrong swept me up into his arms and plodded through the mud, holding me carefully above it.

"Sir Walter Raleigh?" I asked, laughing.

"That's right," he responded. "Nothing's too good for my girl." And with that he planted a quick kiss on my nose, a gesture so spontaneous and affectionate that I could not but be touched, and set me down, unsullied by mud, on the other side of the street.

Sometimes we sat by the fire and talked, long and deep conversations about the future, with Armstrong still talking about being a general and making a name for himself in the army.

"You've already made a name for yourself," I said. "And you're too young to be a general."

He almost bristled. "That's not true," he said shortly, but then his good humor returned. "And you? I still think you'll be a general's wife."

He'd said that to me years before, and I thought nothing of it, but now I heard it as a faint proposal. A general's wife. General George Armstrong Custer's wife. It had a certain lilt to it that captivated me, and later that day, after he'd left, my mind wandered, much as it had when I imagined myself the

mistress of Lane Murphy's plantation. This time I saw myself
as a general's wife, following him from one exciting post to
another, free forever of the bonds of Monroe. My reverie
broke when Betsy called us to dinner, and I found myself
again at that formal dining table, saying, "And how was your
day, Papa?"

Papa inevitably heard gossip about Captain Custer and
me, and one particular incident disturbed him almost beyond
words. Armstrong and I had been at a party at the home of
Maggie Goodman, one of my school friends. The evening
being warm—I think it was March—Armstrong asked me to
step out on the veranda. We stood for a moment, looking at
the quiet town, and I heard him begin to hum under his
breath, a tune I vaguely recognized. Before I knew it, he had
caught me in his arms and was waltzing me around the
porch, keeping time to his own humming. I had longed always to dance, but Papa forbade it as un-Christian, and now I
felt suddenly free, whirling about that veranda, my head almost light from the sheer joy of it. But Papa heard, from
Maggie's parents, I suspect, and let me know in stern tones
that he expected me never to dance again. I wept at the
thought.

Other gossip about Judge Bacon's daughter and Captain
Custer flew about Monroe. Once when we arrived separately
at a party, rumor spread that we had quarreled. Some rumors
had us engaged, with me ready to elope if necessary.

But there was other talk, too, because for all his atten-
tiveness to me, Armstrong still favored several other girls
with his company. "Mama saw him driving a buckboard with
two girls she did not recognize," Nettie reported.

"It's nothing to me," I said quickly, "but perhaps they
were his nieces. I believe the Reeds have several children."

"I don't think so," Nettie replied. "From what Mama
said, these were girls our age."

"Well," I said practically, "it's certainly none of my affair."

Though I tried not to show it, I was a little less compla-
cent when Papa reported one day that Custer had been seen
in the company of Fanny Fifeld, she who had always over-

dressed and overacted at the seminary. "Saw them walking downtown," he said without inflection in his voice. "You know the girl, don't you?"

"Yes," I replied, and said no more.

But later I confided this latest development to Nettie, ending with a complaint that Captain Custer was not showing very good taste in women.

"He likes you, doesn't he?" she asked, grinning.

"Well, yes, but I mean . . . Fanny Fifeld? What can he possibly see in her?"

"Oh," Nettie said, "Fanny was always lively and fun. She just . . . well, she just isn't the same as you are, Libbie."

"Thank you," I muttered.

Just before he was recalled to duty in April, Custer received Papa's reluctant permission to take me on a buggy ride into the countryside. It was a bright, sunny day, though still cool, with spring barely hinted at and few buds yet on the trees. He'd rented the horse, and a fine buggy with black leather seats and a storm curtain with isinglass lights, though we'd rolled the curtain back because the day was sunny. He explained without embarrassment that he'd rented this outfit because his brother-in-law, David Reed, being a farmer, had no suitable buggy.

"Why must it be a suitable buggy?" I asked. "We could have walked."

"No," he said enigmatically, "not today."

He seemed to know exactly where he wanted to go and moved the horse along smartly, heading north out of town on the road that went past the cemetery where Mother lay buried and on up a hillside. I didn't ask where we were going, and he concentrated his attention on the horses, though every once in a while he turned to look at me, each time with a wide smile.

We passed through a grove of pine trees, coming out on the edge of a bluff that looked over the lake. Custer pulled the buggy to the edge of the road, tied the reins, and put the whip back in its socket.

Below us a tangle of marshes reached almost to the edge of the water—it was land where Papa and others sometimes hunted duck and geese. Beyond it the lake was a bright blue, with sunlight sparkling on it and an occasional whitecap ruffling its surface. If I turned my head to the right, I could see the shoreline of the city, the steamers docked at the wharves, and men who looked like small ants bustling about.

"Would you ever leave Monroe?" he asked.

"What an odd question." I drew back in my corner of the buggy to look at him. "I doubt that I shall ever have cause to leave."

"What if you were married and your husband's profession took him away?"

"I would follow him," I said confidently, but then added, "Marriage is a long way off for me." That vision of myself as a peripatetic general's wife flashed through my mind, but I quelled it instantly . . . or tried to.

"I hope not," he muttered, reaching to take one of my hands in both of his. "Libbie, you must know that I want you to be Mrs. Custer. I've been in love with you since Thanksgiving, since before that, probably since the day I saw you swinging on the gate, so brave in spite of your loss. Say you'll let me approach your father."

I pulled my hand back, but he looked so hurt that I reached again for his and began tracing the back of his hand with my finger. "I . . . I can't. Papa would never consent." I could, I knew, have left it at that, hiding behind Papa's authority, but that was not true. "I'm very fond of you, sir, and very flattered by your attentions—but I'm not ready to marry you or anyone else. If I loved you, and if Papa's consent could be obtained, then, yes, I would marry you—and leave Monroe," I added with a smile.

"Well," he said lightly, "at least there's no one else, and I still have a chance. I do, don't I?"

"Yes, of course." I smiled, though I wasn't at all sure that was true.

"Good. May I write you?"

"Of course."

"And will you give me your picture to carry into battle with me?"

"Of course."

"Let's walk to the edge of the bluff," he said abruptly, jumping out of the buggy and coming around to my side. Instead of holding a dignified hand out to help me, he held up both his arms and grasped me around the waist, setting me gently down directly in front of him. Then, before I could protest, he took my face in his hands and kissed me full on the mouth.

It was my first kiss, beyond childish pecks on the cheek, though I did not let him know that—at least, I hoped afterward that he had not been able to tell. Nettie told me that men who were sophisticated about women could tell these things, and I suspected that Armstrong was very sophisticated about women. But then, what did Nettie know? She'd never been kissed either.

"I'm sorry if I've offended," he said, stepping back, but I could see by the smile on his face that he was neither sorry nor afraid he'd offended.

"I think we best return to town," I said, trying hard to be a proper young lady and act, well, not offended, but concerned. Actually I had been hoping for some time that he would kiss me, and I'd rather liked it.

I never thought Papa had any sixth sense, but that day I suspected him of it. Not two hours after Armstrong deposited me at home, again with a promise to write and a plea that I think about his request, Papa called me into the library where he sat, staring at the coals of a small fire in the grate.

"You've been out with Captain Custer again?" he asked.

"Yes, Papa. You know he took me for a ride in the country. You gave your permission."

"Yes, I know," he said. "I gave permission because I knew that he was leaving, going off again to fight for the Union. As you know, I very much respect that man's efforts for his country." Papa had met Armstrong at Humphrey House, where the men of town gathered to talk, and he'd been impressed with his military skill and his devotion to his duty. Papa was very patriotic and admired that quality in others.

"Yes, Papa." I sat gingerly on the edge of the straight chair that sat before his desk and waited. The library was an intimidating room, lined with shelves of leather-bound books, many of them Papa's law books, but some the classics that I had read in school. An Oriental rug rich with deep blues and reds covered the floor, and Papa sat in the only comfortable chair in the room, a brocade-covered armchair flanked by a marble-topped walnut occasional table. It was not a room to which I was often invited, and I was always a little uncomfortable there.

"But I have given much thought to Captain Custer's continued attention to you. Your mother and I have discussed it again and again, and we are in agreement that you must not be seen with him again and not write him when he leaves."

I was astonished. I knew Papa was uncomfortable about the possibility of my becoming involved with a military man, but I never expected an edict so strong. I managed to keep my voice level as I asked, "Why, Papa?"

Papa's expression grew even more serious. "There are several things, daughter, that concern me. By now, this terrible war is two years old, and we've seen several young men come home severely crippled. Look at the Beckman boy, who lost a leg . . . or worse yet, the Crampton boy, who was killed in battle. I would spare you such grief."

"But, Papa, if I loved a man, I would love him with one less leg, and I would devote my life to him," I said with passion. "And if I loved him and he was killed, I would want to have had some time with him."

"And do you love Armstrong Custer?" he asked.

"I'm not sure," I said, to my own surprise. It was as though someone else inside me had said the words, for it was less than half a day since I had assured the man in question that I did not love him.

"You are young," Papa said, "and you have yet to learn of love. Meantime, there are other, ah, matters that concern me. Young Custer drinks." He said the last flatly, without elaborating on the evils of whiskey. He knew that my upbringing had left me well versed in those evils.

"No, Papa, he does not. He has taken an oath never to touch whiskey." Armstrong had told me this, recalling the very evening Papa had in mind and saying that the experience had so horrified him, he swore he would never again drink.

"I saw him once . . . in front of this house." Papa got up from his chair and moved to stir the coals in the grate. Bending over, he turned to look at me, his expression still solemn.

"I know," I said. "I heard the noise, too. But that was the night he took the oath . . . and the last time he's touched liquor. I believe him that it is an oath he will keep forever."

He snorted. "Well enough, if true. But there's another thing. I hear . . . and I've seen with my own eyes . . . that Custer has been courting other young ladies as well as you. The world has no tolerance for a womanizer."

Womanizer! I wasn't exactly sure what the term meant, but I thought it harsh to apply to Armstrong. "He enjoys the company of many people," I said. "He had no reason to limit his attentions to me. Indeed, I discouraged him from doing so."

"Well, he should have chosen someone else better than Fanny Fifield," Papa said, in a completely uncharacteristic tone that made him sound as gossipy as Nettie at her best.

I smothered a smile. "Papa, it's not for us to choose his friends."

"No, but the friends he chooses for himself betray his taste. The plain truth, Elizabeth, is that he is not of your social class."

My mind flashed back to our Thanksgiving meeting, where he'd made it plain that he was aware of the distance between Methodists and Presbyterians. "Because he's Methodist?" I asked.

"No. Because his father is a farrier, and his brother-in-law a farmer. It's not a world you could be comfortable in, daughter, after the advantages you've had."

And that effectively ended the discussion. I was all too aware that no matter what I said, Papa would forbid me any further contact with Armstrong. Without another word I rose and left the room. Papa, who never could tolerate bad manners, must have been sorely tempted to call me back, but he said nothing.

Upstairs, safely in my own room, I sobbed into my pillow, hoping Mama wouldn't hear and come hover over me. When I recovered, I went to my desk, took out paper and pen, and wrote Armstrong a long letter in which I explained Papa's admiration for him as a soldier and loyal patriot but his misgivings about our continued friendship, and asked that he not, after all, write to me.

> As you requested, I am enclosing a most recent ambrotype of myself. I beg you to show it to no one, as my father would not have wished me to give it to you. With it, I hope you will remember me and all the happy times we shared in Monroe. I shall be waiting to hear from others about your great triumphs on the battlefield and shall always think of you with great fondness.
>
> Sincerely,
> Elizabeth Bacon

Nettie delivered the letter to Armstrong the next time he was at Humphrey House—his farewell visit, since he had received orders—and she reported that the look on his face when he read it nearly tore my heart out. But, then, Nettie was given to dramatics.

"He uttered an oath," she said sadly.

"I know that he has learned profanity on the battlefield," I said righteously. "I would hope that he can cure himself of the habit."

Nettie merely smiled at me, as though I were an infant. If she was given to dramatics, she was also given to scheming. Unbeknownst to me, Nettie and Armstrong concocted an arrangement whereby he would write to her, though the letters were patently meant for me. And Nettie would pen back my replies. It would be an awkward way to conduct a love affair by mail, but Armstrong was proud of his ingenuity in thinking of the scheme.

I, meantime, not knowing of this plan, was devastated that he was going off to war where he might very well be killed, sent home in a box like the Crampton boy, and I was forbidden to see or write him. And I could see no way of changing things, of altering Papa's firm decision.

Late spring of 1863 was a momentous time in the history of the Civil War. Heavy fighting during the month of June led to the Battle of Gettysburg, a three-day battle of immense proportions that signaled the eventual triumph of the Union forces. Those days were also momentous for Armstrong, as his letters to Nettie revealed.

One afternoon at Humphrey House, she handed me a letter. "Here, you'll want to read this. It's meant for you," she said, smiling mischievously.

I looked first at the signature and saw the scrawled word "Armstrong." Then I read feverishly, especially the last, where he wrote, "Please give Libbie my very best and tell her that I think of her *every day* and especially before going into battle. I shall wait anxiously for word of her, from you."

After that I pored over each of his letters, reading them two and three times, seeing in my mind's eye a picture of him dashing into battle, sword waving on high, hair blowing in the breeze.

Once back on duty, Armstrong was detailed to the staff of Brigadier General Alfred Pleasanton and almost immediately sent on a reconnaissance mission deep into enemy territory in Virginia. With a few well-chosen troops, he traveled by boat and then horseback behind the enemy lines, through land he described as marshy, weedy territory and totally unfamiliar to him. He wrote that when they stopped at night, they dared not have a camp fire, and there was little chance for either food or sleep. But he was triumphant and captured prisoners, horses, Confederate money, and supplies. They also captured two barrels of whiskey, but then he underlined the words, *which we destroyed.*

"Now, if he'll just give up profanity," I said, and Nettie laughed at me for wanting him to be a saint.

When fighting became heaviest in June, he had other hair-raising experiences, and I found my heart in my mouth as I read the letters. Once he and his horsemen made a fierce charge but advanced so far, they found themselves cut off by Rebels behind them. They fought their way out with sabers, though not all of them survived. Still, Armstrong was untouched, and his men kept talking about "Custer's Luck." Then in another battle he lost control of his horse—something that happened to him rarely, I would learn, and then only in the most dramatic of moments. The horse, a black called Harry, which he had captured on his excursion into enemy territory, bolted across the line, carrying him into the midst of the enemy. But he was wearing a large gray hat, captured from a Confederate, because it kept the sun off his face and prevented sunburn, to which he was very subject. At first the Rebels thought he was one of them. By the time they realized their error, Armstrong had brought the horse under control and bolted back across the battle line. "Custer's Luck," he wrote to Nettie.

Near the end of June he was promoted to the rank of brigadier general. He had jumped four grades to become, at twenty-three, the youngest general in the U.S. Army. His happiness echoed in the letter he sent Nettie: "Please be sure that Libbie hears of this honor." He, who had hoped desperately for a colonelcy to command the Michigan Seventh, was now in charge of the Second Brigade of the Third Division, which included not only the Seventh but three other regiments of the Michigan cavalry.

I heard of the promotion not only in his letters but in the headlines of *The Monroe Commercial,* which boasted of our hometown hero's great promotion. "Monroe Boy Becomes Youngest General in Army" it read, and then a long story detailed Armstrong's background—conveniently overlooking his Ohio childhood and managing to make him appear a lifelong resident of Monroe—and praised his military accomplishments. I longed to shout to the whole town that this man had asked me to be his wife, but I dared not say a word, except to Nettie.

Even Papa mentioned Custer's promotion and added that Monroe was justifiably proud to have such a young man representing it on the field of battle. But he said it in a distant tone, as though talking about someone he greatly respected but did not know personally—the kind of tone in which he often spoke of President Lincoln. The promotion did nothing to change his opinion of Armstrong as a possible son-in-law, and I despaired anew, running to Nettie for comfort.

Then, just after his promotion, came Gettysburg. Armstrong led his Michigan troops to the center of the battle time and again, finally against the famed "Jeb" Stuart, the Confederate general who had never been turned back. At Gettysburg, for the first time, Stuart was forced to retreat, and Armstrong was responsible, according to all reports. He inspired his troops by yelling, "Come on, Wolverines!" and they responded, to a man. Custer's Luck held again, for three horses were shot from under him, with the bullets undoubtedly meant for the man and not the beast.

While I gloried in his triumphs, I fell hard in love with George Armstrong Custer. It may be, as the old saying goes, that forbidden fruit is the sweetest and that I loved him because I was sternly instructed not to do so, or it could be—and probably was—that I was swept away by his theatrical glory on the battlefield. There was a wildness about him, a freedom and daring, that woke something in me that would have horrified Papa.

Whatever the cause, I quickly decided that I could not live without Armstrong. Aside from Nettie, I had to keep my peace. Publicly, when I heard his triumphs repeated throughout the town, I took no more than a passing interest, calmly saying, "My, yes, isn't he amazing!" or "Aren't we proud to be from the same city as General Custer!"

Fanny Fifield, however, voiced more than a passing interest. Whenever the Monroe newspaper reported another triumph by the local hero, she made it known loud and long that she was corresponding with Captain Custer and eagerly awaiting his return. Not only that, she told it abroad that Armstrong carried her picture as well as mine, and that he had shown her my ambrotype.

"How could she have known about the ambrotype if he hadn't shown it to her?" I demanded from Nettie.

"Perhaps a lucky invention on her part," said the ever-peaceful Nettie, who immediately wrote to Armstrong about this latest uproar. "This will certainly take his mind off the battle," she said philosophically after she mailed the letter.

His reply was immediate and emphatic. He had *never* shown the picture to Fanny, nor had he ever mentioned it to her. "You know her quickness at guessing," he wrote. "Perhaps she learned about the ambrotype from the studio where it was taken and supposed that Libbie had given it to me. Be *sure* to tell Libbie how distressed I am that she is upset about this."

"Upset?" I railed. "Why is he even corresponding with her if he wants to marry me as desperately as he says?" Six months earlier I had been mildly interested in his flirtation with Fanny. Now I was in a rage about it. Love made all the difference.

During the rest of the summer, I lost track of the war in my concern over the flirtation war at home in Monroe. When I chanced to pass Fanny on the street—only twice in the whole summer—I deliberately looked the other way, and Papa, fortunately, never made mention of the gossip, though I knew he must have heard it. I often had the sense that he was watching me, with worry on his face and in his heart.

In September the tempo of fighting resumed, and Armstrong triumphed again, this time capturing Jeb Stuart's headquarters and even the general's dinner. But a bullet grazed his leg, forcing him out of action and home to Monroe to recover.

I was about to have to choose between Armstrong and Papa, a choice that terrified me.

Chapter Three

 THE MONROE COMMERCIAL HEADLINE PROCLAIMED, "Wounded Hero Given Huge Welcome" and claimed that "nearly one hundred citizens turned out to welcome home General George Armstrong Custer, who has suffered a minor wound in one leg. He will recuperate in Monroe for several weeks." And then the story, once again, recounted his military triumphs.

Papa read the paper at breakfast and said enigmatically, "I see Custer's come home." He peered at me over the top of his paper but said nothing more than, "I do not want you to see him, daughter."

I was sure my face burned as I toyed with my breakfast, for I knew that I would disobey my father. I had, it seemed to me, no choice, for I had to see him, to tell him how much I loved him, even if I could never see him again. All these years later, it sounds most melodramatic, but then I was wrapped up in the bittersweet agony of my thwarted love affair. However, I did face the practical problem of seeing him.

Nettie and I discussed it at length.

"He would never come calling at the house," I wailed. "What shall I do?"

"Go where he'll go," said the ever-practical Nettie. "You know he'll come to Humphrey House to sit with the men and tell them tales about the war. And your father will think nothing of your being at the hotel with me."

"But what if my father is there, too?" The world seemed to conspire against my passion.

"We'll see," Nettie said calmly. I thought it fine for her to be calm, since she was not the one whose affections were at stake.

For three days after he returned home, Custer did not appear at Humphrey House, though I joined Nettie there each afternoon. When Mama quizzed me at spending so many days in a row at Nettie's, I explained that we were working on a quilt with her mother. And then I lived in fear that Mama would meet Mrs. Humphrey on the street and comment on the nonexistent quilt.

Finally, when I'd begun to think that Armstrong obviously didn't care a fig if he saw me or not, he appeared at the hotel in the afternoon, walking with a cane. We were in the Humphrey family quarters when he arrived, but Nettie contrived frequent errands into the public part of the hotel and came back breathless in midafternoon to report, "He's here. And your father is not."

My hands flew to my hair. "Do I look all right? What shall I do? May I dust my face with some of your powder?" I fluttered around the room, nearly tripping over a chair in my haste to get to a mirror.

"We will walk calmly into the lobby together," she said, "and you will be surprised to see him."

And that's just how it happened. We sauntered through the lobby, deliberately looking away from the group of leather chairs where the men gathered. But out of the corner of my eye, I saw Armstrong reach for his cane and raise himself out of his chair. He came toward us, trying to cover his slight limp, and the next thing I knew, Nettie had vanished.

He stood before me, staring but saying nothing.

Flustered, I stammered, "You've been hurt."

"The wound in my leg is nothing," he said. "It will heal. But there are other wounds. . . ."

"I . . . I read your letters and found them fascinating."

"I know, and I thank you for the answers you sent through Nettie."

We were standing, eyes locked now, in the midst of a very public place, and I became aware that the old men had stopped talking to watch us. I glanced toward them, and Armstrong's eyes followed mine.

"We're being observed," he said. "Might we go someplace private?"

Papa, I thought, forgive me! "The garden," I said. "There's a bench, and it's a pleasant afternoon."

Nettie's father had spent a good deal of time and money on the gardens around the restored hotel, and we sat on a wooden bench tucked privately into a grove of pine trees. We were hidden and yet could enjoy the fragrance of the woods, the view of the lawns in front of us, where a stretch of green was broken with carefully arranged flower beds, now blooming with the mums of fall.

We sat silently for a long time, staring at each other. Uncertainly, once or twice I started to lower my eyes, but my gaze was held by the intensity of his look. When at last he spoke, I thought he was almost laughing at me, for he said, "And have you reached a decision? Do you love me?"

"Yes," I stammered. "I find you fascinating." Strange later to think that I confused fascination with love.

"Hallelujah!" he shouted. "The prettiest girl in all of Monroe loves me."

I reached for his arm, to quiet him. "Shhh! Someone will hear you!"

"I want the whole world to hear me," he cried, jumping up from the bench and doing a kind of limping dance of jubilation in front of me.

"You mustn't," I said. "Papa."

"Ah, Papa." His voice grew serious. "I will ask him for your hand."

"He will never consent." It occurred to me that General Custer was used to winning in battle, and he approached this much like a battle, expecting victory, never defeat. The thought gave me a thrill of apprehension.

"Well," he said philosophically, "I have won half the battle, apparently. You love me. . . ." He paused, waiting for me to confirm it, and I nodded. "Now I'll attack the second half. I will speak to your father immediately."

"You can't!" I cried. "If you do, he'll know I broke my word and have been communicating with you."

"Communicating? Is that what we're doing?" He reached out a tender hand and brushed my hair off my forehead. "I like it."

"I do, too," I breathed, lost in the moment.

"If I cannot speak to your father, and we cannot communicate, what is next?" he asked very seriously in slow, measured words. "Do you mean for us to meet on the street or at parties, and neither speak nor look at each other?"

"No . . . yes . . . it must be so," I sobbed. It all seemed very dramatic to me, and I suddenly saw myself at the center of a novel, the love-struck maiden kept forever from her lover by a wicked father. Of course, Papa was anything but wicked—but at that moment, he was my adversary, the person who stood between me and happiness.

Reaching for my hands, Armstrong pulled me to my feet and then, once I was standing, kissed me, a hard kiss, his mouth pressing against mine, his hands holding my shoulders tightly. At first I pulled away, but then as though another being were taking over my body, I responded to that kiss, my mouth meeting his, my hands at the back of his neck, lost in those blond curls.

I pulled away, embarrassed, and turned my back on him. No young woman of proper upbringing would respond to a kiss as I had. "Sir . . . ," I mumbled.

"Don't you dare try to cancel out that kiss with words," he said.

I looked at the ground, unable to look at him, my face flaming. To my mind, I had behaved in a way more fitting to Fanny Fifeld.

"Remember that I told you once, a long time ago, you were strong?" he asked. "I believe it as much now as then. I knew you would not let that boarding school defeat you. And I know that together we will win again—your father will not defeat us. I will ask him for your hand."

"You mustn't!" I cried again.

"If I cannot go to your father, we will meet on the street and pass each other by," he said firmly, and I saw no hint of the laughter I'd come to look for in his eyes. "We'll be missed inside," he said, businesslike.

I didn't care who missed us, but obediently, I took his arm and let him lead me back to the lobby. The old men still sat in their chairs, and this time they deliberately did not look at us. Armstrong bowed formally to me, and I made my way back to Nettie's quarters.

She asked me a thousand questions, but I could not answer them. I just sat on her bed and stared at the flowered wallpaper, trying to think what I would do about Papa.

For days I dared not mention the subject, and Papa appeared blind to my distress. Mama asked if I was feeling well —"You're a trifle pâle, daughter."—but I assured her it was nothing. Papa read the paper at breakfast, his law books at night, and seemed oblivious. I saw nothing of Armstrong, nor did I hear from him, and I began to think I'd dreamed that scene in the garden of Humphrey House.

Then one day I chanced to pass him on the street, quite innocently. Walking with his sister, Ann Reed, he tipped his hat in the barest of polite gestures, then returned immediately to the lively conversation the two of them were having.

Crushed, I hurried home to sob into my pillow.

Then Nettie came to me. "Armstrong's been seeing Fanny again," she reported bluntly. "He took her for a picnic yesterday."

"A picnic? How do you know that?" I asked incredulously.

"I just know," she said, refusing to say any more.

Things went on that way for a week. I saw him twice

more on the street, and each time he was civil but certainly not cordial. Nettie reported that he and Fanny had been seen again, once at a card party that I'd not felt well enough to attend—was Mama right? was something wrong with me that I felt so tired?—and once when a group of people gathered spontaneously at Humphrey House.

Then he escorted Fanny to church on Sunday. I arrived with Mama and Papa, as was my custom, and seated myself between them in the family pew, bowing my head in devotion. But something drew my eyes, and I chanced to look up. There, in front of me and far off to the opposite side of the church, were Armstrong's long blond curls. And beyond him I saw the equally blond head of Fanny. I barely smothered a small gasp by covering my mouth with my hand, and Papa gave me a sharp look. Then his eye followed mine, and he, too, saw Armstrong. Glancing for just a moment, Papa frowned and bowed his head again in prayer.

But before I bowed my head again, I saw Armstrong turn ever so slightly and look directly at me for a long minute, with neither laughter nor love in his look.

Armstrong had the gall to greet Papa after church, while Mama and I were detained complimenting Mr. Smythers on his fine sermon. Vaguely, I heard him say, "Mr. Bacon, a pleasure, sir. I've missed you at Humphrey House this week."

"I've been busy," Papa said curtly.

"Well, I do look forward to a visit before I'm returned to duty," Armstrong said. Then, "I believe you know Miss Fifeld?"

"Yes, of course," Papa grunted, and then turned away almost rudely to collect Mama and me. We walked home from church in absolute silence, and I pleaded a headache to keep me from Sunday dinner.

As I went up the stairs, I heard Mama whispering frantically to Papa, but only a word here or there made sense. ". . . can't continue . . . she's so unhappy . . ." Papa's responses were too low for me to hear anything.

I did not, as I'd expected, sob into my pillow. Instead, as I lay on my bed, reliving the church scene, anger swept over me in a wave. How dare he humiliate me? How dare he profess his love for me and then frolic with a cheap girl like Fanny?

"I'd hardly call attending church a frolic," he said smoothly, when I asked that question, my tone full of indignation.

We met by prearrangement, the result of much planning, at the secluded bench in the Humphrey House garden. Nettie, at first worried about my pallor and then frightened by my anger, had arranged our meeting.

"You say you love me," I said, "and then you begin to escort a girl who you know lied about my picture. . . . She did lie, didn't she? You didn't show her the picture." I pulled my shawl closer around me, less against the fall chill in the air than as a defensive gesture.

He shrugged, his face half-turned away from me. "No, I didn't show her the picture. But I am not going to become a monk because your father forbids us to meet. When you decide that I can present my case to your father . . ." He let the sentence hang in the air between us.

"You have used Fanny to make me jealous!" I accused, stamping my foot.

"No," he said wearily, "I have used Fanny to keep me company."

I searched his face, looking for a sign of love and seeing instead stubborn determination. "I will speak to Papa," I said.

He looked at me sternly, and there was still no laughter in his eyes. "I thought that was a man's prerogative. Will you wear the pants once we are married?"

I blushed furiously. "I . . . I just thought that . . . I might make Papa understand. . . ."

"I will not shirk my responsibilities . . . nor let it be said that I let a woman do my duty." He stood, arms folded in front of him, a picture of determination.

"You still want to marry me?" I asked, feeling almost that I must throw my voice across the great gulf that separated us.

"Yes," he said firmly, though it later occurred to me that

he never asked if my mind was still set on marriage. He just assumed that, having once said I loved him, I would always love him.

"Do I have your agreement that I should approach your father?"

"Yes," I said miserably, for I could not imagine any outcome of this but the worst. Papa would forbid the marriage and would scorn me for having disobeyed him, while Armstrong, rejected, would return to Fanny Fifeld. I would be left with much less than I had started.

"Good," Armstrong said. And then he kissed me, tenderly, on the forehead, and we went back to the hotel, but I had the strange sensation that what for me was misery was for him high excitement. He welcomed the challenge just given him, as though he were in battle, albeit on a different battlefield. He intended to win as decisively as he had at Gettysburg.

Papa, much to my distress, left town the next day. He had business, he said, in northern New York, where we had family ties. "I am sorry to leave you just now, with you looking so pale," he said to me as we stood at the railroad station, "but your mother will be of great comfort to you." It was the closest he had ever come to mentioning my obvious distress.

All around us were people we knew, waiting to board the train or to meet someone arriving, and it was no time to stamp my foot and say, "But Papa, Armstrong wants to talk to you."

"We'll be just fine," Mama said, pushing a strand of hair back under her bonnet and smiling reassuringly at Papa. I wondered if she ever disagreed with him about anything.

With great belching of steam and a roaring whistle, the train came into the station, sending cinders flying. Papa pushed us almost roughly out of the way, and then said, "Good-bye to you both. I will hope to return in two weeks." He took Mama's hand formally, and she replied, "Good day, Mr. Bacon. I do hope you have a pleasant trip," as though she were bidding good-bye to a casual acquaintance. Armstrong and I would never be that casual, I vowed.

Mama and I walked from the train station to Monroe

Street, through the downtown business district. We passed
the small shop of Mrs. Morrison, the dressmaker, and I remembered a day shortly after I'd met Armstrong. I'd been
headed to Mrs. Morrison's with a coat that needed to be
altered. I rang her bell and then chanced to turn around and
look at the street—and there he was, watching me! It made
my heart jump.

Armstrong didn't appear this day, though. There was a
cool October breeze off the lake, and Mama and I pulled our
shawls tighter around us and walked in silence. As we passed
the newspaper office, I heard a newsboy yelling, "South wins
another battle!" and my heart sank. Armstrong had now been
home over two weeks, and if the South had won another
battle, all the more reason he would have to return to duty
quickly. By the time Papa returned to Monroe, Armstrong
would have left . . . and I would be no closer to being a
bride.

Things happened just as I predicted. Armstrong left a
full week before Papa returned. "I cannot write you," I told
him at our last meeting, another clandestine affair arranged
by Nettie. Sometimes I wonder what course my life would
have taken if Nettie Humphrey had not been so interested in
the drama of a forbidden romance. Perhaps she, even more
than I, was drawn into the theatricality of the situation.

"I would not have you disobey your father," he said
firmly. "I shall continue to write Nettie and hope to hear
from you through her. And I shall write your father." Clearly,
he was displeased that he'd missed his chance to talk to Papa.
Someone else was dictating the terms of his battle.

"I will miss you," I said tremulously. "I always fear that a
Rebel minié ball will get you."

He laughed confidently. "It won't. Remember Custer's
Luck. We will be together for a lifetime."

I believed him and managed to behave with some decorum in the crowd that gathered at the railroad station the
next day to see him off.

"Will your stepmother suspect your being here?" Nettie
asked.

"Why?" I replied airily. "He's a hero and one of our

friends to boot. It's only natural that I join the crowd seeing him off." I'd had on a dark heavy skirt and short gown with a wool shawl, but a bright red scarf at my throat was worn specifically for Armstrong, to echo his own red scarf—as well as to help him spot me in the crowd, for more than fifty people had gathered at the station, and there were cries of "Hurrah for Custer!"

"Look!" Nettie poked me and slanted her head to one side. I looked beyond her and saw Fanny Fifield making her way through the crowd. If I behaved with decorum, she knew no such. Her blond hair was in tight curls that bounced unbecomingly as she walked, and she wore a fancy silk "Sunday dress," totally inappropriate for the railroad station.

"Armstrong!" she called loudly, as though she had no manners.

Startled, he turned, one foot on the step of the railroad car, and saw her approaching. Hesitantly, he smiled.

"I wanted you to have this," she said, waving a fine lace handkerchief. "For luck."

The crowd stared and Armstrong grinned at Fanny, enjoying the attention. "I have Custer's Luck," he said.

"Now you have Fanny's luck, too." She smiled.

Armstrong Custer, before my very eyes, leaned down and planted a quick kiss on Fanny's nose. Then he straightened, smiling, waved at the crowd, with a glance in my direction and a slight grin, and disappeared into the railroad car.

I was seething. Without a word to Nettie, I turned and made my way past the crowd, saying, "Excuse me, please" so brusquely that Conway Noble looked startled and asked if I was feeling well.

"Fine," I said sharply, and continued on. It took Nettie the better part of a block to catch up with me. When she did, I let loose with the temper that I'd never known I'd had but was only recently discovering. "How could he?" I demanded. "How could he disgrace me like that?"

"He didn't disgrace you," she said with her usual calm. "No one in that crowd except you, me, and him knows of the agreement between you, so no one would know that his kiss to Fanny had any meaning for you."

"He knew!"

"Ah, that's another story. Yes, he knew. But I doubt he did it deliberately, especially not to upset you."

"Why, then?"

"On the spur of the moment. Because Armstrong loves being the center of the crowd, loves the dramatic gesture. And it surely was that."

Her answer did little to lessen my rage. "That's easy for you to say," I said.

"Yes," she agreed, "it is. It's not my beau who kissed Fanny."

Nettie, too, had an admirer these days, though Jacob Greene lacked the fire and strength of Armstrong, at least in my eyes. Jacob was tall and blond, like Nettie, with a sort of uneasy grace in his stride and an ever-present grin on his good-natured face. A follower, not a leader, he was a local boy we'd known all our lives who'd joined the Seventh and was serving under Armstrong. On his last leave home, some months earlier, he and Nettie had struck a spark, and now she had two soldiers to correspond with. She shared Armstrong's letters but never those from Jacob, though as far as I knew, their correspondence had not progressed beyond friendship.

Armstrong never mentioned the kiss to Fanny in his letters to Nettie, and she finally convinced me that it was because he thought so little of the incident, he didn't think it merited comment, let alone apology. His letters to Nettie resumed regularly as soon as he returned to the battlefield, and again my heart was in my mouth when I read them. Each letter tossed me between fears for his life and thrills at the glory of his heroism in battle.

In October, the Seventh was forced to retreat after days of hard fighting, some of it hand-to-hand. Armstrong wrote to Nettie from Gainesville, Virginia, that he had taken my ambrotype from his pocket just before the charge and looked at it for what he knew might be the last time. His message to me was that he thought of me often and always looked at my picture just before going into battle—how my heart thrilled with fear to read those words! And how I shuddered to read of the death of his orderly, a young man with a wife and small child. "It made me realize," Armstrong wrote, "how close death is to us each and every moment." Of the defeat he said, "My consolation is that I was not responsible, but I cannot but regret the loss of so many brave men." I was innocently pleased that he felt free of responsibility and was sure other officers had blocked what would have been a brilliant victory on his part. In my mind George Armstrong Custer loomed larger than life as both a soldier and a future husband.

Just after that battle, Armstrong wrote to my father, a long letter, parts of which Papa read me much later. He explained that he had hoped to present his suit in person and begged forgiveness for this letter, which was less than satisfactory. "I have often committed errors of judgment," he wrote, "but as I grew older, I learned the necessity of propriety. I am aware of your fear of intemperance, but surely my conduct in recent years—during which I have not violated my solemn promise, with God as my witness, never to touch alcohol—should dispel that fear. . . . You may have thought my conduct trifling because of gossip about me and others in Monroe, but it was to prevent gossip and protect Libbie. . . . I have always had a purpose in life."

"You knew of this letter?" Papa asked solemnly.

We were again in the library. October had passed before Armstrong's letter reached Papa, and this talk occurred on a cold and gray November day. The library was as gloomy as the outdoors, and apprehension nearly smothered me, causing me to tremble as though cold. "Yes, Papa. I knew that he would write you."

Papa, seeing my trembling, rose to stir the embers of the fire. "And you have encouraged him?"

"I have told him that I would marry him if I loved him, and if you gave your permission." Then I added, "And I do love him . . . very much." That last took great courage on my part.

To my great relief—and surprise—Papa said nothing

about my having disregarded his order not to see Custer. "If I withhold my permission," he said, speaking slowly and deliberately, his hand stroking the short beard on his chin, "it will not be to thwart your love . . . nor to prove that I am still your father, with authority over you."

"Yes, Papa." I hung my head, knowing that he was about to refuse Armstrong's petition and uncertain what I would do next. I could not imagine life without my general.

"It will take me a great deal of time to think about this," he said. "In the meantime, we will not discuss it, and I do not expect you to communicate with Custer."

My hopes were dashed, for I had prayed that Papa would at least relent enough to let me correspond with Armstrong. Instead, I was forbidden to communicate, which meant, literally, that I could not even send word through Nettie. But since Papa did not know about Nettie, I did not feel honor bound in that direction. Strange how we can bend the rules of honorable behavior to suit our own needs.

When Armstrong wrote anxiously to Nettie asking if Papa had received his letter and puzzling over the lack of reply, Nettie was forced to answer that Papa was thinking.

"Thinking!" Armstrong wrote, and one could almost hear his explosion on the paper, as though the very ink itself had voice. "What in God's name takes him so long in thinking?" Then, more rationally, "Please assure Libbie that I love only her, and think of her every minute that my poor brain is not engaged in military matters."

My stepmother opposed my involvement with Armstrong more strongly than my father, and I sometimes wondered if she was not the one who was influencing him unduly. One day as we shared an afternoon cup of tea, I asked her point-blank why she disliked him.

"There is a certain wildness about him," she said slowly, staring at her cup as though she could read the future in its tea leaves. "An intensity, something that concerns me. He has not the stability that your father has for a lifetime of happiness together."

Indignantly I jumped up from my chair. "Armstrong and I will have a lifetime together," I declared passionately.

"You may," she said thoughtfully, "live a lifetime in a short span of years, but I cannot see you growing old together. I can see your father and me twenty years hence in our rocking chairs, sharing a quiet companionship. I cannot see that with this man."

I was overwhelmed at these words from a woman I'd always thought so plain, so dominated by Papa that she had no thought of her own. "Oh, Mama," I said, rushing to hug her, "do not say such things to me. And don't hint at them to Papa. Just wish us happiness and let us wed."

She held me tightly. "I'm afraid it is inevitable," she said.

Many years later that conversation would haunt me, and I would see her again, sitting in the parlor in that black-and-gray needlepoint chair, her gray dress making her almost a part of the furniture except for her face. There was a brightness in her eyes that seemed to light the room, and her cheeks were faintly pink—with emotion, I thought.

Armstrong did not get leave for Christmas, and nothing brightened the holidays for me. Christmas morning Mama, Papa, and I sat in the parlor and opened our gifts—a scarf that I'd knitted for Papa and an embroidered collar that I'd handworked for Mama. She had given me the daintiest of small gold lockets, with a little note for my eyes only saying she suspected I could find a picture to go in it. From Papa there was a leather-bound volume of Mr. Longfellow's poetry, but the severity of this gift was counterbalanced by a silver-framed mirror and hairbrush for my dressing table, the silver in an ornate pattern of flowers and vines.

"Thank you both," I said sincerely. "I shall treasure these things."

Beyond that, I thought the holidays dull. There was a round of parties, and Conway Noble was often my patient escort, though he knew my heart lay elsewhere. When Colonel Frank Earle asked me to take a buggy ride with him, I explained that my father preferred that I not associate with military men. And when France Chandler tried to make me jealous by hovering over Fanny Fifield, I merely smiled at him and turned away. The parties were beginning to bore me, and so were the men of Monroe.

In February, Armstrong was in Monroe, the first of many times that he would stand before me, unannounced, and delight in my surprise, no matter to him whether I was pleased or angry at his sudden appearance. To my complete surprise and slight alarm, he bounded up the stairs of the front porch on Monroe Street.

I happened to answer the knock at the door, Betsy being busy in the kitchen, and when I saw Armstrong there, I was overcome with mixed emotions. But the first thing out of my mouth was almost inane. "You've cut your hair!" I cried.

"Like Samson," he said, "I've lost my strength to a woman and so thought it only appropriate to cut my hair."

"Balderdash." I laughed. "Why did you cut it?"

"To be a proper bridegroom. I have a month's leave," he said, brushing the top of my head with his mouth, "enough for a fine wedding and a proper honeymoon."

I pulled away, afraid of any show of intimacy in my own home. And just then I heard the clearing of a throat behind me. Papa had emerged from his library.

"Mr. Bacon, sir," Armstrong said. "I've had no answer to my letter and so came to talk with you in person."

"So I can see," Papa said evenly. "You will step into the library, please. Libbie, I suspect you'll find your mother upstairs."

Clearly I was dismissed. They stayed closeted in the library for more than two hours, while I paced frantically, and Mama, intent on some handwork, clucked from time to time and offered such homilies as "You cannot change your father, dear," or "Why would he rush you into marriage?"

At one point she grew conversational and told me that her first husband had rushed her into marriage. She'd married him within a month, instead of the year-long engagement she'd expected. "I thought by giving in," she said, "that I was giving up my rights, that I would always have to accede to his wishes whenever any decision of import came up in our lives. It didn't work that way at all."

I had been barely listening, my ears intent for a sound, any sound, from below. But something about what she'd just said registered, and I asked, "Are you telling me you always got your way? That letting yourself be rushed into marriage is blackmail for future decisions?" I was incredulous.

"Not exactly," she said demurely, biting off the thread with which she'd been working. "But it's not always bad."

I confronted her. "Are you suggesting I let Armstrong rush me into a marriage?"

"I'm not even suggesting you marry him," she said calmly, and I turned away in frustration.

Finally, when my patience was near gone, Papa called from below. "Betsy has served tea," he said, as though it were an everyday affair.

When Mama and I entered the parlor, we found Armstrong and Papa together, Papa looking grim, and Armstrong, while not smiling, looking content.

"I have told General Custer that I will not prevent his marrying my daughter," Papa said very formally.

I ran to stand next to Armstrong and reached my hand out for his. He had barely given it a reassuring squeeze when Papa continued. "I will not consent to this union, nor give it my blessing, but I will not prevent it."

Crushed, I slumped into a chair. "Papa, will you give me away?"

"Yes, daughter, reluctantly. But the world will not know my true feelings. You may have your church wedding. Your bridegroom"—he nodded his head toward Armstrong—"wishes to make that within the next two weeks. I have told him such haste is unseemly and impossible."

Armstrong had one more battle to win. I glanced at him and, empowered by his look of love, said firmly, "No, Papa, it is not impossible."

Mama gasped and began to mutter about dresses and

plans and the like, but I looked straight at her and said, "I will see that it is done."

And so began the most hectic two weeks of my life, as I planned the event most girls take a year or more to worry over. The two weeks are yet a blur in my mind, a whirlwind of dress fittings, conferences with Mama and Betsy about food, a visit with Headmaster Boyd, who was to perform the ceremony. Nettie and I found time for two long talks about men and marriage—filled with more speculation than knowledge—but Armstrong and I had little time.

"It's all right," he told me. "We have a lifetime ahead of us." The laughing Armstrong, whose eyes twinkled in amusement at me, the one I'd fallen in love with, was back, and I pushed out of my mind that stern, unbending man who'd fled to Fanny when he didn't get his way. I, who had been miserable for months, walked on clouds of happiness and anticipation. The best, I thought, is yet to be.

Two incidents from those two weeks stand out in my mind. The first was one of the few moments Armstrong and I had alone.

"You must call me Autie now, and no more of this formal Armstrong business," he said. "My family and loved ones have always called me Autie, and you are now the first on my list of loved ones." From that moment on he was Autie, my darling boy.

The second memory is of a special day. One cold morning Autie drove up in David Reed's farm buggy, his overcoat buttoned up to the red kerchief that protected his neck, his head almost buried in a large woolen hat. I watched from the window as he threw the reins over the hitching post, stamped the snow and mud from his boots, and mounted the steps. Then I was at the door before he had a chance to open it.

"Good morning," I said happily. "Come in and take off your coat."

"No," he said, sweeping me off my feet and twirling me around. "We're going for a buggy ride."

"La, Autie, it's too cold, and I have too much to do," I protested, but to no avail. In no time at all, I found myself bundled up to the ears and tucked under a lap robe as we crossed town. The cold bit into my face, and I burrowed down under the blanket, but Autie sat straight and tall, waving at first one person and then another and enjoying himself immensely.

"The last time you took me for a surprise ride," I said, "you proposed to me."

"No need to do that again," he said. "I'm taking you to meet my family."

The ice that struck my insides had nothing to do with the cold outside. I was overwhelmed and more than a little afraid at the thought of meeting the Custers and the Reeds, for now they all lived together in a farmhouse several miles beyond town. I had seen Mrs. Custer once at the market, passing so close to her that I could have touched her, as I wrote Autie. But I didn't speak out of shyness. She was with one of Autie's younger sisters, a cunning child who was sweet and obedient.

My fear was not that they would think me a snob, though that was of some concern, for we were of two different social classes in a community small and rigid enough that social class mattered. Hadn't Autie himself once archly pointed out that he was Methodist and I Presbyterian? More than that, though, I was afraid that I shouldn't know how to behave in a household where pranks and teasing set the tone, rather than the controlled quiet and dignity of my own family.

We pulled into a barnyard before a white two-story frame house that would have benefited from paint. Behind it, in much better shape, was a red barn, but there were no animals to be seen—all hiding inside the barn from the cold, no doubt. The ground in front of the house was bare, though I could see the remains of a tiny flower garden right near the front-porch steps. There was a bare look to the house and barnyard that spoke less of poverty than of a lack of concern with appearances.

Autie hitched the horse and let out a loud "Halloo!" even before coming around to help me out of the buggy. Immediately the door opened and three small children tumbled out, one of them the young girl I'd seen with Mrs.

Custer. They wore no coats, although the two girls wore heavy sweaters over their linsey-woolsey dresses, and the boy sported a wool flannel shirt under his coveralls. Still, they should have been shaking with cold, but they seemed oblivious.

"Is this her?" "Can she come in?" "Introduce me first!" They clamored around the side of the buggy so that I could barely find a place to put my feet down on the ground, and Autie, laughing, held me in the air a minute longer than necessary. Tentatively, I smiled down at the upturned faces and was rewarded with a sighed, "Oooh, she's pretty!" Then I blushed heartily.

"Be quiet, you ragamuffins," he commanded. "Move aside and let Miss Bacon have space to walk." He set me on the ground and, taking my elbow, propelled me toward the steps before I could say a word. The children danced alongside us.

"Aren't you cold?" I ventured. "You'll catch your death."

"Naw," the boy said. "Ma says we're hearty."

"They are, too," Autie said in boasting tones, and I gathered that heartiness was a family trait and a source of some pride. Then he spoke sharply to the boy. "Mind your manners. Say 'No, ma'am,' not 'naw.' "

"Yes, sir," he said dutifully, his spirits not at all dashed by the reprimand.

We were through the door and into a warm and cozy parlor by now. A quick glance around showed me mismatched furniture that had obviously seen lots of wear. A sheet-iron stove in the center of the room gave off a comforting warmth, and Autie placed me directly in front of it with a command to warm myself.

Mrs. Custer came through a doorway, pushing aside a chintz curtain that apparently blocked one room from the other. "My dear," she said, holding out both hands to take mine, "I am glad to meet you. You are making my Armstrong very happy."

"Thank you, Mrs. Custer," I said, taking the offered hands. "I'm very happy, too."

She was a small and frail woman, so faded looking that it

was difficult for me to believe that Autie had sprung from her. She had none of the vibrant energy that distinguished Autie, though her voice was firm when she ordered the children into the other room, and I noticed that they obeyed immediately.

It was not long before I discovered where Autie had inherited his energy. Father Custer burst into the room like the proverbial bull in a china shop, booming, "Where is this lady who's stolen our boy away?" In contrast to my papa's balding head with its fringe of hair, Father Custer's head seemed to sprout gray, wiry hair in every direction, even sideburns, which grew down into a full beard as brushlike as the rest of his hair. But it was his eyes I noticed—the same blue as Autie's and with the twinkle that sometimes graced the son's eyes. I liked him immediately.

There was laughter in his voice as he said, "We thought no one would capture Autie," he said, "but you've got him hog-tied."

Those were not the terms in which I thought of our relationship, and I could think of not one thing to say. My silence didn't seem to bother Father Custer at all, and he went on, "You're as pretty as Autie told us, every bit!" And he walked around me, surveying, until I felt like a horse on the auction block.

Within minutes the entire family was gathered in the room—Autie's parents, the youngest children—Boston, who was nine years behind Autie, and little Margaret, who was then only eleven, Ann and David Reed and their two small children, one a boy named after Autie, and Nevin, Autie's older brother, who stayed home and farmed because rheumatism had caused the army to reject him. They made, to me, an enormous crowd, especially when they all talked at once. I stood silently in the middle, grateful for Autie's comforting arm at my elbow.

"Hush now," Father Custer said loudly, "you're overwhelming. You back off and let the little lady take off her greatcoat and get warmed up." The room fell silent for perhaps a minute, and then the hubbub started over again.

Amid all the commotion, Ann Reed serenely put a

steaming pot of apple cider on the lace-covered table in the dining room and followed that with a tray of slices of freshly made pound cake. I was served first as the guest of honor, though little Lydia had to be reminded twice to wait her turn, and finally I was seated in a wood rocking chair, balancing my cake and cider, while trying to talk to Mrs. Custer, who sat next to me on a straight and very uncomfortable-looking chair.

"He's a good boy," she said, peering at me through wire-rimmed spectacles, "and has never caused me any worry. I'm sure he will bring you nothing but happiness."

Oh, Mother Custer, I think so often of those words!

"They liked you," Autie said with satisfaction as we headed back to Monroe Street. "You'll love them," he predicted, and I murmured that of course I already did, for they were his family, were they not?

Papa was reading and Mama sewing when I entered our home. Each looked up and greeted me, but the house seemed silent as the grave, and I already longed for the boisterous Custer household.

In spite of the hasty planning, we had a grand and large wedding at the Presbyterian church, with Mr. Boyd, my old headmaster from the seminary, performing the ceremony.

"You don't mind, do you?" I'd asked Autie, and he'd replied, "Not as long as he's got the authority to conduct a legal ceremony. Will we really be married?"

I assured him we would.

Autie's favorite brother—though he always denied favoritism—came home from the war for the wedding. Tom, six years younger than Autie, was with the Twenty-first Ohio Infantry, and he and Autie had not seen each other for four years. I went with Autie to the railroad station to meet Tom, and their reunion fair gave me a glow of happiness. But it took them a moment before that reunion to recognize each other—"Is that you, Tom?" "Autie? Where are your curls?" —and that pause gave them an idea.

"We'll pass you off as my aide, a Major Drew," Autie

said, and Tom laughed enthusiastically. "Even Ma won't know."

I protested they could not do that to poor Mother Custer and added, besides, that a mother would always know her son. But they pooh-poohed me and carried on with their joke. Mother Custer, to my dismay, was properly fooled and greeted the false Major Drew with formal hospitality. It was Father Custer who saw through their ruse and cuffed both boys so soundly that I caught Autie fingering his one ear the rest of the afternoon.

"Serves you right," I whispered.

"Sympathy is what I always look for in a wife," he replied with a grim smile.

Tom was to be in the wedding party, along with Jacob Greene, Nettie's beau, and Conway Noble—"He brought us together," Autie said sanctimoniously when I asked about Conway as a choice. I had asked Nettie, and Laura Noble, Conway's sister, and my cousin from Grand Rapids, Rebecca Richmond, to be my attendants, and they had all agreed in spite of short notice.

Papa caught me once for a solemn talk in the days before the wedding. "Daughter," he said, "I cannot believe you have any idea of the difficulties of military life. I am deeply worried."

"Papa," I begged, "be happy for me. Don't worry. Whatever the difficulties are, Autie and I will meet them together." Oh, how naive the young are!

Three hundred people watched me walk down the aisle of the church on Papa's arm. In spite of having described to Autie a wedding gown of pea-green silk looped with military braid, I wore a rich white silk dress with a bertha of point lace and a veil fixed at the brow with orange blossoms. Autie, who walked down the aisle with his beloved mother, wore his uniform, with all his braid and insignia and the ever-present red scarf, and I thought he looked magnificent—though I longed for the curls.

When Mr. Boyd pronounced us man and wife, I could scarce contain my joy, wanting to shout in exuberance. Instead, I received a subdued kiss from my new husband, and we turned to face a congregation of smiling faces. Papa, I thought, looked a little grim.

We paraded from the church to the house on Monroe Street to the accompaniment of sleigh bells and cheering friends. Three hundred people strained the capacity of the house, but the reception was social, hilarious, and delightful. It being winter, the guests could not easily overflow outside, though I noticed Conway Noble and a few of the other young men standing on the porch to smoke.

"When can we escape this?" Autie whispered in my ear.

"Soon," I said comfortingly. "We are to catch the midnight train."

"I know," he said patiently, "but midnight is four hours away! And even then we shall be surrounded by people."

"Hush," I said, putting my finger to his lips and bidding him to be gracious in greeting family friends and accepting their congratulations. It was, I later agreed, too long.

Finally, bidding this one and that good-bye and thank you, I followed Nettie upstairs to my bedroom to change into my traveling outfit, a dark brown dress of empress cloth trimmed with white buttons, with a hat to match. There I looked around the room that had been my home for twenty-one years. The cross-stitch samplers I had done at the age of eight and Mother had framed for me, the flowered drawings that Mama had given me and framed to match the yellow walls of my room, the poster bed where I'd slept as a maiden and would sleep no more because there was not room for two—all made tears rush to my eyes, and had Nettie not been there to help me change, I think I would have broken down into a good cry.

"Come now," Nettie said, with her usual brisk cheerfulness, "we've got what we wanted all the while. Let's not mess it with tears."

"You're right." I laughed and proceeded to change my clothes.

Against Mama's advice, I had not packed my clothes, fearing they would crush unnecessarily. So at the last minute —past eleven o'clock—everyone pitched in to pack my gowns, which landed in the trunk willy-nilly. But Autie,

charging in to be helpful—and anxious, I knew, to be away—
met his match in a frame of hoops that soon had him hopelessly entangled. Finally, to everyone's delight, he called out
desperately, "I surrender!" At the last minute everything was
packed, and we were rushed away to the station, where I bid
a tearful farewell to my parents and then, happy as a lark,
boarded the train with my new husband.

The honeymoon loomed before us.

CIVIL
WAR
BRIDE

Chapter Four

ONCE OUR LUGGAGE WAS DEPOSITED INSIDE OUR ROOM at the Metropolitan Hotel and the boy who'd carried the bags had left, Autie and I stood and looked at each other uncertainly. It was our first moment alone in almost thirty-six hours of marriage, and we were both awkwardly aware of the privacy. Behind us was a long and tiresome train ride, during which the exhilaration of the wedding and reception had given way to pure, plain fatigue. I'd catnapped with my head on Autie's shoulder and worried that he was not getting any rest, but he assured me he was used to going days without sleep.

"Wait," he said, "until we are in our very own room at the Metropolitan." It was the hotel in New York where West Point cadets held their formal banquet after graduation and where Autie had once stayed while working with General McClellan. He was, I sensed, excited about showing it to me, and I was excited about New York and hotels and honeymoons—so excited that I slept fitfully.

And then, there we were, in our very own private room in the Metropolitan. Gas sconces cast a pale glow throughout the room, brightening it on a wintry gray afternoon. On the wall some unknown general stared at us from a gilt frame, and I thought of Papa's prized portrait of General Winfield Scott.

The room was dominated by a massive double bed, with a solid mahogany headboard of nearly six feet and a footboard of at least four—Autie and I walked uncomfortably around it, avoiding looking either at the bed or at each other. Part of me longed for Autie to sweep me off my feet with passion, but another part of me held back timidly. No one had ever talked to me about the facts of life. Certainly Papa would not have, nor would Mama, and my own mother had died long before such talk would have been appropriate. Aunt Harriet hinted delicately at one thing or another just before the wedding—"I do hope Armstrong will be patient with you, Libbie" and that kind of thing, which meant nothing to me—and Nettie and I had speculated on what we knew was called "the marriage relationship." But I knew virtually nothing about the physical side of marriage.

Still, my woman's intuition was good, and I knew it involved a much-sought-after intimacy, and that it would arouse in me the same feelings I got when Autie kissed me—we'd managed a few long and passionate kisses since the wedding, even on the train when the lights were low for the night, and those kisses, with Autie's probing, insistent tongue, had caused a stirring in the pit of my stomach that puzzled and delighted me. I also knew, from whispers among the girls, that bridegrooms were unbelievably impatient for a marriage to be consummated. I had expected, therefore, that once we were alone—at last—Autie would make love to me.

"Well," he said briskly, pacing about the room, "here we are."

"Yes," I agreed, "here we are." I perched on the edge of a horsehair chair, watching Autie pace for a moment, and then got up to stare out the window. Even on this dull day, the city amazed me—so many people crowded into such a small place. I thought longingly of Monroe and the spaces between houses there.

Coming up behind, Autie put his arms around me and turned me gently toward him. "I love you very much," he said, his voice husky, his eyes looking straight at me, filled now neither with laughter nor sternness, but unmistakably with love.

"Oh, Autie," I cried, throwing my arms around him, "I love you, too. I . . . I just can't imagine we're really married."

I expected perhaps another long, passionate kiss, which would this time lead us to the bed. Instead, he suggested a sight-seeing trip! "Freshen up and we'll go see the sights."

Bewildered, I said as lightly as I could, "Of course. Just let me wash my face and rearrange my hair." I made my toilette in the lavatory, while Autie stood and stared out the window, occupying the very spot I'd just vacated.

When I was ready, I crept up behind him and kissed him gently on the ear. He turned and crushed me in his arms, his mouth reaching for mine. But then he pulled away, laughing about my having caught him by surprise. Autie, I decided with amusement, was as nervous as I was. What a pair we'd make!

From that first sight-seeing tour with Autie, New York was always a special place to me. There were people on the streets in such numbers—more in three blocks than one saw in the whole of Monroe. And the buildings and houses sat so close to the sidewalk.

"Where," I asked, "are the lawns?"

Autie only laughed and squeezed my hand as it lay on his arm. A block later he said, "See that young boy?"

"Yes."

"He'll steal your purse in a flash if you're not careful."

My hand went to my bag even as I protested, "He can't be more than ten!"

"Probably not," Autie said. "Don't worry. He won't bother you with me around."

And then a tinge of fear, never lost, crept into my feelings for New York. Still, I was fascinated with its energy—

horse-drawn carriages going in every direction, people walking in the streets, buildings taller and closer together than I'd ever seen. In New York I began to believe that the whole world was a more crowded, busier place than I'd guessed in Monroe.

We had a wonderful time seeing the sights in New York. I would never have applied the term "sheltered" to my childhood, but of course that was the best description. And now I —the sheltered girl from a small town—was in an enormous, busy city. People surrounded me, and noises assailed my ears from every direction. Buildings were taller, and traffic faster, and everything fascinating but bewildering.

We passed one poor old lady, seventy if she was a day, painfully making her way down the street leaning on a cane, her face screwed into a tight frown.

"Is that what you'll look like when you're old?" Autie asked me in a teasing voice. He started to mimic her walk until I poked him and begged him not to be rude.

"Probably I'll look just like that," I said. "And you?"

"I'll never live to be that old," he said confidently, and I shuddered as though someone had just walked on his grave. Then I brightened, knowing he was wrong. We would grow old together.

There was February snow on the ground that day, and Autie laughingly recalled the time he'd nearly hit me with a snowball. This city snow was old and gray with the dirt of New York, and he made no suggestion that we throw it. He did offer to race me to the next tree, but I refused on the grounds that it would look unladylike and unseemly for the wife of a general. He took great delight in telling me I was just afraid of being beaten, and I willingly agreed with him. I was so in love, I would have agreed had he told the proverbial story about the moon being made of green cheese.

"I've no wish to beat you," I said, and he kissed me soundly.

"That's what I want in a wife," he said.

We ate supper in a dim and dark restaurant where Autie ordered oysters and I acted horrified, convinced I never could eat anything that slimy. Autie laughed and made a great show of tossing them down whole. I remember clearly that he drank coffee, refusing the host's suggestion of dark beer, and so I, too, contented myself with coffee, though I longed to try the recommended claret. Once free of Monroe, I intended to shed all my youthful prohibitions—and I badly wanted to taste wine. We held hands while we sipped coffee and talked about the future, our future together, complete with a rose-covered cottage and lots of little Custers.

"Will you always go off to war?" I asked.

"Probably," he said, "but I'll always come home. And sometimes I'll take you with me. Will you go? The accommodations are not always as fine as the Metropolitan."

"I'll follow you anywhere," I said, and I meant it.

"I knew it," he said. "I knew the day I found you in that cold house that you . . . well, that you were game."

Game, that's what I was to be.

It was dark when we left the restaurant, and by mutual agreement we headed to the Metropolitan. Once inside our room, I confessed, "I'm exhausted, Autie."

"Of course you are," he said gently. "I'll just take a stroll around the lobby while you prepare for bed."

When he came back, half an hour later, I was sitting up in the large double bed, pillows behind me, a lace wrapper covering my new satin gown. "What a picture you look!" he cried, rushing toward me to sit on the edge of the bed and stare at me. "Mrs. George Armstrong Custer," he said softly. "I cannot believe that I am such a lucky man."

"Nor I such a lucky girl," I said, laughing. "Come along, Autie, get ready for bed."

He disappeared into the lavatory, emerged sometime later wearing a white flannel nightshirt, and immediately turned down the lights in the room before climbing into bed.

And then Autie made love to me with all the intensity that rumor had led me to expect from my bridegroom. It both frightened and delighted me, though at moments I felt almost like a spectator.

"Autie," I whispered, "what do I do with my hands?"

"Nothing," he panted. "Let me do it. You just lie still."

That, somehow, did not seem right to me, and every

instinct in my body fought against lying still, fought to move along with Autie. It was, however, over in minutes, and then Autie kissed me ever so tenderly, told me I was a wonderful wife, and fell sound asleep, his back pressed close against me. I lay awake for hours, wishing for Nettie or someone I could talk to and knowing none of them, not even Mama, would have had the answers I needed.

By the fourth night we were at the hotel, I had become a full participant in our lovemaking, reaching out to touch Autie in intimate and personal spots, moving with him in a rhythm of lovemaking, finding in myself sensations I'd never believed could exist. But Autie often pulled my hands away and withdrew temporarily until I, quivering, lay still.

During the days, our honeymoon was a delight. We went once, because we had promised Papa, to see a phrenologist. Papa truly believed that the bumps on a person's head gave clues to character, and I guess, worried as he was about my future, he was ready to take any possible advice. Professor Fowler, who had been recommended to Papa by who knows who, had little to say to me beyond that I was a beautiful bride and should have a long life of happiness with my bridegroom. But to Autie, he cautioned, "You must avoid overdoing and learn to take pleasure for its own sake. You contrive, somehow, to overdo everything."

"Autie," I asked as we left Fowler's quarters, "what do you suppose he meant?"

He tucked my hand under his arm and smiled at me, that charming smile that banished all my worries. "Nothing to worry about, Libbie. If I didn't overdo things, I would not be the officer I am. I'm afraid you'll have to love me as I am and not expect any great changes."

"I do," I told him laughingly. "Oh, I do!"

We went once to the theater to see the melodrama *East Lynn,* and both of us laughed at the fun and cried at the sadness. I was startled to see Autie with tears streaming down his face, but he was unembarrassed about it, and when I borrowed his handkerchief, my own being soaked, he cautioned me to save a dry corner for him. Afterward he praised the play highly. I thought it wonderful to be married to a man of such sensitivity.

We were young and in love, and the war was far away from our thoughts. But it was brought home to us by the many people in New York who recognized Autie's uniform everywhere we went. It was the uniform he'd concocted for himself when he was made a general: a black hat with a wide brim—to protect from the sun, no doubt—a blue sailor's shirt under a black velveteen jacket, ornamented with two rows of brass buttons and gold braid spangling the sleeves from cuff to elbow. His trousers were of the same material, with twin gold stripes down the outside seams. Silver stars glittered on each shoulder and on the brim of his hat. On the battlefield he wore gold spurs on his high boots and carried on his belt a straight sword, captured from some enemy soldier, but in the city he left these off naturally. His trademark was a scarlet necktie, which he chose, he told me, because it was important to be conspicuous on the battlefield. It certainly made him conspicuous in the city.

In restaurants, even on the street, people would stop and say, "Aren't you Custer?" and Autie would hang his head just a little and reply, "Yes, I am." Then would follow some compliment on his service: "Read about you at Gettysburg— really showed that old Stuart, didn't you?" or "Youngest general we've got—you surely must be brave!" I wanted to echo, "Of course he is!" but rarely introduced to these admiring citizens, I kept my peace, and Autie accepted their praise with great modesty. I always basked in it and afterward wanted to discuss it at length with Autie, analyzing his popularity.

"I am a soldier," he would say, dismissing the subject, and I loved him for it.

The highlight of our trip, to me, was a visit to West Point, where Autie, his dismal scholastic record apparently forgotten, was greeted as a distinguished alumnus. While he talked with some of his old professors, a group of cadets took me in tow and showed me all the sights, including Lovers' Walk, where, they assured me, General Custer had never walked with anyone else.

"Of course not," I responded jokingly. "He never looked at another girl until he met me." A vision of Fanny Fifield flashed across my mind, but I kept my good humor and laughed at their teasing.

"It must be wonderful," one of the cadets remarked, "to be married to such a famous soldier."

"I wouldn't really know," I told him. "I've only been married five days." I stared at him for a moment, my laughter gone, for he was a young lad, much younger than Autie, and I wondered if he would go off to battle soon and how he would fare. Behind that lurked the thought I'd refused to face: Autie would go off to battle soon, too. Life had been so hectic that I'd been able to imagine that possibility lay far into the future. Somehow the young man's question brought reality home to me. I clung to Autie's promise to take me with him whenever he could.

"Here, here," boomed a deep voice, "I must kiss the bride."

I turned quickly to see a man surprisingly short for such a voice. Bald, with wire-framed glasses and a slight stoop as he walked, he was probably in his sixties and was obviously, from the way the cadets parted to make way for him, a professor. But instead of a military uniform, he wore a commodious black cape. The big cape draped on his small frame created the effect of a gnome.

"Martin Grenwich," he said, his voice no softer, even though he was now closer to me. "I teach mathematics at the academy, and I remember Custer well. One of my, ah, more unusual students." He laughed heartily at his own joke and then went on breathlessly. "Caught himself quite a pretty bride, didn't he? Tell me your name, my dear."

"I'm Elizabeth Bacon of Monroe, Michigan," I said.

"No, you're not!" he cackled. "You're Elizabeth Custer now."

"Yes, of course." I laughed. "But I'm still not used to it."

"May you have many long years to get used to it," he said, raising his hat as though in a salute. And then, before I could protest, he reached up—he was actually shorter than I —to plant a kiss on my cheek. "Good fortune to the prettiest bride I've seen in decades. . . . You may need it with that rascal you've married." He added the latter as a joke, but I sensed an underlying tone of seriousness.

Autie walked up just then. "Professor Grenwich," he said cordially, "how nice to see you."

"Good to see you, Custer," Grenwich said, almost in a mutter. "Fine bride you've got here." And he was gone before Autie could say any more.

On the train back to New York Autie was upset with me. "You let that Grenwich kiss you!" he accused.

"I didn't really let him," I said with a smile. "He just kissed me, suddenly, without any announcement."

"I don't like anyone being familiar with you." Autie was unbending in his disapproval.

"Pshaw!" I said. "He's a harmless old man and endearing, like a puppy."

"You don't know who's harmless and who isn't," Autie said intently. "You must hold yourself above such behavior. Remember, you set a standard of womanhood for my troops."

That sounded like an awesome responsibility to me, and I thought it an unfair burden placed on me by my husband. Besides, I was miffed at Autie's suspicions of my behavior. We rode the rest of the way in silence.

From New York we went to Washington, where I was all prepared for a round of parties and theater trips. But we had no more than settled in our hotel room, even more elegant than the Metropolitan, when a telegram was delivered to Autie. He had received several telegrams while we were in New York, each urging him back to battle, but he had said no harm would come from prolonging his honeymoon. This one was different, for he read it with a darkening face.

"I will not be accused of featherbedding," he said, his voice rising in agitation. "I must return to my troops at once."

The war was about to begin for me.

I hastened to pack, folding Autie's clothes neatly first and then attacking my own. All the while, Autie lounged on the bed, watching me, his face showing a sort of wry amusement.

"Autie, help me with these hoops," I said, struggling with the ungainly things.

"Never again," he vowed without moving from the bed. "They defeated me once. Besides, why are you packing your things?"

"I'm going with you, of course."

He rose from the bed and came toward me, still smiling at me as though I were a wayward child. "Of course you're not. It's far too dangerous."

"I will not be left behind." I stamped my foot in a spoiled manner.

Autie imitated me, stamping his foot. "You will," he said, and then laughed at me. After a moment, though, he turned serious and put his arms around me. "Right now I have rooms in a plantation house—three rooms—and you'd be fairly comfortable. But you'd be alone a great deal, and I have no idea when I'll have to move on. It just wouldn't be fair to you, dear girl."

"Fair is not the issue," I stormed determinedly. "I'll decide what's fair to me. Hardship won't bother me one bit."

"How do you know?" he asked, his grin returning. "You've never suffered any."

Stung, I walked away from him. What he said was true. I'd been petted and spoiled and protected all my life, and so far marriage—all ten days of it—was no different. "Autie, if I don't prove to you now that I can put up with hardship to be with you, we'll never have any kind of a marriage. You'll be off and gone, here and there, and I'll grow old alone in Monroe, or Washington, or wherever you hide me." I bit my lower lip to keep it from trembling and tried to blink back a tear.

"Tears are not a fair way to argue, dear girl," he said. And then he picked me up and whirled me around the room, my feet never touching the floor. "You shall go with me, everywhere you possibly can," he said happily, plunking me down on the bed.

I had won a battle, small though it may have seemed.

We went to Stevensburg, a small town in northeast Virginia. And I went from the luxury of elegant hotels to three rooms upstairs in a plantation house, with displaced southerners living grumpily downstairs and never speaking to us. The house had once been grand—you could tell from little things, the drapes, now tattered, that still hung in the great reception room downstairs, or the elaborate porcelain bowl and pitcher in our bedroom. I could envision the house full of grand furniture—walnut poster beds and great oak chiffoniers and delicate desks with inlaid tops and fragile curved legs—but whatever had happened to that furniture, I didn't know. Surely not chopped for firewood as some stories told! At any rate, now our rooms were sparsely furnished—an iron bedstead, a plain wooden chest of drawers, and two straight chairs did not make for cozy bedtime visiting; and the dining table with four chairs was terribly impractical since there was no kitchen, and we would take all our meals with Autie's troops.

Autie deposited me, gave me a quick kiss, and said, "I'll return as soon as I can."

I watched him race down that once-gracious, curving staircase, taking the stairs two at a time, and nearly leaping off the front veranda to grab the reins of a horse held by a young boy—I judged him to be about fourteen. Without another word or look in my direction, Autie galloped away, and the young boy disappeared back to wherever he had come from. I was left utterly alone.

For a while I busied myself straightening out our clothes, hanging them as best I could, on hooks in a wardrobe. But soon the utter emptiness and quiet began to weigh on me, and my thoughts dwelt on the fact that I'd now been married twelve days and was alone, a thousand or more miles from home, with no idea of when my husband might return —if ever. What, I wondered, would I do if he never returned, if he was—God forbid—killed in battle that very day? Such morbid and self-pitying thoughts soon gave way to tears, and I threw myself on that hard bed with its scratchy coverlet.

"Miz Custer?" A gentle knock on the door was followed by a soft voice. "All right I come in?"

Eliza stood in the doorway. I knew exactly who she was, for Autie had described her several times. A runaway slave, she had been in camp just after he'd been made a general, and when he knew he needed a cook, he'd asked her, "Would you like to come live with me?" She'd replied, "I reckon I would." And she'd taken care of him ever since—cooked his meals, sometimes under fire, cleaned his clothes, kept his quarters neat and clean.

"I clearly married you for love," Autie told me once, "for I don't need a wife. I have Eliza."

"Ginnel go off and leave you?" she asked. Then, without waiting for an answer, "Men's that way. Can't trust them, and that ginnel, he's the worst of the lot. Don't you worry none, though. You and I going to be fine, just fine." She bustled into the room and began to rearrange the clothes I'd worked so hard to straighten, clucking as she found a patch of dirt on the general's pants or sighing in appreciation over some garment of mine.

"I can take care of our clothes," I said hesitantly. "Thank you, but . . ."

"I been doing it and I'll just keep on," she said. She talked on while she shook and pressed with her hands and folded, all the while telling me how grateful she was to the general. "Course I don't let him know that," she said firmly. "Got to keep him knowing he's lucky to have me take care of him." She laughed heartily.

By the time the clothes were arranged to Eliza's satisfaction, I was through with self-pity but very tired. "You rest now," she said, "and I'll fetch you some supper in a bit. I sure am glad to have a woman to talk to. . . . I miss my mammy something fierce." And with that she was gone.

She reappeared about suppertime, bearing a thick steak that she had somehow produced—I would later learn that she could provide foods almost as magically as He who turned loaves into fishes.

Autie arrived in the middle of the night and found me sleeping soundly as though I had not a care in the world. "I knew you'd be all right," he whispered as he woke me to his urgent need for love.

I was a rarity in camp. The men stared at me with open curiosity when I rode into camp for dinner. "Why are they staring?" I asked Autie.

"It's . . . ah . . . not usual to see a woman like you in camp," he said cautiously.

"What do you mean, a woman like me?" I demanded. We had just driven up to the mess tent in the wonderful carriage that Autie had "confiscated" for me—it had silver trim and was drawn by two fine matching black horses. Whenever I went out in it, Autie and four or five troopers rode alongside. "Too close to the enemy," Autie had explained. "They'd like nothing better than to capture Custer's wife."

Now he looked patiently at me. "An officer's wife," he said.

"Well, what women are in camp?"

He shrugged. "We have laundresses."

"Like Eliza?"

"Some are," he said noncommittally, though his eyes told me he was laughing at me. "And a few are camp followers."

"Camp followers?" I echoed.

"They trade the soldiers, ah, certain favors for money or other things they need."

"Oh," I said, blushing clear to my hairline. "And do your men think I'm like a camp follower?"

"They best not," he said vehemently, and all the laughter was gone from his eyes.

Actually I was a trifle flattered that men could think me that wanton. It made me—that sheltered girl who had only recently discovered the physical pleasures of intimacy—feel alluring, and I liked it. Years later I would remember with gratitude that Autie's soldiers had thought me attractive—and slightly naughty.

Later Autie told me the story of Annie Elinor Jones,

who had hung about his camp for a week or more, mostly out of curiosity. Somehow she had access to passes that allowed her to cross Rebel lines back and forth until one day she was arrested as a spy by the Federal authorities. Then she named Autie as someone who could testify for her and said that her trouble had started when Autie paid attention to her and made another general jealous.

"Imagine that!" Autie said, and I nodded, agreeing that she must be a foolish girl, desperate for a daring experience. It never occurred to me that Autie might really have paid attention to her.

I was amazed at the men of his command and their respect for him. Gray-headed men, old enough almost to be my father, snapped to attention when Autie spoke and said, "Yes, sir!"

"Do they always obey you so?" I asked.

"Of course," he replied without a doubt.

"I wouldn't," I said, and laughed at him.

One who not only obeyed but worshiped Autie was Johnny Cisco, the young boy who'd held the horse the night we arrived. He was Autie's other personal servant, as it were, along with Eliza. Johnny was fifteen, a year older than I had guessed, and he had blond hair that hung limply over his forehead, filling me with an urge to grab the shears and cut it for him. He was thin and freckle-faced and lost looking, except when he was around Autie. Then Johnny Cisco blossomed. He took care of Autie's horses, waited on his dining table, and slept with a hound puppy that Autie had adopted. "Just attached himself to the ginnel, he did, that poor chile," Eliza said. "Hangin' 'round camp mostly starving to death."

Autie, who would always attract stray dogs and orphans, dressed the boy in soldier's clothes, including a red scarf at his neck, saw that Eliza fed him, and earned his undying devotion. Johnny was less fond of me, treating me civilly but with a certain distance that said clearly he considered me an interloper. At dinner he always served Autie first, in spite of frequent—and loud—lectures from Eliza about the propriety of serving the lady first.

The first time Autie was gone for a long time, I spent three miserable days at the plantation alone—even Eliza had gone with Autie—and then left for Washington. Autie wanted me to go when he left, and I stubbornly refused. Without comment he left orders with a soldier, also left behind, about my transportation should I change my mind. And change it I did.

I was alone in Washington, ensconced in Mrs. Hyatt's boardinghouse, where Autie had made arrangements before we left for Stevensburg. It was a big, roomy house with probably ten boarders, several of them officers' wives like myself. My rooms were two—a parlor and a bedroom, both more comfortably furnished than the house in Stevensburg. I took my meals at the table with the other boarders and cried myself to sleep at night longing for Autie.

But I had callers to break my loneliness. Congressman Kellogg from Michigan, who had long ago recommended Autie for West Point and who still considered him a protégé, came to see me almost immediately and took me to a reception for some of the military. And then came a summons that intimidated me—Secretary of War Stanton wished me to join him, as Autie's representative, in receiving captured Confederate flags. My heart nearly turned over in my chest as solemn-faced soldiers presented those flags and swore their allegiance to the Union.

In no time I had a fairly busy social life in Washington, and most days I had some engagement on my calendar. Once I even met the President at a reception in the White House. I came away a lifelong Lincoln supporter, for he stopped the whole receiving line to say, "So you are married to the man who goes into battle with a whoop and a yell!"

None of it made up for not having Autie by my side and in my bed at night, though I blushed to think how much I missed him at night. Papa, I thought, would never understand . . . and then I wondered why I thought of Papa.

I had frequent reason to remember Autie's injunctions about the proper role of a wife. "Mrs. Custer," said one congressman, "you're looking particularly lovely tonight. I'll swear Custer doesn't know what he's missing."

"He's defending his country," I said, lowering my eyes.

"He ought to be protecting his wife," the congressman said.

Another suggested that I would enjoy the view of the Potomac from his quarters, but I declined gently.

The only really difficult moment I had was with a senator who cornered me one night at a reception on the pretense of talking about Autie's latest victory.

"Splendid, my dear, just splendid. He's a remarkable man."

I was always willing to talk to anyone who praised Autie. "Thank you, sir. I'm very proud of my husband."

"And he of you, I imagine," he said, moving closer. "It's not every general who has such a pretty bride." He was overweight, and his face glistened slightly with perspiration. When he moved closer, I could smell garlic.

I turned quickly to one side, meaning to avoid him. "Senator . . . ," I said softly, hoping to turn his advance away. Instead, he reached an arm for my shoulders and began to pull me toward him, breathing heavily on me until I thought I might faint. Before I could move quickly enough, he planted a wet kiss on my cheek and whispered, "I could make you proud, too, my dear."

I remembered the night I'd stepped on the foot of lawyer Walter Ashburn in Monroe, and Autie had applauded me for taking charge of the situation. My tactic was different this time—Autie always said a commanding officer had to have several plans. My elbow moved ever so slightly, knocking the senator's hand by accident, and red wine poured down the front of his shirt and coat. I was profuse in my apologies and offered to go fetch a rag to clean his clothes—of course, I didn't return. At my last glance, the senator was lurking in corners, trying to hide his soiled clothes.

Autie had made it plain it was always my duty to make him proud of me, and I grinned with satisfaction, knowing he would approve my actions that particular night. The senator was fairly drunk at the time, and much embarrassed whenever he saw me afterward.

■   ■   ■

"You shall be the treasurer of our marriage," Autie wrote, "for I am notoriously improvident with my funds." I suspect Autie assumed that since I came from a comfortable home, lavish to him, I was adept at managing money, but nothing could have been further from the truth. Papa had always provided, and I had assumed the well would never run dry. In Washington I was appalled at how fast it threatened to do just that.

Autie gave me five hundred dollars, but my board took three hundred dollars, and he had a large commissary bill; before I knew it, I had spent almost the entire sum. I longed for a black silk dress that cost sixty dollars and realized I could not buy it, a situation I'd never found myself in before. Resignedly I began to sew, though I was no seamstress. My stepmother wrote preaching letters about how much men valued frugality in their wives: "A dress," she said, "should never cost above twelve dollars." So I pricked my fingers and ruined my eyes and disposition while laboriously making myself a calico dress and a muslin wrapper, silk being obviously beyond my beginning skills. Autie howled with laughter the first time I wore the wrapper, for it did fit peculiarly. I never got the calico out. Thereafter, I confined myself to embroidery, a useless skill, perhaps, but one I knew.

The most blessed sound I knew in those days was an unmistakable noise on the stair, a determined and rapid step as though someone were climbing the stairs two or three at a time. It meant Autie had come to surprise me again.

He would sweep me off my feet, smothering my face with kisses even as he waltzed me around the room, my feet never touching the floor, my arms locked tight around his neck.

"Come quick!" he said urgently on one of those visits. "We must get a copy of *Harper's Weekly*."

"I have the last one here," I said, unwilling to share him with the public. "Let's just stay here." I looked at the bed, impropriety shining in my eyes.

"No, you minx," he cried. "We must get the brand-new issue."

I asked whatever for but was given no answer, and the next I knew, we were hurrying through the streets in search of the paper. Autie found and bought it without letting me see.

"Hide your eyes," he commanded.

"I will not, Autie. Tell me what it is!" I sensed his excitement but could not rid myself of the fear of some awful catastrophe.

"Hide them!"

Unwillingly I put a gloved hand over my eyes, knowing I could easily peek if I felt the need. Autie led me to a nearby bench and nearly pushed me down, spreading the paper in my lap.

"There! Look!" he ordered.

Cautiously I took my hand away and peered at the paper, to be greeted with a full-size drawing of Autie, charging into battle, his right hand waving a sword while the left quirted a heavily muscled dark horse. "Oh," I gasped, "Autie, how wonderful. He's caught your curls . . . and the expression on your face. . . . Oh, Autie, we must frame it!"

He was obviously pleased beyond measure, marching back and forth in front of me, his chest puffed. "Artist came and drew right there in camp. Even followed me into battle until I sent him back."

I didn't point out that the artist wasn't too good at details, or he would have seen that Autie had to have one hand or the other on the reins of his horse. Autie apparently didn't notice this detail.

That night, as he held me in his arms, Autie talked more gently of the battle and the artist. "I thought to die in that battle," he said, "and it scared me to have the artist draw the picture, as though this were the last look you would have of me."

I put my hand over his mouth to silence him, but he kissed it and held it away. "And then," he said, "I knew I could not die. I could not leave you . . . but I'll never allow another artist to draw me just before a battle. Custer's Luck can't last forever."

It frightened me to hear him say that, as though some-one had walked on that grave that I worried so about. I silenced him this time with a kiss, and he welcomed my advances, moving beneath me with a groan until we were both lost to thought, and the foolish artist long forgotten.

Not a week later I thought that Custer's Luck had run out. I was in my sitting room, idly working at a painting, when I heard a newsboy hawking his wares below my win-dow: "Custer killed! Read all about it! Custer killed!"

I have no doubt that my heart stopped that moment. Unable to move, I sat frozen in the chair, hearing the young boy's cry as he moved away from the boardinghouse. Sud-denly galvanizing myself into action, I flew down the stairs, out the door, and up the street, shouting, "Here, you boy! Here! Let me have a paper!"

When he demanded payment—I had no coins with me —I snatched the paper out of his hand. "Hey, you can't do that!" he complained. He was a ragged young boy, his hair hanging into his eyes, and his too-short pants badly in need of washing and mending.

Just as he reached a dirty hand to grab the paper, I turned away, hand clutched to my mouth. He stopped and stared. "You all right, lady?"

I shook my head. "No," I said. "I . . . I'm General Custer's wife."

His mouth hung open in amazement, and finally, with-out looking at me, he said, "Sorry, ma'am. Keep the paper."

Clutching the paper to me, I headed back to the board-inghouse, though I had no idea of what to do, where to go. Woodenly I climbed the stairs to my room and sat on the bed.

This is a dream, I thought. *Any minute Autie will come bounding up the stairs.* That, of course, I knew was not true. After a bit I began to think about what I must do. Whom to call? My parents and Autie's family were too far away to be of comfort . . . perhaps Congressman Kellogg? He was kind but hardly comforting. Even the officers' wives in Mrs.

Hyatt's house were only casual acquaintances, not people with whom I would share the deepest catastrophe of my life. I was adrift in a sea of strangers, and Autie, my anchor, had been taken from me.

At that moment I wished desperately that I had conceived Autie's child, but my monthly time had been frustratingly regular, a disappointment to us both. If only, I thought, I could have his child, and my mind wandered to picture a young boy, the fair image of his father, wandering around my father's house in Monroe. Then the image of myself, living at home with my parents, a widow at my young age, rose before me, and I choked on the bitterness of it.

It grew dark, and still I sat as though expecting Autie to come bounding up the stairs. At last there were footsteps, far too gentle to be Autie's. The wife of one of Autie's officers entered, took one look at me, and threw her arms around me, crying, "Oh, my dear!" I knew she was overcome with sympathy.

"It was a false rumor," she said. "The secretary of war has said it is not true. Armstrong is alive and well, not even injured."

My foggy brain did not register the words quite. "What?"

She repeated her message, and it slowly dawned on me that her errand was not one of sympathy but reassurance. "He's alive?" I echoed.

"Very," she said, laughing now, and I grabbed her and whirled around the room, just the way Autie whirled me when he was excited. We laughed and cried and hugged until I was exhausted. I slept for twelve hours straight after she left, and never told Autie that I had once thought Custer's Luck had run out. To have told him, to my superstitious mind, might have cast a blight on the famous luck. Custer's Luck was to carry me through for a long time to come.

In the spring of 1864, General Philip Sheridan replaced Pleasanton, whom Autie had so respected and liked, as chief of the cavalry. Sheridan was an ugly man, I thought—short

and chunky, with no neck, and long arms that hung halfway
to his ankles. Convinced that Autie should have had his post,
I was not prepared to like Sheridan, but Autie thought him
an able and good commander, and I kept my silence.

Autie was not as fond of General Grant, who assumed
control of the entire Union Army. Autie disliked him for
having routed General Pleasanton and, more important, for
not giving Autie the promotion he wanted. Proud to be at the
head of the Michigan Cavalry, he was still unsatisfied—he
wanted a division, and he blamed the slowness of that promotion on Grant. Rumor was that Grant was intemperate in
his use of alcohol. By then, in late March, the general already
had victories to his credit, and supposedly President Lincoln
said, "I cannot say whether Grant is a drinking man or not,
but if he is, I should like to know where he buys his liquor as
I wish to present each one of my army commanders with a
barrel of the same brand."

Just after Grant's appointment, Autie was thrown from a
carriage and injured badly enough to warrant ten days' sick
leave. I had been with him in Virginia, and we immediately
took the train to Washington. By luck, or fate, General Grant
was also on that train. He was a short, unassuming man with
sandy hair and gray-green eyes of the most remarkable color.
He talked a great deal on the trip, and as he spoke, his
clenched fist went up and down, from tabletop to thigh, back
and forth, and I watched it, almost mesmerized. Occasionally
he would unloose the fist and stroke his beard, but soon he
clenched it again. I never did see him take a drink that day,
though.

Autie suffered a calamity he thought more devastating
than being dumped out of a carriage when he returned to the
front. He wrote the following to me:

> *My dearest little girl,*
> *The worst calamity of my career has happened.*
> *Eliza and Johnny were captured when our brigade*
> *was hemmed in after a long and hard day. Both*
> *managed to escape as soon as it came dark, but*
> *much to my dismay the Rebels got away with the*

wagon, which had all my personal belongings—and especially my desk, which had in it your ambrotype and your letters.

Oh, my love, you cannot know how I grieve over those letters. When I think of some rough Johnny Reb reading them aloud, no doubt to the high amusement of his fellows, I am mortified for you that you should have expressed your passion so freely in writing. Such matters belong privately between a husband and wife, and I beg you to be more circumspect after this in what you write, never knowing who may see your beloved missives.

Your loving husband,
Autie

In his letter I recognized the same man who would not make love to me in the daylight. Angrily, I replied that he need not be mortified for me and perhaps it was he himself who felt the embarrassment. I had nothing, I assured him, to be ashamed of for loving my husband, and I would not be scolded for it. I thought of the agony I'd endured thinking he was dead, and briefly I hated Autie for being unappreciative of my love and devotion. The thought that I could hate Autie, however briefly, came as a surprise to me, though later it would be a frequent if fleeting emotion.

Mortification was truly his this time, for Autie was apparently alarmed by my anger and answered that he had not meant to scold and of course he treasured my letters. But, he added, he did hope I would be more circumspect in the future.

Autie got his revenge on the Rebs within months, when he defeated forces led by Tom Rosser, a West Point comrade of his. Autie captured Rosser's wagon with many private papers and his trunk of clothes, and in the process retrieved his own papers, which had somehow fallen into Rosser's hands, and which the Confederate general, out of loyalty to Autie, was protecting. Autie laughed about wearing Rosser's coat throughout camp, for the southerner was a much bigger man than Autie, and the coat hung ridiculously on him.

"But," he wrote, "recovering your letters is the most important thing, and now we will never talk of that incident again." Typically Autie closed a subject when he had the last word, and I was left fuming.

Chapter Five

THAT SPRING AUTIE LOST THE ENEMY HE'D CHASED and challenged throughout the war when, at the Battle of Yellow Tavern near Richmond, one of his own Wolverines fired the shot that brought down General Jeb Stuart. Instead of being elated, Autie was heartsick. He had respected and admired Stuart, and he foresaw that the southern cavalry would fall apart after Stuart's death. "The war," he wrote, "is grinding to an end."

Autie soon found another worthy enemy—General Jubal Early, who decided to threaten Washington. Grant had settled troops, including Autie's Michigan Brigade, into what would be the winter-long seige of Petersburg near Richmond, and Early thought to divert attention to the protection of Washington. The entire city went into a panic when Early swept through Maryland and began to harass the city's northern defenses.

"I would be safer in camp with you," I wrote to Autie. "Please say that I may come." Even in the best of circumstances, I preferred to be in camp with Autie, and I was always looking for a way, an excuse, to get there.

I did not, of course, get to visit Autie while those fierce battles raged. Sheridan's troops attacked Early near Winchester, Virginia, and Autie and his saber-swinging Wolverines were so brilliant on the battlefield—and the Union victory so complete—that Autie received the promotion he had wanted so badly in the spring. He was made major general and given charge of the Third Division—it meant he could wear two stars on his shoulder straps instead of one and arrange his buttons in rows of three instead of two. Eliza was kept busy making the necessary changes.

In the late spring battle at Cold Harbor, Jim Christiancy from Monroe, a lieutenant on Autie's staff, was badly wounded with shrapnel in the thigh and hip. Autie immediately notified me that Jim was in a hospital in Washington, and I went at once to see him.

The hospital, a converted public building, appalled me. Wounded men, in all states of desperation, lay in rows of cots in large, open hall-like rooms. Some moaned in pain, a few cried aloud, and others looked to me as if they were already dead. People hurried everywhere—the pitifully few nurses, trying to succor every patient and finding their chore impossible, the two lone physicians, their eyes exhausted and hopeless. And above it all was a horrible stench—the smell of wounds, and decaying flesh, and death. With a hand over my mouth, I sought Jim.

"Jim?" I asked doubtfully when I was pointed to a specific cot. The pale and unshaven man on the cot bore no resemblance to the laughing young boy I remembered. "Is that you?"

His dull eyes lifted a little and he stared at me, almost confused. "Libbie? Libbie Bacon?"

"Libbie Custer," I reminded him. "Autie particularly wanted me to come see you, since he cannot himself."

"He's a great leader, Libbie," Jim said faintly, "a great leader."

Alarmed by his apparent weakness, I sought out a harried and overworked doctor. When I complained that Jim didn't seem to be getting enough care and asked if he was eating, the doctor merely shrugged and motioned around the huge barrackslike room, where men lay on cots and some on the floor, in endless row after row. "We do what we can," he said, and then a loud cry of pain sent him hurtling down a row of bodies. Over his shoulder he said, "He'd be better off somewhere else. I can tell you that."

I had Jim transferred to Mrs. Hyatt's boardinghouse. Unwittingly, I had let myself in for a nasty nursing chore. As fragments of cloth and dirt worked their way out of Jim's wound, it had to be cleaned, and there was no one else at Miss Hyatt's to take on that chore.

Resolutely, I would turn the patient on his side, scrub my hands, and then raise his gown and clean the wound, as the doctor had shown me. When he was most ill, Jim protested only feebly, but as he began to improve, his protests became louder.

"Libbie, it's not fitting for you to be doing this for me."

"Hush, Jim Christiancy. I'm a married woman now, and fitting isn't the question here. We've got to save the use of your hip."

"You're an angel of mercy," he declared. "I thought to die in that hospital."

I remembered the time Autie had "thought to die" in battle and shuddered.

When Jim was better, I sat for long hours reading to him, often from the poetry of Alfred Lord Tennyson, which he particularly enjoyed. Autie had given me a copy of *Enoch Arden*, which I read aloud. And we talked for hours on end, Jim lying in his bed and me sitting in a chair that I had pulled close to the bed.

Jim was a charmer, a ladies' man, who drank far too much, loved all the women, and always had a good time, but he had a good soul. "Libbie," he'd say, "if Armstrong hadn't beaten me to it, you'd be Mrs. Christiancy."

"La, Jim, not unless you changed your ways," I said, laughing.

"You can't tell me Armstrong is a paragon of virtue," he protested.

"He doesn't drink," I replied solemnly.

"And he's given up his eye for the ladies?" he asked.

"Of course he has. He wouldn't dare look at another woman," I said defiantly. The tone behind Jim's words was beginning to make me nervous, as though he found me incredibly naive.

"And you?" There was a seriousness to Jim's tone that sent a chill through me, and when I raised my eyes to his, he was staring intently at me. His hand reached for mine.

"I have no need to look at another man, Jim. Autie makes me happy."

He sighed. "So be it. But let me know if things change."

"Jim Christiancy." I laughed, trying to change the mood. "You're incorrigible."

"That's what my father tells me all the time," he said.

I knew even before that talk that Jim had fallen a little bit in love with me, and I didn't do much to discourage it. Autie was far away, I was lonely, and Jim was charming—I saw no harm in the flirtation.

Autie regarded it otherwise. He appeared at the boardinghouse in one of his surprise visits and barely greeted me before he demanded, "Where's Christiancy?"

"In his room," I said. "Oh, Autie, he can walk ever so slightly on crutches now, and he's getting so much better. You'll be pleased." I was a little slow to catch on to Autie's mood.

"I'll bet," he said grimly, brushing past me to head for Jim's room. "Soldier," he said, "I'm sending you home on extended sick leave. You'll go to Monroe by tomorrow's train."

"Autie," I protested, "he's not well enough to travel."

"He damn well will travel," Autie said, banging out of the room and dragging me with him.

We had a tremendous battle once we reached our room, and though Autie carefully closed the door—without slamming it, which took great forbearance on his part—I know the whole house, and especially Jim Christiancy, heard every word of it, at least every word of Autie's.

"You will not compromise me by being so friendly with a man who serves under me. Not only friendly, you've been intimate with him," Autie said loudly.

"Intimate?" I echoed in disbelief. "Changing his bandages? Hardly a chore to inspire romance, Autie. I suggest you change some bandages yourself. It might change your view of war."

"You should have left him in the hospital! You had no right to bring him here without consulting me."

"Consulting you? You were in battle, and the days it would have taken to get an answer might have meant Jim's life."

"You should have had my permission," he repeated.

Permission? I was stunned. Autie sounded like my father. I could feel my face flame as I repeated, "Autie, you weren't here for me to ask. I just did what I thought was right."

"Well, it sure as hell wasn't right," he roared.

"Autie," I said as calmly as I could, "I've asked you not to swear before."

"And I have asked you to be a model for the officers of the troops. How do you think I feel when I find they're all talking about the man my wife's nursing?"

"Jim's a friend of yours," I answered, my voice growing weak as I realized that I could not win this argument.

"Not close enough that I'd share my wife with him," he hollered.

Autie was riding over me, just as he'd ridden over Confederate troops. And the truth, I saw, was two-pronged: Autie was not jealous of Jim, but he feared that he had been embarrassed in front of his troops and that he had somehow lost his right to dictate what I did, as his wife. Realizing all this did not make me, still a young bride, any better equipped to deal with Autie's anger, and I quailed before it.

Thinking to quiet his voice, I moved closer to him and touched my finger to his lips. Instantly he gathered me in his arms and crushed me to him. "I could not bear to lose you," he said.

Later I would count this as a battle lost on my part.

We had a quiet dinner together, and Autie returned to his troops without even spending the night and without rescinding his orders to Christiancy. Jim, though barely able to move about, left for Monroe the next day, and I saw him off. On the way to the rail station, Jim never mentioned the argument between Autie and me, nor did any glance or word on his part indicate that anything might be less than idyllic in my marriage. In view of the fight he'd heard, I thought him a true gentleman.

Just before he boarded the train, he balanced on his crutches and reached an awkward arm for me. I moved into his embrace, kissing him affectionately.

"Libbie," he said, "I don't think I'd have made it without you." He was still pale, and his uniform hung on his thin bones, but, his eyes now alive, he looked worlds better than he had when I'd found him in the hospital.

"That," I said sincerely, "is reward enough. Go to Monroe and heal, and we'll see you there after the war. Autie will be so looking forward to a visit with you."

Only then did he cock an eyebrow at me, but the look quickly passed from his face. "I'll count on it," he said, kissed me again, and hobbled onto the train with the help of a curious conductor who eyed me once or twice and then shrugged meaninglessly. I hoped the conductor was not somehow in touch with Autie, who would have started the row all over again if he'd seen Jim kiss me.

Autie and I had yet another one-sided argument weeks later when I surprised him near his camp during the heaviest fighting in the Shenandoah Valley.

Autie's camp was some few miles from Harper's Ferry, and I contrived to surprise him by appearing at that small town. Autie was grim-faced when he met me. "You had no right," he stormed, "to come here without my permission."

That word again! "I thought to surprise you."

"You did that," he said grimly, "and nearly scared me half to death to boot. There are guerrillas all around this town—they could have captured you, and don't think *that* wouldn't have delighted them! As it was, they had a perfect chance to take potshots at me—and they did." Ruefully, he took off the battered Rebel hat he always wore and showed me a bullet hole in the brim.

"Custer's Luck," I murmured, hoping to hide my fear. Had Autie died that day, I would have been responsible.

"Either that or I was meant to spend this day with you," he said, drawing me tightly into his arms and kissing me with a demanding strength.

"Autie," I said, backing away, "it's daytime."

He looked disconcerted for just a moment, and then he said, "We'll pull the drapes and pretend it's night."

We spent the day locked in the privacy of my hotel quarters, and Autie's orderly knew to rouse him only if the tide of the war turned irrevocably. It didn't in that twenty-four hours.

And Autie was never again reluctant to make love in the daytime.

In the late fall Autie sent for me, and I took the train to Martinsburg, Virginia, to join him at his headquarters in a big, old farmhouse. He met me at the train, and we drove the few miles to his headquarters, passing rows and rows of army tents, where men lounged about, some working at small tasks I couldn't identify. When they saw Autie, without exception, the men hailed him heartily, and I felt a thrill of pride in him. To think that all these men—there were hundreds—went to battle under Autie's command!

The tents were in much better shape than Autie's farm-house-headquarters, which was shabby and rundown—it might have been freshly painted four years earlier when the war started, but now the white paint was peeling and gray. Around it were untilled, weed-infested fields. I found it depressing.

"I have a surprise for you," Autie said, sweeping me into his arms once we were inside the house.

"What is it?" I could not imagine what he had gotten hold of on the front that would intrigue me, and I loosened myself from his hold to look around for some hidden object.

"You'll see," he smiled. "It's not what you expect."

It certainly wasn't. The surprise was his younger brother, Tom, who'd resigned from the Ohio Infantry to join the Michigan Cavalry. Once that was done, Autie simply requested he be assigned to his troop.

Tom's presence meant a life of practical jokes and little privacy. Autie and his brother often teamed up to tease me. One of their favorite jokes was to ask if I minded if they smoked. When I, trying to be agreeable, said of course not, they would seal all the windows and puff furiously until I was reduced to coughing and wiping my eyes. "Smoke bothering you?" Tom would ask, and Autie would merely nod, though I looked daggers at him.

Once they returned from a skirmish to announce they had a new name for me. They'd stopped at a farmhouse, meaning to use it for temporary headquarters, but the farmer, an old Dutchman, had said no. "The old lady," he said, "is agin it." Autie and Tom had a good laugh over the name, and from that day on, whenever I opposed them, I too was "the old lady."

When I rode my pony—a gentle but short-legged creature that Autie had confiscated for me—they asked if I'd gotten my horseback experience with the infantry. The pony had a choppy little canter, and I could have made better time walking. Autie and Tom would make a great show of holding back their sleek and snorting horses to wait for me to catch up.

I was game about the teasing, as Autie predicted, and occasionally I gave as good as I got. But the lack of privacy bothered me more, for Tom would often rush into our quarters unannounced.

"He's my brother," Autie said, shrugging when I mentioned it.

I said no more for the moment, but our occasional

stolen daytime moments of passion were no more, and, still a bride, I missed them sorely. Autie remained a passionate lover at night, no matter how long the battle he'd been in that day. Once the lights were out and our privacy assured, he would sweep me into bed. Gone were the demure days of my making a toilette and Autie donning a huge white nightshirt. Now morning often found our clothes scattered on the floor where we'd left them in our urgency, though I always picked them up neatly before Eliza came in.

"Come back to bed a moment," Autie invited one morning as he uncharacteristically lingered in the bed. Usually he burst up well before dawn, ready, even eager, for the day's battle, while I sleepily clung to the night.

"I must pick up these clothes. Eliza will be here any moment with coffee."

"Eliza would understand," he said, but I pushed away his inviting arms and dressed myself in a wrapper.

"Don't you have a war to go to today?" I asked impertinently. It always struck me as strange that he went away to war in the mornings and came home to me at night, much like Papa had gone to his law offices.

Eliza and I spent long days together while Autie was off at his war. "That Mistah Tom bothering you some?" she asked one day while I sat lazily writing letters and she stirred a kettle on the fire.

"Some," I said noncommittally, thinking it not proper to discuss family affairs, even with Eliza, who was herself as close as family.

"He's a wild one," she said, "and someday he's gonna get the ginnel in trouble. You mark my words." She stirred the pot even more vigorously, splashing some broth onto her apron. Eliza always wore clean white aprons, and it puzzled me some how she kept them so neat under conditions that were difficult, to say the least. But, then, she kept Autie's clothes in spit-polish condition, too.

"Oh, Eliza, I'm sure they're good for each other," I said, trying to be reassuring. Eliza, I knew, depended on Autie for her security as much as I did—and often feared for him in battle more than I did, for she didn't have much faith in

Custer's Luck and had once scoffed loudly when it was mentioned. Autie silenced her with a dark look, but she continued to brood, as she was now.

Her turbaned head bobbed up and down. "That Tom
and the ginnel are good for each other in wildness. They do
things together neither one ever do alone. . . . My mammy,
she had the sight, and sometimes I think she passed it on to
me. I don't like what I see."

A cold shiver of fear went through me, and I was frantic
to change the subject. "What's for supper, Eliza?" I asked
inanely.

In spite of the war that had brought us there and in spite
of Tom, Winchester was a bit of heaven to me, with comfortable quarters and a constant round of dinners and dances,
even a lively, galloping dance that everyone insisted on calling "Custer's Charge." I may not have tasted much wine, but
Papa would have been dismayed to see how gaily I danced
every dance, each with a different partner, but always saving
the last dance for Autie.

Several officers had their headquarters in local homes,
and we all took turns entertaining, even if it were no more
than a gathering for hot cider in front of a blazing fire, or a
shared supper. The men would tell stories of battle, though
in deference they left out the deaths, and often they were
wry and droll. We laughed a great deal, perhaps to keep fear
from our minds.

Best of all, I was with Autie. I forgot the occasional
spats, intense though they were, that had already marked our
marriage.

The entire country was caught up that fall in the election
campaign between Lincoln and McClellan, a campaign that
caught Autie right in the middle. McClellan was the Democrat, and Autie's family had always been staunch Democrats;
more than that, Autie had served under McClellan early in
the war and been one of his defenders. But Autie had good
reason to be loyal to Lincoln, who was his commander in

chief. He solved his dilemma by refusing to endorse either side. "Soldiers and politics do not mix," he said publicly.

Papa's letters showed no such hesitation. In spite of those who claimed peace would come sooner if McClellan were elected, Papa was firm in his support of Lincoln. Lincoln had, of course, won me over in one sentence with his praise of Autie, but I also believed those who said McClellan might bring peace, though without honor. A corner of me wanted peace at any price, so that I could have my husband home, but I felt, as did most in Washington, that Lincoln would win. I was careful not to voice my opinion, lest it be thought I was speaking for Autie, but I followed the campaign as closely as I did the battle reports.

In November, Lincoln won, much to my relief, and in March Mama and Papa came east for the inauguration. It was only our second visit since my marriage.

All during that long first year of my marriage, I wrote frequently to my parents and heard often from them, mostly pleas that I come back to Monroe until "this terrible conflict is ended." The tension caused by my marriage had not eased, though I'd tried repeatedly to reassure Papa of my safety and happiness, and even Autie had taken to writing him occasionally. Papa answered only my letters, though he often bid me thank Autie for his most recent missive.

We did not make it to Monroe for Christmas—my first Christmas away from home—but in late January we were there for a rousing good visit, which of course was shared between two very different households—the Bacons and the Custers. We stayed with my parents, there being more room there, though it made me nervous, and I insisted we sleep in the spare room with twin beds.

"Are there alligators in this gulf between us?" Autie whispered one night.

"There might as well be," I said. "Stay in your own bed, Autie." It was foolish of me, I know, but I could not have let Autie touch me while I was under my father's roof.

"We should have stayed with Ann and David," he said, referring to his sister and her husband and their house full of children.

"They have no spare room," I answered, "and we'd have slept on sofas."

"Yes," he muttered, "but we could have slept on the same sofa."

During the day Papa and Autie were cordial, even friendly, but when Mama suggested that the Custers might join us for dinner one night, Autie was the one who vetoed the idea. "Thank you, Mother Bacon," he said, "but I fear it would be a strain on you, and my poor parents, unused to dining out, would be too worried about making a good impression."

We visited the Custers and the Reeds several times, and I felt at home enough to regale Autie's parents with tales of the teasing I endured at the hands of their sons. Mother Custer frowned at Autie and admonished him to be more gentle with me, but Father Custer laughed heartily.

"They pick on me, too," he said. "But just you wait, Libbie. One day I'll visit you in camp, and I'll make them change their tune."

"I'll look forward to it," I assured him. I liked Father Custer immensely, finding his company as energetic and irresistible as Autie's.

Papa and I had only one long visit together during the week we were home. It was a sunny day, though chilly, as Michigan always is in midwinter, and Papa asked, almost hesitantly, if I would care to walk out to the marshes with him.

"Oh, Papa, I'd love to," I answered. And then said boldly to Autie, "You stay here with Mama. I'm going to have a visit with Papa."

Papa, beaming, tucked my arm in his as we walked down Monroe Street. "Remember the walks we took when you were very little?" he asked.

"Perfectly," I replied. "One of my very best childhood memories." I almost said something about the many times since I'd wanted to walk with him, but I didn't want to ruin the moment.

Papa ruined it, though I know he didn't mean to. What he said welled up from the great sadness that was still inside him, in spite of Mama. "So much has changed since those days, Libbie. Your mother gone, and now this sad time for our country," he said.

"But," I added, trying to be lighthearted, "a glorious time for Autie."

"Yes," Papa said slowly. "I hear he is making a name for himself, bravest general in the Union Army." Papa spoke deliberately, his praise of Autie sincere, but old wounds still festered. "He is a good leader," he said, "and may the Lord be willing, he will be a good husband to you."

"He is a good husband, Papa. He makes me very happy."

"It is too soon to tell that, daughter," Papa said grimly. Later I would wonder if Papa had all along known something I hadn't. We are always ready to dismiss our parents' caution, but I have often wondered what my life would have brought if I had listened to Papa's fears.

My course was set, though. I was the wife of the famous Civil War general, and I was game.

When Mama and Papa arrived in Washington for the inaugural, I met them at the train. Papa seemed bewildered. "Our luggage?" he asked not once but three times. "How will we find our luggage?"

"I'll send for it, Papa," I assured him. "It will be all right."

"So many people," Mama said, voice fluttering. "I surely do feel lost." She looked dumpier than she had in Monroe, as though the big city made her shrink just a little, and her usual cheerfulness was replaced by a sort of vague apprehension.

"No need," I said. "It's just like Monroe, only bigger." Well, that wasn't quite true, but I wanted to reassure them both, and it tugged at my heart to see Papa, who had always taken charge, look to me for comfort.

As I predicted, their luggage arrived at the boarding-house intact, not long after we got there. Their stay in Washington proved to be a grand adventure for Papa, and Mama tagged uncomplainingly along, though I often felt she would just as soon have stayed at Mrs. Hyatt's. I was pleased that I was able to make the visit more than it would have been for Papa had he been without me . . . or had he not been Armstrong Custer's father-in-law. Papa was presented to Secretary of War Stanton, who spoke highly of Autie and said, "I'm only glad he has been as judicious in love as he is wise in war." He met General Grant, though only long enough for a brief handshake, and I saw to it that he visited with Congressman Kellogg.

But the inauguration was Papa's biggest thrill. We dressed carefully for the occasion, as though, I thought, we were to be the center of attention. Papa wore his best dark suit of worsted wool and carried a walking stick, and Mama wore a tartan plaid with a matching shawl. I told her several times how fetching she looked, and she beamed. I had a velvet-trimmed linen sheath of brown with a flowered hat to match—I didn't tell Mama the outfit had cost considerably more than twelve dollars, though I could see by her eyes that she was curious.

The balcony of the Senate Chamber, where we were fortunate enough to get seats, was crowded, and we sat nearly on top of each other. I could feel Papa stiffen in alarm when Vice President Andrew Johnson, obviously inebriated, took the oath of office and then rambled through a disjointed address.

"Remember," I whispered to Papa, "Autie has forsworn alcohol."

He nodded at me and smiled ever so slightly. Papa took politics and the government very seriously, and in his eyes it was a tragedy that a man so placed in our government would display such weakness. I agreed wholeheartedly, but I had by now seen that very weakness displayed throughout Washington and was less surprised than Papa.

President Lincoln, though, was eloquent, and those words yet ring in my ears: "With malice toward none; with charity for all; with firmness in the right, as God gives us to see the right, let us strive on to finish the work we are in; to bind up the nation's wounds. . . ." It made me very proud of Autie.

Mama and Papa left for Monroe the next day, and I saw

them to the train. Autie had not even been able to get to Washington to see them.

"Tell Armstrong how sorry we are to have missed him," Papa said, standing with his arm resting loosely on my shoulder. I leaned happily against him, relishing the affection.

"Yes," Mama said, "we're so very proud every time we hear people praise him."

"And you're looking well, daughter," Papa said. "I guess we can ease our minds about you a little. Though I do hate your being alone in this city with its . . ." His voice trailed off.

"Its wicked ways, Papa?" I asked mischievously.

"Well, yes," he harrumphed. "I should feel better if Armstrong were with you."

"Or I with him in camp," I said, but Mama gasped and said, "Oh, no, we worry about that even more."

The train whistle blew, and I hurried them to their compartment, giving Mama a tight hug and telling her how glad I was she had come with Papa.

Papa held out his arms for a similar hug, which I gave with pleasure. "I do think he makes you happy, daughter," he said, "and I trust he will take care of you and that you'll be home in Monroe soon."

"I'm sure we will," I said. "Autie writes that the war is grinding down." No need to tell them I was quite sure we would never again live in Monroe.

"I think the awkwardness is easing," I wrote Autie that night. "They are both so very proud of you!"

Had Tom Custer had a West Point education and officer's status, he might well have eclipsed Autie. At the battle of Sayler's Creek, just three days before the Confederate surrender, Tom was shot in the face while capturing a flag. He grabbed the flag and killed the Rebel holding it, then prepared to take another flag. But Autie saw his bloodstained face and clothes and ordered him to the surgeon in the rear. Tom would have refused, but Autie had him placed under arrest.

"He made me proud of the Custer name," Autie said. "He has courage and foolhardiness, all mixed into one. I worry about him and probably always shall, but I am proud of his bravery."

I remembered Eliza's "sight" and shuddered.

We were in Richmond, and Autie was telling me of the last days of the war. I was horrified by the sheer, dogged determination of the Confederates, beaten long before they surrendered, and though I was filled with relief that the war was over—and Autie safe—I could not help but grieve for the vanquished southerners. The story that intrigued me most and frightened me less than Tom's foolhardiness was about the Rebel who carried the flag of truce. "He came on horseback to my camp, waving a dirty white rag on a stick, and asked to be presented to me. He wanted to meet with Grant," Autie said.

"Just think," I responded, much impressed, "the whole end of the war came through you!"

"Well," he said, not very modestly, "that's about right. I'm the one who accepted the truce."

I arrived in Richmond, having traveled from Washington on the presidential gunboat, the *Baltimore,* with a party of officers' wives, under the care of a senator. Autie, who had tried in military terms to get to Richmond for four years, had been beaten there by his wife after the news of the surrender, and I was waiting at the Confederate White House, sleeping in no less than the big walnut bed of Mrs. Jefferson Davis. Autie arrived bearing a small walnut table with spool legs. After the flurry of greetings—and a long look that told me he was thin and drawn and tired—I demanded to know why he was carrying a table.

"It's yours," he said, handing me a note, which I spread out and read.

My dear madam,
     I respectfully present to you the small writing table on which the conditions for the surrender of the Confederate Army of Northern Virginia were written by Lieutenant General Grant—and permit

me to say, madam, that there is scarcely an individ-
ual in our service who has contributed more to
bring about this desirable result than your very gal-
lant husband.

> Very respectfully,
> Phil H. Sheridan
> Major General

I smiled as I read the letter, for I knew that it was
Sheridan's tribute to me for not having spoiled one of his
most brilliant officers. Sheridan thought that marriage utterly
ruined a man for war, and he had once said to Autie, "You're
the only man I know whom matrimony has not spoiled for a
charge." Little did he know how often I would have prevented one of those desperate charges for which Autie was
noted, if only I could have. What I didn't realize at the time
was how valuable a souvenir the general had gifted me with.

Autie fell into an exhausted sleep, and I sat patiently in a
chair in the room. His very presence—and the knowledge
that the war was over—filled me with electricity. So much
good was ahead of us that I was content simply to sit and
watch over him, only occasionally reaching out to touch him.

We had no time in Richmond, for Autie, once refreshed,
was determined that we head immediately to Winchester to
join his troops. From there the column would march to
Washington to be part of the victory parade in late May. I
protested that there was no urgency, since the parade was
nearly six weeks away, but for Autie there was an imperative
to be with his men. I did manage to whisk him through the
Davis mansion, where everything from Sevres china to a
black-and-tan dog had been left behind in the hasty flight
from the besieged city. Autie only grunted as I showed him
these things and urged me to hurry.

Autie had barely left to see about our horses when he
returned, his face ashen. "The President . . . ," he gasped,
"the President . . . has been killed!"

"What President?" I asked shortly, the thought that he
meant Lincoln never occurring to me. I thought perhaps

Jefferson Davis had been killed by angry and uncontrolled Union troops.

"Lincoln!" he shouted, his impatience with me overcoming his shock.

"Lincoln?" I echoed, sinking into one of Mrs. Davis's needlepoint chairs to weep unconsolably, remembering that kind man who had held up a receiving line to talk with me and hearing again those words of his, "With malice toward none; with charity for all . . ."

The nation's joy at peace was utterly broken. Papa, writing on the day the news became known, asked of me, "Oh, daughter, what is to become of us as a nation and as individuals? This is the most gloomy day in the history of the continent." Papa was, of course, not only grieving for Lincoln but remembering Johnson's drunken inaugural address and realizing that the man who had slurred his way through a speech was now leader of our country. Autie expressed great confidence in Johnson's policies, but our sense of triumph was gone as we headed toward Winchester.

"He's yours," Autie said triumphantly. "Do you like him?"

I stared openmouthed at the beautiful blooded bay that Johnny Cisco paraded before us as we stood in a field near Winchester. "He's wonderful, Autie! Don't you want to ride him?"

"No," he said generously, "I have Don Juan. I got him from the provost marshal for twenty-five dollars." I later learned that Don Juan had been confiscated on a march through North Carolina and, because he had a strong record at the race track, was worth at least ten thousand dollars.

"And where did you get this one?" I asked.

"A Confederate just walked up and handed me the reins," Autie said, grinning. "His name is Custis Lee—you know, after Robert E. Lee's son."

I walked over and patted Custis Lee on the nose, fancying that he recognized me as his mistress when he nuzzled his nose into my neck. Laughing, I walked around the beautiful animal, letting one hand run its way around his body.

"You'll have to keep up on the march, now," Autie warned sternly. "No more hanging back on that pony."

"I can ride with you? Not in a carriage?"

"If you can keep up," he said gruffly.

And so I joined Autie in leading his troops to Washington. Autie had also confiscated a beautiful, soft sidesaddle, and I had two or three appropriate riding outfits, though mostly of wool and often too warm on these spring days. Always, no matter the color of my outfit, I wore a scarlet kerchief to signify that I belonged to Autie's troops—and to Autie.

He was a man in his element—victorious, respected by his men, loved by his wife. Pride radiated from him as he rode, and not even the grim looks on the faces of some southerners could daunt him, though I looked at some of them with real heartbreak. In Brandy Station—that crossroads town that had seen a bloody battle between Autie and Jeb Stuart—I saw a young woman holding an infant in her arms. Her dress, though neat and pressed, was obviously worn, and the child was clothed in an oversize hand-me-down. While the child played with a string of beads, the mother stared at us, her head held high but her expression impassive. Instinct told me she was a war widow, and she was watching the triumphal march of those who killed her husband. I looked away.

The column traveled slowly, through Richmond and small towns and on for a rest at camp on the battlefield at Bull Run, where Autie had seen his first action. He insisted on reliving those days for me, walking me over the battlefield and pointing out each and every landmark until I thought my feet, fashionably clad in high-topped shoes, would fall off and I would drop in an exhausted heap at his feet. Autie seemed never to notice.

"There," he said at the bridge at Cedar Run, "that's where we charged the pickets. . . . And there, that's where Smallwood was wounded, the first man in the Army of the Potomac to be wounded."

I shuddered to think of all that had been wounded since.

■   ■   ■

We camped again across the Potomac, just outside Washington. Camp meant quarters not as luxurious as some Autie had shown me, but a good deal more pleasant than the farmhouse at Martinsburg. Orderlies set up two adjoining tents for us, one for a bedroom and the other—with a barn-board floor, as boards were available—for a reception and dining area. Eliza cooked for us, Johnny Cisco looked after us, and we had all the comforts of home. In later years, I always liked sleeping in our tent homes, for Autie would see that they were pitched away from the general camp for privacy, and near trees for comfort. I often felt I was sleeping in a tree house, something I had never done as a youngster, of course.

"You never crept outside to spend the night?" Autie asked incredulously. He still could not always comprehend the difference between being raised in a rowdy family of boys and growing up demurely, the only daughter in the staid and formal household of a judge.

"No," I said laughing, "I never did. Look at all I have to make up for."

"Good," he said, planting a light kiss on my forehead. "I'll never have to build you a house. A tent will always do."

"If we can live like this . . . ," I said dreamily.

"You may, my girl, but I must be off to the city to see about plans for the review. I'll be back by supper." And he was gone.

He returned in a foul humor, flinging his gloves on the table and hurling his hat across the room. "Grant has done it now," he stormed.

"Done what?" I asked, aghast, putting my needlework aside.

"Sent Sheridan west before the review. Wouldn't let him stay to present his troops in victory but sent him off to Texas and Louisiana . . . 'to restore order' I'm told."

"What's happening there?" I asked, with idle curiosity. Texas and Louisiana were far away and of no consequence in my life.

"Holdout Rebels," he said in disgust. "I'd teach them a thing or two if I were there. . . ."

"Fortunately," I said, "you're not. You're headed to Monroe after the review." I'd been living on fantasies about our return to Monroe for weeks, ever since the victory was declared. I could see the whole town lining the streets as Autie got off the train. There'd be a parade, of course, and I'd get to ride with him, even if he was the center of attention, and the headlines of *The Monroe Commercial* would boast his accomplishments. Mama and Papa would have a huge open house to honor Autie, and grateful citizens would have parties to praise him . . . my mind built up one extravaganza after another.

Autie was looking forward to Monroe, too, and when I mentioned it, he agreed with a smile. "But poor Sheridan," he said.

The Grand Review was everything its name implied. There was a presidential reviewing stand, draped with red, white, and blue bunting, in front of the Capitol, and the flag flew at full mast for the first time since Fort Sumter had been fired on. Cheering crowds lined the streets, and little children waved tiny flags and sang patriotic songs. Bands blared, the sun shone as though it hadn't rained torrents two days earlier, and I was almost overcome with excitement.

Long before an early-morning cannon blast signaled the beginning of the review, I found a spot not too far from the reviewing stand, yet far enough back that it gave a perspective—those right up in front, I decided, would see nothing but horses' withers. With me was Mrs. Wesley Merritt, whose husband had been given command of Sheridan's troops. Merritt was a longtime rival of Autie's, but this day I approved heartily of him, for he had put Autie's Third Division first in the line of review.

"Oh!" I clasped my hand to my mouth in sheer wonderment when they came into sight. They rode in battle formation, sixteen abreast, with Autie at the head on Don Juan. Today there was no crushed Rebel hat to keep off the sun— Autie wore the dignified and somewhat subdued formal uniform of a major general, but he and his men still wore their red kerchiefs. Beneath Autie's new hat hung those shining golden curls, long since grown back after he cut them for our wedding.

"He's having trouble with his horse, isn't he?" Mrs. Merritt asked over the noise of the crowd, which had begun to chant, "Custer! Custer!"

"La, Autie can handle Don Juan," I assured her.

The horse was indeed skittish and quivering, no doubt unnerved by the noise of the crowd. Autie held Don Juan in firm control, and they pranced toward the reviewing stand.

"Look there," I said with delight. "Those young girls are throwing flowers at Autie." There were a hundred or more young girls gathered in one spot just before the reviewing stand, all dressed in white—perhaps, I thought, they represent a particular school, on holiday for the occasion. Faintly, over the roar, I could hear them raising their voices in a high-pitched rendition of "Hail to the Chief."

"They're making that horse jumpier than ever," Mrs. Merritt said nervously.

I told her not to worry, but even as the words left my mouth, I saw one girl step forward and try to throw a wreath around Don Juan's neck. She could not have chosen a worse moment, for Autie had just drawn his sword for a salute to the President. As the horse bolted frantically, Autie lost both hat and sword. Of that fearful instant I remember most the sun shining on his now-hatless head.

My heart skipped a beat with worry for Autie and fear that Don Juan would go amok into the crowd, injuring someone. But I had no more time than to blink before Autie had the horse under control again. The moment of drama passed quickly but not before the crowd went wild with renewed enthusiasm for Autie. With great dignity, he retrieved his hat and sword—an orderly had picked them up—and resumed his place at the head of his troops.

"My dear," Mrs. Merritt said, "your husband is truly a remarkable man."

Perhaps it would have been polite to have demurred or said, "And so is yours" or some such, but I simply sighed and

said, "Yes, he is, isn't he?" Wesley Merritt could hold no
candle to Armstrong Custer.

Autie's moment of glory was followed by the most bitter
point of the whole war for me. By prearrangement we met in
the Willard Hotel, where Merritt was quartered—unlike ourselves, the Merritts declined to stay in camp. When Mrs.
Merritt and I walked in, our husbands greeted us with such
grim faces, we were alarmed.

"What . . . ?" I asked, but got no further.

Autie drew me aside and said in low tones, "Merritt and
I have both been ordered to report to Sheridan in New Orleans."

"New Orleans?" I echoed, the full meaning of this not
hitting me.

"Immediately," Autie said. All the spark and fire he had
shown at the parade seemed drained from him now, and he
stood solemnly looking at me. "You go on to Monroe," he
said huskily. "I'll hope to join you there after not too many
months."

Months! Monroe without Autie! "No, Autie, I'll go to
New Orleans," I said firmly.

Oblivious of those who stood around us, he grasped me
tightly in his arms, until I finally had to plead for breath.
"Oh, my dear girl," he said, "how did I ever deserve you?"

I saved my tears until I was alone in our tent.

The most painful part of Autie's new orders was that he
was to take command of a column already in Louisiana. He
bid farewell to his beloved Third Division in a ceremony of
marked contrast to the Grand Review.

At a trumpet call the troops assembled, and Autie rode
down the line, waving that old battered Rebel hat, which
those men had followed so often. The men waved their hats,
cheering wildly and calling out to him. More than once I
heard, "A tiger for Old Curly!" and then a deep-throated
roar of hurrahs. Finally, having reviewed the entire line, Autie rode back to where I waited, mounted on Custis Lee.
Autie's teeth were clenched in an effort to control himself,

and I knew he could not speak to me without coming apart totally. The memory of my husband sobbing at the presentation of *East Lynn* flashed through my mind, and I wondered if I should dig for a handkerchief for him, lest he be forced to use his scarlet kerchief to wipe away tears.

Within minutes I needed the handkerchief for myself. The men called for me, and I tried to respond by riding forward, one hand clutching my hat, which boasted a scarlet feather to match my kerchief. Lacking Autie's iron will and firm control, I was soon awash in tears and could go no farther. They gave me as enthusiastic a cheer as they had Autie, while I retreated to his side.

Autie said nothing but reached a hand out to mine.

We were about to begin life together. Until then the Civil War had dominated our lives, and I knew Autie as a victorious and respected general, a flamboyant commander of the cavalry, who could also be a passionate husband. But we had lived in camps and temporary quarters and had stolen moments together from the war. What did I really know about Autie as a man and about living with him?

I would never have told Papa that those questions flitted through my mind as, still slightly teary, I boarded a southbound train with Autie and his staff.

LOUISIANA
AND
TEXAS

Chapter Six

"COME, ELIZA, WE MUST HURRY OR THE TRAIN WILL leave before we can eat. We only have twenty minutes." Autie's voice sounded impatient.

"I'll jes' wait here, Ginnel," she said carefully.

I sensed her discomfort and quickly assured her that I would bring food from the dining hall, which looked none too promising, anyway. We were in Ohio somewhere, though I've deliberately never remembered where.

"No!" Autie commanded. "Eliza's to come with us." He had on his military tone and bearing, and one look at him was enough for Eliza.

"Yes, sir," she said miserably.

Ignoring me completely, Autie took Eliza's arm and proceeded to rush her out of the train car and toward the dining hall, she looking more miserable with each step. Trailing behind, I was puzzled, uncertain why Autie was making such a fuss and why Eliza was so reluctant.

I knew the moment I saw the dingy dining hall. The

proprietor had no doubt made scandalous sums of money—
trains were loaded with homebound troops in those days, and
since delays of trains and distances between eating houses
made a dining schedule irregular and uncertain, everyone
tended to eat at every chance. But this man hadn't spent any
of that gain on sprucing up his place. The walls were painted
board, the tables long trestle-type with benches on either
side and no cloth thrown over them to hide grease spots and
splinters that threatened the careless diner.

The minute we were through the door, the owner saw
Eliza and said gruffly, "No table for servants. Ain't got the
room." He was fat, no doubt from eating his own greasy
food, and the unclean state of the apron that covered his
wide middle did nothing to inspire confidence in the food we
were about to consume.

Eliza pulled away from Autie. "I'll jes' go on back, Ginnel."

Grabbing her, Autie was firm as ever. "You'll do no such
thing," he said, literally shoving her onto the bench next to
where I had seated myself. He placed himself carefully on
the other side of her, though the bench was so crowded we
were all squeezed together, and I wondered that we would
be able to lift a hand to eat our food.

The proprietor was right behind Autie. "No coloreds at
my table," he said.

Autie rose slowly, command written on his face. "I am
obliged to seat her here since you have provided no other
accommodations," he said.

The proprietor insisted, Autie continued to refuse, and
Eliza and I both sank lower and lower in our seats. My hand
trembled as I tried to take a sip of water to ease my dry
mouth, and when I looked at Eliza, she refused to lift her
eyes even to meet mine.

Autie would of course have whipped the fat man if it
came to fisticuffs, but I could see the headlines: "Boy-
General in Fight at Eating Hall!" A disgraceful way to begin
our tour of duty, to say the least. But as the two stood staring
resolutely at each other, the other officers in our party began
to rise from their seats, one by one.

"We're with you," they said. "Stand your ground. She shall eat."

The proprietor slunk away, and Autie and the others ate heartily, while Eliza and I, our appetites destroyed, toyed with the unappetizing food. The proprietor made a clean gain of a dollar and a half on two women who were too upset to eat.

I suspect Eliza was frightened still, but I, having gotten over my fright, was angry—at Autie. He had made his point, but in doing so, he'd lost sight of Eliza's feelings. He'd embarrassed the one person in the world who was probably more loyal to him than I, and I thought his lack of compassion unforgivable.

I could not mention it until we were miles down the track. Autie had paraded out, right before the owner's eyes, carrying an entire pie and two wrapped sandwiches—"I know how you women are," he said, his eyes now dancing with laughter as if all unpleasantness were forgotten. "You'll be hungry in a bit." But it was some hours before we could eat, and even longer before I could whisper to Autie of my concerns about the scene.

"I will take care of my staff as I see fit," he said coldly, and turned his back on me. Stunned, I stared out the window.

Other than that unpleasant incident, our train trip was more delightful than I would have expected. We were surrounded by a joyous, rollicking, irrepressible throng of officers and enlisted men returning home, and with a happiness tinged with envy, I listened to them shout and sing, watched them tumble off the train into the arms of some waiting woman, while bands tooted a welcome and whole towns lined up behind them as they were lost to our sight down the street, going home. Sometimes the hilarious crowd at the station would turn still in an instant; one silence preceded the careful lifting from the car of a stretcher bearing a wounded soldier, but he was carried away by strong men while the women he loved hovered over him, and I shed a silent tear for him, glad at least that he was returning home alive.

My envy was heightened by some real concern. We were headed to a country that failed to recognize that the war was over. From all we heard, lawlessness, tolerated from necessity during the war, still reigned in Texas. It would be Autie's job to restore order in this wild land. To me Texas sounded like the stepping-off place. I turned my face southward with such regret that Autie said he envisioned being borne southward on a river of tears. I managed to stop up the tears but could not quiet my heart.

It was some comfort to have Autie's staff around us. He was bringing with him the officers who had served him so well in the last days of the war—Fred Nims, James Farningham, Farnham Lyon, George Lee, and Jacob Greene from Monroe. Jacob and my lifelong friend Nettie Humphrey had married in Monroe toward the end of the war, a ceremony modest compared to the fanfare that had attended our wedding, but I still regretted that I had not been able to be there to stand with Nettie and her tall, gangly husband as they swore love undying.

Some of the other officers were Autie's schoolmates from West Point, others friends from his early days in the service, and most special of all, his brother Tom—christened, in my mind, as "the scamp." These men, too, were missing the brass bands and bonfires that should have greeted their homecomings, the welcoming arms to hold them. I had to make up for all the women who were waiting for them, and I tried my hardest to be bright and cheerful.

There was only one among that group of men whom I distrusted—Edward Earle. He, too, was from Michigan, but as I explained in a letter to Nettie, "he doesn't act like it. He's a bore, and he gives the whole staff to believe that he is promised to Mary M. I know that Mary gave him a locket, but it was not with a promise of undying love, and the man cannot take no for an answer. Try to convince Mary not to write him. The whole staff dislikes him, and those that *men* hate must be truly insufferable." Needless to say, Mary

McAllister of Monroe did not marry Edward Earle, but that did not save me from trials while in his company.

"Libbie, give me your portmanteau," the scamp said, beginning a ruse that quickly swept down the line of men on one of the first days of our train journey.

"Mrs. Custer, shall I carry your tote?" asked another, and "I'll take your umbrella," volunteered still another. My coat, a parcel of books, all my belongings, were soon distributed among Autie's aides. Even Eliza was offered help with her luggage, but there was a method to this madness. The ladies' car was off-limits to any man not accompanying a woman, and the brakeman was fierce and firm in turning them away. But once Autie and I were safely seated, with Eliza in her usual place by the door, one by one our men appeared at the door, each demanding entrance because he had a lady inside. As proof he held up whatever portion of my belongings he happened to be carrying, and we were soon all together in the ladies' car, a much more comfortable one than the regular coaches. We sang war songs, told stories loudly, and shouted with laughter, somewhat to the discomfort of the civilians who shared the car with us.

"You what?" I demanded incredulously.

"Left it . . . at the station." Before me stood Jacob Greene. He hung his head in abject shame and refused to look at me.

"You left my bag?"

"Yes, ma'am, Libbie, I did."

Gone were the thousand-and-one things a lady cannot live without—a small personal bar of soap, my mending kit, a small mirror so that I wouldn't look a fright the whole trip, a change of gloves, a slight bit of jewelry—fortunately paste, since I owned no other kind—and who knows what else. But I took pity on poor Jacob.

"You're forgiven," I said, "but only if you promise to bring Nettie to Texas as soon as possible."

"Yes, ma'am, I will," he said gratefully.

∎   ∎   ∎

"Autie, why are we stopped?" I murmured, raising my head from the seat, where I'd been crumpled into a ball of sleepy contentment.

"Engine's broken," he said. "Brakeman tells me we might be here all night. Are you comfortable?" He was slouched down in his seat, long legs stuck forward, hat pulled low over his forehead, and I knew that he could get restful sleep in that position, no matter the circumstances.

"I'm fine," I said happily, reaching a hand for his and curling back into sleep. We slept soundly that way, holding hands all night, only vaguely aware of the civilians who stomped about the still-stopped train, complaining of their inability to sleep.

"Look at the army folks," said one. "They can sleep anywhere, and yet I'm so cramped and stiff from one position that I couldn't possibly doze."

Next morning we laughed to find that Tom had a two-seat cushion all to himself. He was stretched out as comfortably as though he were home in bed; indeed, a few snores had come from his direction.

"Well," he confessed later, "these two old codgers sat down in this seat, and I was behind them, listening to them talk about how rich they'd gotten because of the war, 'cause it made corn prices rise. Seemed unpatriotic to me, so I began to talk loudly to the fellow next to me, telling him how much store I set by my old army coat. 'Just couldn't give it up,' I said, 'even though I had to use it to cover Corporal Smith when he died of the smallpox. Course, I'm not afraid of getting it, having had the varioloid and all.' Well, that coat was on the seat those two old codgers were in, and they were nearly out of their heads with fright. Saw 'em later peering through the window of the next car, and they still looked horrified."

Autie exploded with merriment, and I had to admit it was a good joke.

At Louisville we left the train. The rest of our journey south would be by steamer.

• ■ •

"Libbie, hurry up! Hurry up! You'll miss the fun if you don't scramble!"

"Miss what?" I asked naturally, not knowing that I was walking into the very trap they'd set for me.

"Why, they're going to bury a dead man as soon as we land," Tom said gleefully.

"Another man drowned?" I asked unbelievingly. The first night we were on the steamer, a Negro had fallen in. The boat routinely bumped into the shore, anywhere it happened to be wooded, so that more wood could be loaded. An army of hurrying Negroes, made faster by the first mate's stern voice, would hurry ashore to gather wood. The scene was eerie at night, lit by pine torches and resinous knots burning in iron baskets slung over the side. This first night they made a pretense of looking for a lost Negro but soon gave up their search. Tom was on the upper deck to tell me the tale with no time wasted, and I thought he relished it far too much, embellishing the details as he told the story. Thereafter, at every night landing, I imagined some poor soul swept off into watery depths. Now I was being invited to watch the burial of one of these victims.

"How," I demanded, "can you make so light of death?"

"What difference," Tom asked, "is one more worker, more or less?" And with that, he dragged me to the deck.

Once there, Tom stood gazing solemnly at a great cable, which was used to tie us up, fastened to a strong spar, the two ends of which were buried in the bank. The ground was hollowed out beneath the center, and the rope slipped under to fasten it around a log.

We watched while the boat was secured to the shore, and then Tom said, "The sad ceremony is now ended, and no other will take place until we tie up at the next stop."

It dawned on me, slowly I admit, that the process of tying up was called "burying a dead man." Indignantly I attacked Tom, beating my fists against his chest, but he, laughing, held me at arm's distance. And behind me I heard the

familiar sound of Autie's explosion of laughter. I had once
again been the butt of a good joke on "the old lady."

"General, I don't think it appropriate to play jokes on
the sensibilities of such a lovely lady as your wife," said a
stern voice from the shadows. Major Earle stepped forward,
his frown clearly showing his disapproval.

"My behavior to my wife is best left undiscussed," Autie
said coldly, turning his back on his junior officer.

I just stared, amazed that one of Autie's officers would
dare to chastise him in public, and indignant that he misunderstood my relationship with Autie and Tom. Something
told me in childhood came back to me: "If they didn't love
you, they wouldn't tease you." I was secure in Autie's love for
me—and Tom's more brotherly passion—and I wouldn't
have traded it for a thousand proper Major Earles.

We were on *The Ruth,* one of the most sumptuous
steamers on the Mississippi River, and Autie and I enjoyed
every luxury it had to offer, from lavishly decorated rooms to
delicacies of confectionery served by white-coated waiters.
We prowled the entire ship, with the blessings of a most
patient captain, who even allowed us into his sacrosanct
wheelhouse, where I listened for hours to his stories and
watched with fascination while he pointed out, there, where
the river had burst its banks and made a new channel and,
here, where it had swept over its banks and flooded out
someone's home. Never, I thought, has a girl from Monroe
seen such sights.

Though all worry about our Texas welcome was temporarily thrust aside by my fascination with the river, it was a
melancholy journey, for we saw plantation after plantation
where the grand old home was abandoned, standing in a lake
of water, and the slave cabins and outbuildings had all but
disappeared. It seems these once-rich homesteads were protected by embankments that were not maintained when all
the men were away at war. It was not enough for these poor
people that they suffered the agony of defeat and loss of their
loved ones, but their very homes gave way to the river.

"Wars," I said vehemently, "should be fought on
deserts."

Autie, of course, was intensely interested in every battle site we passed, and he knew them all by name. At one point a tall, dignified man whose very being spoke "soldier" came on board. He turned out to be General Hood of the Confederate forces, come to greet Autie. The war was still too recent for me to be able to understand the cordiality with which the two greeted each other, but I remembered that Autie had sent greetings to his comrades on the other side of the line, and when presented to General Hood, I was as gracious as possible. Even after I was presented, they continued to trade news of various battles.

"The hardest thing," General Hood told us confidentially, "was to fit myself with an artificial leg after I lost my own. For a while I had to carry an extra strapped to my led horse, in case of accident to the one I wore. Once our reserve horses were captured, and I could just imagine the shock of the soldiers who got this horse, with an artificial leg strapped to it." Then he looked directly at me. "You can imagine, Mrs. Custer, that it pains me to admit this, but of all the legs I tried—English, German, French, Yankee, and Confederate—the Yankee was the best of all."

Autie sometimes paced the deck of the steamer late at night, when he thought I was safe asleep in our comfortable cabin. But I lay wide awake, aware that the night was passing and my husband was not with me.

"Autie?" I asked once when he crept into our cabin, almost as the first shards of daylight began to thrust in the window. "Where have you been?"

"Oh, just out on the deck," he said casually, stooping to give me a caressing kiss and brushing my face with the newly grown mustache that he would sport the rest of his life.

I pushed him away. "Why did you dress and leave me?"

"I couldn't sleep, and I didn't want to wake you. For heaven's sake, Libbie, what do you think? I had a tryst with a beautiful maiden on deck?"

"No," I said quietly, "I didn't think that at all. But it worries me that you don't sleep."

He sat down beside me, repentant, and took my hand. "I'm restless," he said. "I'm no good at loafing."

I couldn't hide my amusement. "Loafing? We've been busy as ever, supervising the captain's progress down the river, watching the plantations go by, running down the gangplank so that we could say we'd set foot in Arkansas and Missouri and Tennessee—loafing! Why, Autie, this trip has been fascinating to me. How could you be restless?" I was truly incredulous.

He clutched my hand tightly, and I sensed that Autie was begging me to listen to him. "It's not . . . oh, Libbie, I hate to even say this, but it's not the same as war."

Merrily—and a bit stupidly, I suppose—I replied, "Of course it's not. And aren't we glad?"

Autie stared intently at me. "Are we?"

I sobered instantly. "Autie, you can't be at war your whole life. We're not going to war now. Yours is a peacekeeping assignment. There'll be no battles."

Then he smiled briefly. "I know, Libbie. I'm not that far gone. But I'll be in command again. I'll be responsible for men, for seeing that things are done in military fashion. It'll be all right as soon as I'm in the field again."

"Of course, Autie," I said, rising to dress for the day and pushing away the thoughts that frightened me.

We were detained by orders for some little time in New Orleans, and there I thought briefly that Autie had conquered his restlessness. It was a fascinating city, nearly unscathed by the war. Funny little foreign shopkeepers still held forth in the French Quarter, nearly dragging us off the sidewalk when we walked by to offer rare coffees and spices, imported laces, all manner of goods. Autie even whispered to me that one man had pulled him aside and offered him some guaranteed aphrodisiacs.

"I told him I had no need," Autie said, leering at me until I blushed.

We ate like royalty, in restaurants where dining was raised to a fine art. Seafood was new to a Michigan girl, and I hovered over crabs, lobster, and shrimp, though I shrunk away from a huge live green turtle, upon whose back was painted his epitaph: I will be served for dinner at five P.M.

At one sidewalk café, Autie drank so much coffee that

the old mammy who served him said *"Mon Dieu!"* in surprise at his capacity and proceeded, in voluble French, to tell
her neighbors of what marvels a Yankee man could do in
coffee-sipping. Autie swelled a little with pride—as though, I
later thought, his masculinity had been commented upon,
and I confess to having felt a little of the reflected glory. I
was obviously attached to a man of unusual strengths. The
thought does a girl's heart immeasurable good.

General Winfield Scott was staying at our hotel, and I,
remembering how his picture had hung in my childhood
home, was anxious to meet him, if for nothing more than to
gaze upon my father's hero. Meet him we did, and though
the general knew nothing of my admiration, he remembered
Lieutenant Custer, who had reported to him in 1861, and he
congratulated Autie on his career, congratulations that made
the boy-general's heart leap for joy, I could tell.

General Scott was then very infirm, and though he
begged to be introduced to me, he explained with old-fash-
ioned gallantry that he would be obliged to claim the privi-
lege of remaining seated. But it was too much for him, and
weak as he was, he drew his tall form to a half-standing
position as I entered. I remembered the picture of a colossal
figure on a fiery steed—the Mexican War had seemed to
mythologize the man—and I was almost sorry to see him
now, tottering and decrepit.

General Sheridan was also in New Orleans, having assumed command of the Department of the Mississippi and
established his headquarters in a mansion there. We dined
with him often, sumptuous meals after which I was given
over to the military family to entertain so that Autie and the
general could confer. Autie deliberately left me in absolute
ignorance of what he and Sheridan believed would be a campaign across the border into Mexico. As far as I knew, we
were going to bring peace to Texas and nothing more—Autie
kept me in that state of ignorance, even reading the eastern
papers to me so that he could censor what I read.

"Just think of it," Tom said one day, "me, a wealthy
man!"

"And how," I asked archly, "do you expect to come into this wealth?"

"Why, the spoils of war, Libbie, the spoils of war." He grinned like a disobedient child.

"The spoils of war," I said sarcastically. "In Texas? Tom, you're a dreamer!"

Before he could answer, Autie leapt across the room and boxed him soundly on the ears. When Tom lunged back, they were soon into one of their friendly fisticuff battles, which distracted me totally from the spoils of war, and once peace was restored, I never thought to pursue the subject with Tom. That was just what Autie had in mind when he instigated that sudden bout of roughhousing.

As wonderful as New Orleans was, one afternoon stands out in my mind. We spent it—the entire afternoon!—in a milliner's shop.

"Autie," I complained, "we have no money, probably not even enough to pay our passage up the Red River. I cannot buy a bonnet that I'd never wear in Texas, anyway." I stood with a sensational brown creation of felt and feathers and trim on my head, turning this way and that, admiring my image in the mirror.

"Bother practicality!" Autie said vehemently. "You shall have the best hats of anyone in Texas."

"Eliza says a good practical sunbonnet is what I need," I laughed. "Do you like this brown one . . . or perhaps the bottle green, with its swirl of net."

"Take them both," he replied expansively. Autie sat in a comfortable chair—provided, I'm sure, just to make husbands happy—coffee in his hand, satisfaction written on his face.

"Autie, really . . . ," I protested. "I can't take them both. I have no idea how much these cost, but I know they are dear."

He jingled the money in his pocket. "Never let it be said that I could not provide the best for Elizabeth Bacon of Monroe, Michigan, Judge Bacon's daughter."

"Elizabeth Custer now," I corrected him, smiling.

"Yes, but you shall always be Judge Bacon's daughter to me."

His words caught me off balance. "I think I should prefer to be Armstrong Custer's wife," I said softly.

Unaware that his words had troubled me, Autie leapt up to plant a kiss on my nose. "And so you are, my dear, so you are. Never let it be said that Custer's wife went without the best millinery." He signaled the shopkeeper. "We'll take these two. Please box them carefully for traveling."

I never knew . . . and don't know to this day . . . how much those hats cost in gold currency—I do know their price in peace of mind, and it was dear.

We sailed up the Red River the last week in June on a steamer commanded by a wonderful Yankee captain named Greathouse. The name fit his huge girth as well as the expansive nature of his hospitality.

"You and your men shall be my guests on this trip," the captain said privately to Autie, who breathed, I know, a sigh of relief. After thanking the captain appropriately for his generosity, Autie sought out his staff to inform them. Then he came to me, threw himself on the bed in our cabin, and muttered, "Custer's Luck again!"

"What now?" I asked laughing.

He told me of the captain's offer, explaining that the poor man was not going to lose a pennyworth by such hospitality. "There are government horses and freight aboard," he said, "and Greathouse will be well paid—but not by us."

The army, of course, was responsible for our expenses, but it was such a hassle to secure the money in advance that we often paid our way and waited thirty days or more for reimbursement. This time we had no funds to advance and were saved only by a prudent and calculating steamboat captain.

The scamp saw a chance for a joke. When we were all assembled with the captain, he jingled the last twenty-six cents in his pocket against his knife blade, so that it sounded as though he had gold currency.

"I always like to pay in advance," he said haughtily to Captain Greathouse. "What is the cost of this journey?"

"Sir, I have invited you to be my guests," Greathouse said with formality.

"Well, sir, if you insist," Tom said haughtily, managing to convey the sure impression that he accepted such generosity with condescension and was fully capable of paying his own way.

Behind me I heard a snort, then a choking sound, and I turned just in time to see Autie bolt out the cabin door so fast, he nearly catapulted over the railing into the muddy depths of the river.

"Must have been something he ate," Tom said solemnly.

Our trip on the Red River was a far cry from that down the Mississippi. The crooked river was ugliness itself—dull, reddish-brown water from clay beds, tree trunks gray and slimy from the last sudden rising of the level of the river, muddy banks strewn with brush and fallen trees. Sometimes the pilot wound us around piles of driftwood and logs, covered with moss and jammed so tightly that they looked like solid ground. The surrounding forest was so dense that we could see into it but a short distance, and I imagined it filled with all sorts of horrors, from unrepentant Confederate soldiers to haints who lived in the air and subsisted on the dripping Spanish moss.

There was a more real and present danger.

"I almost got him!" Autie shouted with disgust. He was aiming his rifle at an alligator, trying for the vulnerable spot in their hide just behind the eye.

"What would you do with the disgusting creature if you did kill it?" I asked unhappily.

"Why, turn it into shoes and a bag for you," he said.

"Better you should hit a sand crane," I replied. "They look so miserable standing on one foot. I'm sure it's because they can't bear to put both feet down into the muck of this river!" In spite of my resolve, I don't think I was quite game on that trip.

Captain Greathouse's company was the only thing that made the trip bearable, and with great regret we parted from

him at Alexandria, Louisiana, where we were to stay for some
time before moving on to Texas. The captain seemed to enjoy our silly, joyous bunch, too, and gave us a hogshead of ice
as we departed. Little did I know it was the last ice I would
see for a year or more.

As I stepped off the boat, a worn-looking man in slightly
shabby clothes came toward me. Instinctively I backed a step
toward Autie. Southerners, I knew, were *not* glad to have us
among them.

"Libbie," the man cried, "it's so good to see you after all
these years."

Dubiously, I held out my hand. He did look a little familiar, but only, I thought, because he called to mind someone much younger and much happier. There was something
about those eyes, though. . . .

"It's Lane Murphy, Libbie. We met years ago in
Monroe, when we were both young and carefree." There was
just a touch of regret in his voice, as though he longed to go
back to that "carefree" time.

"Lane!" I cried. Lane Murphy! Once I had fantasized
that he would whisk me away to a charming southern plantation, where I would be waited on hand and foot; now here he
stood before me, obviously no longer the wealthy plantation
owner I had thought him.

"You're to stay in my family's home," he said. "I couldn't
believe it when I heard who the army had quartered there."

"I . . . I hope we won't be putting them to any trouble," I said, appalled at the thought of moving in on someone
and sharing their house with them.

"No . . . no one has lived in the house for over a year,"
he said reluctantly. "My parents are both dead now . . .
and I live in the overseer's quarters *alone*."

Did he emphasize that last word? "Lane, I'm so sorry
. . . the war, I suppose . . ."

"Yes, the war. It's been hard on everyone, I fear." But
then he brightened. "Except you. You look wonderful, Libbie. Fit and healthy and happy."

"Oh, I am, Lane, I truly am. I'm on the greatest adventure of my life."

Autie came up just then, having turned over to Eliza the supervision of the unloading of our belongings. "General Custer," he said brusquely, holding out his hand.

"Yes, General, I know who you are."

"Autie, this is Lane Murphy, who used to visit in Monroe," I said enthusiastically. "Surely you remember!"

"I'm afraid not," Autie said, his voice still not cordial.

Sensing his tone, Lane said quickly, "The house is not far. Libbie? You don't mind a walk?"

"Of course not. I should be glad of it." Actually, the day was warm and muggy, and I was already uncomfortable, but I saw no need of mentioning it.

"Miss Libbie, you wait just one minute!" Eliza's voice rang through the air, and I turned to see her running toward us, waving a parasol. "You don't know this Southern sun," she said scoldingly as she came up close. "Got to keep it off your face at all times." She opened the parasol and handed it to me.

"Yes, Eliza, I will."

"Do you want to order my troops around, too, 'Liza?" Autie asked, but at least this time there was a hint of amusement in his voice. Then, the amusement gone, he turned back to Lane. "Let's be off."

After half a block I was more than grateful for the parasol. The sun seemed much hotter here than at home, and the air was heavy. We left the river and followed a dilapidated white board fence about half a mile before turning into what once was an impressive gate. Now the white-painted bricks were awry, the wrought-iron sign that said "Glen Ellen" dangling.

"Ellen was my mother's name," Lane said when he saw me stare at the sign, "and the Glen . . . well, Father was Celtic, like most Southerners. He named the place for Mother when he bought it."

"Charming," I murmured, but I could not help gazing at the disrepair of the gate.

Lane saw me. "No time, no money, no help for upkeep," he said, shrugging.

I noticed that he limped. "You were in the war yourself?" I asked.

"Wasn't everybody?" he countered, and for just a second he and Autie exchanged looks of comradeship.

Autie softened a bit. "Where were you hurt?"

"Vicksburg. Doubt I ever faced you in battle, General. I fought in the Southern tier of states, not with the Army of Virginia."

"No, it was almost two different wars," Autie acknowledged.

Before us loomed the plantation home of my dreams, only it was not gleaming white with fresh paint, as I'd imagined, and no Southern belles sipped lemonade on the lawn while white-turbaned nannies stood and fanned them. The house, raised above the soft river-bottom ground on piles, had turned gray with old paint. Faded green shutters hung at strange angles, and unkempt bushes nearly grew across the front door. Lane explained that the house had been used as headquarters by a Union general for part of the war—like most of Louisiana, it had been spared the devastation of outright war but had suffered from neglect.

"The general's people took fair care of the inside," he said, "but they weren't much on looking after the outside. I haven't been able to get to it *yet*." His words conveyed a determination that he would soon get to it.

I reached for Autie's arm, awash with sympathy for this man and afraid to ask what had happened to his family. Yet even as I stood there, I was entranced by the song of the mockingbirds. A thick hedge of crape myrtle grew in a semi-circle on the lawn before the house, and it seemed crowded with these song-filled birds. Later I would know that they sang late into the night, as though twilight had made the day too short for them to give voice to all that needed to be sung to their mates.

The house had a wide central hall, upstairs and downstairs, and easily divided itself into two separate wings. We would live in the northern half—"Appropriate," Autie mut-

tered—since it was in better condition. Eliza would have a
sleeping room in the small, detached structure that held the
kitchen. Lane explained that it was built separate to spare the
main house in case of fire, but I moaned over the thought of
carrying food back and forth.

"Slaves did it," Lane shrugged.

He saw us settled, urged us to call on him for any slight
thing we might need, and took his departure.

"He's in love with you," Autie said, his face stern.

"Nonsense, Autie. That poor man has too much grief
and sadness in his life to be in love with anyone, let alone
me."

"You're wrong," Autie said coldly. "I want you to stay
away from him while we're here."

"Autie, I will not be rude," I answered, and I wasn't at
all sure that I would avoid Lane Murphy to appease Autie.

The Murphys' house was a strange contradiction in luxury and primitive living. The sole water supply for the big
house and the servants' quarters was contained in two cisterns at the rear of the house—the water level in these was
low, and the tops uncovered so that bugs and flies, dust and
leaves, were blown in. Nightly the wild cats that roamed the
plantation strolled along the rim of these uncovered cisterns,
singing their plaintive nightly songs. Our drinking water was
so full of gallinippers and pollywogs that a glass stood by the
plate untouched until the sediment and natural history
united at the bottom. Heaven only knows what a microscope
would have revealed.

Animals, of course, are not so fussy, and there was one
wily old cow who knew how to pull the plug out of the cis-
tern—the thing didn't even have a Yankee spout!—to get
herself a drink. Of course, gallons of our precious water supply were wasted. We learned to be alert at the first sound of
rushing water. Once I woke Autie in the night to tell him the
cow had gotten the plug again, and I think his muttered
threats about shooting her were sincere for the moment.

In earlier and better days the place had been carefully
fenced, so that animals could not get near the main house,
but the fences were in disrepair now. And Lane told me that

the open space beneath the house had been protected by latticework, now long gone. That left the underside of the house unprotected, as it were—and it was there that pigs and even calves sought shelter from the sun, making an unholy racket for those of us in the house above.

The bayous about the house were marshy, filled with decaying vegetation, and the frequent rise and fall of the river left mud banks everywhere—all perfect places for the breeding of mosquitoes. I could not exaggerate the size or the ferocity of these insects—Eliza called them gallinippers, which I thought poetically perfect. She took counsel from the other Negroes as to the best method of extermination, and one night we found ourselves asleep in a room with smudge pots. Eliza had filled old kettles with raw cotton and lit the cotton. A Northern mosquito would have wilted in an instant!

"My God," cried Autie, "what is that awful odor?"

"Smudge pots gonna keep the gallinippers from Miss Libbie," Eliza explained calmly.

"I'll not sleep like a piece of dried meat hanging in a smokehouse," he declared. "Get rid of them now!"

Eliza declined and told him in no uncertain tones that he could sleep elsewhere, but I was to be protected from the gallinippers. She removed the smudge pots only when it appeared they had no effect on the insects.

Finally I took refuge, often even in the daytime, behind a netting that enveloped our broad, high bed. I could write or sew, and the nasty things could not get near me—I could watch them batting futilely against the material. Autie, of course, scorned such softness.

"Miss Libbie, I want you to come with me," Eliza said one day when the sun was not quite so bright and the wind not quite high enough to bring in a cloud of mosquitoes.

"Where?" I was willing to go, from boredom, no matter where it was.

"The slave cabins," she replied. "There's nobody left 'cept a few old people, too old to be any use to anybody, even themselves. They're starvin' down there."

"Oh, Eliza, of course we must go."

One old woman was bedridden—Granny Goshen, Eliza called her—and though she appeared ancient, she could not tell me her age. She remembered being in New Orleans with her mistress and other events that finally led me to believe that she was near a hundred. No one had told her, until I did, that she was free, and she raised her eyes to heaven, saying "Praise the Lord!" What, I wondered, could freedom mean to her except that there was no one to take care of her now?

Autie always fussed at Eliza's handouts. "Feeding half the county, I am, anywhere I set up my headquarters," he grumbled. But he had no word of reprimand after I told him about these helpless ex-slaves. Eliza fed them bountifully from our kitchen, the whole six weeks we were in Alexandria, and Autie looked the other way.

He also did a strange thing. One day I heard men laughing and talking outside, and when I went to investigate, I found some of Autie's soldiers busily preparing to trim away the huge bushes and paint the house.

"Autie? Did you do that for Lane?"

"No. I did it because it's a damn shame to see a house like this fall in from rot."

I didn't even reprimand him for swearing, as was my usual custom. Lane had the good sense not to exaggerate his gratefulness. Instead, with Southern politeness, he said, "I'm beholden to you. If ever I can repay you, be sure that I will."

"I understand," Autie said, taking the offered hand.

That night, as we lay in the big bed that once had belonged to Lane's parents, Autie said, "Make no mistake. I've not changed my mind about Murphy."

The best thing about our stay in Alexandria was our evening rides. We had brought Custis Lee and Don Juan with us—Autie would never have left them behind—and each evening a great crowd of us rode in what I soon called a "land of enchantment." The vegetation was lush beyond belief, at least to my Northern eyes, and the sunsets boasted richer, deeper reds and golds than any that Michigan could offer. Sometimes we rode along lanes hedged with Osage orange and double white roses, and the fragrance nearly took my breath away.

Once, though, Autie proposed a new route, off the public highway. We were accompanied by Tom, Jacob, and several others from Autie's staff, all laughing, joking, and singing —and not paying attention to our surroundings, until we found ourselves at the edge of a wide bayou that emptied into the Red River. We could have followed the bayou upward until we came to a narrower and firmer spot, but we were young, foolish, and ignorant of the ground in these parts. Autie, being the bravest among us, dashed across first, and though the crust of mud over the water swayed and sunk under the horse's flying hooves, it held firm. It was a safe crossing, he declared, ignorant of the significance of the seams and fissures that oozed moist mud all around us.

I held back, in spite of Autie's assurances. One by one the others made the crossing and then rode impatiently up and down on the other side, urging me not to be timid.

"You know how Custis Lee follows me, Libbie. Why, he'll just follow me across the patch of mud. Come on, now! I'll come back and lead you across." But Custis Lee and I had once sunk into quicksand in Virginia—an indescribable fear comes over you as the mud sucks your horse's legs down —and we had no wish to repeat the performance. Both of us balked at the crossing. Autie laughed and called us cowards, perfectly suited to each other.

Tom rode boldly back to the side where I waited, and then, crying, "Look how easily I go," headed his horse once more across the infirm terrain. But when Cavalier, his surefooted bay, sprang upon that mud crust, it shattered with a crack like a pistol shot, and that well-dressed, ever-so-confident young brother-in-law of mine found himself waist-deep in thick, black muck.

Cries of "Get some sticks" and "Hold on! We're coming" were intermingled with Tom's desperate pleas for help, for he could feel himself sinking farther and farther. His struggling horse at last put his front hooves on solid ground and began to pull his weight out, and the others thrust tree branches at Tom. I held my breath, quivering to think how close I had come and fearful that they might not be able to save Autie's brother. I may have christened him "the scamp," but there was no better-hearted junior officer among us, and I was truly fond of him.

All was quiet while the men worked, but the minute they got him out, a great cry went up. "Look how easily I go," they taunted, laughing and mimicking him. Tom stood, plastered from head to toe in mud, and took the teasing in good nature. But I could not stop shivering from my narrow escape. Had it been I who'd gone through the mud, they'd have never gotten me out with my long, heavy riding habit—loaded with lead to keep it from blowing.

Needless to say, we proceeded until a safer and narrower place was found for me to cross.

Autie was bent on alligator hunting. "Their scales are as thick as a china plate," he told me. "So far, the balls I've shot bounce off the hide as though they'd hit an ironclad vessel." He insisted that I go on these hunts, sitting in a flimsy rowboat, which seemed hardly any protection to me. The men would yelp and bark like dogs to flush the beast out of its hiding place—apparently, to my disgust, dog meat is an alligator treat—and it would come slowly down the bayou, magnificent in its ugliness and the danger it posed.

Autie dispatched four of the beasts, and I was a little sorry each time, for the carcasses were just left to rot. When I mentioned this to him, he said, "It's the sport, Libbie, the challenge. You don't understand."

Chapter Seven

 "AUTIE," I ASKED, "WILL WE EVER HAVE CHILDREN?" We lay in the big poster bed in Lane's parents' bedroom, my head still thick from lovemaking. We had been married now well over a year and a half, and my monthly female troubles had been regular as always. Each month I waited, half in hope for the sign of a baby to come and half in dread of having to tell Autie that, again, there was no sign. It was Autie I worried about more than myself.

"Of course we will, Libbie," he murmured, gently stroking my hair with the bare arm that held me pressed close to him. "You just mustn't think about it. It's all a question of relaxation."

I smiled wickedly. "And how can I relax with your hands all over me, driving me wild all the time?"

"And if I didn't do that," he hooted, "there'd be no babies ever. Trust me, Libbie, the Lord knew about making babies when he created us the way we are."

"You mean the Lord sanctions . . . ah, our love . . . ?"

"Are you asking if the Lord sanctions the things we do together in bed? You bet he does, Libbie. It's just your father who wouldn't sanction them."

I stiffened and pulled away. "How do you know what Papa and Mama do?" I asked, burned as always by any criticism of Papa and yet entertaining my own doubts. Surely Papa never thought of some of the things Autie did . . . and I enjoyed to the point of nearly screaming aloud.

"I don't know," he said, "but I can guess, can't you? At least, I can guess what they don't do." His hand left my shoulder to travel delicately across my stomach, then on down to my thigh, causing me to shiver involuntarily. "Want to try again?" he muttered, breathing into my ear.

Lost to all sensible thought, I pulled myself over on top of him and let my mouth explore his chest and stomach, while he stroked me in ever-tightening circles. My last sensible thought was that if passion produced babies, we should surely have a dozen children.

Eliza worried about my lack of childbearing almost as much as I did. "Miss Libbie, we got to dose you. I know some remedies, like the folks used to use back in Mississippi. Now, course, if it's the ginnel . . ."

I smothered a giggle. "Eliza, I'm sure it's not the general. He'd be horrified if you even suggested such a thing. The fault is mine, I know."

She was polishing silver—Lane had left his family's belongings intact in the house, and the occupying soldiers had fortunately not carried away the silver and china for souvenirs. Eliza declared it a sin to let silver sit and blacken. So she polished, and we ate from shining sterling and fine bone china. But now she looked up from her work and gave me a sidelong look of amusement. "Still wouldn't hurt none to give him some of this Louisiana red pepper with his eggs . . . and make them eggs near raw when he eats them."

"You want to hear the general roar at the breakfast table?" I asked. "Just try feeding him raw eggs with red pepper on them." I could just see Autie, sitting at the table in his immaculate blue uniform, staring at eggs that ran all over the plate—and would run down his chin should he dare attempt eating them.

"It'd be for a good cause, Miss Libbie," she said defensively, hands on her hips.

"Best not," I said, "tell him what that good cause is. He'd stand no aspersions cast on his manhood . . . and none are merited."

"Miss Libbie, what do all them words you just said mean?"

"They mean leave the general alone, Eliza."

"Yes, ma'am. But now if I can just remember what my mammy used to give Miss Juliette after she married . . . she was just like you, Miss Libbie, wantin' a baby so bad, she could taste it. And after my mammy doctored her, don't you know she had four babies, one right after the other. Like to kill her."

"Maybe," I murmured, "we should forget the cure and let nature take its course."

"Nature," she said knowingly, "sometimes needs a little help." And with that she picked up a tray that met her satisfaction—her face gleamed back at her when she looked in it —and headed for the kitchen, effectively finishing our conversation.

Fortunately, Eliza was never sure what medicine her mammy had used, and so I was spared, though I lived with the fearful vision of a concoction of pollywog tails and frog's blood and who knows what else.

"Figs," she said one day. "Eat a lot of figs, and them's plentiful around here."

Indeed they were. Fresh figs, which I'd never seen before in my life, grew in abundance around Glen Ellen, and to my mind there was no sweeter breakfast than a bowl of figs with heavy cream from the cow that Eliza milked each morning. But my diligent devotion to this breakfast dish did nothing to increase my fertility.

"Eliza thinks she knows what it would take to make me conceive," I told Autie. "Some medicine her mother used to make."

"Horsefeathers," he said, wrapping me in his arms. "I'm all you need."

Autie was not having a glorious time in Louisiana. The general who had once exclaimed, "Oh, glorious war!" and who had led troops so loyal that they imitated his dress and cried genuine tears when he was parted from them, found himself leading rebellious troops who felt that since the war was over, they should be home. They were men who were stationed on the western front during the war, where they'd seen little but scattered guerrilla fighting—never an organized battle like those that had brought Autie glory and had welded fighting men into unified troops. But even though the war was over, the enlistment time for these men was not up, and they were not to be discharged. So there they were—mutinous in Louisiana. And there was Autie, no longer restless but certainly not enjoying command in the way he had assured me he would.

For one thing, the troops foraged liberally, stealing at will from the local population. Autie issued stern orders against such foraging and set the penalty at ten lashes and a shaved head. Several men underwent this punishment before Autie got his point across, and the rest of the men remained angry at the restriction, at the punishment, and most of all, at their general.

"Lashes?" I asked Eliza. "Like we used to hear . . . ?"

"Yes, ma'am, jes' like the worst slave owners did, lashing a man's bare back with a whip. I seen it done when I was nothin' but a young'un, and I tell you, I never want to see such a bloody back again, and I don't want to hear no man yell like that. . . ."

My stomach churned in revolt at the thought. How, I wondered, could Autie expect to inspire loyalty in his troops by such brutal methods? He, who had always handled men better than generals twice his age . . . to resort to this! I blocked the scene from my mind, refusing to think on it, and when once I chanced to pass a soldier with a shaved head, I looked quickly away before I could wonder about his back, and whether he stood straight enough or seemed to stoop in agony.

The returning Confederate soldiers were an equally trying problem—belligerent, angry at finding the army of occupation in their homes, frustrated because the entire way of life they had known was wiped out. Had they but realized, they were more fortunate than their brethren from, say, Virginia, whose homes were literally burned to the ground. In Louisiana, property suffered nothing but neglect—as Lane's Glen Ellen plantation well testified. Still, these men saw their lives gone forever, and they stood on street corners, talking loudly and angrily about what they'd do to Union soldiers, given half the chance. Our men had to listen to gibes and taunts while they were forbidden to return them in kind. Autie issued a declarative couched in welcoming terms, but its underlying message was that continual troublemakers would be arrested and brought to headquarters.

And finally, there were the newly freed slaves. Autie was as disgusted with them as with the soldiers, both blue and gray. "They seem to think that the army will take care of them, and they have no need to support themselves. Once they took orders willingly, but now they resent the least little direction. If you tell a freedman to curry a horse, you're as likely to get an insubordinate remark as you are any help with the horse." To the blacks he was counselor, doctor, lawyer, taskmaster, father, and provider. And he hated every minute of it.

The very air around Alexandria crackled with tension, and Autie was supposed to whip the soldiers into fighting shape so that they could be a peacekeeping force in Texas, as well as encourage the blacks to care for themselves and the returned Confederates to rebuild their lives instead of simply complaining. It was an enormous task for a twenty-five-year-old man, and even I knew it. Autie had, of course, the support of that tight little band of men who became his military family—Tom, whose attitude toward all troublemakers was that they should be immediately shot, and the much more peaceful Jacob Greene, who thought the officers should be able to reason with the men. There were others Autie relied on—Fred Nims, James Farningham, Farnham Lyon, and George Lee; and then the unpleasant Major Earle was still with us.

Autie never talked to me about his troubles. Instead, in the evenings we went on our long rides. "A man," he said one evening, "may do everything to keep a woman from knowledge of official matters, and then she gets so confounded keen in putting trifles together, the first thing you know, she is reading a man's thoughts."

Autie was right. I was putting trifles together. What he didn't know was that I got my trifles from Lane Murphy and, even more reliably, from Eliza.

My days were long, and the afternoons were hot. Sometimes in the midafternoon, when Autie was occupied trying to bring discipline to an unruly army, Lane Murphy would wander up from the overseer's quarters. Autie would disapprove, but I did not expect Autie to know—and I did not feel guilty, for I was merely trying to help Lane. I knew that if my days were long, his were interminable, for as far as I could tell, he didn't have much work to fill his days. There is only so much that one man can do on a dilapidated plantation, and Lane was Southern and relaxed by nature, with none of the Puritan drive of us Yankees. Nor was he in the best of health. I thought of Autie's absolute obsession with his work, and the contrast heightened my love for Autie. I could never bear an idle man.

Some days we walked among the slave cabins, visiting the few who were left. They greeted Lane like a hero, inquiring after his health, calling him "Mistah Lane," and sometimes ever so gently teasing him about some past event. "Remember the time, Mistah Lane . . ." became a familiar refrain in my ears. The other refrain was, "Mistah Lane, we sure do miss Mastah Tom." Master Tom, I learned, was Lane's late father.

"Lane," I asked one day, "they were so anxious to be free. Even old Granny Goshen told me how she praised the Lord she'd lived long enough to see freedom. And yet they obviously love you . . . the man who kept them from being free."

Stifling a smile, he drew himself up in mock indignation. "I wasn't quite that bad, Libbie. Not Simon Legree or anything." Then he sobered. "My family and I provided the only security these people knew. We cared for them—physically and emotionally. We weren't bad slave owners—we saw that they were fed and clothed and lived as well as possible. We didn't raise the whip, and we never sold families apart. Abolishing slavery isn't just a question of freeing poor indentured people, Libbie. You mark my words—it's much more complicated, and that precious husband of yours is already finding that out."

I flinched at his reference to Autie. Neither man cared for the other—that was obvious—but they were both usually polite. Now Lane's anger caused him to cross that fine line, ever so slightly.

He explained the situation to me in more compassionate terms than Autie had used. "The master is used to giving orders, and the slave to taking them. Now neither one knows how to treat the other, and it's leading to disasters. The general's right about one thing—crops are wasting in the fields, because the slaves—excuse me, freedmen—don't think it's their responsibility to harvest them. And no one has ever taught them to think ahead about consequences—they see no relationship between their refusal to work and possible hunger next season." He shook his head in despair.

But Lane, unfortunately, did not always confine his talks to the terrible troubles that beset Louisiana. "Let's walk to the river," he suggested one hot, muggy day.

"Lane," I laughed, "my hair is already hanging in strings in my face from the heat. Surely you don't want to walk *anywhere*." What I didn't say to him was that my petticoats felt damp from sweat and seemed to flap about my legs, and I could feel the perspiration glistening on my face.

"It's important," he said. "I don't want to sit around with Eliza or walk down to the cabins and see ol' Granny Goshen today."

"Of course," I said, fearing that he was upset about his

continued poor health, his bleak future, the disrepair of his family home—Lane had, I thought, any number of reasons to be melancholy, and it was my self-appointed chore to brighten his days.

We tramped down the dirt road by which we'd first approached the plantation, then up onto the dirt levee, Lane leading at a fairly brisk pace. Before us, the dirty river rolled along, depositing silt on the riverbanks, lapping against the exposed roots of trees.

"Lane, where are you going?" I asked, a little breathless from trying to keep up with the pace.

"You'll see. Come on. We're still on the plantation."

Within minutes we rounded a bend in the river and came upon a secluded gazebo—a hexagonal-shaped building, very small, boarded in up to waist level but with remnants of old screening flapping above. Inside, it was surprisingly clean —I'd expected an accumulation of leaves and mold, but instead, the benches, which faced the inside walls, were clean, though badly in need of paint.

"I . . . I come here frequently," Lane said, suddenly hesitant in his speech. "It's a comfort to me."

"It's a beautiful spot, Lane." Indeed, the Red River—in my mind the ugliest river I'd ever seen—looked almost grand from this vantage, the view gentled by weeping willows, which swayed around the edges of the gazebo. Even on this stifling hot afternoon, there was a welcome cooling breeze.

"I thought you'd like it," he said, sounding relieved. "My mother had this built years ago. When I was little, we'd come here on a hot afternoon, and she'd read to us. Now I come here when I'm upset . . . or discouraged . . . or almost every day, I guess." He ended with a wry smile.

"Thank you for bringing me," I said, sincerely moved that he would share such a place with me.

"Surely you know why I brought you here?" he asked, his voice suddenly husky.

I looked at him, standing awkwardly across the gazebo from me, his hands clenched at his sides as though he were trying to quiet an anger . . . or some other intense emotion. I knew, of course, right then, why he'd brought me to this treasured spot, but I had no idea what to do or say next.

"Yes," I murmured, "I guess I do."

To his credit and my relief, he did not take one step toward me. "Libbie, back in Monroe I thought you the prettiest, liveliest girl I'd ever met. But my world was full of pretty girls then, and I took none of them seriously. But now, here, a lifetime since then, I find that each day you are more and more important to me."

"I've wanted to be your friend, Lane," I said lamely.

His impatience was instant. "You know that's not what I mean." He took a deep breath. "Libbie, are you . . . do you really . . . oh, hell, do you love him?"

Startled, I echoed, "Him? Autie? Of course I do, Lane. More than life itself."

"You've been reading bad novels, then," he said bitterly. "He's going to cause you grief."

My loyalty to Autie sprang to the surface. "Autie will always take care of me, Lane Murphy, and it is ungentlemanly of you even to hint at anything else."

"And I am above all else a Southern gentleman," he finished. "You're right, Libbie, and I'll say no more—except that I want you to know that if you *ever* find yourself in need of help, shelter, whatever . . . I'm here. I'm yours."

Quickly, before embarrassment could cause me to stumble, I moved toward him, took his hands in mine, and planted a kiss on his cheek. "Lane, I am most grateful . . . and most appreciative. I shall never forget, *never*. But I'm not sure we should spend our afternoons together anymore."

"Whatever you wish," he said stiffly.

After that, I missed Lane Murphy sorely. He would never, I was sure, have been the passionate husband that Autie was, but he was a companion, a friend of the heart, in a way that Autie could never be. I didn't try to explain that even to myself.

Things went along with relative smoothness—Autie irritable and preoccupied, me bored and miserable—until the night a rock came through the parlor window. Autie, as usual, was pacing, and I sat in a Windsor chair underneath the lamp, stitching on something—I was always stitching on something merely because I thought ladies were supposed to be busy with needlework and it would make the time go by. Autie asked me once what we were to do with all the linens I embroidered—set up a hotel?—and I threw my embroidery hoop at him. But he loved the nightgowns I did for myself.

The rock came from nowhere with a crashing suddenness that startled even Autie. No matter that it brought me screaming from my chair—my nerves were notably unstable —but to startle Autie was a feat in itself.

"What in thunder . . . ?" Autie sprang across the room to the windows, though I, rooted to the spot where I'd been, screamed, "Get back, Autie, don't go near the windows."

Deliberately he turned to me. "Libbie, *be quiet!*" Then he turned again to peer out the long, tall windows of the Murphy parlor while I held my breath and fought off tears simultaneously.

"Nothing," he said calmly, finally turning back toward me. "Whoever it was rode on by in a hurry." He bent to pick up the rock—an ordinary red rock, from the river bottom, no doubt—and held it in his hand, thoughtfully turning it over and over.

I had by then sunk onto the horsehair sofa—not a soft place to sink, but nonetheless, I was glad to be off my feet. "Autie," I asked, my voice trembling, "who would have done such a thing? You have no enemies!" Ah, how love blinds us!

He whirled to look at me, the rock still clasped in his fist. "Yes, but I do, my darling. I haven't talked with you about it because . . . well, there was no need to upset you. But some of my troops are unhappy . . . to say the least."

Before I could ask further, a great commotion erupted in the back of the house, most of the noise being Eliza's voice raised to fever pitch. "Ginnel? Miss Libbie? What the tarnation's goin' on around here?" She stormed unceremoniously into the parlor to stand staring at both of us, hands on her hips in a defiant, somehow threatening pose. "You tell me what this noise is, *now.*"

And with that, Autie began to laugh. He stood still for a moment, shoulders twitching, one hand vainly trying to cover his mouth, and then he sank into a convenient chair and put his head almost between his knees while great, loud laughter rumbled up from his very boots.

"Autie," I said sternly, still half-scared to death, "stop that now and tell us what's going on!"

Finally he had himself in control enough to gasp, "If the troops knew they'd have to fight you two, they'd never give me a minute's trouble." A loud guffaw broke up whatever he intended to say, and then, "Ladies, I thank you for your concern."

Suddenly he was back to himself, General George Armstrong Custer in command. "I can take care of it, ladies," he said. "Believe me, you are in no danger."

I rushed across the room. "Autie, we're not worried about our danger. What about you? What's going on?"

"Major Earle came to me today," he said slowly, "to ask that I appear before his command to explain my orders. I refused."

"Ginnel, why couldn't you just go and explain?" Eliza demanded. Her hands were still on her hips.

"Because once I start to explain or justify, I've weakened my position," he answered firmly. "I'm in charge here, and my orders stand, no matter what the reason for them. I don't intend to start bargaining with my troops. Besides," he added wearily, "Earle doesn't know how to handle his troops. They once fired into his tent at night, and if he hadn't been asleep on the ground, he'd have been killed."

"You let that happen?" I asked, incredulous.

Autie stared at me in disbelief. "Let it happen? If I knew the men responsible, they'd be standing before a firing squad, but I cannot prove who did it." He was getting angry now—at me, Eliza, the men, everyone!

"But Miss Libbie . . ." Eliza was not to be silenced easily, and I admired her pluck, even as I bit my tongue to keep from voicing my worries over and over in a repetitious song.

"Miss Libbie will always be safe, Eliza. I promise you that."

I felt none of the relief one would think I should at this calm, strong statement. "Autie," I whispered, "I'm not worried about myself. That rock wasn't thrown at me . . . it was a threat to you."

"I know that," he answered, looking straight at me with those intense blue eyes, "but I cannot give in to threats. I will not explain my actions to my underlings." Autie stood very straight as he said this, his chin raised ever so slightly, his eyes looking out the window.

Briefly, I wished for a portraitist to capture him as he looked that very moment. But the practical side of me asked, "Will you take precautions?"

From haughtiness to amusement, his face changed instantly. "Precautions? Libbie, no one is going to gun me down when I appear in front of the troops tomorrow."

"No," I persisted, made strong by my fear, "but they might attack you at night. Will you put your pistol under the pillow at night?"

He guffawed again. "If that's all it will take to make you comfortable, of course I shall. Come to me, my love."

I walked unsteadily toward him, to be enfolded in his embrace, where everything seemed safe and certain. Eliza, a grin on her face, slipped quietly out of the room just before Autie hoisted me in his arms and carried me upstairs to the bedroom.

Before he got in bed, he ceremoniously placed his pistol on the floor next to his pillow. "It would make a lump under the pillow," he explained to me.

As the innocent often do, I slept soundly that night. Unbeknownst to me, other precautions were taken, principally by Autie's officers, who slept in a tent campground not yards from the mansion. Having decided among themselves that the situation was serious, they divided up the watch and guarded the house all the night. Their suggestion later that Autie lock the doors and windows at night fell on deaf ears.

■   ■   ■

Autie grew progressively more distracted. At night, sitting at that long dining table with gleaming silver dishes and Eliza hovering over us to see to our every comfort, he would be silent, eating his food with no enjoyment and, I'm sure, no taste.

"Autie, what troubles you tonight?" I felt I had to shout the length of the table between us, and I knew Eliza listened at the door to the servants' pantry.

"It's nothing," he said, with no emotion in his voice.

"Autie, what *is* it?" I became almost desperate, after days of seeing my beloved husband lost in a fog of concern.

He sighed deeply. "The men. Nothing to worry your head over, my darling."

"Autie," I stormed, "I will not be dismissed like that. If the problem is so severe as to cause you such concern, I deserve to know about it."

"Does your father know you talk to me this way?" he asked wickedly, then sobered immediately. "Earle's men, he insists, are used to apologies and explanations. That buffoon came to me again, asking that I talk to his men. You should have seen him, Libbie—pompous as could be. You'd have thought he was the general in charge, and he spoke just so precisely, as though explaining a very simple matter to a half-wit. I tell you I had a hard time to keep from boxing him one. 'The men are not regulars, sir, as you know' "—here Autie's voice rose in imitation of the major, then fell again into his own normal range—"and they do not understand military formality. It seems their former officer would issue an order and then go among them—to, ahem, stand on a barrel and explain the order to the men."

It was as though a faucet within Autie had been let open, for he talked on, seemingly glad to have an audience for this story, which made him so indignant.

"Can you imagine, Libbie? He tells me with a straight face that he thinks it would be wise in this instance for me to explain my orders. And he even expects me to stand on a barrel while I explain myself to a bunch of soldiers!" Autie slammed his fist into his other hand in exasperation and began to pace while I sat quietly, waiting for what would come next with an unexplainable dread running through me.

"Now they've gone and signed a petition—soldiers drawing up a petition like they had some rights! They're demanding Earle's resignation. He's afraid for his life—the coward—and came to me for protection. Frankly, I think he should resign, but it's not up to his men to make that decision. It's up to me!" Autie was more intent, more angry, than he had ever been during the whole of the Great War.

I said nothing, but that night before retiring, I walked in a wide circle around the bed to make sure the pistol was in its place.

The next day, Autie came home looking more jaunty, more like himself.

"Autie?"

"The men have all apologized to Earle," he said triumphantly, "and the matter is closed." Then, almost as an afterthought, he added, "All except one."

Something in the way he said that caught my attention. "And that one?"

"He'll be executed," Autie said firmly. "I cannot brook disobedience."

Executed! The very thought sent shivers through me, and I spent a sleepless night, tossing, turning, and worrying about the poor man who was to die within a week.

Next morning, as soon as Autie was gone, I cornered Eliza for the whole story.

"He's a nice gentleman, so they say, Miss Libbie. Got a wife and child back up North somewheres. . . . I hear he wears a lock of the child's hair next to his heart, so you know he's a good man . . . but he won't apologize. Says he was not wrong in signing that petition, and he'll stand by his word. I 'spect he doesn't think the ginnel'll go through with it . . . but he doesn't know our ginnel."

Grimly I shook my head in agreement. This man had underestimated Autie, in this case a fatal mistake. "Is he to be executed alone?"

"No, there's some deserter gonna be shot with him. Bad man, though, Miss Libbie. He done been caught stealing from folks, runnin' away from the army, 'most everything bad a man can do."

"But the other . . . ?"

She simply shrugged, and I put my hands to my ears, wanting to hear no more as I fled to our bedroom for refuge.

Autie refused to discuss the matter further with me, though I frequently sank into tears, pleading with him for the poor man's life.

"It is *not* your business, Libbie."

"But, Autie, think of his wife at home . . . and the child." Knowing his wish for children of his own, and his soft heart with his younger brothers and sisters, I did not see how he could visit such tragedy on an unknown child. But he remained firm.

"Libbie, if you persist in discussing this with me, I will send you back to Monroe and tell your father that I've found you are not suited to military life after all!"

Tears disappeared in anger! "You'd send me home, as unfit for service?" I demanded. "Autie, sometimes you overreach yourself. And you listen to me, for once—if you execute that innocent man, you'll live with guilt . . . and a big blot on your record, no matter what kind of authority Sheridan gave you."

He stared long and hard at me and then left the room without a word. I collapsed on the bed in tears, aghast that I'd stood up to Autie, beside myself with grief for the condemned man and his innocent, unknowing family.

The distance between us for the next few days was like a visible chasm, deep as any gorge in the greatest mountains. We barely spoke, even at dinner, and Eliza, nervous as a cat, broke two of the good Sevres china dishes, trying to be unobtrusive and yet desperately trying to find a way to end the war between the Custers.

"I suppose I shall have to send you back, too," Autie said caustically to her, when she broke the second dish. "But unfortunately there's nowhere to send you. It appears I am stuck with you."

Eliza fled for the kitchen, and I lifted my chin in the air and turned my head to avoid the meaningful look he sent in my direction. There was some place to send me, and Autie wanted to be sure I understood that.

I made the mistake of speaking to Tom, who simply echoed Autie's sentiments, as I should have expected. "Discipline is most important, Libbie. Don't fret yourself about a man you've never met." And with that callous attitude, he dismissed the entire affair.

Jacob Greene sought me out one day, his attitude much different from Tom's.

"I know you're upset, Libbie . . . and I just, well, I wanted to . . . oh, I don't know what I wanted. It's an awful business." He shook his head uncertainly. "I'm sure glad Nettie's not here. I guess that's what I wanted to say, maybe —that I'm sorry you have to go through this."

"Thank you, Jacob," I said, taking his hand in mine. "You don't know how fervently I wish Nettie *were* here, even if that's a selfish wish!"

"I hope to have her in Texas with us soon," he said. "That is, if we ever get out of this hot, wet place!"

I knew what he was feeling. All the richness of Louisiana —the lush growth, the fragrant odors, the musical birds— had turned sour to me. In an odd way, I blamed it all on Major Earle.

Several nights Autie slept in the officers' tents, which were pitched not too far from the main house. The first night he did this, he sent no message of his whereabouts. I ate a lonely dinner—or at least I picked at my food, with Eliza in constant attention—and sat alone with a book until near midnight, though I could tell you not one word that was on the pages.

At midnight I went to waken Eliza, only to find her prowling in the pantry. "Just straightenin' up, Miss Libbie. It sure enough beats me how things get so out of order." She moved a stack of dishes here and another there, but it was obvious she was simply rearranging to be busy. I thought in view of her recent record she might best leave the dishes alone, but I didn't say so.

"He's not come home," I said.

"I know. I been listenin'."

"I suppose he's all right."

She put a warm, comforting arm around me. "Miss Libbie, you know he is. Anything were wrong, them soldiers would come running to tell us. He's just doin' his job, doin' what he has to. . . ." She slept—or dozed—outside the bedroom door all night, while I lay inside, wide awake and miserable.

It was not that I feared Autie would actually send me packing home to my father—not really, anyway, for that would have cost him face. But I could not imagine, not in my wildest dreams, how our marriage could ever go back to its former idyllic state. There was too much anger between us, too much hurt. . . . At dawn, I sobbed myself into a fitful sleep, only to be awakened within an hour by Eliza, who barged into the room, announcing, "Miss Libbie, you gonna sleep all day? The ginnel's downstairs, waitin' on his breakfast."

I splashed water on my face—that tepid, nasty water, which was all we had and did precious little for my tear-swollen eyes—and threw on a clean wrapper, hastily brushing my hair.

Autie greeted me coolly with a kiss on the forehead and explained that he thought it best to sleep in the officers' tents for the next few nights, as a show of support for his officers and to demonstrate his own strength.

I simply nodded.

At last the dread day arrived, in some ways a sweet relief, because the suspense would be over within hours. I'd had nothing else on my mind for days, and my nerves had reached the breaking point, or so I thought—until nerves actually break, I suspect no one knows how far they will stretch.

Eliza, as frightened as I, had confided to me that rumors were abundant that Autie would be murdered before the executions could take place, and if not then, he would be shot as soon as the firing squad had done its job. Undaunted, he had ordered his officers to remain unarmed, although they had begged for sidearms at least to defend him, should the need arise.

Autie left at dawn, and I watched in horror as he rode away, sure that he would never return. Instead of a mutinous deserter and an innocent soldier being shot, Autie would be cut down on the field.

I retreated to my bedroom, to put pillows over my head and deaden the gunshots I expected to hear. Eliza stayed by me, patting my head and reassuring me, until I was momentarily reminded of my mother, who had so stroked and loved me when I was upset as a small child. We seemed to stay in that bedroom, hung in suspense, for hours.

"Eliza, have you heard it yet?" A thousand times I pulled the pillow slightly aside to question her.

"No, Miss Libbie, not yet. You know the ginnel be all right. He always is."

I buried my head again. Later I learned that even executions involved military formality. The entire division, five thousand soldiers, was assembled to witness this execution— the men formed a hollow square in a field outside town. Autie rode slowly around the line, close enough that any hand could have reached out and dealt him harm. Behind him, alive with alarm, were Tom, Jacob, and the other senior officers, including Major Earle, who was, Eliza reported later, actually shaking with fear. Behind the officers came a wagon bearing the two doomed men, sitting on their coffins. They were escorted by the guard and the firing squad of eight men.

When the parade had gone once around the ground, the provost marshal took all eight rifles off to one side and loaded seven, so that each of the eight might forever comfort himself that it was possibly not his shot that dealt the death blow. All the while the condemned men waited and watched— later, from gossip transmitted through Eliza, I learned too much of the white color of their faces, the despair and fear in their eyes, ever to erase the picture from my mind. At last they were blindfolded, while those gathered soldiers held their breath in agony, waiting for the dread command, "Fire!" One soldier later reported that in that moment of absolute silence, the mockingbirds in the hedges around the field even stopped singing briefly, as though aware of the great tragedy being enacted before them.

We heard the shots, of course—pillows can muffle only so much—and Eliza and I clung to each other, speechless. Within an hour we heard Autie mount the stairs.

"It's done?" I asked dully.

"In part," he replied self-confidently. "The deserter is dead."

"And the young sergeant?" My heart did a crazy leap in my chest, and I put a hand to my breast, as though to quiet the beating.

"He was pardoned." Nonchalantly Autie began stripping off his gloves, taking off his dress saber.

"Pardoned? Ginnel, you tell us what happened!" Eliza demanded, propriety sinking before her amazement.

It seems that just before the command to fire was given, the provost marshal stealthily stepped to the sergeant, took his arm, and led him away. Then came the command, and the deserter fell back dead, in blessed ignorance that he went to eternity alone, while the sergeant swooned in the provost marshal's arms.

"I believe he was the victim of undue influence," Autie said properly, "and I had determined from the outset to pardon him. But I could not let the soldiers feel that I was persuaded by threats on my life."

And so, he had subjected one terrified young man to a week of agony beyond endurance. The soldier was also imprisoned for some length of time, and I often wondered if that man were ever whole again, ever but a shell of the loving husband and father he had once been.

Autie never told me, but I later learned that the sergeant's regiment had gone to the execution with loaded rifles. Had Autie known, he probably would not have rescued the young man, and then there would have been even greater disaster, with Autie dead, in all probability. The whole affair was to me proof again that the Lord works in mysterious ways His wonders to accomplish. Either that, or the Lord wasn't ready for Autie yet.

Autie's performance the night after the execution did little to quiet my uncertainties. He began to dance around our bedroom with the air of one who has a secret and wants only to have that hidden knowledge pulled from him. Yet each time I inquired, begged, pleaded, even announced that I didn't care a rap what he was excited about, he chuckled in triumph, insisting that he had a good joke on me. It was, it turned out, a fine joke: there had been no ammunition in the entire house the whole time he'd been under threat. That pistol beside the bed, in which I'd placed so much trust, had been unloaded—and could not have been loaded without a trip to the commissary!

The rift between Autie and me did not heal magically overnight. We were like strangers, awkward and self-conscious around each other, building again a relationship that would never be quite the same as it had been before this traumatic event. I could never forget that Autie had a streak of cruelty in him and a need to prove his authority that blotted out human kindness, though he justified it as military necessity; Autie could never entirely forgive me for questioning his word and judgment.

Fortunately, we were ordered to march to Texas, a long, grueling journey that accomplished the healing that idle days in Louisiana could never have seen. Autie studied his maps for days on end, calling alternately for the quartermaster—to discuss transportation—and the commissar—to discuss supplies. When at length he announced that we would be on the march within days, he was astounded that I replied calmly, "So I've gathered."

"How," he demanded, "did you know?"

I would, I assumed, ride Custis Lee, and Autie would ride Jack Rucker, the new quarter horse he'd recently acquired. Jack Rucker was stronger and tougher than the Thoroughbred Don Juan, but no more beloved by Autie. "I'm shipping Don Juan home," he told me. "He deserves a rest, and my father will take care of him."

I didn't mind, as long as he didn't ship Custis Lee home. I had no spirit for getting acquainted with a new horse on a long march. Distracted by details, I didn't see the real trouble ahead of me.

Chapter Eight

 "YOU AND ELIZA WILL JOURNEY TO TEXAS BY WAY OF New Orleans and the Gulf of Mexico. You'll join me in Hempstead, which is to be our permanent camp." Autie looked up from the maps he was poring over, seated at the desk in the Glen Ellen library, a room now woefully devoid of books.

"Join you in Texas!" I echoed indignantly. "Eliza and I will *accompany* you to Texas."

He assumed that now-familiar look of authority. "You are the only two women in the whole command. And the march will be entirely too difficult for you, especially at this time of year."

It was August, and even our Red River quarters were unbearable, though I had been careful not to complain about mosquitoes, suffocating heat, poor water, even alligators, for I feared that complaint might send me packing back to Monroe. Now I saw that New Orleans, not Monroe, might be my dreaded fate. Perhaps at that point in our marriage, the separation would have been wise, for we were still sleeping stiffly on separate sides of the bed, still distantly polite with each other at the dining table. But I sensed that being sent away would cost me more than a separation from Autie and the possible discomfort of a boat trip. Stubbornly, I dug my heels in for battle.

I also changed my tactics. Walking behind the chair where he sat, I twirled a finger in his long curls and said in my most gentle voice, "Autie, you know I'm a good campaigner. You've said so yourself."

Though he was startled at this unexpected touch of affection, he remained firm. "You've never been tested by anything like this. Your father has written sternly advising me to send you by water, and even other officers are saying they wouldn't take *their* wives on such a journey. I'll not be put in a position of the villain who caused you a miserable trip . . . or worse."

"And if something were to happen to me in New Orleans . . . or perhaps the boat will capsize in the Gulf. . . . Besides, since when do you let Papa's notions govern our relationship?"

He sprang out of the chair, away from my fingers, which had crept from his hair down to the back of his neck, beneath his tight collar. "Libbie, stop! You're not an effective seductress—too obvious. And I won't be swayed by cheap feminine tricks."

I began to laugh aloud. "Did they remind you of Fanny Fifeld?"

Autie had the grace to blush. But then he blustered, "Stop trying to distract me! And I'm not making this decision because of anything your father has written. I simply agree with him this one time."

Autie was right that I was not very good at feminine wiles—most times when I pouted, he simply laughed. I decided that, as always, honesty was the best tack, and there was not a bit of playacting in me when I stood before him at the window where he looked out over the lawns of Glen Ellen.

"Autie, I really don't want to be separated from you." I hesitated and then added, "Not right now."

Autie took that as a step toward reconciliation on my part, for he turned toward me and gave me the first meaningful kiss we'd shared in more than two weeks. Responding, I knew how much I'd hated the distance between us, how badly I wanted things to be just as they had been. I was too young to realize the impossibility of ever going back, but for now, once again, I was in his arms.

"I don't mind hardship, you know I don't, and I'll be no trouble. You know I can do it."

He tilted my head up for another long, slow kiss. "I don't want us to be apart, either," he said. "But, Libbie, I could not bear it if anything happened to you that I could somehow have prevented."

"It won't," I promised, sure that I'd won another small victory. Then, grinning, I asked, "Have you thought how Eliza would react to that pronouncement? If you think I was indignant, I defy you to tell her she's not to accompany you."

He shook his head in agreement. "You're right. I'm tempted to tell her, just to hear her screech."

And screech she did. Autie strode jauntily into the pantry, while I hid just the other side of the door in the dining room, where I could hear the fireworks. "Eliza," I heard him say, "you and Miss Libbie will go by boat to New Orleans and Texas, rather than with the troops."

Loud wails and angry squawls were punctuated by such questions as "Who you think gonna cook for you?" and "Who gonna comfort Miss Libbie when she need you?" The sound of pots and pans being slammed around echoed in the dining room, and in a flash Autie came bursting through the door, hand covering his mouth so that he wouldn't collapse in laughter. Behind him came Eliza, eyes flashing, the skillet in her hands looking like a dangerous weapon.

"Miss Libbie! Did he tell you? I ain't goin' by no boat! Been on enough of them to last me a lifetime!" She sputtered and carried on until at last I could stand it no longer.

"He's not really going to send us by boat, Eliza. He thought it was best . . . but he's seen the error of his ways."

As I said that, I glanced sideways at Autie, who looked pained to say the least.

"You mean he was funnin' with me?" Instead of lessening her anger, the idea that Autie had played a joke on her infuriated Eliza, and she began to swing the skillet.

Autie beat a hasty retreat, and I could hear the library door slam behind him. Once he was out of earshot, Eliza put down the skillet and gave me a broad smile.

"We know how to handle him, don't we, Miss Libbie?"

Autie endured much whispered criticism during the preparations for the march, especially when he ordered an ambulance outfitted as a traveling wagon for me. The seats were arranged so that the leather backs could be unstrapped at the sides and laid down to form a bed—I could rest, even while we were on the move. There was a pocket for my needlework and book, and straps to hold my shawl and traveling bag.

It wasn't that the soldiers resented this work, but that they genuinely felt the trip would be too hard and were concerned about my safety. One whose name I don't know yet, in a touching gesture, covered a canteen with leather and used yellow silk—from the saddler—to embroider on the cover the words "Lady Custer." The soldier advised me to fill the canteen each morning, cover it with a wet blanket, and hang it, with the cork left out, near the roof of the wagon so that it might catch any air that was stirring. This technique assured me of palatable water—well, almost palatable—during the whole trip, but the wet blanket faded the letters out so that by the time we reached Texas, "Lady Custer" was no longer visible.

But, then, I looked far from a lady at the end of that journey. The thought that Autie might have been right to send me by boat flitted through my mind a thousand times, but I never voiced it, even to Eliza, and I never complained.

When the column marched away from Glen Ellen, I rode proudly at the front on Custis Lee, between Autie and Tom. Behind us streamed several thousand men, marching two by two, and a wagon train of supplies. It took hours for the entire train to pass any given point.

Lane stood in the shadows of the trees, watching as we passed, and because Autie was beside me, I gave no notice that I saw him. I wished I could tell him, once more, how important he had been to me. But I suspect that Lane knew, and knew, too, why I bade him no farewell.

Shortly after we left the plantations of the Red River Valley with their fragrant blooms and thick growth, we entered a dense pine forest. The land here was not nearly as rich, so few people lived in the forest. Those that did inhabited small log huts, built low to the ground, with two rooms —one on each side of a floored breezeway. Autie told me these cabins were called "dogtrots" because the dogs—ten of them to one cabin sometimes!—congregated in those open spaces. We saw untidy children and pale-faced, lethargic adults lounging amid the dogs while skin-and-bones pigs rooted near the cabins seeking something, anything, to eat.

"I think we'll not ask accommodations along the way for a while," Autie said. "We'll camp."

I breathed a sigh of relief.

But camping was hard on me. Autie showed me how to roll his overcoat for a pillow, explaining that soldiers slept like a top on such a pillow. But for me the thick, unwieldy material of Uncle Sam's coats made a rocky resting place that forced my neck to assume a steep incline from head to shoulder. I awoke less patriotic than I had retired. But I did not complain, and Autie praised my veteranlike behavior, though I think his praise was an effort to encourage me. At last Eliza provided moss to make a much softer pillow. But the moss had a damp vegetable odor and often held tiny horned toads or lizards that Texans call swifts—neither was dangerous, but they were not my idea of sleeping companions, and it seemed impossible to dislodge them. Eliza tried hay next for my pillow. The hay was soft, clean, and sweet smelling. I closed my eyes in gratitude.

I had begged off sleeping in a tent because there were so many poisonous insects in the forest, so every night Autie had the wagon parked in front of the tent, and he lifted me in and out of this high sleeping room, where I felt safe from scorpions, tarantulas, and centipedes.

One night I was awakened by a munching and crunching in my ear—wisps of hay hanging over the edge of the wagon had proved a temptation to a stray mule, which was busily eating the pillow from beneath my head. Fortunately, we were off to one side, away from the troops, and no one heard my shrieks of indignation, or worse, Autie's peals of laughter. The angrier I got, the harder he laughed, until I was forced to join him.

Finally Eliza traded blankets for a pillow at one of those dogtrot cabins. It was a poor excuse for a pillow—so tiny as near to be lost in your ear—but I welcomed it gratefully.

Each morning, before dawn, Autie lifted me from the wagon and deposited me in our tent—this special treatment kept my feet dry in spite of the drenching dews in the forest. The fear of holding up an entire army taught me to bathe and dress in seven minutes—Autie timed it one morning, to my great discomfort. I combed my hair straight back, as it was too dark that time of the morning to part it, even by candlelight. Nonetheless, I lived in terror that some day thousands of men might be kept waiting because a woman had lost her hairpins—the commanding officers would order the trumpeter to delay sounding "Boots and Saddles," the call to march, and would remind me, again, that "it is easier to command a whole division of cavalry than one woman."

Nothing smothers the air like a pine forest—the fringed top of those trees may have swayed in the breeze, but not a breath descended to us below. When we stopped to rest, we would carefully position ourselves in the strip of shadow made by a tree, only to be forced to move within minutes as the sun followed its path and moved our shadow.

Reveille sounded at two A.M.—causing Autie once to remark that we ought to eat breakfast the night before so as to save time in the morning. It was necessary to move before dawn, because the moment the sun rose, the heat became suffocating. We camped off the road, and it was difficult to find the road in the pitch-darkness, so Autie set me on Custis Lee and commanded me to follow as close as possible while we picked our way over logs and through ditches or under-brush. Custis Lee usually put his hoof exactly in the footprint just left by Jack Rucker, Autie's new horse, and we were safe. Out of the dark we'd hear Autie's cheerful "Are you all right?" "Give Lee his head," or "That old plug of yours will bring you through fine." The latter inevitably inspired some retort on my part in defense of my beautiful Custis Lee—and by this Autie knew that I was safely following behind.

Our guide, a Texan named Sillman, was a talker—there is no other word for it. His mule, named Betty, walked so fast that no one could keep up with her—save her master's tongue, which ran incessantly. During much of the day I rode at the head of the column with Autie, and when we felt we could no longer bear the sun beating down on our heads, we'd call out, "In heaven's name, Sillman, how much longer?" by which we really meant, "How soon shall we find a creek by which to camp?"

"Oh, three miles or so, you're sure to find a bold-flowin' stream," Sillman would reply confidently. Sure enough, the grass began to grow greener, moss hung from the trees, cypress appeared among the dry pines, and hope sprang in our hearts. Our mouths began to taste cool, clean water—and then we'd find ourselves in a dry creek bed, with nothing but pools of muddy water and a coating of green mold. For years, if we ever came to a puny, crawling driblet of water, we said, "Must be one of Sillman's bold-flowing streams." I do not remember one good drink of water on that march—what we had generally tasted of tree roots—and I was grate-ful for the bottle of claret that Lane Murphy had pressed on me, assuring me over my protests that I would welcome it.

I survived most of it unscathed—dealing with seed-tick and chigger bites and even once being rescued from that most deadly snake, the pine-tree rattlesnake—it had looked to me like a small, dried twig. But one morning I was morti-fied to find myself ill—I, who had boasted about being such a good campaigner, could not lift my head from the pillow. It was embarrassing—I could not be sent back, nor could I be left, even under guard, in the woods. The surgeon bade me lie in the wagon during the march, where I was lonely and bored—and nearly jiggled and joggled to death, for I had "breakbone fever." Not dangerous, it was nevertheless extremely painful, and each bounce of the wagon introduced me to a new bone in my body. The surgeon fed me quinine, and in a few days, light-headed and tottering, I was lifted again to the saddle, glad to be back among the shining faces who happily welcomed me.

Both Tom and Jacob also suffered bouts of breakbone fever on the march, and, not having a wagon like mine, they were forced to endure the agony of remaining ahorseback. My insistence that they use my wagon was refused with a stern suggestion from Autie that to do so would embarrass them before their men. Neither man recovered as quickly or as thoroughly as I—Tom suffered from some form of rheumatism for more than a year, and Jacob grew gray and drawn, racked with fever until he looked far worse than he had when released from the Confederate Army's prison. Autie, of course, remained hale and hearty and declared that he had no time for illness, nor it the nerve to attack him.

River crossings provided even more fearful torment than had breakbone fever. Texas is a land of freshets, where the most innocent little stream can rise to a roar in no time, and the banks are high, steep, and slippery. Our train included a pontoon bridge to cross these rivers, but oh! getting down to that bridge was a trial. Often as I could, I rode Custis Lee, my hand wound into his mane, my very soul trusting his surefootedness. But there were those days when, because of heat or some such, the surgeon ordered me to the wagon to avoid a recurrence of the fever.

Then I sat inside the wagon with trembling fear, hands clutching at the sides, head out the window to spot Autie as he directed the driver down the deep descent and, at the same time, tried to encourage me. The soil would have become wet and slippery simply from the transporting of boats and lumber for the bridge, and the brake alone was insufficient to stop the wagon—soldiers had to man the wheels. The four mules who pulled the wagon usually sat down and slid down the bank on their rumps. The driver, a strong burly man who kept the reins knotted around gigantic fists, was alternately grateful for my thanks for his care and patient with my pleadings that he go slowly. I knew that come evening, when the safe crossing was behind us, Eliza would reward him with hot biscuits and coffee, and he would think his job well done.

One of these steep river crossings had a special boon. As soon as we were safely across, Eliza disappeared, only to return triumphant with a fish as long as her arm. We were sorely tired of corn pone and back ribs, and that platter of fish tasted like manna from the gods!

The country improved as we came out of the forest and onto the prairie. Even the farmhouses looked better, and we were soon able to bargain for eggs and butter—ah, heavenly treat! In place of monotonous pines, we had magnolia, mulberry, pecan, persimmon, and live-oak trees. Cactus plants grew four and five feet high, with brilliant red blossoms making gorgeous spots of color in the prairie grass, and wildflowers offered an artist's palette of colors. The air began to smell faintly of the sea and blew softly about us instead of hanging, leaden, on our shoulders.

"Autie?"

"You're a good campaigner, Libbie. I'll never doubt you again." And he never did.

We arrived at Hempstead, where we were to camp, in October, nearly seven weeks after we'd left Alexandria. There we received welcome mail from Monroe and, most important of all, the news that Autie had been brevetted major, lieutenant colonel, and brigadier general in the regular army. General Sheridan came to the camp by way of Galveston, bringing with him Father Custer, whose anger at Autie knew no bounds when he heard of the hardships of our trip.

"You should never have allowed her to make that journey, son!" he stormed, while Autie hung his head like a schoolboy caught stealing apples off a tree.

"Father," I intercepted, "I insisted upon it. Don't be angry at Autie."

"I don't care how you insisted," said that old man, as stubborn as his son, "he should have refused."

Sheridan's purpose on the visit was, of course, more than just to deliver Father Custer. He congratulated Autie on his new rank, praised the discipline of the men on the long, difficult march—there had been no pillaging of farmhouses along the way—and put Autie in charge of the entire cavalry in Texas—thirteen cavalry regiments and an equal number of infantry regiments. Their job was to restore law and order to Texas—a tall order for a land in ferment, beset with jayhawkers, bandits, and bushwhackers.

After the formal ceremonies, Sheridan and Autie and several others retired to our tent for a conference. Autie sent me to Eliza's tent, with apologies. "Confidential matters, Libbie, you understand, don't you?"

I did, until I saw Tom strut into the tent, bold as you please, behind Autie. Little did I know that their discussion centered on the possibility of Autie leading a campaign into Mexico to drive out Maximilian and the French, once and for all. My suspicions were raised, though, by such a secret council, and I badgered Autie to tell me what it was about.

"Military matters, Libbie," he said sternly more than once, knowing full well the reaction I'd have had to the possibility of a campaign in Mexico, for I surely would have been left behind then.

Our camp was on Clear Creek, which was ironically the color of ashes, and Autie and I had a large tent on the bank, with lumber from the pontoon bridge used for flooring. Eliza's cook tent was near us, but the other staff were some distance away, giving us the privacy we desired, and the entire division ranged along the stream where, at last, there was plenty of water. Beyond us fifty miles of prairie stretched out to the sea.

The land was a far corner of the plantation owned by Leonard Groce, one of the oldest residents of Texas, a charming gentleman whose four sons had all fought under General Lee. When he saw that our furniture consisted of a bucket and two camp stools, that good man had his wife send over chairs—with real backs, against which I sank gratefully —along with milk, vegetables, roast of mutton, jelly, and other delicacies. Gratefully, we declined the offer of a room in their house—Autie had no wish to share a house with anyone!—but I did take advantage of their hospitality to improve my appearance at a real dressing table with a mirror.

I'd broken my mirror early in the march and since then had made my toilet by feel. My horror was absolute when I looked into the mirror and saw my face, parboiled and swollen with sunburn, while my hair hung faded and rough about it.

"Autie," I demanded, "why didn't you tell me how awful I look?"

He said nothing but took me in his arms. Eventually I realized that his having told me would have only made things worse, for I could do nothing about my appearance, and I got over my fit of pique.

Groce and his neighbors introduced Autie to what was to become one of the greatest pleasures of his life—hunting with a pack of dogs. Autie was absolutely fascinated to realize that each hunter had his own pack of dogs, and each dog responded to his own master's horn and none other. Neighboring planters gave Autie five hounds, and he immediately secured a horn and began to practice, until I thought—and nearly hoped—he'd split his cheeks in two. The dogs would sit in a semicircle around him, sympathy clearly written on their faces, and tune their voices to the same key as his practicing.

"Autie, please give us a rest!" I covered my ears with my hands, as though that would help.

"I have to practice," he replied. "If anyone thinks it's easy to blow a horn, I defy them to try it."

Tom caught the fever, too, and no matter how we described their red faces and bulging eyes, their bent bodies and ludicrous struggles, we could dissuade neither Autie nor Tom from their practice. Eventually, they were ready for deer hunting, though Tom had an unfortunate accident on his first hunt. When a deer bounded toward him, he got so excited, he fired at the wrong moment—the shot went harmlessly by the buck and instantly killed one of Autie's dogs. Ever after as they set out on hunting expeditions, Autie would say, "Tom's a good shot. He's sure to hit *something*!"

Father Custer went hunting with them, too, though he was the subject of so many jokes by his sons that I wondered he kept his good humor. Still, his eyes would twinkle and his face wreathe into wrinkles as he described the way one son had distracted him while the other rapped his horse smartly across the withers, causing the horse to bolt and nearly unseat the old man. Once Autie pulled the poor man's cape over his head and held it there momentarily, while Tom rapped the horse. But Father Custer was a good horseman and a good sport, for he enjoyed his sons, and when I would beg them to be easy on him, he'd say, "Now, now, Libbie, let the boys be!"

Nettie Humphrey Greene, my best friend from childhood, and our first Texas norther arrived together—Nettie from Galveston and the norther from the plains, she being the more welcome, but the storm surprising us more. After a day of hot, muggy air, the wind howled over the prairie toward us, shaking and rattling the tent as if driven by human fury.

"Autie," I cried, "we have to get dressed."

"Shhh! It will be all right. The tent is secure—it'll hold."

"How can it?" I wailed, as I burrowed into the shelter of his arms.

"Wait," he said, "until the rain starts. It will quiet the wind."

Unbelievably, he was right—but the next morning havoc greeted us—tents blown down, utensils blown about, brush everywhere. Father Custer's tent had collapsed, and he'd had to get himself out from under it, something he accomplished with difficulty but told about with such droll humor that we were soon all laughing.

With Nettie, it was a different story. When the men were off repairing the damage, she clung to me. "Libbie, how have you stood it?"

"Well," I said practically, "it never has blown like that before."

She wore a soft, pale gown, tremendously unsuited to our situation, and matching dainty shoes on her feet, which must, I thought, have been half-frozen. Her hair was parted, though badly, and her eyes were dark with circles. Now she sank into the chair so kindly provided by the Groces.

"I wanted to be with Jacob so badly, but I don't think . . . I can't stand . . ."

Was Nettie going to turn weak-kneed on me? After I'd so looked forward to her arrival? "Nonsense," I said briskly, "you'll be as good a campaigner as I am. It's either that, Nettie, or be sent back to Monroe." She wailed, but I refused to give her any sympathy, which would, I thought, have sent her over the edge into a cauldron of self-pity.

"I . . . I   miss   home . . . and   Monroe . . . and . . ."

"Fresh apples," I said decisively. "I've missed good fresh apples ever since we got here."

Nettie looked startled, for apples, I knew, were not on her mind.

"Remember how you missed Jacob when you were in Monroe," I said heartlessly. "Now, let's fix your face." There was no worry about obtaining water cold enough to brace tear-swollen eyes, as there had been when I'd tried to camouflage a crying spell in Louisiana. Nettie yowled anew when I splashed the water on her face and swore it froze the moment it touched her skin. But by the time Jacob came to collect her, she was mostly recovered and able to smile a little.

"Had a bit of a rough welcome, I'm afraid," Jacob said softly, putting a protective arm around her. "But I certainly am glad this girl's here."

If Nettie didn't behave and make Jacob happy, I vowed, I'd personally take a whip to her!

In November we were ordered to the city of Austin, Texas, where we remained until late January. We marched again from Hempstead to Austin, but it was a far different march —the weather was neither hot nor muggy; indeed, it was almost pleasant, as though Texas had decided to show us what it could do to be welcoming. We crossed a few rivers, but most we could ford—no more that fearful skate down steep banks to a pontoon bridge. Eggs, butter, and poultry were plentiful at the comfortable farms we passed, and sometimes the officers went astray to chase a hare—though much to my relief, the chaparral bushes often provided safe hiding places for the desperate animals. I did not mind eating venison or even rabbit, but I never wanted to see them killed.

We arrived in Austin with at least three kind offers of hospitality from local citizens, for even though loyal Southerners, many of these locals were relieved to see a Federal force coming to restore law and order.

"I won't stay in another man's house," Autie announced, but then immediately softened his proclamation with a query. "You don't mind, do you, Libbie? We can camp here outside the city for a few days and get the lay of the land."

"Here" was on a hillside above the city, with a magnificent view of a charming town of stucco houses, given the look of summer even in November by the perpetual green of its live-oak trees. Looking carefully, we could make out the magnificence of the State House and the governor's mansion —after months of camping, they were indeed wondrous buildings to us.

"No, Autie," I said truthfully, "I should prefer to camp here. I . . . well, I hate to give up our camp life."

Once we were settled—in the Blind Asylum, which had been closed during the war—I missed camp life even more. The ceiling seemed to come down to smother me during the night, and though we kept all three windows in our room open, there was never enough air stirring. And most of all I missed the gentle rocking of the wagon in the wind, where I had been lulled to sleep so many nights, in spite of my fears of scorpions and their fellow creatures.

I had no need, however, to miss the dogs who had surrounded our wagon, for many had come with us.

"Autie, get that dog out of here!" Byron, the lordliest of his hounds—a purebred greyhound—had installed himself on our bed next to Autie, who had, in his usual fashion, simply flung himself down on the bed. "I believe," he once told me, "that I must have got the habit at West Point, where we lived in terror of a wrinkle." Wherever he learned it, Autie was wont to spread his arms and jump backward on a bed, so that he lay spread out, taking most of the room. Adding Byron to this scene left little room for me, even though it was but nap time in the afternoon and not night.

Instead of answering me, Autie crooned to the dog, "Walk right up here on this clean white spread, without troubling yourself to care whether your feet are muddy or not. Your Aunt Eliza wants you to lie on nice, white counterpanes —she washes them especially for you."

Byron responded by licking his master's hand and turning a most venomous look on me. I called Eliza, who entered in her usual state of anger at something or other the general had done. Byron took one look at her and curled back his lip to expose long, white fangs, a greeting accompanied by a low, threatening sound from his throat. Eliza paled visibly.

"Never mind, Eliza. I shall take a broom to him." But Byron declined to move, and growled at me every bit as ferociously. Autie lay there, silent and amused—he had a fondness for not interfering in difficulties between others.

"I shall simply lie down," I announced, to no one in particular, though two humans and one dog watched me intently. I lay down in the small portion of the bed that was left, my angry back toward Autie and his blasted dog. Byron soon planted his feet against my back and began to push, ever so subtly, until I was in danger of edging off the bed and was, in truth, afraid of the dog.

"Now see what you done, Ginnel?" Eliza exclaimed in anger. "You keer more for that pesky, sassy old hound than you do for Miss Libbie, and your mother would be right ashamed of you now."

Autie had had enough. He gave Byron a kick that sent him flying off the bed. "Get out of here," he said to Eliza, though both she and he knew his anger was only put on. Eliza had a way of treating him as though he were a big boy away from home for the first time, and when provoked enough, she always invoked his mother, though she never had met that dear lady. Somehow it had an effect on Autie.

The battle of the dogs continued, however—for one day my beloved Ginnie, a pointer given us in Hempstead, failed to appear. She was always thumping her tail at our door, early in the morning, a gentle hint that it was time to be up. "Autie," I implored, "where can she be?"

"Probably out with some dog," he growled from the comfort of his covers. "You can never trust a bitch."

I threw a pillow at him, and he, laughing, got into his pants to go investigate. In truth, Autie was as concerned as I and as fond of Ginnie. In no time he came bounding back up the stairs to announce that she was fine, but seven small Ginnies were taking breakfast from their mother in quarters under the porch. Breathless, I followed him, and Autie crawled under the porch to hand the babies to me, one by one, while Ginnie paced frantically beside us. With the last one in his hand, Autie led the way to our bedroom and deposited the puppy in the midst of our bed—Ginnie's rag bed in the hall was in no way good enough for such a family. Ginnie and the rest of the brood were soon installed in the same place. Then nothing would do but that we called Eliza.

That not-so-patient woman took one look and demanded, "Did I come all the way out here to this no-count country to wash white counterpanes for dogs?"

In time we had twenty-three dogs at the Blind Asylum, but Byron and Ginnie were the lordliest of all.

"Autie, what will you do when peacetime is declared?" It was an accepted fact that once law and order were restored in Texas, Autie's brevet rank would be meaningless, and his pay would revert to that of his regular rank—from six thousand dollars to about sixteen hundred dollars a year.

We had ridden up Mount Brunnel outside Austin, a path smooth but so steep that we'd dismounted and walked part of the way. The view from the top, though, was magnificent —the river that wound through Austin, and which on close examination was filled with sand bars, looked from this distance like a silver ribbon, and the plowed fields in the lowlands made huge square patterns in the green vista. I was mounted on Custis Lee, and Autie on a fine Thoroughbred that he had traded from a Texan on the march from Hempstead. We hardly looked like people to be concerned about money—and yet I was. I've no idea yet why I determined to bring up the subject at that particular moment, though, and thereby spoil what had been an almost-perfect afternoon for the two of us.

"Are you worried about money?" he asked in a bantering tone.

"Yes," I answered, my tone much more direct, "I am."

"We're living very frugally," Autie said, still in that jaunty tone that was clearly meant to say that I was worrying about nothing and he didn't want to talk about it.

"But we had nothing when we came here. Living frugally may perhaps get us out of debt."

"We spent the money at a milliner's shop, buying hats for you," he railed indignantly.

As patiently as possible, I sighed and refrained from pointing out that he had made those purchases, not I. "But Autie, what will we do when your rank is reduced?"

It was, of course, an event he did not contemplate with joy—and therefore rarely faced with serious thought. "Something will work out," he said.

"My father is concerned," I told him. "He writes me often about investments. . . ."

"I have many investment opportunities here," Autie said loftily. "Horses . . . land . . . even cattle."

"Papa says land would be a bad investment for us, for we'd have to move on and leave it."

"Papa says!" he mocked, pulling too hard on the reins, so that his horse jumped in amazement. "Don't you think I can take care of you without listening to Papa every minute?"

Poor Custis Lee, for I sawed every bit as violently on his reins, turning him away from Autie in my anger at that remark.

"Wait!" Autie cried. "Hear me out! I've provided very well for you, in spite of your father's doubts. . . . Oh, I know, he worried about you living in a wagon like an immigrant. Well, you did . . . and you enjoyed it!"

I could offer no argument, so I remained silent. We had by now reined our horses to a walk, and they, accustomed to all manner of activities by their riders, showed no alarm at the anger that flew between us.

"Well, now he fears poverty for you, and if that happens, I'll make you love that, too!"

I stared at him in amazement. It was such an irrational, childish argument that I had no answer. We rode in silence for several minutes.

"Besides," Autie finally said, "your long-term well-being is in no doubt. Your father will leave you a comfortable inheritance."

And then my anger exploded, scaring both horses, myself, and most of all, Autie. "What do you plan to do?" I screamed. "Kill him off when we need the money!" I spurred Custis Lee more viciously than I ever had—an act I regretted ever after—and left Autie sitting behind, staring at our disappearing dust.

"Libbie," he commanded futilely, "come back here!"

I was settled in our bedroom at the asylum before he spoke to me again, and then he was tentative in his approach. "Libbie?"

"Yes?" I answered coldly, anger still rising in me like bile.

"I didn't mean that . . . I just can't bear for you to think I won't take care of you."

"Autie," I said levelly, "I know you mean to take care of me." And I let the rest of the thought dangle. But I did not rush into the outstretched arms he held toward me.

Later Autie asked me, in serious tones, if our future planning might not eventually include some kind of inheritance from my father, and I had to tell him I would receive the house on the occasion of Papa's death—he was then in poor health, but his death was not expected by any means—and my stepmother would receive the bulk of a pitifully small estate for a man of Papa's prominence.

"He's just borrowed money to fix up the house," I said, "because he's sure people will want to know where General

Custer's father-in-law lives, and the house must be in good enough shape so as not to disgrace you."

"Libbie? Nettie's awful sick. I wonder . . . could you see to her today?" Jacob Greene approached me at breakfast, a meal I would long since have forgone except that Autie warned me the troops would think me a "feather-bed soldier" if I stayed abed instead of rising to eat with the officers. Nettie had so far never appeared this early in the morning, so I'd not been surprised by her absence.

"Of course, Jacob. I'll go to her now."

Nettie and Jacob occupied rooms just down the hall from ours in the asylum, so getting to her was not difficult at all. My knock elicited a weak "Come in," and I found Nettie prostrate on the bed, a cold cloth on her head, still in her nightgown with her hair undone.

"Nettie? Jacob says you're feeling poorly."

She let out a loud groan. "That's a mild understatement. I can't stand up without throwing up. Poor Jacob . . . he's longed to have me with him, and now look at me."

"Are you just sick today?"

"No, but today's worse. I've felt bad every morning for two weeks."

"Nettie . . . are you expecting?"

There was no surprise, no girlish, "Oh, do you think so?" Instead, she said grimly, "I'm quite sure that's the problem."

"Problem?" I exclaimed. "Oh, Nettie, if it were me, I'd be so delighted, you'd have to stop me from singing it from the rooftops."

She put a hand to her head, her expression pained. "That's because you don't feel like I do, Libbie. And if you did, you wouldn't want to be thousands of miles from home in this godforsaken country."

"Oh, Nettie, we won't be here forever. You'll be safely back in Monroe by the time the baby comes . . . and Jacob will be so happy."

I thought, of course, of Autie and the joy he'd have shown if I'd exhibited similar symptoms. As it was, I worried about telling Autie and delayed for several days. In fact, I delayed so long that he heard the news from Tom.

"Ain't it grand?" Tom exploded. "When are you and Libbie goin' to give us the same kind of news?"

"I've no idea," Autie said, tight-lipped, while I wished that the very floor would open and swallow me.

"No," he said that night as we lay in bed, "I'm not upset. I'm happy for Jacob and Nettie." But he turned aside and went to sleep without touching me, and I, of course, thought that he considered making love to me a fruitless exercise. My pillow was wet with tears before I slept that night.

Christmas came and went—we filled the huge parlor of the asylum with evergreens, made canopies of flags, fashioned wax lights in impromptu wooden sconces, and waxed the floor till it shone for dancing. One of the soldiers organized a band, and a sergeant called off quadrilles. We had a grand and festive feast with all the proper courses—soup, roast game, and pudding for dessert.

As Autie raised his glass in toast to the holidays, I looked at our table and the faces of those who meant so much to me —besides Autie, there were Tom and Nettie and Jacob and one or two others who had been with us since our early-summer boat trip down the Mississippi. If I could not be with Papa and Mama, I thought, I surely could have not asked for a better Christmas nor more loving companions.

All good things, it seems, come quickly to an end, for in January it was decided that the civil authorities in Texas were now capable of restoring law and order. The government considered a cavalry division in Texas unnecessary, especially since there was now no longer an expedition going to Mexico. The U.S. government, it seems, wished to avoid offending France. Peacetime was declared—the move we had dreaded so much—and we prepared ourselves to head back to Monroe. Autie was officially between assignments and reduced in rank, his brevetted rank gone, and with it a good portion of our income.

We had scant belongings to pack, for we'd been traveling light and, of late, living with other people's furniture. We could not take all the dogs, though Byron and Ginnie would go, and Jack Rucker, Custis Lee, and the fine new Thoroughbred would be shipped to Michigan while we returned by boat to New Orleans and then north by steamer. We returned the cow a kind citizen had lent us and reluctantly bid good-bye to the many friends we had made. Texas, feared as a wild 'n' woolly place, had been a grand adventure for us, and we would always recall it with special fondness.

With Nettie, Jacob, Tom, and three other senior officers, we rode from Austin to Brennan, a ride made pleasant by good roads and fresh horses and made easier because Autie did not have an entire division to manage. But when we stopped at a small hotel in Brennan, I was alarmed by the knots of men gathered in the courtyard.

"Autie, those men . . ."

"Confederates," he said tersely. "Pay them no mind."

They were hard to ignore, for it was obvious from their looks and gestures that they were talking about us. Jacob, Tom, Autie, and the other men, of course, walked tall and bold in their blue army uniforms, and there was no mistaking their loyalties. We could not reach the dining hall without passing by one particular group of about six men, so I held tight to Autie's arm and lowered my eyes. Still, I could not close my ears.

"Damned Yankees" came the muttered growl. "Ought to teach 'em a thing or two about Southern hospitality . . . send 'em packing back where they belong." The rest of what they said was too vile to repeat, but at each epithet I felt the muscles in Autie's arm tighten. Any moment I expected his blood to be raised to fighting heat, but to my surprise—and relief—he and the others simply walked by as if the men did not exist or were, at the least, silent.

"They're not worth dignifying with anger," Autie said, and when I expressed some fear, he scoffed. "They were only barking, not biting."

Still I decided never to travel in Texas again without a division of cavalry. It was a sad farewell from a state I'd come to like so well.

From Brennan to Galveston we rode in a shaky railroad —once over a trestle that the conductor told us he expected to go down each time he crossed it and then proceeded to describe our danger so graphically that I was terrified out of my wits. Autie later pointed out to all about us that I had met danger in my usual fashion—with my head buried in the folds of my cloak. In Galveston we were detained—the steamer we were to board for New Orleans had not arrived —and we spent a day exploring the glistening white beach. But our sights were really on home and an uncertain future.

Chapter Nine

 WE HAD AN INTERIM IN CIVILIZATION, THOUGH IT WAS
brief and not very pleasant. It began with a night-
marish storm at sea.

When we boarded the steamer in Galveston, both Autie
and I were so besotted with thoughts of going home that we
paid scant attention to the vessel. A captured blockade-run-
ner, it had been built up with two stories of cabins and state-
rooms for passengers. Before that modification, crew and
passengers were quartered in the hull, but now the so-called
prize quarters were on the upper deck. Even so, our state-
rooms were tiny and smelled badly of bilge water.

We were barely out of the harbor when a norther struck.
After a sojourn in Texas, we thought ourselves veterans of
these storms, but a norther on land is mild compared to a
storm on the maelstrom of the Gulf. The waves seemed to
lash themselves from shore to shore, speeding toward the
borders of Texas and Mexico, then rushing back to the Flor-
ida peninsula so fast, I wondered why that strip of land had

not been swept out of existence. No matter which way the waves went, as we proceeded northeast toward New Orleans, the wind seemed dead set against us, and the ship labored to make its way ahead.

By nightfall I crept into my berth, hoping to lose my terror in sleep, but the creaking and groaning of the ship's timbers kept me watchfully awake.

"Autie, doesn't it seem to you that this whole new top part on the boat shall be loosed and washed overboard?"

He laughed and then reached a comforting hand from the berth above me. "Libbie, that's impossible. Calm yourself and sleep."

"I wish we were in the hull," I wailed.

"And then you'd be afraid of being closed in down there and wish yourself above. I'll tell you what I wish. . . ."

"What?"

"That these damn berths were big enough for two!"

I giggled. "Impossible!"

"Right," he sighed.

I slept fitfully, with fierce dreams, until a terrible crashing awoke me. The boat veered quickly and began to roll from side to side, with the immediate result that the water pitcher overturned and deluged me in my berth. For just an instant, I thought myself plunged into the ocean's depths. My scream of terror brought Autie to my side in a moment, but he had no words of comfort as together we listened to the creaking and groaning—and an even more deadly silence, signifying machinery, somewhere, had stopped.

"The ship is sinking," I announced. "It's breaking to pieces."

"Nonsense, Libbie, it's simply a fierce storm . . . a bad one, I'll grant you. But it'll blow over."

Outside we could hear the shouting of the sailors, and orders of the captain coming through his trumpet, then the creaking of chains and flapping of canvas. At the very moment that we heard the sound of the canvas—the sails torn from the spars, I was sure—everything in the cabin broke loose. Furniture broke from fastenings and flew about the tiny cabin, lamps smashed, and crockery in the adjoining dining room shattered. Above it all we could hear the wails of women in nearby cabins.

"Autie, you must go to the captain and find out if we're going down."

"You will stay right here?" he asked. "You promise not to move?"

"I promise." Where in heaven's name would I go?

He threw on some clothes and left, while Eliza crept from her place on the sofa at the far end of the cabin and came to comfort me. Though she must have been as terrified as I was—she had vowed never again to set foot in a boat after our mild journeys on the Mississippi and Red rivers— she held me in her arms, crooning words of comfort. At long last Autie came to the door to report that waves were crashing over the entire deck—he had had to creep on his hands and knees, clinging to ropes and spars as best he could until he reached the pilothouse. I, of course, went into a new tizzy at this description of how close he'd come to being washed overboard.

"The storm broke in the wheelhouse and disabled the machinery," Autie reported, "but we're perfectly safe . . . the sails, that noise we heard, will keep us from being tossed to shipwreck." Only months later did Autie tell me that he had told only part of the truth to two weeping women—the captain had in fact said that our fate was very uncertain in this hurricane.

The storm rolled the boat from side to side in a sickening manner, and everyone soon succumbed to mal de mer except Eliza and me. From the next cabin, we could hear the sounds of Jacob and Nettie becoming violently ill, and more distantly, down the line of cabins, similar sounds from folks we knew less well. I worried particularly about Nettie, who was still suffering from morning sickness and needed no further reason for nausea, but Autie, weakly from his bunk, forbade me to go to her.

"Jacob's with her," he managed to say. To my amazement even Autie was laid low—so miserable, he did not care if the ship went down. He lay in his bunk and was absolutely quiet until morning, when, in a quavery voice, he called out,

"Is something the matter with Jacob and Nettie? Their stomachs?"

"You best be lookin' to your own stomach, Ginnel," Eliza commanded, and when I called out for Autie to reassure us once again that we were safe, she said, "Ginnel, you just look out for yourself—I'll see to Miss Libbie."

Daylight diminishes all terrors, and whether it was true or not, we thought the seas subsided a bit with dawn. Autie's voice began to strengthen, and he went so far as to crawl to Jacob's door to let him know what he thought of those who give in to seasickness, though I begged him to be charitable because of Nettie.

We began to gather in the dining hall for breakfast, and around me I saw officers with white, exhausted faces. Father Custer brought the only merriment when he tottered into the dining cabin and fixed Autie with a steely glare: "The next time I follow you to Texas, it will be when this pond is bridged over."

Even safe seas gave me no security, and I was uneasy until we stepped ashore in New Orleans. That city was again a delight to us, though Autie and I, our thoughts racing ahead to a penurious future, were much more careful of our finances. Then it was onto a steamer for Cairo, where Autie bid farewell to some of his officers, and then to Detroit, where others left us. By the time we arrived in Monroe, our traveling party had shrunk to include only Tom and Father Custer, Jacob and Nettie, and Autie and myself.

We arrived in Monroe on March 3, and oh! such a homecoming as we had! What with the local band turned out at the station and bonfires built late into the night of our arrival, we had all the glory of the welcome we'd missed some months earlier.

Papa puffed with pride. "Your husband honors us all," he said, beaming with satisfaction, when we'd settled to a late-night cup of Mama's hot chocolate. "You've made a fine choice of a husband, Libbie."

Autie darted me a devilish look that I knew hinted at all the objections to our marriage, but he was gracious and polite. "Father Bacon, you give me too much credit. All that I do, I do because of Libbie."

Someone walked on my grave again, I suppose, for I remember shuddering ever so slightly. But I managed to laugh away Autie's compliment. "It's amazing to me you can do all you do while also putting up with a squeamish, scaredy-cat wife."

"I wouldn't have it any other way," he said, putting a protective arm around me.

We were playacting for Mama and Papa, but they were a most easily convinced audience.

For four days we were busy every minute—the Boyds had an evening's social for us, and some of our own friends prepared a party another night. Mama took me in the daytime to have tea with several of her friends and mine— women like Mrs. Oldman, who had watched me grow up, and even Mrs. Morrison, the dressmaker, who'd made so many of my clothes, including my wedding dress. Mama said Mrs. Fifield asked us to tea, but that she declined for the time being—Fanny Fifield having been my archrival for Autie's affections before our marriage. And, of course, we spent a great deal of time with Autie's family, where the boys continued to harass poor Father Custer until I thought I could stand it no more.

One evening they attached firecrackers to his chair before the fire, then howled in glee as the old man jumped up in alarm, sure that his house was ablaze. I thought it a wonder he didn't have a heart attack, but he simply glowered at his sons and stored away the memory. Frequently at the dinner table they would entice him into an argument—such an ardent Democrat as he was, they simply had to take the other side for a brief moment, and then he would be off, spouting and lecturing, ignoring his dinner plate all the while.

Tom, meantime, would sneak his father's plate away, eat heartily from it, and return it empty to its place in front of his parent. Then he'd say, "Come, come, Father, eat your dinner and stop all this foolish talk." Father Custer's face would turn completely blank as he looked at his empty plate, as though he were not sure if he'd really eaten yet or not. And then it would dawn on him that his sons had played yet another joke, and a sly grin would appear on his face.

"Libbie, I must leave for New York tomorrow."

We were staying with my parents, again in the spare bedroom where Autie had once declared the gulf between us large enough to be filled with alligators.

"Autie," I complained, "you've given me no notice. How can I be ready to go so soon?" The million details of packing flitted through my mind.

"I . . . ah, I thought . . . that you should stay here, Libbie." He spoke slowly; then all of a sudden, the words came in a rush. "Not that I wouldn't want you with me everywhere I go, but because of our financial problems . . . I thought it more economical for me to go alone."

I knew he was right. "Oh, but Autie, I shall miss you so, and shall hate hearing all the wonderful things you're doing."

"They won't be wonderful without you," he said passionately, tiptoeing from his bed to mine and planting himself firmly—and suggestively—next to me on the bed.

"Autie . . . ," I began.

He kissed the words away. "We'll talk about it tomorrow. Shhh! We don't want to wake Mama and Papa."

Given more warning, I would have rejected his advances because of Mama and Papa—promising to keep quiet was a bit chancy for me—but Autie sneaked up on me and, lost in passion, I could only echo "Shhh!"

We did not talk about New York the next day—at least, Autie and I did not talk privately. Instead, he talked to Papa at the breakfast table.

"I'm off to New York today, sir. Wish me luck?"

"Luck?" Papa exclaimed. "You never need anybody else's luck. You carry it with you! But what takes you to New York?"

"Perhaps Custer's Luck." Autie smiled, and then said seriously, "I've had several business opportunities put before me, now that I'm at loose ends. I thought it best to explore them in person."

"Very wise." Papa nodded sagaciously. "Offers from whom?"

"Oh," Autie said, a trifle too nonchalantly, "some bankers and some railroad people both seem to think I could make a great killing in their business."

"Autie!" I broke in. "You know nothing about railroads, and as for banking . . . what would you do?"

He did not like being doubted. "That's what I intend to explore, Libbie," he said very formally, his words seeming to come through his nose rather than out his mouth. It was a tone I'd noticed from Autie of late when he was uncertain and trying to be impressive.

Papa said nothing more, and shortly we escorted Autie to the railroad station. It was a particularly sad leave-taking for me, for Nettie and Jacob had gone to visit his family in New England—later Jacob would decide the army too uncertain a career and would accept a position with an insurance company there, robbing me of Nettie's company permanently. And Eliza left on the same train to return to Virginia.

"My ol' missus," she said, "I got to check on her—and show her where I buried everything during the war. I 'spect she needs that silver now. But, Miss Libbie, don't you fret— I'll come right back to Monroe."

When Autie tried to hurry her onto the train, she fixed him with a stern look and said, "Ginnel, I ain't eatin' no meals with you in no railroad restaurants." Then, skirts swishing, she mounted the stairs into the train.

Autie enveloped me in one last embrace, declaring his undying love and his hatred of being alone.

"Autie, I'll miss you ever as much, and I'll be lonely. Do hurry home . . . but do whatever you need to." I felt very noble, sending my husband off without a selfish care of my own, even though days of boredom—possibly weeks—were staring me in the face.

"I'll probably go down to Washington, too," he said hurriedly, and was then gone before I could protest. Washington, where I had friends, where many of our shared friends would be! My nobleness collapsed into a fit of anger and jealousy.

Papa and I walked home from the railroad station, and, of course, he noticed that I was more quiet than usual. "Libbie?"

"I should be with him if he's going to Washington," I said angrily. "I don't mind missing New York, but Washington . . ." I saw myself briefly as a bit of a snob, for I knew I would be jealous of Autie hobnobbing with those in power.

"And why didn't you go with him?"

"We have no money, Papa. Autie has to find work soon, and at a good income."

Papa sighed. "I suspected this was coming, and I'm in no position to do more than shelter you, but that I shall do as long as needed. But, daughter, I hope Armstrong's head is not swayed by glamorous business offers. The man is a born soldier, and that is where he belongs."

"Papa! You would have me be an army wife?" I was still angry at Autie, and now my anger sent a barb toward my father.

But he simply smiled. "I know, I fought against it. I remember fearing that you would end traveling in a wagon like some emigrant's wife. . . ."

"I've already done that," I interrupted, "and it wasn't half-bad, though I fear my complexion is ruined forever."

"Mama mentioned your skin did not look as delicate as usual," he admitted, "but such fineries are lost on me. You are beautiful, and I am glad to have you home." He patted the hand I had slipped through his arm.

"But, Papa, why have you changed your mind about my being an army wife?"

He stopped in the midst of Monroe Street, regardless of those who looked curiously as they walked by and tipped their hats. "Because of Armstrong," he said. "He has convinced me that the army is a noble calling simply by his own nobility, and you could do no better than to follow him wherever he takes you, daughter."

Had Papa been a fly on our bedroom wall some nights, I thought irreverently, he would change his ideas about nobility. And then it occurred to me to wonder what Papa's reaction would have been to the execution ceremony in Louisiana. I did not ever tell him the story.

Autie wrote of offers and rumors . . . he should be appointed foreign minister, with a salary of ten thousand in gold, though the appointment would be brief . . . he should consider running for either congressman or governor, as the people wanted to be led by those who had defended them so bravely . . . most alarming of all, he should take temporary service with Mexico, where the trouble was far from over. Carvajal, head of the Juarez military government, offered Autie the post of adjutant general with a salary in gold twice that of a major general in the regular army.

Autie met the rich and famous—he breakfasted one day with poet William Cullen Bryant and lunched another with historian George Bancroft. After a rehearsal of *A Child of Fortune,* he was privileged to walk actress Maggie Mitchell to her quarters, and another night he dined at the home of the chief justice of the Supreme Court, who dwelt on Autie's record as the youngest general ever brevetted in the army.

In New York and Washington both, he spent long evenings in the theater and, I began to suspect, as many hours in photographers' studios. In Washington, sculptress Vinnie Ream wanted to make a medallion of him, and another wanted to cast his head for a bust; in New York he visited the studio of artist Ole Balling to see his large painting, *Heroes of the Republic,* which featured Autie himself with twelve other generals. Only Autie had his sword raised as if to smite the enemy. "It is extremely good," he wrote me, "but would have been more natural if my hair were not such a perfect golden hue."

I read these letters with growing impatience, in spite of passages that spoke of his loneliness—once he suffered a bad cold and had the nerve to wish that I were there to nurse him —and of his undying love for me. "I shall never again travel without you, Libbie—you *must* go everywhere I go." Fine, I thought, and yet I did not see him rushing home. Instead his visit lengthened, drawn out by this possibility and that.

I nearly lost my patience completely the day I received a

letter describing a party at the home of some general or other. The company included Mrs. General Frémont and a baroness, whose dress was so low that Autie was inspired to write, "I have not seen such sights since I was weaned." He went on to add, "Of course, it did not make my passions rise . . . or *nuthin'* else, for I miss you, my darling girl." I burned the letter in anger and pondered how I could get Autie back to Monroe.

In truth, I did not want to stay in Monroe, for the days were long and deadly dull to me after the variety of life in our several camps. I breakfasted with Mama and Papa, sewed with Mama in the mornings, dined with them both, and napped after dinner, then took tea with various ladies in town. Then it was suppertime and an early bedtime, for Papa never had stayed upright past nine o'clock save on rare occasions. I began to feel sleep-logged among other things, and I longed for the gaiety of our small army family, the camaraderie and good times we'd known most recently in Austin. Occasional visits with the Custer family broke my routine—but even the scamp was generally away with Autie, who had managed to secure an officer's commission for his brother. I almost wrote to Autie, suggesting he reconsider the offer from Mexico, for I would follow him anywhere rather than spend my days in Monroe.

"Libbie?" A tentative, scared voice woke me from my sleep.

"Mama? What is it?" Awakened suddenly in the night, anyone is subject to a quick flash of fear, and I sat upright in bed, clutching at my heart.

"Your father," she said, poking a night-capped head around the door. "I'm afraid he's ill."

"Have you sent for the doctor?"

She gave me a pained look. "I've no one to send."

I was too used to army life, where there were always soldiers available to run errands and do needed chores. A shake of the head brought me back to the reality of Monroe. "Of course. I'll go myself."

"Libbie, you mustn't. It's three o'clock in the morning. Oh, if only Eliza were back."

Throwing the covers aside, I thrust my feet into shoes. "She's not," I said, "and we must do what must be done. I'll go for Dr. Jameson. Let me see Papa a minute first, so that I know what to tell the doctor."

Papa's color was bad, and though he tried to wave away my concern, I could tell that he was somewhat alarmed himself. He was suffering from both nausea and diarrhea, sometimes doubled with pains in his belly, though he tried to deny any pain in our presence.

"Papa, I'll be right back with Dr. Jameson. You rest." My heart was in my throat as I spoke. Papa had been unwell for some time—just old age approaching, I thought—though this was different, a more acute illness that seemed to have struck him suddenly. Still, I thought a man of his age—sixty-eight years old—hardly had the strength to resist a major illness.

Dr. Jameson, routed out of bed and hurried into his carriage by my impatience, confirmed my worst fears. "Cholera," he said. "We'll do the best we can."

Mama wrung her hands and wept aloud, until I was forced to lead her from the room. For the next two days I lived on faith and black coffee, served by the faithful Betsy, who still worked for my family. Mama lived on air, as far as I could tell—air and sobs, until I wanted to hush her however I could. I longed for Autie but could not reach him, and the only word I had from him was the letter about the baroness and her low-cut, cleavage-revealing gown—hardly the reassurance I sought.

Papa weakened each hour, and I spent long stretches sitting by his bedside, holding the thin hand that began to feel like tissue paper. Much of the time he slept, a restless sleep punctuated by deep gulps as he sought to catch his breath. I found myself more alarmed by his sleep than by his waking state.

"Daughter," he said in the wee hours of one morning, "you have done well for yourself." He motioned for me to lean closer to him. "Armstrong is a good man. Follow him wherever he goes, for he'll take care of you. Forget yourself. And remember, he is a born soldier."

"Yes, Papa," I whispered.

Those were the last words I heard from my father, for he died at dawn that morning. I knew he was gone, and yet I sat by his bed, still holding that limp hand, for more than an hour. The strange thought came to me that I had lost the one person in the world who would take care of me. I remembered what Papa said about Autie taking care of me, and yet the thought lingered and left a feeling of desperation hidden in the back of my mind. At long last, I went to waken Mama and tell her the news.

Autie made it to Monroe in time for the funeral, and he was kindness itself. "Libbie, I can't believe you had to endure this without me. I should have been by your side."

Truthfully, I replied, "I wished for you many times, Autie. And Papa . . . he spoke of you."

He slapped his hand hard against his forehead. "I should have known. . . . I should have sensed that you needed me." Autie had long had a belief in mystical communication between us, though it had never yet been tried. Now, tested, it had failed dismally.

"Autie," I said, reaching a hand for him, "you would have been here if you could. That is enough for me." I told him neither about my strange feeling when Papa died nor about Papa's last words to me. Though I wondered why I kept silent.

Papa's funeral was large, with dignitaries from all over Michigan and plain folk from Monroe coming to pay their last respects. Mama and I greeted the mourners afterward at the house on Monroe Street, and I thought perhaps I should never sit down again, never stop smiling and saying, "We appreciate your kindness." Mama bore up as well as she could, but not being strong, she was given to fits of weeping, which discomforted those who had come to offer their sympathy. Twice I caught Autie's eye and had him lead her aside until she recovered herself.

There was the matter of the will, a matter that neither Autie nor I wished to bring up between ourselves, given the unpleasantness of our earlier conversation about it. As I predicted, there was no money save the bit set aside to draw interest and provide for Mama. I was left owner of a house on Monroe Street in which I knew we would not live.

"Libbie, you mustn't wear that black!" Autie swept me into his arms. "It depresses you even more to dress in mourning. Please . . . for my sake . . . wear your everyday clothes."

I remembered the trauma of wearing mourning for my mother and instantly agreed with Autie, though a time or two I thought I saw townsfolk frowning at my conservative brown or blue or gray outfits.

"What others think is no matter, Libbie," Autie counseled. "We know you mourn for your father, and we know he wouldn't want you to be any more unhappy than necessary."

I lifted my chin and walked proudly beside him through the town.

Somewhat to my discomfort, Autie became a less cautious lover once the threat of Papa hearing us was removed. We were still in the guest room—we could hardly budge Mama out of the parental suite so quickly—but Autie made light now of the gulf between our beds.

"I think I'll take the Mexico offer," he said one night while I lay with my head on his chest, still spent from our lovemaking. "What with your father gone and your having no security, I've got to have an income!"

I sat upright. "Autie, I can't follow you to Mexico!"

"I know, my love, but it would not be for long. Sheridan thinks it could be accomplished in six months."

"Six months!" I wailed. "Autie, I was barely able to stand two weeks in Monroe without you."

"You'll appreciate me all the more when I return," he said wickedly.

Papa's words returned to me. "Forget yourself. He is born to be a soldier."

"If you think it's best," I said softly, but inwardly, Papa or no, I rebelled in anger.

Within days Autie told me that General Grant and Secretary of War Stanton had both written their approval of his temporary appointment in Mexico, and it seemed as though we should be preparing for a year's absence from the regular U.S. Army. I began to think in terms of a year in Austin, as close to Mexico as I thought I dared go.

But then one day Autie came home from the post office with a defeated look. "Seward has refused my application for a year's leave of absence. Even that would offend France—since I'm still officially an officer in the army. He's told me he'd grant any other reasonable request for me."

I saw Autie's disappointment, and I hurt for him, but I was also relieved. What I didn't see was that Autie was already pondering the latitude covered by "any reasonable request."

My relief was short-lived, and my concern soon took another turn. Autie was invited to take a "swing around the circle" with President Andrew Johnson as he made a whistle-stop campaign for his policy of appeasement toward the South.

"Autie, you can't!" I cried. "You have always supported Reconstruction. I know you've said we should not give the vote to those who did not support the Union cause."

"No . . . Libbie, I meant we should punish those Northerners who did not support us, even put obstacles in our way. I think we must consider clemency to those who opposed us in good faith, or this country will be at war again."

I could not believe that war could come again—the South could not possibly fight—and the whole argument did not sound like Autie to me, though I knew he still valued some of his Southern schoolmates from West Point. Perhaps that explained his new, lenient attitude, though somehow I doubted it.

"Besides, Libbie, it's politically sound for me. . . ."

"You've sworn off a career in politics, said it wasn't for you," I reminded him, and held my breath, for I thought politics the most dangerous and uncertain of arenas, far worse than the army. And I could see that building a political career might doom us to years in Monroe, when my feet itched to be gone on new adventures.

"Libbie"— his voice was cold—"I'll handle my own career."

We parted on that unfriendly note, he to join the President, who was beginning his tour in New York State. After several stops in New York and Ohio, the presidential train backed off the main line onto the spur leading to Monroe, and Autie, with great pride, introduced President Johnson to our own community. I stood in the audience, swelled with glory for him, and thinking perhaps I had been wrong about this tour. Then, from nowhere, came a raucous cry.

"Custer! You got that commission yet? Isn't that what you're on this train for?"

Autie, with superb control, ignored the heckler and went on with his introduction of Johnson, though I, standing close to him, could see the muscles in his cheek twitch. I was reminded of the former Confederates who had heckled us at the small hotel in Texas, and of Autie's refusal to sink to their level. Apparently the same control was going to carry him through now.

The crowd heard Johnson politely, though without distinct enthusiasm—the wounds of the war ran deep in Monroe, as in other cities, and forgiveness could not easily be given that soon. But *The Monroe Commercial,* an admittedly radical paper, was less polite, calling Autie an egotist and accusing him of fawning to receive a commission:

> The President was marshaling his forces in opposition to the policy of Reconstruction, which General Custer had declared to be the right one, and needed every man he could get. A set of political demagogues flattered General Custer that by going into support of "my policy" he could either get the nomination for Congress in this district, or secure a promotion in the army. Either the bait was too strong for the general; or the general was too weak for the bait; . . . the general ungloriously yielded, and we now find him doing all in his power to prevent just what he declared under oath ought to be done.

"Blast and damn!" Autie exploded when he read the paper in our compartment on the train, for I had joined the presidential party and was to continue on to Chicago and back to Washington with them. "Some yellow-bellied reporter who knows nothing of war dares to criticize my position! I spoke for Reconstruction before I had spent time in the South." He grew red in anger, and I thought it a blessing the yellow-bellied reporter was not in front of him at that moment.

The tour continued that way, with respectful crowds in Detroit, but wild and rowdy hecklers in Chicago, St. Louis, Terre Haute, and Louisville. The President, his patience worn to a nub, often made the mistake of trying to answer these radicals.

Autie slumped in the chair in our compartment. "Johnson should know better. You cannot argue with irrational people. He ought to just keep quiet."

Rising from the bunk where I sat in our cramped quarters, I went to stroke his head and said, gently, "Politics is not for us, Autie. It's too brutal."

He pulled back the curtain and watched the Ohio landscape speeding by for a long, silent moment. Then, pressing my hand to his mouth, he said, "You're right, Libbie. We'll leave the train at Steubenville."

"And then what, Autie? You still have no position, and we have no income." Despair crept into my voice, much as I wanted to be supportive.

With a triumphant grin he rose, dug his hand into his breast pocket, and unfurled before me a commission in the United States Regular Army for Lieutenant Colonel George Armstrong Custer. "Do you remember that it was my policy never to comment on political matters as a soldier, and therefore a paid employee, of the government? It is by far the safer policy, and I shall never again abandon it all the length of my days."

I smiled. "That's a long promise, Autie. Perhaps you should make one you're more likely to keep." But my mind was whirling—Autie did have the commission. How long had he had it? Was there—no, I could not bear to think it—was there a hint of truth in the charge of fawning? I never asked how he came by that commission.

Late that night Autie whispered, "Custer's Luck protects us again, Libbie. You are happy to be going on assignment, aren't you?"

"Yes," I answered, "I guess I am. But I'll reserve the full answer until I see where your assignment is."

He was first posted to Fort Garland, and diligently prowling over the map, he finally discovered the fort in the space given over to the Rocky Mountains. "There'll be deer . . . and trout fishing." Autie began to wax eloquent at the prospect of a veritable hunter's paradise. I, who cared nothing for fishing and was still afraid of guns, found that my veins didn't bound as his did at the prospect. To me Fort Garland meant a small, obscure post several hundred miles from any railroad, with only a handful of men to command, and little prospect of an active campaign, for the Indian troubles were another world away from this remote post. I thought the latter a mixed blessing. I feared Indians more than I had any Rebel minié ball that might have cut down my husband, but I also knew that he thrived on action and grew testy and unpleasant with inaction.

Before we could come to grips with the good and the bad of this assignment, Autie received new orders to Fort Riley, a good-sized, well-established post in Kansas, with the Kansas Pacific Railroad tracks no more than ten miles away. I breathed an enormous sigh of relief.

Mama was beside herself with grief that we would be leaving. She had visibly shrunk since Papa's death—I swear she'd lost an inch and a half in height—and she seemed incapable of making any decisions.

"Miss Libbie, what are we to have for dinner?" Betsy would appear before me with a quizzical expression on her face.

"Why, I don't know, Betsy. Did you ask Mama?"

"I most certainly did"—her head would bob emphatically—"and she just shook her head. I wasn't sure she even knew what I was talking about."

"What can you fix easily from what's on hand?" I asked, and we settled the menu in those practical terms.

In the days following Papa's death, I had taken charge—cleaning out his desk and closet, dealing with bankers and lawyers, doing what I knew needed to be done, because Mama seemed too uncertain. Struck down with grief, I thought. But now Papa had been gone more than six months, and she showed no recovery.

"I cannot leave her," I told Autie.

"Do you intend to stay behind when I go to Riley?" he asked coldly.

"No . . . no, not for anything!" My voice rose passionately, for I was terrified at the thought of being left in Monroe to wither. "But what shall I do?"

In the end we sent Mama to a sister in Ohio and closed the house on Monroe Street, a task that was bittersweet for me, made more so by the memory of this house closed once before, years ago, and of a young girl who'd escaped her prison to build a fire in the fireplace . . . and the young man with long blond curls who had rescued her.

Tom was a more thorny problem. As Autie and I sorted through pots and pans in Mama's kitchen one day, I finally gave vent to my exasperation. "Autie, Tom must stop this disgraceful behavior!"

He sat on the floor, stretching his arm into the far reaches of a cabinet. "What disgraceful behavior? Carrying on with the Widow McAnally? Libbie, do you want to take these pots with us?"

"Of course I mean Lydia McAnally. The whole town's talking. . . . Autie, you know she expects him to marry her."

"Tom's only a boy, barely twenty-one. Tom isn't going to marry anyone. Now, Libbie, about this cast-iron skillet . . ."

"Bother the skillet, Autie! Tom is disgracing the family, running around with that woman. . . . She's thirty if she's a day, older than you and me."

"They say older women are good for young men," Autie said softly, a wicked grin appearing. "Of course, I wouldn't know. . . ."

"Autie!"

"All right, Libbie, I give in. I'll speak to Tom, though precious little good that will do. What if Tom had spoken to me about the impropriety of my courting Judge Bacon's daughter?"

"That was entirely different, and you know it." I stamped my foot in impatience with his attitude.

"Libbie, you don't like Mrs. McAnally, do you?"

I bent my head, searching through a drawer of napkins. "She reminds me of Fanny Fifeld."

He was across the room in a flash, scattering pots and pans with his leap. "Aha! I knew it! You're jealous of her!"

"Tom is our younger brother," I said righteously, "and I feel honor bound to look after his welfare."

"Of course," Autie said, smiling knowingly at me.

I swatted him with a cup towel and went back to my sorting. In the end we simply closed the house on Monroe and left the pots and pans in their places, figuring that transporting them was more trouble than buying new when we got to Kansas.

"Can we afford that?" I asked.

"Libbie, I'm a lieutenant colonel," was the answer.

Eliza returned from her "Ole Missus" to accompany us, along with Diana, a pretty Monroe girl whom we took to brighten our lives and those of the officers at Fort Riley. It had not been easy to find a girl whose mother would let her accompany us. One mother had looked right at me and said, "Why, Libbie, she might marry an officer!" and another whispered behind my back until I was sure she was saying, "Look at Libbie's skin. It is hopelessly darkened and thickened by exposure. I shall not let my daughter suffer the same fate!"

But Diana's mother had consented to let her go with us, Diana of the bright eye and curling hair, who talked delightedly of going among the "brass buttons and epaulets." She would, we knew, beautify our quarters more than all the bric-a-brac we were leaving behind on Monroe Street.

Once again we left Monroe by train, this time headed to St. Louis.

KANSAS
AND
COURTMARTIAL

Chapter Ten

FORT RILEY WAS A HUGE DISAPPOINTMENT TO ME, AND nothing in our journey had prepared me for it. We'd stopped in St. Louis to visit the Great Fair, where everyone made merry in an effort to put away the gloom cast by the late Great War, and then it was on to Leavenworth, where we shopped to buy all those things we'd left behind in the kitchen on Monroe Street—the cookstove was most important, for we took the advice of an officer who found us browsing, bewildered, in one of the surprisingly excellent stores in that city. We bought pots, pans, dishes, and a small supply of linens—still, it was a scant store with which to start housekeeping. In all my married life—now well over two years—I'd never had a home of my own. Fort Riley would be my first real home.

Riding in the ambulance that brought us from the railhead, I shaded my eyes with my hand to peer ahead, anxious for the first glimpse of the fort. And then, there, magically, it appeared on the horizon—a cluster of story-and-a-half limestone buildings placed around a parade ground. As we drew closer, I saw that the sutler's store, the quartermaster and commissary storehouses, and the stables were outside the parade ground, but nothing else. There were no trees and precious little vegetation, save the buffalo grass that curled close to the ground. The post sat on a wide plateau at the junction of the Republican and Smoky Hills rivers, and the only trees to be seen were cottonwoods, which bordered the banks of the rivers. Otherwise the eye saw nothing but the plains, waving away on all sides of us, like the surface of a vast ocean.

"I've never seen so far at one time," Autie breathed, clearly awestruck, as the green seemed to roll before us toward the setting sun.

"Where is the moat?" I asked without thinking.

"Moat?" Autie hooted in derision. "Old lady, what are you thinking of?"

"Fort Monroe," I answered indignantly, my mind conjuring up a picture of the only fort I'd known, with its stone walls and turrets for the sentinels, and a moat surrounding the whole. That, I had innocently thought, would repel any Indians. And yet there wasn't even a fence around this fort, nor a tree to hide behind.

Autie ignored me. "You know that transparent veil of faint color in Bierstadt's paintings?" he asked. "Now, for the first time, I realize what it means."

"Autie, it's dusk, and we've yet to find our quarters," I prodded, ever the faithful, complaining wife. We—Diana, Eliza, and I—had bumped over the country, sometimes jammed against the framework of the ambulance's canvas cover and most of the time sliding off the slippery cushions onto the insulted dogs at our feet—Byron and a newly acquired ugly white bulldog named Turkey.

Promising to install us quickly in our quarters, Autie reported to the commanding officer. We three women were left in the ambulance with the dogs. Turk was indignant, and I stared him down as best I could, trying to keep from smiling at the twist in his lumpy tail, the curve in his bowlegs, the ambitious nose, which drew the upper lip above the heaviest of protruding jaws. Byron and Turk had tangled, but usually it needed only a deep growl and an uprising of the bristles on the back for Byron to recall lessons earlier administered by Turk. This time Byron, made cross as we all were by hunger, thirst, and exhaustion, seemed less likely to give way when they renewed hostilities.

After an eternity Autie returned to find Diana clenching Byron's collar with both hands while I sat at the other end of the ambulance, Turk on my lap swelling with rage because my fingers, twisted in his chain, held him motionless. Never mind that both Diana and I were shaking in terror, and Eliza, situated in the middle, was near screaming with fright of "them dogs."

"You there," Autie cried to Turk, "get on out of here!" A well-aimed boot gave direction to the order, and then he turned his attention to Lord Byron. "Don't you ever fight with ladies present!" he blazed, as the boot aided Byron out of the ambulance.

But then Autie created chaos anew. "There are no quarters for us. We will have to stay with the Gibbses."

"Autie," I exclaimed, "we can't. We'll pay whatever we have to for a room."

He looked at me pityingly. "There are no rooms, not for all the king's ransom. Our quarters are not inhabitable to-night—we can't even cook." Then he concluded firmly, "We're staying with the Gibbses."

So all of us traipsed into the commanding officer's house, where the one spare room had already been taken by General Sherman, who'd arrived before us. His first words to me were, "Child, you'll find the air of the plains is like champagne."

I was less interested in champagne than I was worried about inconveniencing Mrs. Gibbs.

"Oh, don't bother about it," Mrs. Gibbs said. "Out here one gets used to making do. I'm surely used to making room for whoever needs it."

I'd no idea how those words would haunt me in the next ten years.

■　　■　　■

"Autie, it's enormous!" I wandered through a house twice as large as the one on Monroe Street. In truth, it had been made by pulling two houses together, with the result that the parlors on one side alone were so huge as to dwarf our few, pitiful pieces of furniture—six wooden chairs looked lost upon a sea of wooden floor in need of waxing.

"Perhaps," Autie said thoughtfully, "someone will come and rank us out, and we can retire to more modest quarters."

That's exactly what happened. An officer who outranked Autie—even though Autie was now in command—came and requested the house, and then, according to army custom, we had to move. But we had our choice of all the houses among those officers below us in rank—we could displace whoever had a house that pleased us. Sometimes on remote posts when the process of ranking out began at the top, families fell before it like so many dominoes—I remember once when eight families were required to move, the lowest in rank having to move into a two-room cabin formerly occupied by a noncommissioned officer.

In this instance, ranking worked to our advantage, for we were soon settled in a house more proportionate to our furniture—and to us.

"Autie, there's a huge crowd of people outside." Fearfully, I held back the dreary curtain at the window of our new quarters. "Whoever are they?"

"Tourists," he replied. "They've come to see where General Custer lives."

"And, no doubt, to see General Custer," I said. "Do we have to let them in?"

Autie crossed his arms thoughtfully. "I rather think you should."

"We have no chairs to seat them . . . and Eliza and I could not possibly begin to feed them," I wailed, my notions of propriety upset by a crowd of what looked to be at least fifty people.

"Oh," Autie said, "I doubt that's expected. Just let them in."

Obediently, I crossed the hall to open the door, and before I could offer a word of cordial greetings, utter strangers thrust themselves into my new home. "General Custer . . . ," I said futilely, "General Custer will be glad to greet you." But then I turned and looked for him, and Autie was nowhere to be seen.

"He gone outside the back," Eliza whispered, while I frantically tried to welcome the group. None of them spoke to me, though they seemed to peer into every corner and to be particularly curious about six wooden chairs sitting lonely in our parlor. "I'm sorry I can't seat you all. . . ." But my apologies fell on deaf ears, and soon, having satisfied their curiosity, they trooped back outside.

Autie reappeared almost immediately. "I just stepped outside," he said innocently.

"If you ever dare leave me again like that . . . ," I fumed. But I knew that Autie had a habit of disappearing before strangers—was he shy?—and I learned to refuse those eager tourists their peek at my home.

One afternoon Autie and I sat in the library—a fancy name for a room we'd fixed with a desk and several makeshift bookcases to hold the volumes that Autie could not bear to leave behind. He liked to work at the desk, with me seated by his side working on my infernal needlework.

"He's coming to pay his call," Tom cried, bursting into the room without so much as a by-your-leave. "Pritchett—the new officer. I've helped him dress."

"I bet you have," Autie said, laughing heartily. "Libbie, stay and see this."

"Whatever is going on?" I asked, completely puzzled.

"Just what you hear. A new officer is coming to pay his formal call, and Tom and the others have given him some pointers. We'll receive him in the parlor."

Within minutes Lieutenant Pritchett entered our parlor —a large man in full uniform, though it fit poorly on his portly body. The first thing I saw was that he wore cavalry boots—strictly out of order with a dress uniform—and then I saw the red sash spread from under his arms to below his waistline. A sword belt, with saber attached, surrounded this, and over the whole he folded large hands encased in white cotton gloves. He looked like a child dressed so carefully that he is afraid to move, and he had no idea how ridiculous the other officers had made him appear.

Diana left the room hurriedly, hand over her mouth, and Autie's mustache quivered as he shook hands and bid the man welcome to the regiment. Then, overcome by mirth he could no longer control, Autie dashed out the door, leaving me to deal with the soldier. I tried desperately to entertain him and succeeded so well that he overstayed his welcome. When he finally left, I confronted Autie and Diana in a rage.

"You'll laugh next time," Autie predicted.

"Nonsense," I replied stoutly. "It's absolutely cruel to make such fun of a human being. When he realizes how foolish he's been made to look . . ."

"He's probably already plotting to play the same trick on the next new officer," Autie said calmly, settling himself down to read again.

Life at Fort Riley was full of such high jinks. A game of romps was Autie's favorite. We chased each other upstairs and down, using the furniture as temporary barricades against each other, while the dogs barked and raced around, joining in the excitement. The fracas was frightful, and I was sure neighboring families thought the new commanding officer was beating his wife, for our houses were close together and the walls far from thick.

As we had in Louisiana, we rode frequently—only this time we rode over endless miles of plains, with none of the swamp and quagmire of Michigan nor the quicksands and sloughs of Louisiana. It was a long time before I learned I needn't steer around a darkened patch of ground, for all the plains were safe. And Sherman was right about the air—it was more exhilarating than any bubbly drink. And the prairie sky—surely whoever said, "The sky fits close down all around" was on a Kansas prairie when he uttered those words.

"Come on, old lady, hurry up that old plug of yours! I have one orderly and don't want another." Autie called this back disdainfully, though with a wink at his orderly, who followed the prescribed distance in the rear.

Outraged at the insult to Custis Lee, I bided my time and then when he least expected it, flew by him, leaving man and horse in my wake.

"That's not such a bad nag after all," Autie laughed, coming up behind me.

"Autie, my hair . . ."

"You mean that dead woman's hair," he said, referring to the waterfall that I wore, according to the latest fashion. "All right, let's clear the decks for another race."

"Clearing the decks" meant that I unfastened hairpins, net, and switch and handed them to him, to be hidden in the breast of his coat.

"Just think if your coat opens accidentally in front of, oh, say . . . Lieutenant Pritchett, who still owes you for a mean joke," I teased, getting a head start on him before he knew it.

"Cheat!" he cried, racing to catch up. Soon our horses were going full tilt, side by side, and then Autie, with one powerful arm, lifted me out of my saddle and held me poised in the air for an instant. In that brief moment I found myself suspended between heaven and earth, and I thought, with surprising clarity, that I must cling to the bridle and keep control of my horse. Whether I came down on his ear or his tail was yet to be determined, but the moment I was held aloft was in my mind an hour of uncertainty. My indignation rolled off Autie like the proverbial water off a duck's back.

Another favorite trick of Autie's was to put me on his Thoroughbred, Phil Sheridan, when newcomers rode with us —there were always newcomers, and they were always the butt of jokes. The stranger would be given the honor of riding next to the commanding officer's wife, and as Phil started slowly, the newcomer simply kept pace. But then, as the colt took longer and longer strides, a look of puzzlement would appear on the man's face, until Autie gave me the signal and I spoke in low tones to Phil. Off we would fly, leaving the mystified soldier to urge his nag in vain. It was not quite my idea of hospitality, but my need to be a good sport outweighed social custom, and I participated in these charades.

I am obliged to confess that I belong to the league of those who once went off the horse against their will and then concealed the fact. Autie had asked me to ride on in advance one day, because he and Tom wanted to talk about something not of interest to me. Wallowing in the prairie day, I forgot to watch Phil, and when he took one of those sudden jumps from one side of the road to the other, at some imaginary obstacle, I found myself hanging on to the saddle. There was nothing for it but an ignominious slide, and I landed in a heap in the dust. Autie found Phil wandering riderless and came immediately to look for me.

"All right," I called from my seat on the ground, waving a feeble arm. I surely was not hurt—except for my crushed spirits. "Autie," I pleaded as soon as I was righted in the saddle again, "you must not tell anyone! Promise me!"

"Of course, Libbie," he said, his mustache jerking and twisting suspiciously. Then, turning to Tom, who had ridden up, he asked, "Have you heard of the famous Japanese acrobat, All Right?"

Solemnly and somewhat mystified, Tom denied any knowledge of such a creature, and Autie merely nodded and said, "I see."

But for weeks he would bring up All Right in who-knows-what situation, or he would wonder aloud, "How could an old campaigner be unseated, under *any* circumstances?"

"I don't know, General," some flunky would reply, while I blushed a furious red.

Diana rode a pretty little sorrel horse, though we rarely saw her—all we saw was an avalanche of flying curls as she dashed off beside first this young officer and then that one. But once Custis Lee was temporarily disabled and Autie was on Phil, so I rode the sorrel.

"Old lady, pay attention to your horse. It's crowding Phil something awful, irritating him."

The little horse had indeed snuggled right up to Phil. I used the reins harshly and pulled him aside, but as soon as my attention wandered, we were right back at Autie's side, too close even for lovers.

"My leg!" Autie complained. "It's crushed beyond repair."

"I can't keep him away," I said, baffled.

Autie let out a long laugh. "I suspect someone has taught this horse to ride so close . . . someone who wants the rider close to him."

And then it dawned on me, and I joined him in laughter. Autie told the whole story, the minute he was back among the officers, of how a perfectly good cavalry horse could be demoralized in the hands of a belle. Diana blushed while all the young men joined in the laughter, though no doubt each of them had been guilty of encouraging the little horse in its new trick.

Diana had more cause to blush a few nights later, at a party given at our house. Major Joel Elliott and the unfortunate Lieutenant Pritchett tangled over whose turn it was to dance with Diana. Too courteous to enter into the discussion in her presence, they retired to the small veranda outside our house, but from there their voices could be clearly heard.

"It is *not* your turn," Elliott accused. "You danced two dances with her, and this one's promised to me."

"It'll be over while we stand out here arguing," Pritchett said pompously, his tongue suspiciously thick. "Stand aside."

"Try and make me," came the dire threat.

"Just watch me and I will," was the answer.

Then, in a lower voice, Elliott muttered, "Custer'll arrest both of us."

"Not if I tell him what you've done," taunted Pritchett confidently.

Autie was called outside to join the men, while Diana and I stood poised inside the door, clasping each other in horror.

"Pritchett's at fault," Elliott said, "and I ask your permission to pound him."

Autie was infamous for the escapade at West Point when he had encouraged two cadets to solve their differences in a fair fight, and I, breath held in anticipation, remembered this incident. Surely he wouldn't consent as commanding officer.

I also remembered that Pritchett's gait had been unsteady when last I looked at him.

"You have my permission," Autie said.

All dancing inside stopped as we heard the thud of blows hitting flesh, the grunts of the recipient, and the oaths muttered on both sides. Neither man came back into the dance that night, so we were never sure who triumphed, but both lost. Diana refused to ride, or dance, with either of them for weeks.

When I reprimanded Autie for having allowed such a fracas, he merely shrugged. "It was a diversion, wasn't it?"

"Autie, Lieutenant Pritchett was drunk."

He shrugged again. "It's a continual problem. The men are bored."

The men were not the only ones bored. Life was not all romps and races for Autie. The post was understaffed. The Seventh should have had twelve companies of 100 enlisted men each, with three officers for each company, but the most we ever had at Riley was about 950 enlisted men and fewer than 20 officers. The actual training of the troops and the day-to-day discipline were handled by the field-grade officers, the corporals and sergeants. Autie had the challenge of gaining the loyalty of these men and of forming them into crack Indian fighters—but he had little in the way of daily duties.

Still, he was in charge.

"Autie, who are those two men marching around the parade ground?" I stood at the window, holding the glass curtain to one side to peer out at two men marching round and round, apparently observed by four or five other soldiers who stood on the sidelines.

"Insubordinates," he replied. "They were insubordinate to their officers."

"And so they must march forever?"

"With their heads shaved," he added.

I shook my head, grateful that he had not called the riflemen to execute these men, as he had in Louisiana. Still, I suspected that such harsh discipline as shaving heads was not earning him the loyalty of his troops—and he needed that when and if a battle should come.

From October to February, eighty men deserted. Autie did not understand. "A man," he railed, "does not walk away from his post. How can they?"

"They were bored, like you," I suggested.

"I am *not* bored," he said indignantly. "I am preparing for an expedition against hostile Indians."

Autie didn't know much about Indians, and both he and I knew that, though we never talked about it. My ideas about savages were based on such frightening accounts that I preferred to comfort myself with the thought that the perpetrators of horrible deeds were still miles to the west of Fort Riley and might never be seen. The inevitable fact that Autie must one day march out in search of them was put far to the back of my mind.

If Autie did not know about Indians, he did know about alcohol. "Libbie, you know I've sworn never to touch liquor. . . ."

Startled, I looked up from the bed, where I was propped up with my book. "Yes?"

"The men . . . they want me to drink with them." He twisted his hands around, unfastening the tight buttons of his collar.

"And you?"

"I've truthfully no desire to drink. But I wonder if they would accept me better. I have to do something about drinking on this post, and I'm not sure abstinence is the answer."

"Autie, I would not see you go back on your pledge."

He was at the side of the bed in an instant, kneeling before me. "Nor would I. I . . . I'm just seeking advice. . . . What are you reading? That trash again?" He had no patience with novels, which helped me pass the long days.

"It's a new novel," I said patiently.

"Garbage," he said derisively, and then, startling me, grabbed the book and threw it across the room. "Your father wouldn't approve," he said, and stalked from the room.

Autie was not angry at me—nor at the book—and I knew it; but he was frustrated. Some mornings, after he'd finished his morning duties at his desk, he'd pace the floor saying, "Libbie, what shall I do?"

"Read a good book," I suggested, quickly hiding yet another novel in my skirts.

"There is no company library worth looking at," he said. "I believe I'll start my memoirs."

"Autie, at twenty-eight, aren't you a little young to be writing your memoirs?"

"Only the first volume, Libbie, about the war. God, how I wish for another war."

My heart did a funny leap, for I knew the next war would be against Indians—and they were a fierce, new enemy who followed none of the rules of war known by the Confederates.

As Autie's impatience and dissatisfaction grew, so did the rift between us. A two-month trip on his part to Washington, D.C., to testify before the examining board for his new commission was almost a welcome respite for me, though I would never have let him know that. And when he returned —bringing a trunk of gowns and material, stockings, ribbons, and hats—I greeted him as though he'd been gone for six months. But within a week we were testy with each other.

"You're thinking of Lane Murphy," he announced one day as he sat at his desk, and I, by his request, sat next to him, working on a small painting I'd begun.

"No," I said calmly, "I'm not. I'm trying to puzzle out that faint veil of purple over the landscape that you talked about in . . . whose paintings were they?"

"Bierstadt. You may not be thinking about him now, but you've thought about him recently."

"Of course I have, Autie. He was a friend, and he's pitiful in many ways. I worry about him."

"You could have stayed in Louisiana," he taunted, carried away with his own unhappiness.

"Autie, for heaven's sake . . . !" I stood up abruptly, only to be greeted by a growl from Byron, who slept at his master's feet.

I left the room and stood, despite the cold February air, on the veranda, staring at the endless plain. In my mind I could see Autie leading a troop of men off across that sea of grass, and the vision brought both sorrow and joy. Then I shivered, for I had always before fought desperately against being separated from him.

"Autie," I whispered, "you need a war."

One of the great blessings of Fort Riley to me was the company of other women. For so long in Louisiana and on the march, I'd been the only woman, save Eliza. In Texas, of course, I'd had my beloved Nettie for company, but we had all known that our duty in Texas was temporary. Now I was settled with a community of women, and I loved it—we gossiped and giggled together, often over poor Diana's latest suitor, as she was the only single lady among us except one nanny who had accompanied a family.

Mrs. Gibbs was a mother to all of us, sharing her experiences on the plains with those of us who were new, comforting some who were homesick and lonely but would not dare tell a husband, rejoicing with those who celebrated a birthday or an anniversary.

She had raised her children on the prairie, having been stationed there well before 1860, and sometimes she recalled stories of their childhood. One in particular proved a significant omen: she told us of a prairie fire in which she nearly lost her two young sons. A private had taken the boys to the river to fish and turned his back for just a minute—in that second, a fire leapt up between the man and the river, leaving the two boys screaming on the other side. Like all little children, they called for their mother and would, Mrs. Gibbs was sure, have rushed through that wall of flames to find her had not the brave soldier himself jumped the flames and pulled the boys into the river, where they were perfectly safe until the fire passed. It was not the first horror story I'd heard about fire on the prairie, but perhaps because it involved children, it was the most frightening.

Having women around me meant that I was also surrounded by children, and that proved an ever more difficult thing for Autie and me. Captain Jonathan Myers and his wife, Elizabeth, had two towheaded sons, about five and six years of age, who toddled along after their father every chance they got, and I often saw Autie eyeing his fellow officer wistfully. I knew he wished for youngsters with long blond curls who would follow him everywhere.

When Melissa Thompson whispered to us at tea that she was expecting, news traveled rapidly over the post and soon reached Autie.

"Good news for Thompson, isn't it?" he said casually.

"Yes," I replied. "Melissa is overjoyed."

He stared at me so long that I nearly began to squirm in my chair. "It must be hard on a woman to have a baby out here. I'm glad it's not you."

I wanted to ask, "Autie, are you sure?" but I was afraid to pursue the subject further.

Another time as we rode on the prairie, Autie said, "See, if we had children, you would not be as free to go everywhere with me."

"Nonsense." I laughed, and before I thought, said, "Eliza would take care of them." And then I wished I'd been silent, for if he was finding blessings in childlessness, I should let him be.

Annabelle Coker also became enceinte while at Riley, but she was nowhere near as overjoyed as Melissa Thompson. "I won't have a baby in this godforsaken place," she said plainly one day as all of the officers' wives sat in a sewing circle. "I don't know how you can be so calm about living out here."

"Lord love us, we have no choice," Mrs. Gibbs said good-naturedly. "We have to follow our husbands."

She put into my mind my father's last words to me, but Annabelle had no such sentimental memory, apparently, for she said harshly, "Well, mine may have to follow me."

Lieutenant James Coker was a puzzle to me, but an extremely pleasant man, perhaps a year or two younger than Autie. His wife, from a wealthy family back east, was spoiled and unhappy and generally making his life unpleasant, and

yet I think he loved her deeply . . . or wanted to. Sometimes he would seek me out privately to ask advice about
making Annabelle happy, until one day I finally said to him,
"You cannot make Annabelle happy. She will have to do that
for herself."

He sighed. "Libbie, I wish she were more like you."

I thanked him for the compliment.

Two months after announcing her pregnancy, Annabelle
Coker departed for her family home in New York. We all
wished her well and voiced various good wishes for the baby
and the safe return of both to Riley next year.

"That's hardly likely," she said ungraciously. "I shall not
bring a baby out here. James will have to ask for a transfer."

After she left, with all of us a little relieved at her going,
James seemed to me lonely, and I often went out of my way
to talk with him.

"I hear you've asked for a transfer," I said brightly one
evening at a gathering.

He looked weary. "No, Annabelle told me to, but that
doesn't mean I've done it."

Startled, I hardly knew what to say and decided silence
might be best.

"I cannot let her run my life," he said, "and I'm not sure
she'd be happy, even if I did ask for a transfer. I think all she
wants is for me to go back and live in that mausoleum her
family calls a home, and I can't do that. I don't know what
shall become of us."

I felt a great pity for him. But James Coker remained a
puzzle to me. Though he was increasingly friendly with me
and relaxed in my company, he stayed aloof from the other
officers. He never rode with us on our afternoons on the
prairie, never joined the men when they drank, never took
part in the general merriment and high jinks that went on.

"I think he reads a lot," volunteered Tom, somewhat
scornfully.

Eyeing him across a room, Autie commented, "Reminds
me of Lane Murphy," and then looked long and hard at me.

■   ■   ■

"More soup?" I asked the young officer to my right. Our table was crowded with officers, several of whom had just arrived, and a journalist who had come to see what life on the frontier was really like.

When the soup tureen was emptied, Eliza set the platter in front of Autie. From where I sat at the other end of the table, I could see that his expression first changed to surprise, then confusion, and finally he collapsed in one of his shoulder-shaking fits of laughter.

Curious beyond control, I stood up to get a better view and was rewarded with the sight of a tiny steak, hardly the size of a man's fist, afloat in the center of that huge platter. Blushing, I gazed about the table and would have offered my guests some apologies, except that Autie abhorred having me do that.

"Eliza!" he called, still laughing.

"Ginnel, don't you be complainin' about that steak. Them cattle stampeded this mornin', and nobody could get them back in time to kill them."

"Wise cattle," murmured Autie, who then did explain to our guests that in the fall we'd feasted on prairie chickens he'd shot on his hunting trips, but with that supply gone, we were dependent on government beef and ate a great deal of oxtail soup. "Please," he finished, "do the best you can with vegetables and bread and butter."

No one seemed to suffer unduly from our meager fare—no one except me, that is, for I suffered a terrible attack of domestic responsibility. Although Autie had been a perfect gentleman about the lack of meat—and the disappearance of potatoes the next day—I could not bear the possibility that he considered me less than efficient in putting food on his table. Nothing would do but that I was going to the little town near us for provisions. Normally Autie forbade me to go there because it was inhabited largely by outlaws and desperadoes. But I did not tell him where I was going. Instead, once he was away and busy, I set out for town with a driver and an ambulance. We crossed the river on the chain bridge.

To my dismay, when I returned, the chain bridge had been washed away, and the river, which had been fairly calm that morning, had turned into a roaring torrent, carrying earth and trees with it as it rushed downstream. For nearly two hours I sat on the riverbank, despairing over what to do, looking every once in a while with distaste at the potatoes and eggs I had risked so much to secure, watching with awe the power of the water. From where I sat, the buildings of the garrison were in plain sight—so near and yet so far.

"Libbie, we're not going to make it back before nightfall."

Startled, I turned to see James Coker riding up behind me. "James! I didn't know you were here."

"Didn't mean to startle you. I'd gone for a ride alone and thought to ford the river here . . . but I guess not. You best have your driver take you back to town. Mrs. James—her husband runs the mercantile store—will be glad to put you up overnight."

"Autie will be frantic!" I wailed.

"I'll see that word gets to him," he said reassuringly, and I didn't ask how he would cross the river if I couldn't. Mrs. James did indeed make me welcome, and the next morning I was down on the riverbank almost at the break of day. James Coker was there, too. Both of us were disappointed that the river had not subsided at all.

"I . . . I thought you'd returned to the post."

"I couldn't," he said, shrugging. "But I hollered across to a soldier and got word to Custer that you're safe."

"James, I must get across. I'll get the sergeant there to take me in his boat."

"Libbie, that's not a very good idea," he said deliberately.

"James, I will go with or without you," I said, doing all but stamping my foot in my impatience.

He dismounted and hitched his horse to the back of my ambulance. "Bring him when you can," he said to the driver, who carefully avoided looking at either of us. Then, turning to me, James asked, "One last time—I can't dissuade you from this folly?"

"Absolutely not." I stood firm, my chin jutting forward, I'm sure.

"It's dangerous, Libbie . . . more so than you realize."

"If the sergeant can take us . . ."

"Of course he'll take us if you tell him to—you're Custer's wife." With that James spread his hands helplessly, looked at me a minute, then walked over to the sergeant in charge of the boat. He acquiesced, as James predicted.

The wind blew so fiercely that it was difficult for the two men to hold the tiny boat near enough to the slippery landing to hand me in. Behind us, the wind rushed through the riverbank trees, causing their branches to creak and moan eerily.

"Can't steer," the sergeant told James, while I nearly held my hands over my ears. "We'll pole out to the middle best we can, then let the current take us to that bend down there."

"Just tell me what to do," James said, spray from the river already drenching him.

"Just take care of Mrs. Custer," the sergeant said, nodding to where I sat huddled in the rear of the boat. I closed my eyes to the wild rush of water and debris on all sides of us and tried to close my ears to the sound it made. Faintly over the roar came the voices of soldiers from the opposite bank, shouting encouragement to our brave captain, who used his pole and all the energy he could muster to push away logs that threatened to swamp us.

When we got close enough to the other shore, James literally jumped into the air—while I held my breath—to catch the limbs of an overhanging tree. Clutching at branches and rocks, he pulled while the sergeant used his pole to push us toward the bank.

Within an hour I was safe in my own home—but not safe from Autie.

"You ordered a sergeant to do what?" he asked incredulously, pacing the perimeter of the library in his anger.

"I didn't *order* him—I *asked* him, and he was kind enough to agree."

"Kind enough! I don't know whether to commend the man or court-martial him. But I know that you will not be allowed out alone again. I can't trust you!"

"Autie, I only wanted eggs and potatoes. . . ."

"For eggs and potatoes you risk your life, along with the lives of one of my enlisted men . . . and an officer." He swung around to face me. "And how did you happen to be with Coker, of all people?"

"He was in town. I met him coincidentally."

Autie gave me a long look, which spoke volumes. Rationally, he knew that I told the truth, for I'd never lied to him about anything, let alone a man. But the jealous, irrational part of Autie almost wanted to believe that he had been betrayed . . . even cuckolded, and I could see the two sides warring.

With the muscles in his jaw twitching in anger, he stormed out of the room.

"Miss Libbie?" Eliza's tentative voice brought me back to reality a few minutes later. "Where's them potatoes and eggs?"

"I left them in the ambulance," I said wearily. "They may be here in a day or two."

General Hancock, head of the Department of the Missouri, arrived with seven companies of infantry and a battery of artillery. He was to lead an expedition to threaten the Indians—though it was couched in far different terms—and Autie's Seventh Cavalry would be accompanying them.

For days, even weeks, I'd heard the sounds from the blacksmith's shop of the shoeing of horses and sharpening of sabers, seen the drilling on the parade ground outside the post, watched the loading of wagons about the quartermaster and commissary storehouses. An idiot would have known the Seventh was preparing to move out, and though inexperienced in cavalry affairs, I was no idiot.

Still, I had little idea of the dangers of Indian warfare, and Autie tried to hide the seriousness of the expedition from me.

"Those Indians see how many of us there are and how well equipped," he said, "and they'll walk the path of peace." Or, "We're going to council with the Indians, Libbie, not fight." Fourteen hundred men would be moving out, a vast expedition for the plains fighting forces.

In his effort to reassure me, Autie seemed to forget the differences between us. He grew less critical and more passionate, and I welcomed his advances eagerly, as I had when I was a bride, though the thought flickered through my mind that now Autie had a war—or almost the equivalent—and things were back on an even keel between us.

Neither of us slept the night before he left. Our passion rose to fever pitch, subsided, and then, sparked by the least little touch and fanned by our uncertainties, burst forth again, until I was left breathless and exhausted. In the quiet between storms, we talked.

"Libbie, I trust you, you know that, don't you?"

"Of course, Autie. Why would you not trust me?"

"Because every man in this post would like to have you for himself . . . some more than others."

"Pshaw! Most of them are happily married."

"And some," he said darkly, "are not."

My mind flew to James Coker, for I knew he was in Autie's thoughts at the moment.

Another time: "It's a great expedition, Libbie—those Indians are going to see what a fighting force we have and abandon the warpath. They'll know they can't win."

I was filled with terrors and wished I could believe as easily as he did.

And finally: "Libbie, don't let me see you cry, for I could not bear it."

Chin in the air, I replied, "I won't." But then, unable to hold back the tears in the privacy of our bedroom, I collapsed in great sobs, and Autie stroked me until, once again, despair was replaced by passion.

Next morning I stood straight and tall as the band played "The Girl I Left Behind Me" and then endured the absolute silence that prevailed as the column left the garrison. We army wives were too well trained to give in to weeping and wailing as our men marched out, but oh! it overtook us when they were out of sight.

Melissa Thompson, bereft, came to stay at my house for

a night or two, to gain comfort, and I listened to her say the Lord's Prayer backward and count to ten thousand, all in an effort to put herself to sleep.

"Libbie, are you awake?"

"Yes, and have been for ever so long."

"Oh, say something to me, for I'm past all hope of sleep," she implored, and so I recited a single verse of poetry that leapt to my mind:

> There's something in the parting hour
>   That chills the warmest heart;
> But kindred, comrade, lover, friend
>   Are fated all to part.
> But this I've seen, and many a pang
>   Has pressed it on my mind—
> The one that goes is happier
>   Than he who stays behind.

When at last Melissa slept, I lay awake, haunted by my own thoughts. I loved Autie desperately, and I could not face the thought of his death on the field of battle—at the hands of savages, no less—but there was a corner of my mind that wondered what life without Autie would be like. And I could not quiet that corner, despite my best efforts. I began, again, to recite poetry to myself, over and over.

Chapter Eleven

 ALL AROUND US, AS FAR AS WE COULD SEE, THE ROLL-
ing land was covered with prairie grass. It grew
thick and matted down into close clumps on the
plains and in the valley along the river near us.

"Libbie? Look at that, like a ribbon of smoke." Diana
stood, shielding her eyes with one hand while she gazed to
the west. With a group of officers' wives, now all abandoned
like myself, we were out for a walk around the parade
ground.

I looked for a long minute. "It is smoke. It looks like a
tiny thin line of fire far out on the prairie. I'll sound the
alarm."

"Why?" she asked, shrugging. "It's a long way away. It's
not going to bother us."

But I knew better. Hadn't Autie made me read about
fires as part of what he called my indoctrination into life on
the plains? In Kansas, where the wind blows so constantly
and fiercely, the least flame, seen from miles away, is life
threatening.

Unfortunately, that was about all I knew about fires, and none at the post—even Autie before he left—had been enough of a plainsman to have taken the precautions so common to ranchers. We should have had double furrows plowed around the entire post, so as to stop any leaping fire. And at the first sight, we should have burned a stretch of grass between the post and the fire, to rob the advancing blaze of its food.

The men left at the post discovered the fire almost at the same time. Behind us we heard a roar and shout from the soldiers' barracks as they were marshaled into a fighting line. But transfixed, we women stood and watched as that slender tongue of fire, curling and creeping toward us, began to ascend in waves. In seconds the sky had turned black, the sun shut out by a dark pall of smoke. This dark canopy was broken by flashes of light when flames, fanned by a fresh gust of wind, rose heavenward.

The blaze swept on toward us, surging in waves, coming ever closer, until it seemed that the end of the world, when all shall be rolled together as a scroll, had really come. The whole earth appeared to be on fire.

The river was half a mile away, and our feet could not fly fast enough to reach it before the flames overtook us. There was no such thing as a fire engine; we did not even have Babcock Extinguishers. All the men—citizen employees, soldiers, and officers—seized gunnysacks, blankets, anything that came to hand, and raced wildly beyond the post to the fire. Forming a cordon, they beat and lashed the flames with blankets, twisted so as to deliver a more powerful blow. Soldiers yelled, swore, and leapt in a frenzy as the flames darted around them. They would stamp the flames out in one spot, only to run madly across the prairie to another island of flame and begin stamping and thrashing anew.

Clutching Diana with one hand, I stood motionless. Not a woman around me spoke—all were nearly paralyzed in horror. Those with young children clutched the youngsters to them and tried, vainly, to quiet the cries of terror. But beyond these whimperings, there was no sound except the roar of the fire and frantic cries of the soldiers.

The wind, which sent the danger toward us, saved us. Capriciously, in its usual Kansas fashion, it swept the flames off in a new direction, away over the bluffs. And then, in that smoky air, we stood and looked at devastation. The green that had begun to appear on the prairie with spring was gone, and the land looked more desolate than ever, a blackened desert surrounding us.

Within days of the fire, a unit arrived to replace the departed cavalry. They were black infantrymen, garrisoned to the post for the summer under the command of Colonel John Williamson, a courteous, quiet, and scholarly man, who was baffled by the behavior of his untrained charges. While they danced and turned cartwheels on the parade ground, he stood by with obvious perplexity. When they were issued their first rifles and in great joy fired round after round from the barracks, he was incapable of restoring them to order.

One afternoon as we sat on the veranda, the sound of a shot came from the barracks, followed by a wild rush of men out the doors, running back and forth, yelling with alarm. My needlework dropped unseen from my hands—I was trying to repair the damage done to my riding habit by hard use and the Kansas wind—as I stared in horror, wondering what had happened.

"Eliza?" I called.

Sticking her head out the door, she stared a minute, then said grimly, "I bet they done shot someone. Fools can't handle a gun."

And that is exactly what happened. One soldier trustingly allowed himself to be cast for the part of William Tell's son. He was shot and killed by a man who had held a gun in his hand for the first time that week.

Eliza tried to counter my growing concern about the lack of discipline on the post. "Nothin's gonna happen, Miss Libbie. They're jes' havin' some fun." She was actually enjoying having the new troops at Riley, for never before had she been courted by so many. She would flirt with a new beau one day, quarrel and discard him for a new one the next. The men hovered around her—and around our kitchen, where I suspect they ate very well during their brief time in Eliza's favor.

Eliza was having fun, but I knew what Autie thought of the inappropriate combination of soldiers and fun, and I worried about the lack of discipline. Williamson simply watched benevolently, though he had locked up the accidental murderer for one night and issued a stern command against use of firearms inside a building. Nonetheless, we still heard shots from the barracks.

One night I was wakened from a sound sleep by the tramp of feet over the ground. I lay, listening for the sentinel to call out, but heard nothing. Diana crept into my room to ask what was going on, and I, equally puzzled, called for Eliza.

"Lord, I don't know what they's doin'," Eliza said, joining us at the bedroom window, where we knelt clutching our wrappers about us and feeling ill prepared—and poorly dressed—to meet any crisis.

Muttered threats and a low rumble, like a constant growl, reached our ears, though we could not make out anything that was said. But we could see fists waved threateningly in the air and feet stamped impatiently as the men milled about, not yards from our house.

Diana clutched my arm. "Libbie, I . . . I wish Autie were here."

"So do I," I answered grimly. "It appears to be a mutiny." The very thought sent a shiver through me. If Autie had been at Riley, there would have never been a mutiny . . . and we women would not be helplessly alone with no one to call for help. I remembered the shaved heads of insubordinates and, worse, the young man nearly executed in Louisiana. No, there would have been no mutiny with Autie present. As it was, those who were supposed to protect us were the very ones threatening us.

The men were demanding that Williamson come out of his house, the very dwelling that adjoined ours, and I feared at any moment they would storm the doors.

"Miss Libbie, you know we's safe inside here."

"In a house with no locks?" I asked. "Not that locks would stop them." Surely black soldiers were not as cruel to women as Indians, I thought to myself, not wanting to ask Eliza's opinion on the subject.

"They won't come near here, Miss Libbie. Too many of them done ate your good food. And remember the one you wrote a letter for? Or the one you gave the ginnel's shirt to because he didn't have one without patches? They'll protect this house, you mark my words."

To my everlasting relief, the men dispersed without violence, though their muttering could be heard the rest of the long, sleepless night. Next day we learned that it was a mutiny over sugar—Colonel Williamson had, rightly, refused to issue the entire ration of sugar at once.

My letters to Autie were grim and desperate, filled with fire and mutiny, and his in return told of a snowstorm so fierce that the horses had to be whipped to keep them moving and thus prevent death from freezing. One of Autie's fellow officers, suffering from the cold, begged to borrow Lord Byron as a sleeping companion for warmth. Autie agreed and then howled with laughter when the man complained the dog had slept on top of him and nearly suffocated him.

But the expedition was not going well. They had tried to parley with a band of Pawnee Indians, who had, in fear— even Autie admitted that—slipped away in the night. They split up into small groups, so that the army could not follow them—leading, I knew as I read between the lines of the letters, to great frustration on Autie's part. Then a stage station was burned on the Smoky Hill Trail, and in retaliation Hancock burned the village left behind by the Pawnee. Autie insisted, however, that it was Sioux who attacked the stage station, not Pawnee—and later, too late for the Pawnee, he would be proved right. The Sioux chief Pawnee Killer, whom Autie had councilled with and trusted, was responsible for the carnage. Meanwhile, his frustration was growing . . . and his loneliness.

"I could bear all this better," he wrote, "if my dear girl were by my side. I am nothing without you. . . ."

Holding that letter in my hand, I stared out over the plains and thought what a wild land we had come to, how far from Monroe, with its predictable climate and peaceful, civilized ways. For all my differences with Autie, I would not have gone back for anything. He loved me.

My next letter from Autie said that I might safely join him at Fort Hays, where a temporary camp was being set up. Autie never asked if I preferred to stay at Riley; he simply expected me at Hays with all possible haste. He had left in March, and it was now May—we had been apart two months, and though we'd endured longer separations during the war, this seemed interminable to both of us. "I did not marry you to live in separate houses," he wrote. "One bed shall accommodate us both. . . . Bring a good supply of bacon—one hundred pounds or more; three or four cans of lard, vegetables—potatoes, onions, etc. You will need calico dresses . . . and bring a set of field croquet."

From Autie's letter, I began to think I was going to a house party—field croquet, indeed!

When I heard that General Sherman and a party were to stop at Riley on their way by train to Fort Harker, I ordered Diana to pack what she could into a valise. Sherman was more than willing to do anything to keep his boy-general happy and applauded my decision to join Autie.

"Every cavalryman needs a wife as brave as you," he said benevolently, and I blushed. Little did I realize what I, with my so-called bravery, would be called on to face.

Eliza fixed us a huge roll of bedding, and that, with our two valises, was handed into the general's special railroad car —somewhat to my embarrassment, for the bedding hardly looked like ladies' baggage. But I anticipated sleeping on the ground once we got to Fort Hays, and experience had by now taught me to be practical.

The railroad line was littered with deserted town sites. Towns sprung up overnight and disappeared as quickly, the one-story buildings and tents moved on to the next spot to form a new street of saloons. Devastation was left behind—

broken kegs; short, rough chimneys made of small stones; tin cans everywhere; broken bottles littering the ground; great gaping holes where canvas-roofed buildings had stood. Civilization was, I thought, making a mess of the West.

"Libbie, if that is Fort Harker, Riley looks a paradise," Diana whispered to me as we descended from the train.

Before us was a scene barely better than the abandoned towns we had passed—dismal wooden buildings huddled together against the Kansas wind, and no trees nor vegetation softened the landscape. Even the soldiers looked disheartened, I thought. Diana and I shared a room with a floor of boards so uneven that enough prairie sand had sifted in to plant a good crop of something.

James Coker was at Harker with a detachment of men and was to escort us the eighty miles to Fort Hays. He looked at me with amusement once he settled his two female charges into the ambulance. "Well, Libbie, if it's not a swollen river, it's an Indian-infested prairie."

"Pshaw, James," I answered laughingly, "we're in good hands, and we know it." It never occurred to me that the march was really dangerous, nor did I understand the quick, dark look that James shot in my direction.

Stage stops appeared along the route every ten or fifteen miles—log or stone huts huddled together for protection, with doors and window coverings of rough-hewn timber that would withstand an attack. Supplies were kept inside so that the occupants could hold out against a seige, and nearby was always a dugout—a dwelling dug into the earth, with its roof level with the ground—for escape in case of fire. This subterranean dwelling was connected to the station by an underground tunnel, but one look at it made me utter a desperate prayer that I would never be forced to crawl through such a tiny space under the ground. Apparently the Indians' favorite trick was to shoot a flaming arrow into the hay stored in the barns—if I were in a station when that happened, James assured me, I would be grateful for the tunnel and the dugout.

James occasionally reined his horse beside the ambulance and chatted as we rode. Once he startled me by saying, "I was sorry to hear about your horse."

Leaning out of the ambulance, I thought perhaps I'd misunderstood. "My horse?"

"Custis Lee? Wasn't that his name?"

The use of the past tense alarmed me. "He's with Autie," I said.

James gave me a strange look. "You haven't heard? Armstrong hasn't written you?"

"James," I fairly shouted, "what is it?" Diana, seated on the other side of the ambulance, inched closer to me and put a comforting arm around my shoulders.

"He was shot, Libbie. God, I'm sorry to be the one to tell you."

"No!" I screamed. "Not Custis Lee." After several minutes, my eyes swollen with tears, I managed to ask, "How?"

"Armstrong was buffalo hunting. . . . I don't know how it happened exactly, except that he found himself in a pretty sticky situation. Horse down, no troops around, and an angry bull in front of him . . . you're lucky you didn't lose both horse and husband."

His humor was lost on me. "Autie shot Custis Lee?" I echoed.

"That's what the story is. Libbie, please, wait until he tells you. . . . I . . . I didn't mean to be the bearer of bad tales." He spurred his horse quickly away.

While Diana held me tight, I wept for Custis Lee, the most gentlemanly, beautiful horse I had ever known. I truly believe that we have some animals who are soul mates—just as some people are lucky enough to find marriage partners who are soul mates—and for me, Custis Lee was such an animal. I would never again feel quite the same about another horse.

And Autie? Why hadn't he written me?

At last we reached Hays—another log-hut post, treeless and desolate, except that beyond it stretched the white tents of the Seventh Cavalry.

Autie greeted me enthusiastically, bouncing me out of the ambulance and holding me high off the ground, as though to get a good look. Then, his manner turning much more proper, he faced James and said, "I'm obliged, Coker. No trouble, I presume?"

"None, thank God," James said with more fervor than I thought our uneventful trip justified.

Then Autie whisked me off to his tent for a private reunion.

"Autie," I protested as he reached for the buttons on my dress, "in the middle of the day? The entire command will know what we're doing . . . and so will Diana."

"Diana's too young," he murmured, his mouth at my throat, "and the men will be jealous."

"They'll think me a harlot."

"I told you they'd be jealous." He laughed softly, the buttons loosening under his efforts and my resistance melting away. We had parted on a passionate note at Riley, and Autie and I were both ready to resume our relationship on that level, ignoring the differences that had plagued us. After all, Autie had his war now—or almost.

We spent the entire afternoon in bed and not much of it talking. By the time we reappeared for supper—my face a furious red, I was sure, from embarrassment and from Autie's whiskers—we were reunited.

"Autie," I whispered once when he lay contentedly close to me, "where's Custis Lee?"

Startled, he sat straight up. "Shot, Libbie, I wrote you about that."

"I never got the letter."

He rocked me in his arms. "Oh, Libbie, I can't believe . . . I wrote you right away. It was a terrible accident. . . . I can't tell you how I felt. . . ." Autie talked on at an accelerated pace, until at last I turned away from him. I knew he hadn't written the letter, and that if James Coker hadn't told me, I might never have known what had happened to Custis Lee. I never asked about the angry buffalo bull.

■   ■   ■

"Libbie, what is it?" Impatience tinged Autie's voice, for I'd jiggled his shoulder and punched his side until at last he'd roused from a sound sleep in the middle of the night.

"It's lightning," I whispered.

"Oh," he groaned, "thanks for telling me." He rolled over to go back to sleep.

"Autie! Listen to the wind. . . . The tent pole is swaying like it won't last another minute." The tent pole was indeed weaving in the wind, and the tent flap rattled and swung loose at one end. I felt like a rag doll in a rag house.

Grumpily he sat up and looked, then said soothingly, "It's just a Kansas storm, Libbie. This is the rainy season." But as he spoke, he was fumbling for pants and boots. At last, dressed, he said, "I'll go out and pound the tent pins in and check the tether ropes."

I huddled in terror in the bed, which was now growing damp as the moisture-laden tent began to leak; outside I could hear Autie alternately pounding and shouting, and over it all, the roar of the wind and rain, the crash of thunder and crack of lightning. Lanterns appeared, and I knew men had come to help Autie. In the shadows cast by their lights, I could see them clinging to ropes to keep them from sailing off in the air—taking the tent with them—and trying desperately to keep the ridgepole steady by strengthening the poles. Then a corner of the tent tore away, seeming to take on a life of its own, and Autie rushed in, gathered me in his arms, blanket over my head, and rushed out just as the tent collapsed, the men still clinging to it and trying to guide its fall so that it would not collapse nearby tents.

We ended the night sleeping in a neighboring Sibley tent, which, having no square corners to catch the wind, was more stable. When Autie carried me in, I saw several forms rolled in blankets and radiating out from the center like the spokes of a wagon wheel—this tent, fortunately, had a wooden floor. Autie and I were soon two more spokes in the human wheel, asleep in a trice. But there would be no more passion that night.

Next morning I found myself alone, with a pitcher and bowl supplied for my toilette. My shoes were hopeless, so I was dropped into cavalry boots and carried to the mess tent, wearing a soaking-wet dress.

"Kansas," I said to Autie, "has shown us enough."

"I doubt it's through," he said wryly.

"Libbie," Autie said sternly, "there are Indians all around, even if you can't see any sign. You *must* not walk out from the post while I'm on scout."

I had been at Fort Hays only two weeks, and already Autie and the cavalry were preparing to march; Eliza, Diana, and I would stay behind in the care of a handful of officers and soldiers who were being left to bolster defenses. I tried not to let Autie see my pleasure when I learned that James Coker was one of those to stay behind.

"I promise," I said solemnly. "But, Autie, the Indians surely wouldn't come close to the fort."

"I repeat, you know nothing about Indians," he said, and I wanted to ask how he'd gotten to be an expert in one brief expedition.

The days dragged after Autie left, though I soon learned that he was right about the Indians. Twice the sentinels were driven into the fort by small bands of savages, and several times attempts were made to stampede the horses and mules that grazed about the post. These events, dreaded though they were, provided about the only excitement in our daily routine.

But James Coker was a blessing to me. He spent long hours sitting in front of our tent talking, or walking around the fort with me, though we made its slight perimeter in no time at all, so small was Fort Hays.

"What do you hear from Annabelle?" I asked the first afternoon we talked alone.

"Not much. We're . . . ah, not in communication. 'Estranged' is the word, I guess." He laughed bitterly.

"The baby?"

"She lost it," he said harshly. "Blames it on Kansas, the army, and me, mostly me."

"Oh, James, I am so sorry."

He managed a rueful smile. "So am I. . . . I don't sup-pose I can ever say how sorry. But it wouldn't be good for a tyke to be raised between the two of us—me out here, and Annabelle hating my life, and all. I don't suppose we'll ever be together again."

I thought of Autie and our differences, and they paled in the face of a relationship like that between James and Anna-belle. Then, improperly, I wondered at their private life and concluded that it had not been as wild and wonderful as ours or they would have salvaged their marriage. Ah, to be young and think passion solves all problems! I felt sorry for James that he had not had the pleasure of a passionate marriage, but of course I said nothing—and probably blushed.

As our talks increased, our closeness grew, and though I never talked to James Coker about the lack of passion in his marriage, we did talk about subjects generally avoided be-tween men and women not married to each other. One was my marriage to Autie.

"You and Armstrong are getting along better, I see," he commented.

"Oh, you do?" I asked. "And how?"

"You look less strained, less drawn, and Armstrong is less prickly. I didn't tangle with him for a week before they left."

"Autie needs a war," I said, grinning and taking his arm companionably. "Danger improves his disposition."

"And what does it do for yours?" he asked, putting his hand over mine, which rested inside his arm.

"La, I've not been in danger, so I don't know. Autie always sees that I'm safe."

James pulled away abruptly, withdrawing his arm and turning from me. "Yes," he said curtly, "he does."

"James, what is it?"

He whirled around to stare intensely at me. "Did you know that I was ordered to shoot you?"

"Shoot me? Whatever are you talking about?" Had this man of whom I was so fond gone suddenly mad in front of me?

"Shoot you," he repeated. "On that march from Harker, if we were attacked and I was certain the outcome would go against us, Armstrong ordered me to shoot you . . . in the forehead. An instant, painless death."

"James!" I was unable to catch my breath, unable to think. "We really were in danger?"

"Grim danger. But Armstrong's request isn't all that unusual, Libbie. It's a fairly common feeling among officers out here that they'd rather their wives were dead than captured."

I could say nothing, though later I wondered if that was supreme love on Autie's part . . . or a careless toying with my life.

Autie had been gone two weeks when James confessed that he loved me. "I've tried not to, Libbie, but . . . well, there it is." He gave me one of his wry grins. "Will you run away with me?"

I laughed aloud, delighted and flattered and very naive. "Where would we run away to?" My eyes swept the plains around us. "The Indians would get us, and then you'd shoot me."

"Oh, no, never. I don't think I could have followed Armstrong's orders . . . and now I know I couldn't."

"Then," I teased, "you'd let the Indians have me."

"No," he said gallantly, "I'd see that the choice never came to that. Pack your valise."

We were both joking, and yet there was a thread most serious beneath our banter. I took his arm again, and we walked in silence for a long time. I kept my eyes down, but sideways I was aware of him looking at me, and I wondered if the whole post was also aware.

Diana twitted me about James, but as she was young and in love with a new officer a day, she took flirtations lightly. "Lieutenant Coker certainly enjoys your company, Libbie."

"And I his," I replied lightly. "Autie has asked him to look after me, and he's doing an excellent job."

Eliza took the whole thing much more seriously. "You mark my words, gonna be trouble the ginnel hears about that lieutenant and you," she warned.

"Bother, Eliza, he's simply helping me pass the time while Autie's gone."

"Done passed too much, you ask me," she said grumpily. "You be careful, Miss Libbie."

I thought that remarkable advice from one whose loyalty was to the general and not to his wife, or so I supposed.

The most serious objection to my friendship with James came from Tom Custer, who had, in spite of his protests, been left behind when Autie marched out. Tom was angry at being left behind, angry because there were few other officers for him to carouse with and no liquor on post to spark that carousing. "Libbie," he said one day, "you best stay away from Coker. I know Autie always told you not to be too friendly with any officer."

"Don't be silly," I said in a big-sister tone of voice. "Autie would be grateful to James for helping me pass the time."

Tom gave me a dark look, and thereafter, sometimes, when James and I talked, I would see Tom staring at us from a distance.

Beyond the post the prairie wore the soft green of spring, and prairie flowers added bright touches here and there.

"James, I would so love to go and pick some flowers," I said one afternoon after supper. "Couldn't we just walk out there a ways? The sentinels will always have us in view." My tone was coaxing, and I knew it.

"Is this another swollen river, Libbie?" he asked, laughing. "All right, my love, if you wish to go, we'll go."

I wandered among the blue and pink and red flowers, picking this and that until I had a nice bouquet, savoring the fresh air—the Kansas wind had gentled into a welcoming breeze—and loving being away from the post, while James lounged and watched me.

"I wish dark would never come," I said. "I want to stay out here, *today*, forever!"

"So do I," he said huskily. "But dark is coming, Libbie, and we have to get back. Come." He held out an arm, and as I took it, he put his other hand on my shoulder, turning me toward him. Then he bent his head to give me a gentle kiss, full of love and none of the demands of Autie's kisses. Without fully meaning to, I responded, until the kiss deepened in intensity and sent fire rushing through me. Had James not held both my arms firmly in front of him, I would have thrown them around his neck.

"We must go," he said firmly. "But, Libbie . . . thank you. That was worth a lifetime."

"James, I . . ."

"Please," he said, "don't say anything."

Dark falls fast on the prairie, and we had not gotten halfway back to the post before the shadows deepened into twilight, and the sentinels, who had once seemed so close— did they see us?—disappeared from sight. I could no longer make them out, but with my arm linked in James's I felt perfectly safe.

Suddenly I saw a flash from the direction of the post, followed by a whistling sound that sang past our ears. While we stood puzzled, a second whiz and zip indicated another bullet, passing dangerously close.

"Drop!" James commanded, throwing me to the ground. "We're being fired on. They think we're Indians."

"Of course we're not," I said indignantly. "Tell them so!"

"Keep your head down," he said sternly, pushing the back of my head with his hand. Then, raising his head only a slight bit, he halloed the post, saying, "This is Lieutenant James Coker—"

A third barrage of gunfire was the answer.

"I can't tell them from here. I'll have to creep up to the sentinels. Libbie, you must stay here, flat to the ground. Bury your nose in the grass."

"I want to go with you," I wailed.

"No—for several reasons. I may get shot, prime among them. And I can move faster without you."

"How will you know where I am, if you leave me here?" I asked, well aware that at dark the prairie was indeed a sea upon which to be lost.

"I'll know," he said, and then, tenderly, he kissed my forehead and inched away from me, cautioning once more, "Stay very quiet."

And so, nose in the buffalo grass, I tried to melt into the

prairie, thankful for my slimness. Yet my body seemed to rise above the earth in such a heap that even the dullest marksman could have hit it. My thoughts were a turmoil—if James was hit, no one would know that I was out here, and I would lie until daybreak. That is, if Indians didn't find me—everyone knew they could see at night, even if we couldn't. And what if, in spite of his guarantees, James lost track of where I was? And through all this, the memory of his kiss burned, etched onto my mouth like acid because of my guilty thoughts of Autie.

James rescued me, and the sentinels apologized profoundly, begging me not to tell the general they had fired on his wife.

"I don't think I'll mention this to the general at all," I assured them, for reasons of my own.

Awkwardly James escorted me to my quarters. Outside, he stammered, "Libbie . . . I . . ."

"James," I said, my calm by now having returned, "let's not mention any of it."

But our walks were over. James Coker and I were not quite comfortable with each other, though we watched one another furtively about the post. When I thought he wasn't looking, I studied James, knowing that he had not the fire and brilliance of Autie but that life with James would be smoother, calmer, even more secure. Then I would shake my head, for my future was committed. In the long run, I knew I loved Autie over James Coker.

"Mrs. Custer! Mrs. Custer! Make haste for your lives. It's a flood!" The frantic voice drew me out of a sound sleep, though Lord knows how I slept with the thunder and lightning crashing around us.

"A flood?" I echoed stupidly.

"Creek's risin' at an alarming rate," said the soldier. "You best be out of there *right now.*"

"One moment," I called, desperately reaching under my pillow for the clothes that I had hidden, hoping to protect them from the wetness all around us. It was useless—they were soaked and difficult to get into. At last—though it was probably only seconds—I scrambled out of the tent.

With the next flash of lightning I saw that the creek—only a little trickle of water the night before—was level with the high banks. Good-sized trees had fringed its banks—now I could see only the tops of those trees. The water had risen some thirty-five feet in less than no time.

"My kitchen!" Eliza screamed. "The river's takin' my kitchen."

"Let it be," I called, rushing to pull her away from the threatened kitchen tent. "We can't save it, Eliza. Come!"

"Lordy, Lordy, Miss Libbie. How's I gonna feed the ginnel now?"

"How could you feed him if you were washed away in the stream?" I countered, and she did me the favor of grinning. Appalled as we were by the storm, neither of us yet realized how awful the tragedy was.

Our sleeping tents, fortunately, were high enough on a rise to be safe, at least for the present. But a group of tents had been pitched on a bend in the crooked stream—the men had chosen that spot because of the circle of trees that edged the water. But now it was the worst possible location. The water swept over that strip of earth, creating a new island and marooning several men who were, one by one, swept into the torrent.

Then, piercing our ears even over the uproar of the storm, came sounds that no one, once hearing, ever forgets—the despairing cries of drowning men. Eliza and I were both completely undone. As we ran up and down the bank, wringing our hands, she called to me, "Miss Libbie, what shall we do? What shall we do?" We tried to scream encouragement to the flailing forms we could see in the water, but our voices were lost on the wind. When the lightning flashed, we could see men swept along with tree trunks, masses of earth, and heaps of rubbish, their arms reaching toward us, imploring us to help them. There is no more helpless feeling than to stand and watch a fellow creature beg for his life, while you are unable to help.

"The ropes!" I cried. "The tent ropes." I ran to the tent

to unwind a rope but found it lashed to the poles, stiff with moisture, and tied with intricate sailors' knots. In a frenzy I tugged at the fastenings, bruising my hands and tearing the nails.

Eliza came up to where I was insanely tugging. "Miss Libbie, there's a chance with one man. He's caught in the branches of a tree, but I see his face and he's alive. There's my clothesline—but I can't do it, I *can't*. Miss Libbie, where would we get another clothesline?"

She was so used to protecting our things, so used to frugality, that even in this extreme circumstance she couldn't sacrifice a rope. Without another word I flew to the kitchen for the clothesline.

We saw a man's face with hue of death—that terrible blue look—and the current battering so badly that he was afraid to leave go of the trees to grasp our rope. We threw it to him over and over again, only to have his benumbed fingers grab at it and then lose hold. I thought he would disappear before us any minute. At long last we made a loop and tried to call to him to put it over his head, and all the while we could hear him bubbling and bellowing and gagging as the water dragged him under, then released him momentarily.

Eliza, she who was terrified of water, was waist-deep when we finally pulled him ashore—cold and blue, his teeth chattering, his eyes perfectly wild.

When we had pulled him to shore, I screamed with amazement, "Tom!" There before me was Tom, he who always had laughter in his eyes and mischief in his heart—only now he was more than half-dead, a pitiful and frightening sight.

He could not answer me but only turned away, retching up river water. We wrapped him in a blanket and put him in my tent. "Coffee, Eliza. Pour hot coffee into him. I'll get whiskey. Can you get the red pepper from your tent?" I was frantic out of my concern for Tom and my sense that Autie could not survive the death of his beloved brother.

She gave me a strange look but without asking did as I bid. We saved two more men that night, filling them with whiskey, rubbing them with hot pepper, keeping them warm and talking to them all the while, trying to get the scare out of them.

Still, seven men drowned near our tent that night, and their cries echo yet in my ears. When day broke, we found ourselves on a narrow strip of land, surrounded on all sides by water, cut off from the main body of the camp by a wide and deep river, the water too swift to contemplate crossing it, though some of the cavalry officers thought of plunging their horses in until we begged them not to try. The place looked like a laundry, with blankets, bedding, and clothes strewn everywhere.

But the water was receding, and we were alive. We were grateful.

Tom stumbled toward me in that early-morning light. "Libbie, you saved my life. I'm . . . I'm grateful. . . ."

"Tom, you're my brother," I said, "and I would do anything for you. But I'd have worked as hard to save any soldier last night."

He looked humbled as he said, "God bless you, Libbie. I hope Autie knows what a jewel he has."

I wondered if Tom would ever again be the laughing, carefree boy I had known all these years, the one who had teased me so in Louisiana and Texas, even the man who drank too much in Kansas and led other officers astray. While I might have hoped for his reform, I would not have had it come this way.

"Miss Libbie, look!" Horror was etched in Eliza's voice. "No, don't look!"

But I did, and saw a soldier's drowned body embedded in the side of the bank, swollen beyond recognition. No one could reach it, and we could not escape the sight of it. That vision remains etched in my mind, along with the terrible screams.

We were three days on that strip of land, until the water receded enough for us to be moved across the soggy prairie to an even higher spot. They were three sodden, sleepless days and nights, and Diana, Eliza, and I suffered from exhaustion. Mrs. Gibbs, who with her two sons had been marooned with us, maintained a rare composure that I envied but could not copy. I would never, I thought, be the perfect army wife.

Fort Hays after the storm was a dreary place, but still I was devastated when word came that we women were to return immediately to Fort Harker, because Hays was considered unsafe for us. We left with two officers—James Coker was not one of them—and an escort of ten mounted soldiers.

"Libbie, look at that soldier." Diana spoke under her breath and barely nodded her head in the direction of a soldier riding directly behind our ambulance. When I looked, I gasped aloud, for he reeled in the seat so badly that he was in imminent danger of falling out of the saddle. Within minutes steadier hands removed him from his horse and dumped him, unceremoniously, in the wagon that held forage for the mules and the horses.

"Drunk," I muttered in disgust.

"Plains whiskey," Eliza said. "They only needs to smell it, it's such deadly poison."

Autie had told me that sometimes a barrel of tolerably good whiskey, sent from the East, was made into several barrels on the plains by the addition of drugs. Such a brew had the power to lay out like a dead person even a hard-drinking old cavalryman in no time at all.

And one by one, that's what happened to our escort. The teamsters, who fortunately remained sober, laid them in the supply wagons, and we rode across the prairie without an escort. Had the Indians only known, here was their golden chance for a free attack.

In that country, the air is so clear that every object on the brow of a small ascent of ground is silhouetted against the deep blue of the sky. The Indians placed little heaps of stones on these rises to hide behind, and to my strained eyes every little pile of rocks seemed to move, an effect heightened by the waves of heat that hovered over the surface of the earth. At each rise we looked anxiously into the depression ahead, no sooner relieved to find it safe than we were torn with terrors about the next rise. Had I been going over such ground to join Autie, I've no doubt the prospect of reunion would have quieted my terrors—but I had no such joyous prospect to distract me.

In spite of my fright, I could not help being struck by the wildflowers—their reds and oranges made the earth glow, and yet I knew that no soldier would allow me to stop and gather some as I had done in other days—the danger now, in this strip of land, was too great. I thought of James Coker and the night we had gathered wildflowers but soon brushed the thought from my mind.

Buffalo, antelope, black-tailed deer, coyote, and jackrabbits all scurried out of our way, and I thought how delighted Autie would have been to take off after one or all of them. Once we saw a herd of wild horses, with the leader bearing his head in a proud, lofty manner, mane and tail flowing, neck splendidly arched, proud head carried loftily. But we saw them only momentarily, for wild horses run like the wind when they are alarmed—and we alarmed them.

At Fort Harker we were all invited to stay with the commanding officer, but I thought that too much of an imposition. Sending Mrs. Gibbs to accept that hospitality with her two young sons, I announced that Diana, Eliza, and I would sleep in the ambulance. It was, after all, perfectly covered and for our comfort was placed in a narrow space between two storehouses.

Kansas did it once again! A storm arose in the night, and the flapping of the tarpaulin over our ambulance awoke us. With ropes and picket pins thrashing, it was finally lifted on high and soared off into space. Still, we had the curtains and cover of the ambulance, and we huddled together, trying to hide our eyes from the lightning and our ears from the roar of the storm—I had heard enough of storms to last me a lifetime. The rain beat in and soaked our blankets, and then the curtain at the end of the ambulance jerked itself free, and water deluged us from a new direction.

I longed to scream out for the sentinel, but one of the earliest lessons Autie had taught me was that one never spoke to the guard on post. We saw that poor soldier with every lightning flash, tramping his way around our wagons without ever looking at us.

But then, suddenly, we found ourselves in motion, spinning down the incline behind the wagons. And I screamed, regardless of military rules and procedure. The sentinel rushed to our aid—blessed be him for answering a higher law that forbids neglecting a woman in danger.

The wagon was dragged back and secured with stronger picket pins, but sleep was murdered for the night. The guard had, of course, reported to the commanding officer, and soon there came a lantern or two zigzagging over the parade ground in our direction. There was no arguing—we were fished out of our watery beds and followed the officers to drier quarters, those that I had first resisted because I wished not to make trouble.

Next morning I prepared to regain control of my world, but was startled by the approach of the commanding officer.

"Mrs. Custer? I'm sorry to say I cannot offer you the hospitality of Fort Harker. You and your party are to return to Fort Riley immediately."

"Return to Fort Riley? I had hoped, sir, to be going in the other direction, to join my husband." I fought for composure as I spoke.

"I know that," he said kindly, "but the way west is too dangerous . . . and you cannot stay here, because we have an outbreak of cholera. We've lost platoons of soldiers within days. I cannot . . . will not take responsibility for your health and well-being."

Chapter Twelve

THERE WAS NOTHING FOR IT. WE RETURNED TO FORT Riley, with every step taking me farther from Autie. As we rode, each turn of the ambulance wheels seemed to raise a new question in my troubled mind. I'd endured a summer like none I'd ever known—floods and fire, pestilence and mutiny—and I'd survived just fine *without Autie*. When I tried to imagine those same catastrophes with Autie present, my stomach churned uneasily and I saw myself cowering before his stern discipline of rebellious soldiers or his cavalier disregard for disease, which he made plain he regarded as an affliction of the weak. I saw myself, to speak flatly, embarrassed for my husband, uncomfortable about his behavior.

And yet I loved Autie, did I not? Was ours not the passionate storybook romance? And was he not the reason I was traipsing around the West, exposing myself not only to the dangers I'd already met but to the ever-present threat of Indian violence—or, as James Coker had told me, the threat of a supposedly merciful bullet from a friend in case of enemy attack. Why, but for love, had I chanced out to the remote posts of Hays and Harker? Of course I loved Autie—there could be no doubt about it—and if I loved him, then I must needs spend every possible minute with him. So returning to Riley was a setback.

"Libbie, are you all right?" Diana spoke from her perch next to me as the ambulance bounced over the prairie. "I saw a tear, I thought. . . ."

"Must be Miss Libbie got some dust in her eye," Eliza said with a mischievous grin. "Can't be that she's missin' the ginnel."

I gave her a long look and said nothing.

Later I learned that the company that would have escorted me to Wallace was ambushed by Indians and caught in a fierce battle. I remembered James Coker and the bullet he saved for me, and I decided the Lord was looking after me by returning me to Riley. But I never told Autie about that feeling.

Days at Fort Riley dragged on for all of us. Mrs. Gibbs had also returned there, and we had a little community of wives whose husbands were off fighting John—the frontier name for the Indian. Autie wrote frequently, as did the other men, and we lived for the mail, spending long hours on the gallery of the house we occupied, watching for the door of the office to open.

"Here he comes, one step at a time," Mrs. Gibbs said wryly, and we all turned to look.

The mail was delivered by a cavalryman who had been left behind, ostensibly to take care of company property. Privately we believed it was because his brain was addled. He had become inflated with his importance from the joy with which we greeted his daily visit, and now his walk across the parade ground became a spectacle. This soldier—whose name I never did learn—was over six feet tall, a lumbering, bearish kind of a man, but one set on military perfection. Stalking across the parade ground, he would not demean himself by hastening but took one measured step after another, as though he were on drill. When he drew near enough to see us watching—which we always were—his head went back loftily, and his steps seemed to slow even more.

"Napoleon would not have run for an impatient woman," Diana giggled, "and neither shall he." Then she looked long at me. "Autie wouldn't either."

Once this mutton of a man presented himself before us, he insisted on observing all the form and ceremony he considered suitable to the occasion. I wanted merely to grab the letters from his hand and dismiss him, but no such luck.

With a flourish of his huge arm, he gave me a salute that took in a wide semicircle of Kansas air. "Good morning, Mrs. General George Armstrong Custer."

"Good morning," I answered as courteously as I could manage.

When the mail was at last safely handed over—he always gave it to me to deliver, presumably because he was in Autie's command and considered me therefore in command of the wives—he turned on his heel with military precision, a perfect "right about-face," flourished that arm again, and marched away as slowly as he'd come.

"What does Autie write that you want to share?" Diana asked impishly.

Scanning the pages, I said, "That he is desperate with worry because he believes we are at Harker, where cholera is raging." Autie was then at Fort Wallace. The Seventh had its first outright fight with the enemy when a band of three hundred Cheyenne, under Roman Nose, attacked a stage station near Fort Wallace and ran off all the stock. Inflated by success, they then proceeded to attack Wallace, a pitifully indefensible group of log huts and mud cabins. When attacked, though, the cavalry charged out in defense and fought as bravely as though they had a battery of artillery behind them. In overwhelming numbers the Indians countercharged, lances poised and arrows on the string, and Autie wrote me of hand-to-hand combat. He did not say exactly that he had been involved, but my heart leapt in fear at the thought of Autie locked in a death struggle with an Indian. And when I read that "one of the soldiers" wounded Roman Nose himself with a Spencer rifle, I of course assumed that it was Autie who had fired that rifle.

Much later Autie told me the wonderful story of a black trooper who rushed into a dangerously unprotected place during that battle. Those watching in horror saw him throw up his hands, kick his feet in the air, and collapse—dead to all appearances. "He's a goner," said one soldier to the other. But after the battle, the dead man—restored to life—walked back to the post, gun in hand. "I just did that to fool 'em," he said. "I thought they'd try to get my scalp, thinkin' I was dead, and then I'd git one of 'em."

Within months, Wallace, a small fort of two hundred men, sprouted sixty new graves, the result of repeated Indian attacks. The stage stations they were sent to protect were repeatedly attacked, men mercilessly butchered. Inside the fort things went from bad to worse—bacon and flour, stored unprotected out of necessity, went rancid and moldy. Men deserted, many to seek their fortunes in the gold mines in the Rocky Mountains—an easy escape that was seldom tracked, though many of them probably lost their lives to Roman Nose's warriors instead of finding their fortunes. Usually the deserters took arms, ammunition, horses, and food with them, knowing that officers could not search for them without leaving the fort dangerously undermanned.

Autie wrote to me of all these discouragements, and my heart went out to him. One battle does not make a war, and the fight with Roman Nose had not been enough to mesh Autie's units into a fighting army. They were, instead, involved in a battle they didn't understand, with an enemy who didn't follow the rules they knew. Autie's depression increased, and with it my concern.

One day I sat alone on the gallery sewing a new gown for Eliza—she had complained about being the worst-dressed darkie in the garrison—when I heard the peculiar sound of military steps approaching, far too rapidly for the mail carrier. Biting off the thread with which I worked, I looked up . . . and saw Autie standing before me.

"Autie?" My sewing fell from my lap as I stood to walk toward him, expecting to be enfolded in a passionate embrace.

Instead Autie stared at me, arms held stiffly at his side. "I've just come from Harker," he said, his voice stiff and strained. "Coker's been hurt."

"James?" I asked. Then, fearing the worst, "Indians?" Now I saw that a yellowish bruise on Autie's cheekbone was just beginning to purple up, and he had plasters on the knuckles of one hand. His lower lip appeared to have been recently split, and there was a small scratch over his right eye. Before he spoke, I knew instinctively what had happened.

"No. I beat him senseless."

Even though I sensed the truth, my mind refused to comprehend the words. "Autie, what are you saying?"

"I beat him." His expression never changed. "He'll have some permanent reminders not to dally with my wife."

"I . . . what . . ." I stammered badly, but nothing sensible came from me. The scene was not real. I felt as though it were a dream, as though I were detached and watching myself from a distance and would soon wake to find it all changed. Or perhaps Autie would finally break into a smile and say, "Fooled you, old lady!" But neither happened.

At last, gathering a measure of calm, I suggested we go inside. "We need not discuss this with the whole world listening," I said, though in truth even Diana had disappeared.

"I don't care who knows, I will not be cuckolded," he said loudly.

Knowing that arguing with Autie was going to be pointless, I simply turned and went inside. He followed me, and soon we were in the room given me for a bedroom—since Autie was not officially at Riley, we had no house of our own, and I was charitably treated as a guest in another officer's home. There we faced each other across a double bed, and the mind taking one of its odd, unpredictable turns, I briefly saw us facing each other across a huge hotel bed in New York on the first night of our honeymoon. Then the air had crackled with anticipation; now it bristled with pent-up anger.

I took a deep breath. "I don't know where you got the notion that anything went on between James Coker and me, but you're wrong. Dead wrong."

"Coker was almost dead wrong," he replied with an ironic grin. "Word travels fast in an army, Libbie. I heard of your nightly walks on the prairie . . . from someone who cares about you. . . . and the time you were nearly shot. I would have expected you to know better."

Autie still stood stiff as though on parade. What frightened me most was that he showed no sign of anger. His attitude was instead one of cold, calm deliberation. I would have preferred, I think, that he flew in a rage and threatened to begin throwing the china.

In spite of my almost uncontrollable anger, I began to do just what I knew I should not—apologize, explain, cajole. "I was lonely, Autie, missing *you*, and James was kind to me. He's had a bad marriage. . . .

"James Coker never courted me," I said, willing him to believe me. Briefly I wished that I had Autie's control and could withstand his anger. Instead, his cold rage overpowered my own indignation and—yes, it frightened me—left me the one trying to make everything all right. "He was . . . and is . . . a friend . . . and if you've hurt him badly . . ."

"He'll recover."

Deep down I know that I should have at that moment confessed my love for Autie, reassured him that it was he and he alone whom I loved, but something—that remnant of anger, perhaps—held me back, and I never said those words. I had humbled myself, but there was a limit.

"Now what?" I asked, wondering if he planned divorce, disgrace, separation, or a brave face to the world.

"We will go on as usual," he said. "No one need know about this, and I trust it will not happen again."

All that I had said had been lost on him! It was too much for me. "Autie," I screamed, "it never happened at all. You're wrong—can't you get that through your head?"

"Libbie, you were the one who requested privacy for

this discussion, and now you're inviting the entire post to hear it by your yelling. Can't you keep your voice down?"

Frustrated, I bit my knuckles and turned away. Autie would win our battle, just as he won on the battlefield. But Autie never understood those he had conquered, not even me.

We ate a silent meal that night, served by a cautious Eliza, whose eyes darted from one to the other of us without a word. Diana stayed wherever she had hidden, and Mrs. Gibbs had taken her two boys elsewhere, too. So the dining room, which had seen us all share happy meals, now housed two strained and uncomfortable souls.

"Autie, tell me how you got here. Do you have orders . . . ?" I thought I should choke on food and toyed with the steak that Eliza had prepared.

He drew himself straighter. "Of necessity, I wrote my own orders. We marched to Harker for supplies and new orders . . . but neither were there." He shook his head in exasperation and grew conversational, the old and familiar Autie. "This is a poorly run war, Libbie. . . . At Wallace, we have few rations, no decent horses, no medicine to fight cholera."

A premonition of disaster ran through me. "How did you get from Harker to Riley?"

"By train," he answered confidently. "I told Smith I could not return without seeing to my wife's health. I was frantic when I heard of the cholera. You are well, aren't you?"

Smith was, of course, Colonel A. J. Smith, the district commander who had been at Riley when we first arrived. "He gave permission?" I asked unbelievingly.

"Of course he did. Your boy has done so much for this man's army, no one would deny him a reunion with his wife. Now I can take you to Wallace personally."

He was going to take me to Fort Wallace! I could hardly believe my ears. Autie had written long, long letters about the perilous position of Wallace, the mutinous men, the failing supplies . . . and yet he was going to take me there.

"When do we leave?" I asked. The thought of refusing

to go never occurred to me, for in my mind I heard my father saying, "Follow Autie wherever he takes you."

"Tomorrow."

We retired soon after dinner. Wounded to my very core, I crept into one side of the bed, desperately wishing for my own house so that I would not be confined to the same room with Autie. He, however, had no inclination to stay on his side of the bed. His hands began their sensuous stroking—he rubbed my back, almost kneading the knots that had appeared between my shoulders. And then gradually, ever so slowly, his hands worked their way downward until he was stroking the length of my leg, moving those insistent fingers toward my inner thighs. I shuddered but lay perfectly still.

"I missed you, Libbie," he murmured, inching himself toward me until I felt the length of his body along my back and the hard, strong force of his member pushing at me. "I . . . I can't exist without you, and the thought that another man might possess you. It drove me crazy. . . . Say you'll forgive me."

"Autie," I whispered, tears running down my cheeks as I turned toward him, "how could you hurt James Coker? He's a good man. You once trusted him to put a bullet in my brain."

He jerked upright. "Coker told you that? He's a worse fool than I thought. Libbie, if you had to dally, how could you choose someone like Coker?"

Stiff with renewed anger, I turned away from him.

I lay awake all the night, sometimes crying quietly into my handkerchief, more often trying to make sense out of something absolutely incomprehensible. For now, I could not forgive Autie for doubting me, for beating James, for being Autie—his rushing, insistent fingers with all their probing and stroking would arouse not one whit of passion in me. But I prayed it would not always be so, for I could see a miserable lifetime ahead if passion did not hold us together. And Fort Wallace? I would think about that in the morning.

The morning spared me from thinking about Wallace. Autie was as usual up and about early, cheerful as though nothing had ever happened. I dragged myself from bed, avoiding the mirror so as not to see the dark circles that I knew marked my eyes, and stood for several long minutes, bewildered, in the middle of the room.

"Best get packed," Autie said. "We'll leave in an hour."

Listlessly I moved toward the wardrobe, my mind not up to the task of choosing clothes, rolling them in bedding, gathering my toilette. Where, I wondered, was Eliza, and then I knew—she was probably hiding from Autie.

At a knock on the door, I expected to see her face bringing coffee. Instead, a young soldier stood very erect. When Autie opened the door, he saluted and then said in a staccato voice, "Official orders for you, sir," before fleeing as fast as his military dignity would allow.

"Orders?" I asked.

Autie unfolded the papers and read, his frown deepening. Then, wordlessly, he wadded the papers into a ball and threw them across the room. Next he began to pace, back and forth, back and forth. I crept to the comfort of the bed, watching and waiting.

At long last he spoke. "Court-martialed," he said bitterly. "I've been court-martialed."

This whole bizarre episode was going from bad to worse, and I heard him in disbelief. "For what? Beating James Coker?"

Autie came closer that moment to hitting me than he ever yet had. Striding across the room to place his face in front of mine, he raised his fist and then lowered it. "No," he said in a mimicking tone of voice, "not for beating James Coker." Then his voice deepened. "For absence without leave and conduct to the prejudice of good order and military discipline." He had, it appeared, memorized the words of the document.

"What does that mean?" I asked. "I know about absence without leave . . . that means you're here and you should be at Fort Wallace. But the other?"

"I shouldn't be at Fort Wallace!" he said, raising his voice. "I told Smith where I was coming . . . and the other, I don't know." He paused a long time, then spoke dramatically. "I tell you what I think it means. Hancock's Indian campaign this summer has been a bust, and he needs a scapegoat. So here I am. But I'll not let them ruin me this way. Believe me, Libbie, I'll fight."

With a shudder, I nodded.

Trial would commence in September—it was now late July—and until then Autie was to remain at Riley, so we were given our own quarters, small blessing that that proved to be. Autie spent long hours convincing me of his innocence and of the necessity that we fight the charges together.

"We must, above all, not appear worried," he lectured time and again. "We'll give parties, go on with our lives as though nothing were the matter."

And so, newly ensconced in temporary—and draftily unsatisfactory—quarters, I began again to give dinner parties. Autie was always the charming host, laughing with his guests, urging them to have more to eat, more to drink, telling another joke. I watched it all with a peculiar sense of detachment I'd developed after Autie returned to Riley.

The guests who enjoyed Autie's hospitality, however, did not see him during the hours he spent poring over military law books and official records in his study. He would leave those papers in the late afternoon, having worked at least ten hours, with eyes red-rimmed and spirits dejected. But by dinner he would be affable and bright.

His scars from the fight with James had healed, and gradually the distance between us lessened. Not that I ever understood or forgave his attack on James, nor his distrust of me, but the circumstances of being united against the world inevitably drew us back together again. We began with those little gestures of caring—a touch here, a light kiss there—and within three weeks we were again lovers. Sometimes, exhausted in the early-morning hours, I thought that Autie took out all his frustrations in an extraordinary sexual energy, an energy that swept me along, unwilling, and ultimately left me like a shipwrecked sailor washed ashore. Somehow I deemed it my conjugal duty to match his intensity, and my responses were ardent enough that he never sensed my doubts.

"Libbie," he whispered, panting, one night, "I can't bear

it when we're not happy like this. Promise me . . . *promise me* that you'll never look at another man."

I evaded the promise with a rebuke. "You know I never have, Autie," I said, stroking the sweating head that lay on my bosom.

Passion had weakened him. "I know," he whispered, almost pitifully. "I was wrong. Forgive me?" He could, when it suited his purposes, be almost a little boy, pathetic in his need to be loved and forgiven.

"Do you forgive James?" I wanted to ask, but I said nothing. Instead my hands traveled over his back, his arms, his chest, feeling him stiffen into arousal again. Somehow, as my absolute faith in Autie crumbled, my physical reticence lessened, and I often became the aggressor. Autie was delighted.

James Coker's division rode into Riley about two weeks after Autie's returned. I heard the news, of course, and watched them from a distance, but it was two more days before I chanced to come face-to-face with James while on a walk about the parade ground with Diana.

He took off his cap and bowed, saluting me in a formally correct manner. I looked for scars but saw none obvious beyond a thick scab that still clung above one eyebrow. With relief I realized that my fears of permanent maiming had been an exaggeration. But his eyes were different—they glittered with a hardness I'd not seen before.

"Libbie, you are well?"

"Very, James, and you?" It was like a formal dance, where the partners barely touch, following a prescribed and impersonal form.

"I am well," he said. "And Armstrong?"

"He is well. You've heard . . . ?"

"I've heard," he said grimly. Then, nodding to Diana a few steps away, he made bold to say, "I'm the one who reported him, Libbie. I think it only fair to tell you that."

"Reported him? James, why? Because you fought?"

"No. That was a private affair between two men. But,

Libbie, the men who died on the trail, the others who marched one hundred fifty miles in fifty-five hours, the horses that had to be destroyed . . ." His voice trailed off bitterly.

"James!" I commanded. "Whatever are you talking about? Men and horses dying? Autie has simply been court-martialed for being absent without leave and for something about military order . . . I don't remember the words."

"Nor," he said sarcastically, "do you know their meaning. Libbie, we must talk, privately."

I looked around, expecting to see Autie leap from the door of our quarters and come bounding across the parade ground to confront James again. "That's impossible, James. You and I both know it."

"It's important . . . important that you understand the situation."

His face was earnest, and I, God help me, wanted to know what he had to say. James Coker was perhaps infatuated with me—or had been—but he was not blind enough in love to fabricate stories. I had to hear what he wanted to say.

"Be at Mrs. Gibbs's house for tea tomorrow at four P.M." I said boldly, counting on that dear lady's cooperation. "I'll be there, and I'll arrange a *brief* private talk." Autie detested our afternoon teas and always remained at his desk at that hour.

He nodded and resumed his formal manner. "Delighted to see you again, Libbie, and you, Miss Diana."

When Diana heard of my plan, she was appalled. "Libbie, you wouldn't! Meeting him in secret!"

"It's for Autie's sake," I said, admitting to myself that it was only in part a white lie. I also admitted that I was running a terrible risk.

Mrs. Gibbs was one of the world's nonjudgmental persons. She never asked, she never blinked, she simply said, "If it's important to you, Libbie, I'll arrange it." And so, next afternoon, James Coker and I found ourselves in a small study in the Gibbses' home.

"Conduct to the prejudice of good order and military discipline," James said, standing stiffly before the chair where I sat, "means that one hundred fifty men were on a forced march, two were sent after deserters, attacked by Indians, and never searched for, ten horses were left to die along the road, troops were subjected to agonizing unbroken travel, with hardships of exhaustion, thirst, and starvation. Twenty men deserted." He reeled these charges off as though he had been reciting them over and over to himself.

"Why?" I managed to ask, though my voice was faint and I was grateful for the chair that supported me. Had I been standing, I was sure my weak knees would have given way.

"So Autie could get to you. He was panicked about reports that you had cholera," James said, straight-faced.

"And rumors that I was having an affair with you," I added softly.

"That too," he admitted.

"Why are you telling me this?"

"Because it is your right to know before you leap to his defense." His correct military manner dropped, replaced by an impassioned, personal pleading. "Libbie, you've got to know what kind of a man you're married to."

I saw the pain—and love—in his eyes, and I cringed. Those thoughts of what life would be like without Autie flitted through my poor brain, but I could not allow myself to take them seriously. "Thank you for your concern, James. I'll certainly consider this," I said most formally, sweeping from the room and leaving behind me a confused and crushed man. Unfortunately, my put-up front was so good that James Coker did not at that moment know of my own confusion and uncertainty.

The mind plays strange tricks to protect itself. Because I could not, or would not, leave Autie, I could not believe James's accusations. So I discounted them, convincing myself that James had exaggerated, even fabricated the charges out of jealousy and misguided love. And then, by one of those inexplicable twists of logic, James became the enemy for Autie and me to vanquish, and Autie, to my mind, was an innocent victim—well, almost.

Poor James . . . all he ever did was offer me his love and follow his conscience.

"Of course, Autie knew he risked the consequences of leaving Wallace," I wrote blithely to his mother, "but he did what he thought was right at the time. His troops, who have always been his first concern, needed supplies. Surely he will be vindicated." Then from my superior military knowledge, I added the reassuring thought that court-martial was neither serious nor unusual in this man's army. "Almost half the men have been court-martialed at one time or another." I half came to believe my reassurances myself.

In early September we were transferred to Fort Leavenworth, where the court convened on September 15 with a jury of nine men. I sat with Autie each day, convinced that the trial would go our way . . . until Captain Robert M. West took the stand.

I had been convinced that James Coker was the only man who could testify against Autie with any impact, and that he would not do so because of me. Perhaps I was smug, but nonetheless, I knew it true, and I was right—James stayed well away from Leavenworth and the trial. But Captain West was a surprise to me. Sitting beside Autie, I watched as he was sworn in, a man much older—in his fifties —with the florid face that often bespeaks too much consumption of the grape.

"He's a drunk," Autie whispered to me too loudly. "I had him court-martialed for being drunk on duty. I guess he wants his revenge."

Surely, I thought, the army is more systematic or businesslike than to allow petty revenge in its most serious proceedings.

West charged Autie with ordering the pursuit of deserters, causing "three men to be severely wounded" and then "persistently refusing to allow said soldiers to receive treatment," so that one subsequently died.

"Didn't Sheridan order you to shoot deserters without trial?" I whispered to Autie.

"Yes," he replied. "Nine men deserted—we went after them and recovered six. Three of them were . . . ah, . . .

unfortunately shot, but I saw that they had medical attention." He paused for a moment and then muttered, "I just didn't want everyone to know that they got care. Wanted them to think I was willing to let them die. But, Libbie, I wouldn't have done that. . . ."

I remembered the execution in Louisiana, and I could not look at Autie.

Autie was also charged with responsibility for the death of the two troopers lost on the march from Wallace to Harker. The prosecution's description of their mutilated, scalped bodies was so graphic that horror almost made me gag. "Autie?" I whispered.

"I did not have time to go searching for every man jack of them," Autie whispered back defensively. "Besides, if they'd fought back when they were attacked, instead of running, they'd be alive today, sitting in this damn courtroom."

I turned away from him again.

In spite of eloquent testimony on Autie's behalf—and a widespread belief that the whole trial was a whitewash for Hancock and an exercise in envy for officers who'd resented Autie since his graduation from West Point—the verdict was guilty on all counts. Autie was sentenced "to be suspended from rank and pay for one year, and forfeit his pay for the same time."

Phil Sheridan had at first offered to testify as to his orders concerning the treatment of deserters, but his campaign kept him from Leavenworth. After Autie's conviction he wanted to intervene to obtain a remission of the sentence, but Autie would not accept this. "How would that look?" he asked me bitterly.

"We shall remain in Leavenworth for the winter," he said solemnly, "and I shall work on my book, the story of my adventures from West Point to Appomattox."

Sheridan had invited us to stay at his residence at Leavenworth, since he would be away on campaign, so it was settled. In the spring, Autie said, perhaps we should go to Europe.

If my joy at the turn of events was less than Autie expected—after all, he would now be my constant companion, and I would be relieved of worry over his fate at the hands of savages—I could only explain it by financial concerns. Autie had certain emoluments, so that the loss of his regular pay did not render us penniless, but still we would have to conserve. Europe, indeed!

Beyond pleading the strain of financial worries, I could not have explained my reserve to Autie. Indeed, I myself never made sense of the tangled web of truth and deceit woven by Autie and James and the court-martial.

We spent the winter at Leavenworth, dancing merrily to keep our own personal ghosts at bay. There were gay dances and lavish dinners, long walks on the post grounds near the river, hunting with the dogs once spring arrived. But Europe was farther and farther away—Autie was unable to secure the sponsorship he wanted, and we could not afford to go without backing. Autie worked at his memoirs.

In June we left for Monroe, taking Eliza and Diana with us. Autie had grown increasingly uncomfortable, watching patrols head out from the post in pursuit of deserters and Indians. Autie, who needed a war, was now not only forced to be inactive but also to watch others marching off to a war that he knew he could have conducted better. It was too much for him.

"We'll stay in Monroe until October, when the year is up," he said.

I was miserable in Monroe, though I kept my spirits up to fool Autie . . . and to avoid having to talk to him about how I felt. In Leavenworth, surrounded by our cavalry family, who understood the politics of Autie's court-martial and who saw no disgrace in our situation, I had managed a good face, laughing and dancing with the best of them. But Monroe was different—it was home, and its people had little understanding of army ways. Though no one ever spoke a critical word to me, I felt on display, the subject of curiosity and—dare I say it?—scorn from our fellow citizens. And I was more acutely aware of my own hidden doubts now that there was no dancing to keep them away.

Autie, by contrast, loved being in Monroe and acted as though he were still the national hero—perhaps he truly didn't realize he was not. He spent long days fishing for bass in the Raisin River. Other days he held forth in the lobby of Humphrey House, talking to the men gathered there—the one day I chanced to enter the lobby, I was heartbroken to see that group and know that my father was no longer one of them.

Autie also favored long walks through the town, with me on his arm. He was marvelous when on parade like that—always affable, always positive. "How are you? . . . Good to see you. . . . Yes, we're very glad to be back home in Monroe." So it went as he greeted people on the street, while I, a pale shadow, clung to him, smiling weakly.

"Libbie," he would say paternally when we were safely back in the house on Monroe Street, "you must be more cheerful. These good people will think you're ashamed of something. Are you?"

"Of course not," I assured him. But I kept my eyes down to avoid looking at him. In my heart I longed to be back at a frontier post. The months from June to October stretched dishearteningly before me.

Autie watched me hawkishly in Monroe. Tom was there for much of the summer, though officially assigned to the Seventh. Autie seemed to grow jealous even of his own brother, for Tom spent a great deal of time at the house on Monroe Street, and I, as always, became the surrogate mother, even though his own mother was not five miles away.

"Tom, have you had breakfast?" or "Tom, won't you eat those fresh berries that Eliza picked?"

"Libbie!" Autie would interrupt impatiently. "I'm waiting for you in the library so that I can work on my memoirs."

And why, I wondered, could he not work on his memoirs without my sitting by his side?

"You spend so much time worrying over Tom," Autie said peevishly, "one would wonder which Custer you're married to."

"Now, Autie," I would say soothingly.

Jim Christiancy, whom I'd nursed during the Civil War, was back in Monroe, still a semi-invalid from his wounds, now living with his parents. He came to call, putting one crutch aside to hold out an arm to me for a hug.

"Libbie! My God, how good it is to see you! I owe you my life! You know that, don't you, Armstrong?" he asked, turning to Autie. "I owe her my life!"

"A great debt," Autie said grimly, his eyes flashing dangerously.

"Autie," I said, "isn't it wonderful to see how well Jim looks?"

Jim shook his head. "Don't toy with me, Libbie. I'll never be a whole man again. But I'm happy as I can be under the circumstances." Then he looked at Autie. "I envy you this woman, Armstrong."

Autie just nodded grimly, and the rest of the visit went from bad to worse. I saw Jim throughout the summer from time to time, but only casually. He never felt welcome enough to return to the house, nor did I feel comfortable in asking him. I thought it a pity, for his life needed whatever brightening it could get.

The final straw came when no less a figure than General Phil Sheridan came to Monroe for a visit. He was on his way to Washington from the Indian frontier and stopped, I was sure, as a way of publicly expressing his support of Autie.

"Libbie," Little Phil said—everyone, even Autie, called him Little Phil behind his back, and I'd begun to think of him that way—"you're as beautiful as ever. Exile has not harmed you." He bent to kiss my hand.

"La, Phil," I said, trying to laugh, "it's been good to be home among friends. But Autie and I are ready to be back in the army."

"I'm sure you are," he said, looking intently at me and then gazing at Autie, who stood silently to one side. "I'm sure you are."

Autie was furious after he'd left. "You needn't be begging for me, especially not from one of your conquests."

"Autie, do be serious. Phil Sheridan is an old friend of

yours, from the war days . . . and I was not begging. I was stating a truth."

"He's a better friend of yours," Autie countered harshly, "ever since you and he rode that train together."

My mind flitted back to that train ride to Washington with Sheridan—it seemed a lifetime ago—when I had been young and green and overwhelmed by generals. "Yes," I said softly, "he is an old friend of mine, too."

"I have to watch you with every pair of army pants that happens along," Autie said with venom.

Stung, I stared at him, unbelieving. Autie was accusing me of infidelity . . . or as good as. It was as though he'd exaggerated his fears about James Coker a thousandfold. "Autie?" I managed to whisper. "Do you believe I've been unfaithful to you?"

He turned red, that famous Custer blush revealing his discomfort. "No," he muttered, "not exactly."

"Then why?" I demanded. "Why are you so suspicious of every little thing I do? You've even questioned my relationship with Tom this summer. . . . Perhaps you protest too much, as the saying goes." A sudden light was going on in my head.

"Libbie, what are you talking about?" he demanded, ill at ease.

"Perhaps you suspect me of infidelity because you yourself have been guilty," I said.

"Libbie, for heaven's sake . . ."

"All those trips to New York and Washington without me," I went on, now riding the crest of my anger and indignation, "all those times you wrote me about how the women fawned over you and you resisted. Maybe that was what you wanted me to believe. . . ."

"Libbie . . ." His voice had a note of desperation in it.

"And Kansas City," my monologue went on, almost musing, as though I'd not even heard him, ". . . I remember a night when you came in late, very late, and you smelled to high heaven of French perfume. . . . You told me that you'd had to fight off a society lady, and we both laughed about it." I paused. "Maybe I shouldn't have laughed, Autie."

I stared at him, my eyes wide with my new but very certain knowledge.

"Libbie, don't be silly. I love you, only you."

"Oh, I don't doubt that, Autie. But that has nothing to do with your being faithful. I know your appetites."

He had the poor taste to look almost proud, and I turned away in disgust. For days, unable to go near him, I slept in the guest room. Mama had long since occupied my old bedroom on her visits back to the house, and Autie and I shared my father's bedroom—the room in which he and my stepmother had slept. Sometimes I had felt uncomfortable about making love to Autie in that same room. Now I just felt uncomfortable about Autie.

"Libbie," he asked plaintively after five days, "aren't you ever coming back to my bed?"

"Perhaps," I said unconvincingly.

It was two weeks before I returned to his bed, and my ardor never returned all that long summer. Waiting for October and our reprieve, we were testy with each other, always ready for a disagreement. Sometimes I found myself provoking arguments.

"You really want a son, don't you, Autie?" I asked one night as we sat, some distance apart, in uncomfortable old wooden chairs set upon the grass behind the house.

He chewed on the stem of grass he had plucked and looked beyond me, as though he could see clear to the West. After a long pause he said, "No, Libbie, I don't think I do. That has been a big problem for me . . . and for you . . . but I think I've got a grip on it. The truth is, there's no place in our lives for children. If you had to tend to youngsters, you could not be with me on the plains—and I prefer that."

"But family is so important to you," I protested. I missed children, even wanted them, but I had long since decided I really wanted them mostly to please Autie, mostly because I thought he was unhappy without them. Now I wanted to push that point to its limits.

He brightened, as though I'd suggested a wonderful solution. "I've thought perhaps we could adopt Autie Reed."

"Autie Reed!" I exploded. "Your ten-year-old nephew? And what does his mother say about that?"

"Well," he admitted reluctantly, "I thought it best to discuss it with you first. I haven't talked to her."

"I wouldn't, if I were you," I said to Autie, and the subject was dropped. But gradually Autie did convince me that our childlessness was not at the root of our unhappiness.

But we never, that long summer, dug out that root. I used to catch Eliza staring at us, as though she could shake both of us, and I thought she knew more about us than we did ourselves.

As it turned out, we did not have to wait until October. Autie's rescue came early in September, with a knock on the door.

"Message for the general," the young boy said, holding a telegraph in his hand.

"I'll take it," I replied, but he pulled back the hand holding the paper.

"I'm to wait for a reply, Miz Custer," he said apologetically.

"Of course. Come in." My mind whirled, for I knew without ever looking at that message that Autie was returning to the army. It could be nothing else. Was I losing him . . . or was a bitter, unhappy summer coming to an end? I wasn't sure whether to laugh or cry.

"Autie?" There was a tremor in my voice, I was sure. "There's a wire for you."

He was at the door in an instant, tearing open the message. His eyes widened as he read, then a grin spread across his face while I stood nearby, my breath held tight.

"Let me read it," he said. "It's from Phil. Says, 'Generals Sherman, Sully, and myself, and nearly all the officers of your regiment, have asked for you, and I hope the application will be successful. Can you come at once? Eleven companies of your regiment will move about the first of October against the hostile Indians.' Libbie," he said, grabbing me and whirling me around as in the old, happier days, "they need me!"

"You'll go?" I asked softly.

"Of course. I'll go tomorrow." Then he paused to look at me. "Don't look so downcast, old lady. Isn't this what you've wanted all summer, too?"

He forgot the young boy standing there, forgot my step-mother and Tom Custer seated within earshot at the dining table, forgot Eliza hovering at the swinging door into the kitchen. "I swear to God," he said forcefully, "I don't know how to make you happy."

I hung my head, feeling very much the fool but for some reason unable to control the emotions that rose to the surface. Indeed, I was unable to puzzle them out myself. "I suppose I'm to stay here?" I, who had spent half the summer avoiding Autie, was now, suddenly, desperate to be with him.

"And could you be ready to go tomorrow?" he asked sarcastically, and then softened instantly. "It won't be for long. I'll be on march right away . . . but we'll be together again soon."

Neither he nor I had any way of knowing that "soon" would stretch far beyond the Christmas holidays.

Autie's summons to duty came on the heels of a turbulent summer on the western plains. In July there had been the Medicine Lodge Council, a triumph of peacemaking, so the Michigan newspapers told us. But Al Barnitz, a captain with one of the Seventh Cavalry companies, had written Autie that the Cheyenne had agreed to the treaty without any idea or understanding of what they were giving up. "The treaty amounts to nothing, and we will certainly have another war soon or later," he wrote.

Then, as though fulfilling Captain Barnitz's prophecy, came the Battle of Beecher's Island, where scouts, under Major George A. Forsyth, were pinned down for a week on an island in the dry bed of the Arikara Fork of the Republican River in Kansas. They were finally rescued by buffalo soldiers from the Tenth, but their plight enraged the army. Easterners, who read of it in newspapers and knew neither the drama nor the intensity, still thought that a peaceable solution was possible.

But Autie knew better. And he had told his views to the old men gathered in the Humphrey House lobby, who nodded sagely and thought he was wonderful. Now he was off to prove that he was right.

"Libbie, you will help me pack?" He looked the little boy, lost as he stood among his bags and clothes.

"Of course I'll help you," I said, moving to fold the pile of pants he had thrown on the floor, a blue carpet of cavalry uniforms sparked by an occasional red bandanna—he still considered those bandannas his trademark—and punctuated by a lone sock here or undershirt there. I began the task of organizing at which I was, by now, very proficient.

"Old lady, look at me," he said.

I noted without comment that he had twice called me "old lady" that night, a term of affection that he had not used for some time.

When I turned toward him, he folded me in his arms and said fiercely, "I need a victory, Libbie. I need a victory."

The next day I was the bright and cheerful army wife at the rail station in Monroe, kissing my husband good-bye and waving long after the train had become a speck in the distance. But as I turned back toward Monroe Street, Eliza and Mama both at my side, I carried with me an indelible picture of the intense look Autie had given me as he boarded the train.

He was, of course, off to fight Indians. There was no denying the danger, in spite of Custer's Luck. What if I'd sent him off to his death without truly smoothing the differences between us? When all the house was quiet that night, I lay sobbing into my pillow in Papa's bed, reaching in vain for the spot where Autie should be.

VICTORY
AND
DEFEAT

Chapter Thirteen

 AUTIE GOT HIS VICTORY AT WASHITA, AND I WAS WITH
him. Oh, not really. Even Autie wouldn't have
taken me into battle. But his letters were so vivid
that I lived that battle with him—after the fact, of course.

In reality, the first part of that fall of 1868 I was fuming
in Monroe—bored, lonely, and angry. All that long summer
we had been distant with each other, uncomfortable, my anger at his accusations still high, my belief that he had dallied
with other women too strong to ignore. But once really separated from him, I was desperate to be with him. I could not
explain my feelings then and cannot now.

And I was sick to death of Monroe—with Mama now
living back there, full of her aches and pains, even the Custers, sweet and kind as they were. Father Custer jollied me
into good spirits whenever he could, and Mother Custer
fussed over me in her quiet way. But I longed for the company of men who called me "old lady" and laughed at my
fears, danced with me far into the night and loved me be-

cause I was fun. I missed the army . . . and I missed Autie. Sometimes his letters sent me into gales of laughter, like the time poor Tom needed a change of clothes:

> *His dog, Brandy, tangled with a polecat, and Tom, in rushing to pull him off, got enough perfume to last him several months. This is not exactly the country to allow a man parting with his clothes, as he can't very well go back several hundred miles to replace them. Tom partially turned the joke, concluding to call on all the other officers in camp while so highly, if not fashionably, perfumed. He would enter a tent, and soon the remark would arise, "Some dog has been killing a skunk. I wonder where the damn brute is!" Someone else would say, "It's evidently close about here, you can bet!" So the conversation would go until Tom could contain his laughter no longer and thus betrayed his awful secret.*

Another time, more seriously, he wrote that Fort Dodge was a terrible place, where most of the officers had laundresses for mistresses, and some quickly became drunkards. He knew of one officer, he wrote, who took to drink because he suspected his wife of infidelity:

> *From the excellent officer that he was, he has descended to one of the most inefficient. Poor man, I am deeply sorry for him and cannot censure him. I would do no better if as well were I in his place. . . . How blessed I am that I am united to a pure, virtuous, and devoted wife and I feel immeasurably thankful for it.*

James Coker, I thought, get thee behind me! But I knew that Autie's letter held hidden barbs beneath its sugary words.

More often his letters moved me to fear rather than laughter or anger. In October he wrote,

*We have been on the warpath but one week. I
joined the regiment near our present camp a week
since, and within two hours the Indians attacked.
. . . You would never ask to go to a circus after
seeing Indians ride and perform in a fight. I took
my rifle and went out on the line, hoping to obtain a
good shot, but it was like shooting swallows on the
wing, so rapid were they in their movements. . . .
Sometimes a warrior, all feathered and painted, in
order to show his bravery to his comrades, started
alone on his pony, and with the speed of a quarter
horse would dash along the entire length of my line,
and even within three or four hundred yards of it,
my men pouring in their rifle balls by hundreds, yet
none bringing down the game. I could see the bullets knock up the dust around and beneath his
pony's feet, but none apparently striking him.*

My heart leapt in terror when I thought of Autie actually
facing Indians—though what else, I wondered, did I expect?
A few days later he wrote,

*Sherman has finally decided on a winter cam-
paign. We are going to the heart of Indian country,
where the troops have never been before. The Indians have grown up in the belief that the soldiers
cannot and dare not follow them there. They are
now convinced that all the tribes that have been
committing depredations on the plains in the past
season have gone south and are near each other in
the vicinity of the Washita Mountains. They will
doubtless combine against us.*

"Eliza! Eliza!" My frantic voice echoed through the
house on Monroe Street.

"What is it, Miss Libbie? I'se right here. You don't need
to go yellin' so." She poked her head out of the kitchen,
curiosity and concern written on her face.

"The general!" I gasped, breathless as though I'd run a mile. "We must go to the general."

"Now, Miss Libbie," she said patiently. "He's off fightin' them Indians, and you know we can't go to him. We got to stay here until he sends for us. Miss Libbie, you come and let me fix a good cup of tea."

"No!" I said frantically. "We've got to go . . ." I turned and began to mount the stairs.

"Go where?"

"To Leavenworth," I said desperately. "At least we'll be closer to him."

"Not much," she muttered, as she watched me pull clothes out of the wardrobe like a madwoman.

When Autie fought in the Civil War, I used to think superstitiously that I had to wish him luck each time he left me. If I didn't, he would be injured . . . or killed. Now that feeling came back, though different. It wasn't that I had to wish him luck, but I had to be close, I had to be on the frontier as though, somehow, I could spread my wings and shelter him. Autie would have laughed and called me "old lady" if he could have read my mind.

He probably missed Eliza more than me, for he wrote that he wished her to bake him some rolls "instead of the solid shot our cook gives us." And Eliza missed Autie. She was as glad as I when we finally left for Leavenworth in early November.

I was greeted gaily at Leavenworth by those who had missed us, and though I settled like a star boarder in the quarters of Lieutenant Major Thomas Brown and his wife Lucille, rather than in my own house, I was glad to be home among my army friends. They understood my anxieties and fears in a way that even good, kind Father Custer never could. We talked of Indians and soldiers, of generals and enlisted men, of the newness of a winter campaign.

"Even Jim Bridger came from St. Louis to advise against it," said Lucille. "Said you can't hunt Indians on the plains in winter for fear of blizzards." A new hazard for us to think about.

Such anxieties were heightened by the letter waiting for

me when I arrived. "A white woman has just come into our
camp deranged and can give no account of herself. She has
been four days without food. Our cook is now giving her
something to eat. I can only explain her coming by supposing
her to have been captured by the Indians, and their barba-
rous treatment having rendered her insane. I send her tonight, by the mail party, to Fort Dodge." The story brought
to my mind once again, with instant clarity, James Coker and
the bullet he had been instructed to save for me.

Autie's orders for moving toward the Indian village were
issued on the evening of November 22, and so good were
army communications—even the grapevine—that we at
Leavenworth knew of it almost immediately. Our vigil began.

From Autie's letters after the battle, I know that it
started to snow that morning, and by breakfast the men stood
in knee-deep drifts. Autie thought it all the better, for the
army could move through the snow; the Indian villages could
not. Still, the guides could see no landmarks, the men were
soaked with cold and wet, and no halt was made for food
through the long day. When at last they camped for the
night, small fires could be built under the deep banks of the
stream, so the men had coffee and the horses oats; but no
bugle sounded, no voice was raised, no pipe lit for fear of a
spark.

By the ashes of a fire recently extinguished, then the
barking of a dog, and finally the cry of a baby, the Indian
camp was discovered. The night was spent in fitful sleep and
long preparations, and before dawn a single shot and the
sounds of "Garryowen" piped the eight hundred horsemen
into battle. Magazine accounts, official reports, even Autie's
personal letters chronicle the military details—half-clad Indians pouring out of tepees to run in all directions, cavalrymen
blasting at them with six-shooters, slashing with sabers, even
running their prey down with galloping horses. Indians
plunged into the icy river, and a few escaped in ravines and
clumps of bushes, but their defense was ragged, pitiful. Autie
was in possession of the village within ten minutes. To this
day I hear the cry of the Indian baby, see the captured white

woman, feel the cold of winter and the frozen river. Autie, of course, reveled in the fighting:

> The entire village, numbering forty-seven lodges of Black Kettle's band of Cheyenne, two lodges of Arapaho, two lodges of Sioux—fifty-one lodges in all, under the command of their principal chief, Black Kettle—was conquered. The Indians left on the ground 103 warriors, including Black Kettle, whose scalp was taken by an Osage guide.

Black Kettle. I had heard even Autie say that he was a peace chief, one who sought no war with the white man but who often could not control the young men of his tribe. Now he lay dead, scalped, on the battlefield. I shuddered as I continued to read Autie's official report.

> Eight hundred seventy-five horses and mules were captured, 241 saddles, 573 buffalo robes, 390 buffalo skins for lodges, 160 untanned robes, 210 axes, 140 hatchets, 4,000 arrows and arrowheads, 1,050 pounds of lead, 300 pounds of bullets . . .

The list began to fog my brain, and I skipped over it to the next paragraph, which was no more comforting.

> Everything of value was destroyed. Fifty-three prisoners were taken, squaws and their children. Two white children, captives with the Indians, were taken. One white woman in their possession was murdered by her captors the moment the attack was made.

Autie's report concluded with the information that two officers—Major Elliott and Captain Hamilton—and nineteen enlisted men were killed. Captain Barnitz—my old friend—was seriously wounded through the abdomen, though miraculously no vital organs were struck and he later recovered. Joel Elliott was not so lucky.

Ah, Autie, there was the rub in your grand and glorious victory. The death of Major Joel Elliott almost robbed you of your glory. The stories that came back varied, depending on who was telling them, but to the best I could understand, Joel Elliott had taken a detachment and ridden off toward the river, pursuing some fleeing Indians. When one of the lieutenants suggested to Autie that the detachment might be under attack, Autie was scornful: Captain Myers, he said, had been fighting down there all morning and would have reported any unit in difficulty.

But Elliott was under attack—and he and his men were all killed. When they didn't return, speculation ran through the camp where men were burning saddles, clothing, utensils, weapons, ammunition, and the winter supply of dried buffalo meat. Such appalling waste troubles me to this day, but Autie assured me that impoverishment was the only road to victory in the battle against the Indians. Nonetheless, I shook with sobs when told about the nine hundred ponies that were either shot or had their throats cut.

A scout party went in search of the missing detachment, but returned reporting no sight of them within two miles of the camp. And Autie deemed it time to withdraw, for there were other large Indian camps nearby, and large groups of warriors had begun to gather on the bluffs, watching the soldiers in that silent, ominous way that Indians had. The soldiers then numbered nine hundred men, but they had no count of the Indians. As it later turned out, the Indians outnumbered them. But Autie judged at the time that being so far from a base of supplies, his men exhausted from a long fast, horses worn out with a difficult march through the snow, he could not risk the lives of the whole command in further search for Joel Elliott's unit. At Autie's command the company band struck up "Garryowen," boldly leading the troops on a march carefully designed to fool the watching Indians—first toward their tepees, then suddenly countermarching to head toward the supply train. Joel Elliott and his men were left behind.

Autie believed, he told me later, that Elliott had become lost without a compass and would soon make his way to Camp Supply. Not until November 27 did they return to the Washita . . . and then they found the badly butchered bodies of Joel and his men.

The news filtered to the newspapers back east. An anonymous letter, obviously written by an officer who'd been at Washita, published in the St. Louis paper, charged Autie with having callously left the battlefield without secure knowledge of all the men in his command. Back at Leavenworth, within my hearing, some defended Autie, saying that Joel was already dead and it would have done no good to endanger the remainder of the troops to search for him. Besides, they argued, Joel had taken off on an independent, unauthorized glory-seeking mission; his fate was not Autie's responsibility. Still, there was a public outcry that Elliott and his men had been abandoned . . . and Autie was the villain.

Autie, so another officer later told me, demanded to know of his officers who had written the letter to the St. Louis paper. "I will horsewhip the culprit," he thundered.

Shifting his pistol, James Coker stepped forward. "I wrote the letter," he said, "and I stand by what I wrote."

Autie glared, for James Coker was now the one enemy he could not defeat. He could not horsewhip him again, nor could he court-martial him—though I know Autie tried to scheme a way to make that possible.

I kept deliberately aloof when the Washita battle was discussed at Leavenworth, but I had always thought Joel Elliott a charming young man, and I grieved for him.

Autie did not join me for Christmas, for the Seventh continued out in the field. The holiday was a rather melancholy affair for me, in spite of the efforts of those around me to be of good spirits. I had thought of going back to Monroe, but only briefly, for hadn't I just gratefully escaped from there? Eliza, once returned to the frontier, declared herself firmly planted there, to await the "ginnel's" return from campaign.

Sighing, I agreed with her, and spent the holiday watching Lucille Brown fix makeshift holidays for her little ones.

"We've oranges for their stockings," she told me on Christmas Eve, "and candy canes. But I can't help thinking how grand their surprises would be were they back home."

Next morning it seemed to me those children were perfectly elated, and I could not imagine that their joy could have been any greater were they back in Ohio with doting grandparents.

As I watched them—a towheaded boy of six and a sister, slightly darker, no more than four—I felt a pang again, for now it was clear to me that I would never give Autie the son he now denied wanting. Sometimes the idea of our barrenness made me angry at Autie, in a kind of perverse reasoning that I could never explain.

His letters over that holiday were warm and loving, full of references to his "darling girl" and of declarations of loneliness and love. In some letters he wrote in a stilted manner in the third person. "She has been to him more than his fondest hopes ever pictured a wife could be. And he owes her a life of devotion, of pure unbounded and undivided affection for the pure love she bears him, for her unselfish devotion to him and to his interests, and for the perfect type of a true, pure, and loving wife she is and ever has been to him." Autie, with selective memory, had wiped out the differences that had simmered all the past year and come to a boil in Monroe over the last summer.

Forgetfulness was not so easy for me, in spite of my strange and frantic anxiety about his safety. Once I was back in the world of the army, among those who shared my daily fears but among whom a stiff upper lip was the required code, I worried less about Autie's safety . . . and fretted more about our relationship. Loving letters did not flow as easily from my pen.

Autie, nobody's fool, responded to the distant tone of my letters. "While I am absent, you may perhaps think kindly of me and remember much that is good of me, but when I return, that spark of distrust, which I alone am responsible for first placing in your mind but which others have fanned into a flame, will be rekindled, and little burning words will be the result. . . . You are and ever will be the one single object of my love."

Those little flames, though, whispered to me of past indiscretions and of present doubts: Was Autie a ruthless killer of innocent women and children at Washita or was he, as all around me thought, a heroic Indian fighter, the man destined to bring peace to the frontier? Was he a faithful husband or, as rumors hinted, a habitué of ladies of the night, a ladies' man who charmed the youngest and the oldest, and bedded whom he could? At least, I told myself more than once, I needn't worry about indiscretions when he was off on campaign.

Washita was the high point of Autie's year. The rest of the winter was unmarked by any battle and spent instead in parleyings, ruses, subterfuges, councils, and promises of peace on the part of the Indians. In December, slopping through mud, the Seventh forced a group of Kiowa into Fort Cobb, and in January they moved south to the Wichita Mountains, where Phil Sheridan ordered the construction of Fort Sill, Oklahoma. Both Indians and soldiers were hungry and cold, and Autie's troops were able to round up several bands of the hostiles and move them toward the reservation.

"The arrogance and pride is whipped out of the Indians," he wrote in February. "Yesterday we made peace with the Kiowa and released their two head chiefs, Satanta and Lone Wolf. . . . We will set out in a westerly direction, intending to treat with the Cheyenne."

By the first of March, the Seventh was living on quarter rations of bread. "I wish," Autie wrote, "that some of those who are responsible for this state of affairs and who are living in luxury and comfort could be made to share at least the discomforts and privations of troops serving in the field."

The column returned by late March to the Washita battlefield, from where Autie wrote that he had been successful against the Cheyenne. "I outmarched them, outwitted them at their own game, proved to them they were in my power, and could and would have annihilated the entire village." What prevented that annihilation—I breathed a sigh of relief as I read—was the presence of two captive white women, who were eventually released. After a few days' rest Autie's troops moved toward Fort Hays for their summer encampment.

I was in the throng that edged the parade ground at Hays when the Seventh rode in, the band playing "Garryowen" and the men riding as smartly as possible. But they were a sad lot, ragged and tired, their horses thin. Only Autie looked unscathed by the winter of hardship. I caught my breath when I saw him.

Gone were the army blues. Instead he wore a fine, fringed suit of buckskin, topped with his trademark red scarf. Momentarily, I almost did not recognize him, for in addition to changing his outfit, he wore a full beard . . . and his curls had been cut short. He looked to me an entirely different man, and I wasn't sure if that was good or bad.

There was much shouting and hugging once the men were dismissed to greet their families. Autie strode purposefully to where I waited and then stood in front of me, perhaps a foot away.

"Libbie?" He sounded the little boy again.

"You look wonderful, Autie," I said, throwing myself into his arms.

"I . . . I wasn't even sure you'd be here," he muttered into my hair. "I was afraid . . ."

"Where else would I be, Autie? I belong wherever you are."

"Please God we'll have no more of these long separations," he said fervently.

In spite of his obvious desperation—I use the word advisedly—to be with me again, Autie was not as ardent as I'd expected. After previous, briefer separations in our marriage, Autie had sometimes been so impatient a lover as to be rough and inconsiderate. This night, when we finally retired to our tent alone, he was slow, deliberate, stroking and teasing rather than rushing headlong into passion. There was none of the loud and almost violent passion that sometimes

made me worry about the ears of the sentry. This night Autie
seemed to have less immediate need of his own pleasure.

At the time, I thought perhaps he was growing up, that
somehow a new and stronger man had come back to me
from the Indian Wars. I was only partly right . . . and partly
wrong.

We camped again on Big Creek that summer, though my
mind still swam with memories of the flood two years earlier.
I was one of three women in camp, most of the others being
prevented from joining the unit by the need to care for small
children. But General Miles had his bride, Katherine, with
him, and my cousin from New York, Rebecca Richmond, was
with us. We three braved it among all those men.

"See?" Autie triumphed. "If we had children, you'd be
back in Monroe, and I'd dutifully have to go visit you. At the
very least, you'd be in those awful quarters at Hays, and we'd
have to retire to the parade ground to have our battles, lest
everyone on officers' row know our every secret. Either way,
we'd miss all this." He waved his arm expansively to take in
our tent home, the cottonwood trees that ringed it, and beyond, the endless plains, naked and glaring in the sunlight.

Our home for the summer was a generous-sized hospital
tent, which served as a sitting room, and an adjoining wall
tent, which made our bedroom. Since we were camped on
the slope of the riverbank, the tent had been shored up at
the rear until it was almost to the level of the trees. Autie
had the carpenter continue the floor right on out around one
tree, and we had a gallery for sitting. A huge tarpaulin,
spread over the larger tent, extended enough to create a
porch, where we spent many hours. Our tent was discreetly
away from the others—General and Mrs. Miles had pitched
their tents farther on in the bend of the river, Rebecca's was
between theirs and ours, and the rows of tents for the
soldiers were beyond the Mileses' tent.

Fort Hays was not far at all and often afforded us
wagonloads of visitors. But the post itself was dreary beyond
measure—plain, bare officers' quarters that resembled bar-

racks; a dull-brown parade ground with only sparse, stunted grass; nary a tree on the whole place. And Hays City, the town that grew up around the fort, was no better. It was mostly built of crude frames covered with canvas. Shanties had been made of slabs, bits of driftwood, and logs, and sometimes the roofs were covered with tin that had once been fruit or vegetable cans, now flattened out.

Pistol shots were heard so often in Hays City that it was like a perpetual Fourth of July. The graveyard had been begun with the interment of men who had died violent deaths, and thirty-six new graves were added in the summer we were there. In all the times we went to town, I asked to avoid the railroad track, for I was never sure if we would come upon a body swinging from the beams that supported the bridge. And Autie cautioned me severely about casual looking—on trips to the railroad station to greet visitors, I was not to look out of the ambulance, for fear of attracting the wrong kind of attention. I was grateful beyond words that I could camp with Autie and live far away from both the post and the town.

I wish I could say it was a blissful summer. Autie and I did agree, without ever speaking of it, to let bygones be bygones. There was no mention of Monroe, nor St. Louis, nor James Coker—he was now stationed with another unit of the Seventh at Harker, and so he and Autie were mercifully separated. I heard, however, here and there, that he was still loudly critical of Autie, and not just for the deaths of Joel Elliott and his men. He now accused Autie publicly of having an affair with a married woman at Fort Hays—I wracked my brain but could come up with no suitable candidate—and of habituating demimonde dives in Leavenworth. The latter rumor cut through me like knives, because it reinforced my own suspicions.

Autie denied these accusations vehemently to my face, his anger turning on me. "It's all your fault," he would say, "for letting Coker get enthralled with you. He's just doing this to embarrass me, so he can have free run at you. I'll have to take him on again."

And then I would beg and plead and assure Autie that I believed none of what James Coker said. But gnawing doubts

stayed in my mind. Sometimes I sat and stared at Autie and
wondered if I even knew him. Maybe, I thought, Autie was
someone I didn't know at all, had never known. I was sure, at
least, that he was a different man now than the one I'd married. His victory at Washita had made him, overnight, the
nation's most prominent Indian fighter . . . and it had
given him a new self-confidence—Autie, who'd never lacked
in that department to begin with. Sometimes I thought he
bordered on arrogant.

But what did that have to do with ladies of the night and
married women in St. Louis? Sometimes my brain reeled in
confusion, and I put Autie off at night when we came to bed.
I couldn't bear for him to touch me, though at other times—
my doubts momentarily quieted—I welcomed him passionately. *Ah, Libbie*, I thought to myself, *you are a fickle and
weak woman.*

"Old lady, come with me to see the Indians. I have to do
some parleying with them."

There were some sixty prisoners from Washita still quartered at Hays, and Autie frequently had to go to them since
he had learned their language.

"I believe not," I said, lightly as I could. "They wouldn't
want me peering at them, and I . . ."

"Libbie, you're afraid!" He hooted around, doing a little
dance and clapping his hands as though he'd caught me in
the most embarrassing situation.

"I am not!" I declared. "It's just . . ." There was nothing for it; I went to visit the Indians. In truth, I was more
than a little afraid. The chiefs among these Indians were
apart, preparing for their council with Autie—or, I should
say, being prepared by their squaws, who fluttered over them
like lords and ladies over royalty. But I'd heard enough tales
about the desperate work squaws and children had done in
battle to fear going in among them, chiefs or no. The reins
shook in my hand as I rode quietly along beside Autie, and
the shaking hand unnerved Phil, my new quarter horse, who
was used to a firm, guiding hand.

"You're awfully quiet, Libbie. I keep telling you there's

nothing to fear. These are peaceful Indians . . . they are
conquered Indians."

My failure to reply goaded him into further reassurances. "You don't think I'd take you where there is any danger, do you?"

I simply shook my head.

As we neared the stockade, Phil began to tremble from
more than the shaking hands that guided him, and I had all I
could do to keep him from turning back toward camp.

"He's afraid of Indians," Autie said matter-of-factly. "He
can smell them, and he's afraid."

If I hadn't known that Autie would accuse me of losing
control of my horse, I'd have given Phil his head, for I
wanted to go back home as much as he did. By the time I
dismounted, the animal had nearly torn my arms from the
sockets.

Boldly Autie walked past the sentinel and into the midst
of a crowd of Indian women and children, dragging me with
him. So great was my distress that I was sure I could see
knives being fondled under bulky garments, even feel the
points of weapons aimed in my direction.

Autie began signing to the women. "What are you telling
them?" I asked curiously.

"That you are my wife. They want to know if you are the
only one."

I looked at him archly. "You told them yes?"

"They pity me. It means I am not a chief of much consequence."

The squaws moved closer, reaching out to touch my
shoulder, my hair, my gown. One took my hand in her rough
palm, and I realized that hard work had turned her hand to
leather. Then another, with a wrinkled and rough face, laid
her cheek against mine, and I thought instantly of sandpaper.
Her hair was thin and wiry, scattering over her shoulders and
hanging over her eyes, and her lined face spoke of weather
and work beyond my imagining. Her ears were ragged, having once been punctured from top to lobe to hold rings, but
now torn out by the weight of these ornaments. It was all I

could do to keep from drawing back, but I forced a smile of pleasure onto my face and hid my revulsion.

I looked for Autie and, to my alarm, found him some distance away, with an old woman pulling his head down so that she could lay her cheek against his. Later I asked why he was so popular with old women, and he told me that it was not considered acceptable for young women to show any attention to strangers. But it was eminently proper for old women to do so.

I felt my hair being examined at the back, and then sensed that the bird on my hat was being fingered. Children were called to admire the buttons on my riding habit, and my hand was imprisoned while an old woman stroked the kid of my glove.

"They admire your gloves," Autie whispered, coming behind me, "to the point of possession should they catch you alone outside the post." It was all I could do to keep from snatching my hand away and running from the post.

There were mothers with babies among them, babies who were gathered into little cocoonlike rolls, their limbs lashed into absolute quietude. One special infant, born just before the battle, belonged to Monahsetah, a Cheyenne princess. She offered the infant proudly for inspection, her eyes fastened on Autie as though desperate for his approval. When he favored her with a smile, she muttered something guttural to him.

"Who is she?" I asked.

Autie explained that she was a princess of some intelligence whose advice had been used to bring in tribes over the winter. "She can read a trail better than any scout I ever knew," he said enthusiastically. "The bones of the game killed by a war party, the fur or skin of the animals, the ashes of the camp fire, all these little details mean an enormous amount to her. She could tell how long ago game had been killed by the marrow in the bones."

"But I thought she was imprisoned here," I said curiously.

"Monahsetah? No, she was on the march with us much

of the winter. Until time for the papoose. Tom called her Sallie Ann, and she took to the name."

Did he look away from me deliberately as he said that?

"Where is the baby's father?" I expected to hear that he had been killed at Washita.

"Crippled," Autie said. "She shot him."

"She shot her husband!"

He grinned. "Well, I don't know the whole story, but he apparently wanted her to do more work than she thought was appropriate for a princess. It was an arranged marriage."

Could she just as easily pull a knife and cripple the wife of the man who'd captured her? I looked again into soft eyes that seemed to smile at me, but I was leery and uncomfortable. I was as charmed by her baby, with his dark, darting eyes, as I was puzzled by Monahsetah.

At last the chiefs were ready. Autie had secured permission for me to attend the council, a great honor, he told me, but one I could have done without. In the presence of those fierce and gloomy men, I began to tremble anew. In honor of the occasion, women and children—usually barred—were admitted, and their excitement was so high, it filled the air with anticipation.

When the traditional clay pipe was passed, I feared I should be further honored. Fortunately, it circulated only among Autie and the three chiefs; I was spared. Even so, as we waited for those taciturn men to speak, I began to feel faint. To be shut up in a Sibley tent with a crowd of Indians on a warm summer day is not an experience that one longs to repeat. Kinnikinnick—a mixture of willow bark, sumac leaves, sage leaf, and tobacco, mingled with buffalo marrow —saved our nostrils from the odors and the closeness, but still I buried my rebellious nose in my handkerchief. Etiquette forbade my leaving for open air until the general and the chiefs had agreed—every captive white man, woman, and child must be released before the Indian prisoners could return to their homes—and shaken hands. Then, at long last, we escaped.

These visits became routine, though I can't say that I ever became more comfortable with them. Once Autie took

Eliza, but he never repeated that experiment, for she proved to be more scared than I. When she couldn't see Autie, she "took one leap and lit out of thar in a jiffy," as she described it.

Neither Eliza nor I were foolish in our apprehensions. One day in the summer an orderly from the post rode to our tent in a lather, barely pausing to present his commander's compliments before spilling out that the general was wanted at the post, for there'd been an uprising among the Indians, and all they could be induced to say was that they wanted "Ouchess," meaning "Creeping Panther," a name they had given Autie some time before.

It seems there were rumors that hostile bands lurked near the post, intent on rescuing the three chiefs. The commanding officer decided to separate the chiefs from the others, but the soldiers sent to effect this were unable to explain in terms the Indians understood. Typically, the Indians resisted when force was applied, and the women and children, once they saw a fight, joined in. Knives were drawn, and one sergeant was stabbed so badly, his life was despaired of. The remainder of the guard came to the rescue, and soon one chief—Big Head—was dead, and another—Dull Knife—lay mortally wounded. Far Bear, the third chief, was felled by a rifle butt, but uninjured.

Autie walked alone into the midst of the women and children, and with remarkable ability and calm was able to quiet them. Soon they were keening their grief over the dead, some of the women gashing their legs and cutting off their fingers.

I never again visited the stockade with Autie, for the Indians were now dissatisfied and restless, and we had seen how skillfully they hid knives, how quickly they used them. When at last the white captives were released and word came that the Indians would return to their homes, there was general rejoicing on both sides.

The Indians—who had come to us with no possessions —left with wagonloads of goods, "all kinds of truck," as one soldier told me. When Monahsetah left, the soldiers all cried, "Good-bye, Sallie Ann," and she bowed as though acknowledging an ovation. Then she came directly to where Autie and I stood watching the goings-on. Standing before us, she ignored me and raised her eyes coyly to Autie to murmur, "Good-bye, Creeping Panther."

Autie blushed, a weakness he had not been able to overcome, even now that he wore buckskin and was an Indian fighter.

Chapter Fourteen

 YEARS AFTER BIGHORN SOMEONE WROTE IN *HARPER'S* that the Custers were "the most romantic couple on the frontier, their total absorption in each other making them comparable to the great lovers of the Ages." I read that grimly, suppressing an urge to write the author and explain that apparent absorption, though I never did write the letter.

Still, I suppose it was true. There were times—instant, electric moments that would flash upon us—when Autie and I were so acutely aware of each other that it was a physical sensation. Across a room, I could feel his slightest move, the gesture of a hand, the turn of an eye, and he would feel the same tension at the same moment. In a roomful of people, we would then exist only for each other, boldly cutting an entire crowd out of our consciousnesses and barely managing the politest of nods, the murmured monosyllable in response to a question.

These moments were not physical passion alone, though

that was surely a strong element, and more than once Autie whisked me off early from a party, explaining, "I fear Libbie is overtired," when in truth, desire had swept over both of us in waves. But more often those instances were of the spirit rather than the flesh, psychic if you will, rather than physical. And they grew more infrequent over the years.

In spite of romantic rumor, Autie's suspicions, and my great doubts about his fidelity, our marriage settled into the dailiness of most marriages—the taking for granted, even the small irritations and quarrels that sometimes seem to drive away the joy. Oh, Autie insisted that I sit by his side when he wrote, and everyone thought that romantic, but it was simply that he wanted me to divert him from boredom. And I took it as my chore to save him from hyperbole.

Around me I saw marriages that were more or less like ours—especially less when there were children involved on the frontier, for the wives had to raise their children mostly alone, and they tended to be too tired and frazzled for any joy. Lucille Brown, with whom I'd stayed in Leavenworth, was charming, bright, and witty . . . but she rarely left her home, never left the post because of her constant obligation to her two children. No rides across the prairie on a cool spring evening for her!

But even those fortunately childless, like Katherine Miles and myself, who followed their husbands from camp to camp, seemed ecstatic only once in a blue moon, moderately happy some of the time, and curiously discontent the majority of their days.

As I sailed blindly past the crises in our lives and sometimes wondered what life without Autie would be like, I firmly believed that each man and each woman should have a mate. It was fixed in me since childhood that man and woman walked the road of life together, and I was constantly scheming to marry off this one or that . . . my cousin Rebecca, who spent much of the summer at Big Creek with us, Autie's sister Maggie, even my stepmother if I could. But my most dedicated efforts were directed toward finding a wife for Tom Custer. A wife, I told Autie, would civilize Tom.

"I know he's my brother, and I may be prejudiced,"

Autie laughed, "but why does he need civilizing? I think Tom is a delightful fellow."

"Have you been to his tent lately?"

"No. Have you?"

"Yes, I have," I said vehemently. Tom had invited me there almost as soon as we camped on Big Creek to see his collection of Indian mementos. I was used to necklaces of the fore claws of the bear, war bonnets with eagle feathers extending from head to heels, buffalo-hide shields, and even scalp locks, which were frequently stretched over small willow hoops to keep them from shrinking.

But Tom also had a box of rattlesnakes . . . live rattlesnakes. Whenever he saw a snake with seven or more rattles, he would leap off his horse, take off his coat, and tie up one end of a sleeve, commanding his long-suffering orderly to hold the sleeve open for the prisoner. Then, with the butt of the carbine, he pinioned the reptile near the head, holding it down with one hand and using the other to seize it by the back of the neck. Then he was back on his horse, seven rattles ominously threatening him from the sleeve of the jacket rolled behind him.

The snakes were kept in patched-up hardtack boxes and had to be lifted out to be seen and fully appreciated. While I perched on the bed, carefully holding my petticoats about me lest a stray snake be curled in the bedclothes, Tom lifted these monsters one by one so that they could show their full length and shake their rattles in rage.

"There's one missing," he exclaimed in genuine regret.

"One missing?" I echoed, my eyeballs wide in horror as I began to peer under the bed.

"Oh, you needn't be looking for it," he said more cheerily. "The other in that box ate it apparently. I shouldn't have put those two together."

Thereafter I tried to argue with Tom that he should keep all his snakes in one box—was that, I wondered, like all your eggs in one basket?—because they surely craved companionship.

"If you think, old lady, that after all the trouble I have

taken to catch these snakes, I am going to make it easy for them to eat each other up, you are mightily mistaken."

"Tom," I exploded, "how are you ever going to interest a nice young lady in marriage if you persist in having snakes, cannibalistic snakes at that, around you?"

"The only girl I want is married," he said, giving me a long look that I could not possibly have misinterpreted.

I'm sure I blushed. In all the years Autie and I had been married, Tom had been part of our household, a happy conspirator in Autie's high jinks, another wayward man for me to boss and cajole, sometimes almost the son I'd never raised. That laughing Tom, with his face always open and smiling, could feel any other way about me had never occurred to me.

There was no smile now. "I'll say it once, Libbie, and I'll never say it again." He approached me and grabbed one wrist almost hurtfully, holding me so that I could not move from him, could not easily evade his eyes. "My brother is married to the woman I love. Should he ever mistreat her, I'll take action. Beyond that, I'll stay a happy bachelor."

He released me and turned his back, and I, a speechless coward, fled back to my own tent, where, as fate would have it, I encountered Autie.

"Any luck in taming Tom?" he asked jokingly.

"No," I muttered, "none."

"Why, Libbie," Autie said, perceptive as always, "I do believe you're upset. Is it the snakes . . . or Tom's perpetual bachelorhood?"

"Both," I managed to say as lightly as possible. "He's hopeless." Autie would never know how I meant that.

"Well," he replied, "I doubt you'll find a young lady who will appreciate Tom's snakes well enough, but keep trotting out candidates, Libbie."

And keep trying I did, though Tom went to his grave a bachelor.

That summer on Big Creek had many highlights—the time we took our Thoroughbred to Leavenworth for a race; the great slow mule race in which Autie had to literally beat his reluctant beast across the finish line; murderous storms, which put me in mind of the earlier terrifying flood; even the hanging of a horse thief in town. But the events that remain most clear in my mind are the buffalo hunts.

Buffalo were in such enormous herds all about us that it seemed as if nothing could diminish their numbers. General Sherman told me, not long since, that from the time Autie and I were in Kansas until the date of the almost total annihilation of the buffalo, nine million of the brutes had been killed.

The prairie was stamped with the presence of buffalo. There were, for instance, trails leading to streams, narrow ruts so deep we had to check our horses to cross safely. Each hoofprint evenly replaced the next in a steady march—not for the buffalo the wild, exultant run of the deer or the antelope. The lumbering buffalo led a solid, practical existence.

Then there were the strange circles beaten in the prairie grass, fifteen feet or more in circumference. They were made by a buffalo calf's mother walking round and round to protect her newly born sleeping calf from wolves at night. I, who had been so often the gullible victim of western stories, thought this the crowning example of a tall tale. But it proved to be true, and ever after those pathetic circles roused in me the deepest sympathy for the mother who vigilantly kept up the ceaseless tramp during the long night. It was rather how I felt about watching over Autie.

The buffalo wallow was another serious obstacle to riding, one that nearly threw me more than once. Ten to fifteen feet in circumference, these were great basins hollowed out by buffalo rolling in the mud. The sun-baked rim did not give under a horse's hooves, but woe to him who tried to leap into the depression and spring out again.

"Libbie, we're going on a hunt tomorrow," Autie announced one day. "You'll ride in an ambulance with Mrs. Miles and Rebecca."

"Fine," I said enthusiastically, though inwardly I wondered if it was safe. It had not been long since the killing of the Indian chiefs, and I feared hostiles at every corner, though I was not about to let Autie see me being anything less than game again so soon. My fear of the Indians had disgraced me enough. Besides, no women had been taken on hunts before, at least not that I knew of, and it was, I sensed, Autie's way of giving me a gift.

Still, when we were settled in the ambulance and I discovered a cavalry detachment waiting to escort us, I grew more nervous—why so much protection unless trouble was expected? And when Katherine Miles began to moan that she wished her husband would ride with her instead of ahorseback, my anxiety increased—what could be severe enough to make a cavalryman leave his horse for a wagon? I listened for, and heard, the small signs of change on a cavalry march—the sudden rattle of steel, short and low exclamations from the troopers, horses' ears jumping into erect alertness from a listless droop, the click of the hoof that evidenced a change of gait. Each small signal set me to scanning the horizon to find the cause, and each time I saw behind every tuft of grass, every sagebrush and clump of cactus, the hidden movements of a hostile Indian. Once, coming to a stream, I felt the whole train suddenly jerk to a halt. In alarm, I stuck my head out the side, only to have the company physician explain that a well-armed foe had stopped us.

"As soon as the essence-peddler sees fit to move on, we'll march," the doctor said laughingly, and the whole command waited on the pleasure of a skunk.

But then the cry was heard. "Buffalo!" My eyes saw only great black blotches against the faultless sky, for I had not then ever seen a buffalo, and I attributed to them the ferocity of the tiger, the strength of the lion. I had no idea how peaceful the big beasts were if left alone.

In a low voice Autie gave orders for the hunt, and instantly all the merry bantering of the horsemen stopped. They murmured, each soldier examining his girth, bit, bridle, stirrups, and firearms. Then, at a low signal, they all gave rein to their excited horses and dashed up from the little divide where they had hidden, leeward so that the quick nostrils of the buffalo picket might not sniff danger. Within minutes they were lost to our sight over a rise, and we had nothing for it but to wait patiently.

After a bit Tom came riding up to announce that Autie had wounded a buffalo and waited for us before he put in the death shot. I saw Katherine pale, and I felt a trifle weak myself, but on we went until we were confronted with a huge beast pawing the ground, his short tail waving defiance and rage, his bloodshot eyes glittering from beneath the thick mat of bushy hair on his forehead, his horns ripping up the sod. As the officers darted up to him, he plunged forward to gore their horses and, failing, dug his hoofs into the soil and tore up the earth, throwing the dust about him in his fury.

Autie gave the telling shot, and mercifully the big beast rolled over, shook his frame once, and struggled no more. We had left the ambulance to walk around him, using up adjectives at an alarming rate trying to describe our surprise at the size of the beast when suddenly Autie grabbed Katherine Miles—a general's wife! had he no better sense?—and placed her on the dead carcass. Though she screamed in terror, Autie handed her a knife and told her to cut a tuft from the head as a trophy. The poor woman's hands trembled so much that Tom had to cut it for her. Autie told her she was now the queen of the hunt, and she managed to thank him graciously, though it was plain she was miserably uncomfortable. Rebecca and I were each given a tuft, and we retired to the carriage rather than watch the cutting up of the animal. Our soldiers were unskilled at this butchery—not having the long practice of the Indians—and, as Autie told me later, they made a bloody job worse by their inexperience.

Later in the day, during an attack on a particularly ferocious bull, one of the riders went down. We watched from our safe distance with our hearts in our throats. None could identify the wounded man. Rebecca, who had captivated all the single men but had not given her heart to any one soldier, was in deep sympathy but curiously removed from the anxiety Katherine and I felt, each wondering for our husband's safety. At last the doctor rode toward us, saying that a certain sergeant had been thrown after his horse stepped in a prairie-dog hole. Though he lay motionless for an alarming time, he soon enough jumped up and declared himself "all right." It was suspected, however, that his arm was sprained. What was really needed, the doctor explained, was some whiskey to insure that the injured man did not faint.

Quietly Katherine Miles produced a small vial of whiskey and offered it to the doctor. We all hid smiles of amazement, for she was well-known as a vociferous teetotaler. "You never know," she explained haughtily, "when there might be an emergency."

"You don't mean Mrs. Miles," Autie exclaimed that night. "Old lady, you're wrong. She's never had a drop."

"No, Autie," I said, "she must carry it for emergencies."

"I wonder what she considers an emergency," he mused, and I threw a pillow at him for his suspicions.

"Old lady, we're going on our last buffalo hunt of the summer, and J. C. Evans is coming to join us," Autie announced triumphantly one day.

"The politician?" I asked with surprise.

"Yes. I've been after him ever so long, and he's finally found time to come. You will make him welcome, won't you?" He looked like a pleading young boy, asking me please to like his friends.

I wanted to remind him that I'd entertained almost two hundred people since the summer began—friends of his, lady friends of mine, official army visitors, even two English dukes—and I suspected I could make one more guest welcome. But Mr. Evans was more important to Autie than most of our visitors—Autie still harbored political ambitions, though he never voiced them to me. Still, I knew that he sometimes wanted a way out of the army and saw politics as the answer.

"Yes, Autie," I sighed. "Eliza will cook buffalo steaks for him, and I shall ramble on at length about the glories of life on the prairie."

"Libbie, there's no need to be sarcastic!" he replied indignantly.

J. C. Evans, whom I'd never met, turned out to be an enormous man, surely almost three hundred pounds and far too much for any of our horses. He rode in the ambulance with me, and I found him distasteful after we'd driven ten feet from camp.

"Well, well, so you're Libbie! Armstrong talks a great deal of you and how game you are."

I smiled but could think of no appropriate reply.

"How game are you, Mrs. Custer?"

Was it my imagination or was that question accompanied by a leer? "Not very," I replied. "I'm afraid many things on the prairie alarm me. Like vermin."

"Armstrong tells me you take everything in stride and are always ready for a little fun," he said, inching closer to me on the bench that ran the side of the ambulance. He was not an attractive man, his bulk coming not just from large stature but from an indulgence in food and drink. His face tended toward the florid, and his chin hung in folds from his face. As he spoke to me, sweat glistened on his forehead, in spite of a pleasant prairie breeze.

Autie came riding back just then. "Are you two getting along famously?" he asked in the too-hearty tone that he used when he was uncertain.

I smiled at him, my expression a frozen imitation of someone who is "getting along famously," but my adversary said, "Yes, yes, of course, Armstrong. You just go on and find those buffalo for us."

Autie shot me one curious look and then rode away. For the rest of the ride to the hunt, I dodged Mr. Evans's innuendos and denied his suggestions. If things really got sticky, I reasoned, I could always call on the ambulance driver for help. It seemed to me we rode farther that day to find buffalo than we ever had before. Mr. Evans, when his attention could be diverted from me, was enthralled with the jackrabbits, the speed with which the staghounds chased them, the hawks that circled the prairie—in short, everything he saw.

We camped on the prairie that night without much privacy, so that I had little occasion to tell Autie of his friend's advances. Next morning the hunters were off at dawn—Mr.

Evans having been trusted to a sturdy horse—and I was mercifully left behind to follow more leisurely in the ambulance.

After a good run the hunters returned triumphant. Twenty-four buffalo had been shot, but the buffalo had extracted their toll. One of the party had been literally herded into the creek by an angry bull; one horse had been gored, and another had the hide scraped off the length of its side by a horn; a newcomer to buffalo hunting sported a hole in his sleeve, which revealed that the aim of his pistol had not been quite what he intended it to be; and still another complained that the palm of his hand, blackened by powder, smarted a great deal, though he could not explain where the ball went. But it was J. C. Evans who had suffered the worst.

Having spotted his buffalo, he'd taken off at a breakneck speed—a foolish thing for any novice in country dotted with prairie-dog holes, but doubly so for a man of his weight. Trying to circle his buffalo, Evans positioned his horse so that its flank was scraped by the enraged buffalo's horns. The horse in turn bolted, and though Evans—to hear Autie tell it—made a valiant effort to keep his seat, he lost his balance and went headlong to the ground, right in front of the furious buffalo bull.

Every soldier within sight rushed the bull, who fortunately decided it was more valiant to run than to fight and left the country before Evans regained consciousness. When Autie told me this, I had to restrain myself from saying, "My compliments to the buffalo." After a period of insensibility, Evans rebounded with a black eye and bruised cheek to show for his adventure—"no money could buy these souvenirs," he declared—and went on with the hunt. Grudgingly, I gave him credit for boldness in that, but his other boldness solicited only my disgust.

Autie was perfectly blind to the man's advances to me, but not Tom. "Libbie," he cried, riding alongside the ambulance that bore us back to camp, "wasn't Evans here a bully sport?"

I stared at him. A bully sport? Tom had never, ever used those words in his life! "Yes," I managed to agree, "bully."

Thereafter Tom rode alongside us, bragging all the while

on Mr. Evans's sportsmanship, in spite of dark and threatening glances from the latter. And I had all I could do to keep
from laughing aloud. In addition to humiliating Evans, Tom
showed me that our friendship could continue.

Late that night, as we three sat under the fly of our tent,
Tom said jokingly, "You know, Autie, I think Evans is sweet
on Libbie."

"Of course he is," Autie agreed casually, "who wouldn't
be?"

Tom's face clouded for just a minute, but when he answered, his tone was light again. "I'm serious. You'd better
watch out for competition."

"My friends," Autie said calmly, "know better than to
have designs on my wife. I'd kill the man who looked at her
in the wrong way."

Or beat him senseless, I thought with a shudder, remembering James Coker.

The next day the hunters went out again, but Autie
loosed his staghounds ahead of them. Contrary to their usual
habit, the dogs became separated from Autie and followed
others of the party. Several of the dogs were hounding a
buffalo when some of the party thoughtlessly opened fire.
Autie's favorite dog, Maida, the companion of all his marches
the past winter, was killed instantly by a shot from Evans's
rifle.

"Terribly sorry," he apologized, "but you know how it
goes. Dog got in the way." Mr. Evans, not devoted to animals
himself, could not fathom Autie's attachment to his animals,
and his apology reflected his inability to understand.

One night as summer drew to a close I came upon Eliza
sitting on a stump, staring off into the Kansas sunset. When I
spoke to her—"Eliza, is something the matter?"—she looked
at me with the most solemn face I've ever seen.

"Miss Libbie," she said, "I'm lonely out here."

"Lonely?" I laughed at first, not believing her. "Eliza,
you have us, and we're family."

"No, you're not," she said deliberately. "You and the

ginnel are good to me, but it's not the same. I'se alone. You's always got the ginnel, but I ain't got nobody, and there ain't no picnics, nor church sociables, nor buryings out here."

"But, Eliza," I said, absolutely dumbfounded as she brushed aside a tear, "you've always been so happy, so cheerful . . . and you've always had more men around you than any other woman I know." It was true—she'd fed them all from the bounty of our table, increasing our food bills by no small amount.

"That don't matter, Miss Libbie," she said. "What good's men if'n they's just after a good time? It's not like you and the ginnel."

Little you understand about that, I thought. "What can I do to help?"

"Nothin'. I'se gonna leave, go to Leavenworth. I know a few other cooks there. . . ." She looked half-afraid that I would forbid her to go.

"The general won't eat without you here," I said.

"Yes, ma'am, he will. There's cooks in Hays City waiting for work. He'll be just fine. And Miss Libbie, I got to go."

When I reported all this to Autie, he stormed and ranted and took off for Eliza's tent in the dark of the night. I heard loud voices raised—both Autie's deep voice and Eliza's lighter one—but I could not make out the words.

"She's going," he said when he came back, in a tone that clearly indicated that he couldn't believe any of his inner circle, even his cook, would leave him. "She's been with me since the war, and she's leaving. What will I do?"

"Look at it from her point of view, Autie. She's not getting any younger . . . and she probably wants a home and family."

"Insolent, that's what she was," he said, ignoring the fact that I'd spoken. "Just plain insolent. Told me I'd have to make do without her."

I hardly saw that as insolent, but I didn't think this was the time to tell Autie that.

Autie ranted and raved, working himself into such a fit that by the time Eliza left, two days later, he barely nodded at her, and I could see that her heart was broken. I followed her to the ambulance that was to take her to Hays City and said, "Remember not to look right or left," a joking reference to the scare that had been put into all of us about the evils of Hays City.

"No, ma'am," she said dully. "The ginnel? He ain't forgiven me?"

"He'll get over it, Eliza," I said. "You must do what you feel you have to. Here." And I handed her thirty dollars, the most I could spare from my meager housekeeping fund.

"Miss Libbie, I think these last years I done worked for you and not him, and I'll never forget you."

We hugged, and I watched her ride off. She never looked back, and I could tell from her rigid back that she was having a hard time controlling her emotions.

"The disloyal wretch gone?" Autie asked when I returned.

"Yes, Autie, she's gone . . . with no 'God's blessing' from you." He ignored me, and I went boldly on. "You know, Autie, for years the rumor has been that she was your mistress as well as your cook. Whether or not that was true, you could at least have bid her farewell."

He looked astounded. "You've heard those rumors?"

"Of course. Haven't you?"

"Well . . . yes, but I . . . I always thought you were protected from them."

"Were they true, Autie?" I asked my question directly, looking straight at him.

"Of course not," he said with predictable indignation. "Libbie, how could you even think that, you who are the one love of my life?"

Ah, Autie, sometimes you protested too much. But I guess we'll never know about Eliza.

The summer ended with a blow that once again destroyed my confidence in Autie—and threatened my love for him. Rebecca and I had walked out one evening to the edge of the camp to catch the breeze. It had been one of those stifling days on the prairie when nothing moves, not one blade of

grass, and the air hangs heavy, as though in anticipation of a
storm. Toward evening great dark clouds began to pile up to
the west, and we thought to catch the breeze and watch the
storm approach.

When the lightning looked to be moving closer, we reluctantly returned to camp, Rebecca to her small tent and I
to our larger quarters. But as I approached, loud voices
stopped me.

"I know Monahsetah had another baby," Autie was saying. "What has that to do with me?"

"Everything," Tom replied. "The baby has blue eyes and
red in its hair."

"There's no proof," Autie retorted too quickly.

"Monahsetah is all the proof that's needed, Autie. For
God's sake . . ."

"Libbie will never see that baby," Autie said fiercely,
"and if she does, we'll attribute the red hair and blue eyes to
you."

"No, brother, we won't," Tom said in tones of steel that
I'd never heard from him before. "I have lied to Libbie for
the last time."

"You won't tell her. . . ." Was there just a hint of begging in Autie's voice?

"No, I won't tell her, unless you force me to. But, Autie,
be warned . . . you best treat Libbie with all the kindness
she deserves, or I'll do worse than tell her about Monahsetah."

Tom left our tent so abruptly that I barely had time to
round one corner and get out of his sight. He marched away,
his back straight and stiff. Hidden by the side of the tent, I
stood motionless as a wave of nausea swept over me. Then I
fled to the river and was sick.

"Libbie!" Autie said when I returned, having dabbed
river water on my face in an effort to hide swollen eyes.
"Where have you been? Even with the sentries, you know
better than to be out at night. I was scared half out of my
mind." His arms reached to enfold me.

"I'm sure you were, Autie," I said, moving away from his
open arms. But I said nothing about Monahsetah. To have

mentioned her new baby would have been to admit to eaves-
dropping . . . and besides, I had no idea what to say. How
did I tell my husband that I knew he had dallied with an
Indian woman? And if I told him, what did I do next? What
would life without Autie be like?

AN
INTERLUDE

Chapter Fifteen

 I FOUND OUT SOON ENOUGH WHAT LIFE WITHOUT AU-
tie would be like. We returned to Leavenworth in
October, and by November he was in Chicago
visiting Phil Sheridan, who was then quite ill. "The general,"
he wrote, "is improving but requires 'setters-up' with him at
night." Phil, weak as he was, sent kindest regards, which
recalled to my mind Autie's terrible jealousy, leading him
once to imply that even Little Phil was sweet on me. Now,
with campaigns in his mind, Autie was only too glad to sit up
at night with Phil, with apparently no jealousy. Autie, no one
could ever accuse you of being consistent!

I had never told Autie what I knew about Monahsetah
. . . what I had long suspected and now knew for the truth.
Instead of confronting him, I simply withdrew, as though
into my own little shell. Oh, I had withdrawn before, after
he'd beaten James Coker and after I'd first realized that Autie had cheated on me, but this was different . . . and he
knew it. At first Autie was puzzled and overcareful of me,

always trying to please in a way that was unlike a man who generally wanted things to go his way. But I was curiously unaffected by his eagerness, neither scorning his advances nor accepting them.

"Libbie," he said one night, "we have not been man and wife for some time now."

"That's true, Autie," I said.

"Why? I . . . I miss you. You know I love you."

"I love you, too, Autie." It was true. I did love him. I was not even angry with him. I was just . . . distanced.

"Is it . . . because we've not had children?" He looked away, as though the subject were painful. "I thought we'd decided . . ."

"Decided what, Autie? That we are fortunate? You decided that . . . but I always thought you were convincing yourself."

"No," he said a trifle too quickly, "I really mean it. It's much more important to me to have you with me."

"That's not the thing, anyway," I said, wearying of the discussion. "I just need time . . ."

"Time away from me?"

"Perhaps."

Autie's puzzlement turned to anger later. He paced the floor and talked loudly about the naturalness of marital relationships, the unnaturalness of abstinence. And finally he resorted to threats. "There are always women interested in me," he said haughtily. "I've never . . . *never* even considered another woman, but by God, Libbie, you force a man too far. . . ."

Oh, Autie, why did you lie to me? I thought back on my own temptations . . . mostly James Coker . . . and how seriously I took the marriage vow. And I knew that Autie had never taken the vow as seriously. To know that meant that I lived in a house built on shifting sand—what else would suddenly give way and leave me facing a yawning abyss? In odd moments I longed for my father—he who had opposed my marriage to Autie and who was, I now saw, the one person on earth who would protect me no matter what.

Life without Autie? It was like looking through a glass

darkly. I could not see a future without Autie, but neither could I see a return to our happier days. And I knew we couldn't go on as we were for the rest of our lives.

After visiting Phil Sheridan in Chicago, Autie went on to see Evans, the politician whom I despised. I thought Autie would have no more to do with him after he carelessly shot Maida, but Autie protested, "It was an accident, Libbie, just an accident. And he might do me some good politically." Autie grew proportionately more calculating as his army career grew more threatened.

He reported a grand reception at Evans's private club in Detroit, where he played euchre and met "some very influential men." Next it was Washington, where he testified in hearings about the reorganization of the army.

All the while I was at Leavenworth, keeping company with the ladies of the post during the day, fretting in loneliness at night, remembering the happy summer we'd just spent, and trying to puzzle out our future. Ah, Autie, I could have done without you . . . if you'd not been such grand company and made such a lark of life.

Autie wrote of his festive travels as if there were no rift between us. From Chicago: "We had seen a performance of Lydia Thompson's *Blondes* at the Opera House, and the *Times*—a bitter, copperhead sheet—informed the public that I was pursuing blondes instead of the dusky maidens of the Prairies." In his self-absorption, Autie was so blind to the cause of the rift between us that he could make untimely jokes that were not funny at all.

I was no more encouraged by the report from New York, where he had stopped on his way to Washington: "In New York I went with Mrs. Cram to see Jefferson in *Rip Van Winkle*. The acting surpassed anything I have ever seen. . . . When the daughter, grown to a young lady, recognizes in the decrepit, tattered old man her lost father, there was not one person not affected by it. . . . I never saw the play before, nor, so deep an impression has it made on me, do I desire ever to see it again." Indifferently, I wondered who

Mrs. Cram was but could not place her and was thus left with my imagination to fill in the possibilities. I truly doubted that she was eighty years old, blind, and fat. My mind recalled only too well Autie's 1866 adventures in New York City, when he'd dined at Delmonico's, attended theater and opera with beautiful women on his arm, mingled with wealthy capitalists, and then came home to Monroe to tell me all about it, leaving me wondering how much of the story I was not hearing.

By mid-December, Autie was in Monroe, where he decided to stay for the holidays . . . which left me alone at Leavenworth, sunk in self-pity over my second Christmas alone. Autie returned in February, ostensibly to settle down to writing those memoirs he always talked of but did little to accomplish. Now, fidgety and uncertain, he would insist I take my usual position at his right elbow to watch while he scribbled furiously on sheets of foolscap for five, perhaps ten, minutes. Then he would bound up.

"Prospects for the Seventh are not good, Libbie, not good at all," he would declaim, as though I'd not heard this speech ten times already. "A regiment from the Pacific Coast department wants to take our place. I've made application for a position at West Point." Nothing came either of the West Point position or the Pacific Coast troops, and we stayed, uneasily, at Leavenworth. The rift between us did not heal, and we were edgily polite with each other. Abroad in the post, we were happy and gay, laughing together, me always clinging to Autie's arm. Inside our private quarters, we were strangers.

A new rumor stirred his anxieties. "The Seventh will be broken up," he said. "I've made an application to accompany its headquarters to whatever post it is assigned, but I don't know. . . ."

By April Autie could stand it no longer and was off to New York on extended leave, taking me as far as Monroe.

"Autie, I'll go with you," I said at the last minute, pushing aside my indifference because I hated the thought of being left alone again in Monroe. Mama, unable to care for the house on Monroe Street, again lived in a nearby town with a distant relative, and I would be truly alone except for Autie's parents. "I've got to see about a position that will bring us some money," he answered earnestly. "You'd be bored to tears, darling girl."

"Autie," I asked directly, "what are you going to do?"

He'd been packing—usually my chore—because throwing gloves and socks into a suitcase kept him from looking directly at me. Now he almost mumbled as he lost himself in the closet, supposedly gathering clothes. "You know," he said, halfway over his shoulder, "that silver mine."

The Stevens silver mine, near Georgetown, Colorado, was a wild hare of an idea that he'd become involved with the previous year, along with Tom and that infamous Mr. Evans. Autie saw it as the route to fortune for us. "Can it be," he wrote earlier that year when we were apart, "that my little Standby and I who have long wished to possess a fortune are about to have our hopes realized?"

"Astor's for it," he now said loftily, referring to none other than John Jacob Astor, one of the wealthiest men I'd ever heard of. "So's Levi Morton, and Jay Gould . . . you watch, Libbie, the list will grow."

"Autie," I said, "there are no miracles, there is no instant wealth. You can't pin our hopes on this wild scheme."

"I've subscribed thirty-five thousand dollars to the mines," he said indignantly. "I know this is a worthwhile project."

Now, any other wife would have been alarmed by the sum Autie named, but I simply stood and laughed aloud.

"What are you laughing about?" That old Custer blush, which he never could hide when embarrassed, began to creep upon him, and I watched, fascinated, as his face turned red.

"You don't have thirty-five thousand dollars."

"No," he admitted, "but my name's worth something."

So that was it. Autie had sold his name to attract other investors . . . men like Astor and Gould. It was rather like Judas and the thirty pieces of silver. I wanted to cry that a war hero, a man who'd led troops so loyal they'd have died for him in an instant, could have sunk to selling shares in a questionable silver mine. But hating myself, I said nothing, and Autie left for New York.

"Within an hour," he wrote from that city, "I had received more invitations than I can accept. . . . A friend has taken a box at the Academy of Music for ten nights. He has invited me to occupy a seat in it whenever I choose. Miss Kellogg also expects me behind the scenes." Miss Kellogg, the actress, loomed large in Autie's letters: "Tonight I am to sit with Miss Kellogg in her box at the Academy of Music— she does not sing. At her request I am sending you a paper with an account of her, with her compliments." *How kind of her,* I thought. And then, "This morning I took a walk with Miss Kellogg on Broadway. . . . To show you how careful Miss Kellogg is in her conduct with gentlemen, she told me she has never ridden with a gentleman alone but twice in New York." *Did Autie run along behind the carriage?* I wondered, though I never put the question in my letters. Later he wrote, "The old Irish servant who takes care of my rooms looks at me with suspicion when I return, sometimes not till morning, the bed not having been touched. I think she believes I do not pass my nights in the most reputable manner. In fact, circumstances, as she sees them, are against me." And how, Autie dear, *were* you passing your nights?

Autie wrote of fashions—pongee parasols were the style, but chignons unpopular; and of investments—the Morton and Bliss firm of lawyers took ten thousand dollars of mining stock, $60,000 was now disposed of; but never what I wanted to hear: that he was coming home.

Autie was like a bad habit. I did not expect to fall into his arms when he returned, but I was used to having him with me, and without him I felt anchorless. That long period in Monroe—taking Sunday supper with his ailing mother, laughing at Father Custer's jokes, strolling about town and nodding to all those people I'd known all my life—gave me a new perspective on my relationship with Autie. I might never —would never—trust him again nor feel as passionately in love as I once had, but I missed him. I missed the excitement, the vitality he brought to his own life and to mine. I longed for Autie . . . and the frontier, in spite of Indians, rattlesnakes, floods, and storms. Could I, I wondered, have all that again without renewing our passion? Perhaps I knew that if I once let Autie touch me, all that longing would come flooding back and I would succumb, Monahsetah or not. Ah, how naive we can be sometimes.

In September he wrote unhappily, "I presume you have seen the announcements of the War Department in the papers. Personally I should have preferred the plains, but for your sake. Duty in the South has somewhat of a political aspect, which I always seek to avoid." The Seventh had been scattered among several small posts in the South, and Autie was assigned command of a two-company contingent at Elizabethtown, Kentucky, near Louisville. His silver mine had collapsed in thin air, and Autie was once more a penniless soldier on active duty.

"Well," Autie demanded, "how do you like it?"

I turned to look out the long parlor window. Below me lay Elizabethtown—Betsytown, as Autie was already calling it. Even at midday the streets were nearly empty. Before me stretched one main road, with wooden buildings sadly in need of paint, their disrepair not hidden by the lush green trees that lined the road. At a distance I saw a church spire and the courthouse—on closer inspection I would find both needed repair. But Autie had located a fine house, one completely furnished with four bedrooms, a good well, a stable for the horses, and a view.

"The house is fine, Autie," I said, "but the town is dull, dull as dishwater." At his look of dismay I protested, "You can't tell me you wouldn't rather be at Leavenworth!"

"Yes," he admitted, "I would. But I thought . . . well, I hoped . . . oh, Libbie, I thought we could concentrate on each other here."

I looked long and hard at him. "Perhaps we can, Autie." And I knew that I was giving in again, that I was captured by the force of his personality. To change the mood, I asked lightly, "When can we have a ball? All the time I was in Monroe, I longed to dance until my feet fell off."

"And dance you shall," he said happily, sweeping me into an impromptu waltz for which he whistled the accompaniment. It was comfortable to have Autie's arms about me again, and I smiled at him. "Libbie, Libbie," he said hoarsely, wrapping me in his arms.

Response is a puzzling thing, and totally without logic or reason. As he kissed me gently, I found myself responding with a passion that I thought I'd conquered. We hurried back to the hotel, brushing aside curious questions from Tom— "Did you like the house, old lady?"—to retire to the privacy of our room.

We were neither tentative nor shy in our reunion, the old longing rising to sweep us away as though there had been no distance between us.

"Libbie," Autie panted, spent at last, "why have we been apart so long?"

"It was time, Autie," I said, "it was time." And I never mentioned Monahsetah, banishing her at that moment from my memory—or so I thought.

"And what," I asked laughingly at supper, as our pleasure in each other seemed to radiate around us, "will the Seventh do to earn its pay in Elizabethtown? There are no Indians here."

He smiled and put a finger to his lips, as though telling a great secret. "There's the Ku Klux Klan . . . and there are bootleggers who make moonshine in the hills. I thought you'd like the peace."

"Oh," I sighed, "I do. But I miss Kansas . . . this is really dull, Autie."

"I'll keep it from being dull for you," he said, his eyes twinkling.

"Autie," I whispered in protest, "we cannot spend two years in the bedroom."

"No, but we can spend a good portion of it there," he answered, his knee moving against mine under the table. We sat in the dining room of the Hill House hotel where we were staying until we could move into our own house.

Later we took coffee on the veranda with Tom and their sister, Maggie, who had recently married Lieutenant James Calhoun of the Seventh. Jimmi, we called him. We'd been together no more than ten minutes when Jimmi began to yawn and stretch. "Guess we'll turn in," he said, turning to his wife. "Maggie?"

"Of course," she answered, though I thought in the darkness I was conscious of a little nervous gesture, as though she were embarrassed at her groom's haste to retire.

"That's the trouble with you newlyweds," Tom drawled. "You always tire out so quick and have to go to bed."

"Tom Custer!" Maggie's tone became that of an older sister, disciplining a wayward younger sibling.

"Well," he complained, "it's true."

I could see Autie tugging at Tom's sleeve—out of Maggie's line of vision. As soon as the newlyweds left us, Autie began to whisper to Tom, though they refused my pleas to be let in on the secret.

"Lovely night, isn't it, old lady?" Tom asked innocently, while Autie replied, "I bet she misses the plains and those nights where the stars closed down all around us."

"Yes, but not the rustle in the grass that I always thought was Indians, nor the lightning that I always thought meant a flood," I replied. "Now, what are you two whispering about?"

"Nothing," Autie replied. "Old lady, it's been a long day. Don't you think you'd best retire?"

Suspicious, I asked, "Aren't you coming, too?"

"I'll be up directly."

Knowing that I was foolhardy in trusting them, I went to our room in the hotel. I made my toilette, wrapped myself in a gown, brushed my hair a hundred strokes and more, and still wondered where Autie could be. Peering out the window, I saw nothing but darkness—only an occasional gas street lamp—and heard nothing except crickets.

Suddenly that quiet was broken by a wild commotion. Men shouted, horses neighed, someone banged a metal spoon against a heavy pot, and someone else broke into an unharmonious melody on the Jew's harp. The melee slowly developed into a long chant, "Maggie and Jimmi, Maggie and Jimmi!"

Were I dressed, I'd have been on the veranda in a minute to be part of the commotion, but now I felt trapped by my own nightgown. I peered out the window and could see a mob of men below me, some carrying torches. Throwing propriety to the winds, I donned a wrapper and rushed into the hallway, only to meet Maggie and Jimmi in the hall. He was struggling to pull up a pair of suspenders, while she clutched a wrapper about herself.

"Jimmi's going down to quiet them," she said, as he bolted down the stairs.

"Quiet there. A man can't get any sleep!" came a quavery voice from a room down the hall.

"That's that old man from the dinner table," she whispered, "the one who had his eye on you."

"He could hardly see with either eye," I said. "I thought he was ninety-five!" I'd been so indignant that this old man had ogled me that I had made a great show of my attachment to Autie. "Come on, Maggie, we might as well join the fun."

"Oh, Libbie, you wouldn't!"

"Yes, I would, and so will you," I said, grabbing her hand.

We reached the front door in time to see Jimmi being pulled around the circle of men in a wheelbarrow, a nightcap set on his head. Every time he tried to rise, rough hands pushed him back into his inelegant seat, amid much laughter and shouting.

Finally, hoarsely, he cried, "Drinks on me at the tavern!" and a great shout went up among the men. Released from his wheelbarrow, Jimmi bounded up the stairs to put a protective arm around Maggie. "I shall have to go have a drink with them," he said. "Are you all right?"

She nodded, and I murmured, "Of course."

Autie came up the stairs long enough to say, "I won't drink, but I should go with them."

He came in two hours later, but there was not a breath of whiskey about him. I'm sure our passion surpassed that of the honeymooners down the hall.

We had not been in Betsytown long when I began to fidget in my mind. I was not used to living in a house, apart from everyone else, and the spirit of make-do that characterized our army posts was missing. Here the army families were scattered about the town rather than on top of each other as at Hays and Harker, and somehow the whole atmosphere was different. I was homesick for the frontier. And daily I watched Autie grow more restless.

"Wretched dull town," he stormed one day. "The Indians are overrunning the West—did you read about the latest bout of atrocities?—and here I am stuck in this damn small town, chasing an occasional moonshiner!"

"Your memoirs, Autie," I reminded, barely able to hide the amusement in my voice. "They're your ticket to permanent fame."

"Memoirs be damned," he said—and I must add that Autie was rarely profane—"I want action. I want another Washita."

Autie could never understand that at age thirty-three he'd already had more victories than most men are accorded in their lifetimes. He might never have another one—but then, I didn't believe that either.

"Patience, Autie," I said, "patience. Little Phil will send for you again."

"And none too soon," he said forcefully. Then Autie had the grace to laugh at himself. "Oh, Libbie, what would I do without you to keep me humble?"

Eventually during that stay in Betsytown, Autie abandoned his memoirs in favor of a series of articles about his frontier adventures. *Galaxy Magazine* had contracted to publish these pieces, and I guess Autie saw that opportunity as a bird in hand—worth several memoirs that remained in the bush.

"Libbie, pack my bags! I'm going on a buffalo hunt." Autie's voice preceded him up the stairs to the bedroom, where I was at my desk writing a letter.

"Autie, you can't hunt buffalo in Kentucky." I laughed, wondering what he had in mind now.

"No, no," he answered impatiently, waving a piece of paper at me. "I'm going to Leavenworth to take a . . . a czar on a hunt."

I was flabbergasted. "A czar?"

"Well," he admitted, "his third son. But still, Russian nobility. Phil's the host, and he's asked me. . . . Cody is to be the guide." He meant, of course, Buffalo Bill Cody, the wild West show entrepreneur. After the first mention of the famed showman, Autie talked incessantly of "my good friend, Cody." Autie's friendships were often based on fame and had little to do with either interests or time shared.

"And I?" I asked archly.

"You can stay at the Galt House in Louisville. The duke —that's what he is, a duke—will return to Louisville with me. Old lady, you don't mind, do you?"

"No," I lied, "I don't mind, Autie." In truth I had been on enough buffalo hunts in Kansas that I was a seasoned camper and should, I thought, be allowed to go. But if Phil's invitation hadn't included me, there was nothing for it. I would wait in a hotel and once again experience all Autie's joy secondhand. I bit my lip and began packing.

Autie talked nonstop for the next twelve hours, and it was with almost relief that I bid him good-bye in Louisville and settled down to wait for three long weeks. Letters kept me posted: Wild Bill had persuaded the Sioux chief Yellow Tail to camp near the hunting party, with four hundred of his tribe, and they danced for the duke at night, which made my blood crawl with fear; the duke brought down eight buffalo each day and was a "superb but almost reckless rider"; the Indians demonstrated hunting buffalo with a bow and arrow, greatly intriguing the duke; and finally, a telegram told me, "Gen. Sheridan & staff & myself invited by Grand Duke to accompany him to Denver."

In Denver there was a ball, and in St. Louis, Topeka, and Jefferson City, receptions. My mind asked the question no matter how I tried to blot it out: what, Autie, are you doing at all these fancy parties, with women who are much impressed by officers in uniform? Perhaps, I told myself, they were all smitten by the duke and never looked at Autie —but I didn't believe that either.

The duke, Autie reported, was exhausted from the hectic pace and refusing all invitations. Except that he came to Louisville, for the Citizens' Ball and a visit to Mammoth Cave.

"Libbie, Libbie." Autie swept me into his arms the moment he was off the train, forgetting equally the duke and the huge crowd gathered at the Louisville station. He wore his buckskins and smelled of the frontier, though I knew he'd been back in civilization well over ten days. Autie was acting again, but that knowledge made me no less glad to see him.

"Good heavens, the duke," he exclaimed, and turning, pulled me into the railroad car. There he presented me to a strikingly handsome man. Alexis, the grand duke, was tall and solid, a much larger man than Autie, with blond hair that swept back from his forehead in neat, even waves, and sideburns that grew down to meet his muttonchop whiskers, which were strangely dark in color. But it was his eyes that riveted me—blue and direct, like Autie's, only more intense, if that was possible.

"So this is the old lady," he said with evident amusement. "Your husband has been singing your praises, and I hardly thought he'd last out the trip, so anxious was he to return to you. Now I understand why." And with that he bent deep over my hand to kiss it.

I caught my breath, captivated by his charm. Quick as I said, "Your excellency"—Autie had written me that was the proper way to address the duke—I felt myself being tugged at.

"Come, Libbie, we must let the duke and his party detrain."

"Wait, wait, my good man," the duke said. "Don't rush this charming lady away from me. I was just about to have tea and hope that crowd would disappear." He nodded his head toward the window.

"It won't," Autie said curtly. "They've come to see you, and they'll wait until they do."

The duke cocked an eyebrow at Autie in amusement. "Well, so be it. We'll go to the Galt House for tea then." Then he turned to me. "You will save the first dance for me tonight?"

"I'd be honored," I murmured, forcing myself to look directly at him when my every instinct was to avoid those eyes, which could, I was sure, read my very soul.

Autie turned on me in fury as soon as the door to our room closed behind us. "You're captivated by him! You blushed like a schoolgirl . . . you embarrassed me."

"I don't blush, Autie," I reminded him. "You're the one who blushes . . . and if anyone embarrassed you, it was yourself, rushing me out the door so."

"I wanted to make love to my wife," he said in a tone that implied anything but romance. He stood across the room from me, stiff as a board, his face red.

"You're not off to much of a start in that direction," I said hastily, thankful that he'd made me angry enough to hide my confusion.

His mood changed instantly, and he became the contrite little boy. "Sorry, Libbie, I just can't bear to have another man look at you."

"Nor I another woman look at you," I answered, keeping my distance. "How was your trip?" He could not miss my implication.

"What does that mean?" Defensiveness crept into his voice. "You know I've never looked at another woman."

In spite of my resolve to put them behind me, I wanted to invoke Monahsetah and Mrs. Cram—whoever that was— and Miss Kellogg and countless nameless women over the years, but I kept silent, contenting myself with looking directly at him. He apparently found my gaze as hard to face as I had found the duke's, for his eyes shifted downward and he stared at the floor.

"Libbie, must we fight?"

"No," I answered. "But I will dance the first dance with the duke tonight."

He was across the room, his arms around me. "Of course," he said, "it's an honor for you . . . and for me."

His hands began fumbling at the buttons on my dress, and within minutes we were in the bed. As Autie's hands roamed over me, teasing and touching until I was on fire, I closed my eyes and saw only those deep, intense eyes beneath that blond hair. It was not Autie I was seeing.

There is something about having had a man make love to you in the middle of the afternoon that invests a woman with a certain extra charm or appeal—rather like walking around with a secret about yourself that the world doesn't know, yet somehow the world senses your allure. That is the only way I can explain the fact that the duke danced every dance but three with me that night . . . and invited me to New Orleans.

"I don't know if Autie can leave Elizabethtown again so soon," I murmured, "but I'll certainly discuss your invitation with him."

"I suppose you must," he said, "but I'd rather you didn't. I mean to spirit you away from him."

"Your Excellency!" I reproved gently, now looking anywhere but at those blue eyes. Could he, I wondered desperately, see through me and discern my fantasies of the afternoon?

"Oh, I know it's impossible. And your husband is too good a fellow. But you've stolen my heart, old lady." Strangely, it was not out of place for the duke to use Autie's term of affection. "And you must call me Alexis. No more of this 'excellency' business, please."

"Alexis," I murmured.

We did not go to New Orleans. I never even told Autie about the invitation, though I told the duke next day that both Autie and I regretted that his duties would not allow him to accept the kind invitation. I'm sure he wondered why Autie never mentioned it, but so be it. I had lied, yes, but I reasoned it was best to put temptation behind both of us.

We were at the station in Louisville when the duke's train pulled out, and in my last glimpse of him I seemed to feel those blue eyes piercing through my little lie. Grand

Duke Alexis was a memory I held on to . . . and sometimes pulled to the front of my consciousness when I felt the need of comfort.

The knock on our door came late one April afternoon. Autie and I were seated at his desk—those everlasting memoirs!—and he, grateful for any interruption, leapt up to answer. Before I could blink, he was bounding back up the stairs to the study, and I knew exactly what that paper was he was waving in his hand. I had not moved about the country with Autie without learning a few things.

"Libbie? What are you doing sitting on the table?" He froze, one hand holding the paper aloft, as though he were stopped in midgesture as he started to wave it.

"Staying out of your way," I said calmly.

"Not so easy!" he cried, grabbing me to swing me about the room, though my feet never touched the floor. "Orders! We're going to the Dakotas—start packing!"

How many times had I heard those words? And yet, the word "Dakotas" caused a great wrench in my midsection. The end of nowhere, I thought.

Unceremoniously Autie deposited me back on the table-top, grabbed a chair, and threw it against the wall.

"Autie!" I tried to sound more horrified than I was. In truth, I didn't care about the chair, and a part of me . . . a big part, in fact . . . shared Autie's excitement.

"It wasn't much of a chair, Libbie, and I couldn't resist. I just had to do something. I'm going to fight Indians again!" The little boy smiled at me with winning charm, as though to ask how I could resist him. I couldn't.

Within an hour the orderlies were at work and our house was torn up. Our kitchen utensils were plunged into barrels and left uncovered, for it took too much time to cover them. Rolls of bedding were wrapped in waterproof cloth, strapped, and roped; pictures and books were crowded into chests and boxes, and the whole of it loaded on a wagon, where it looked a motley assortment. If my father could have seen the sum total of our household goods, after more than ten years of marriage, he would have been horrified, thinking all his worst fears had come true.

I managed to find a quiet corner, where I retired with an atlas. As my finger traced the route from Kentucky almost up to the border of the British possessions, it seemed to me we would be going to Lapland. I longed for the frontier, yes, but I wanted Leavenworth and Big Creek and the familiar frontier, not a whole strange new territory.

But Autie was going back to his regiment and summer campaigns against the Indians. All the while we were in Kentucky, his spirit had been lumbering about the earth; now it could soar free as he once again had a chance to be a soldier, a *real* soldier.

I really was not sorry to leave Betsytown. Our stay there had perhaps been a good hiatus, but it would have been disastrous had we stayed much longer.

THE
DAKOTAS

Chapter Sixteen

OUR THREE TRIUMPHANT YEARS IN THE DAKOTAS WERE a magical time in our lives together. Those were the years when Autie gloried in his military profession. He was *the* Indian fighter on the frontier, and all others, from Wild Bill to Little Phil, paled before his reputation. There were critics, of course—men like Frederick Benteen, who envied Autie's fame and glory, and James Coker, who still bore him the greatest of personal grudges one man can hold against another. But Autie had the confidence of the generals, the respect of most of his men, and the love of his wife.

Monahsetah and society women from St. Louis to New York faded into obscurity as Autie and I renewed the passion —and yes, "obsession" is the word—of our early marriage. We were gloriously, deliriously happy when we were together . . . and yet always there was, for me, a strange but sure knowledge that tragedy waited around the corner. That conviction came to me even as I figured the distance from

Kentucky to Yankton on the map, and it never left during those three years. I could no longer imagine Autie growing old alongside me, and oftentimes when he was gone, I cried myself to sleep.

Our arrival in the Dakotas was neither auspicious nor pleasant. The railroad ended about a mile from Yankton, and we stepped down from the Pullman car—where we'd been surrounded by inlaid woods, mirrors, and plush—to the barest ground I'd ever seen.

"Autie! Where are the grasses?" It was a sunny, warm April day, and to my way of thinking, the prairie should have been bright with the green of new growth, dotted with the various colors of wildflowers. Instead, I saw only brown.

He hooted. "This is the Dakotas, old lady, not Kansas. Spring is later here . . . if it ever arrives. They say they have eight months of winter and four of very late fall. Hurry now, the ladies are being taken to town to the hotel."

"And you?"

"Why, I'll camp with the men."

"I will camp with you," I said firmly.

"Libbie, you don't have to. . . ." Autie was protesting, but his eyes twinkled with delight. "Here, hold these puppies."

One of the dogs had given birth on the train, of all places, so we were laden down with not only five grown dogs but six newborn pups, along with the canaries in their cages. I'd refused to leave them behind, even though Autie suggested the frigid Dakota winters would do them in.

I sat in a corral made of luggage, guarding puppies and birds, while Autie went about the business of laying out camp. Our tent could be pitched only after the camp as a whole was laid out. Meanwhile I could enjoy the warmth of the sun and the familiar sounds of an army camp. We were home again.

I wished later I'd marked the instant, but suddenly the sun vanished and the air took on a chill—slight at first, but increasing so rapidly that it near took my breath away. I gathered the puppies closer to me, holding them in my skirts lest they get too cold. My eyes scanned the endless horizon as though I could predict the weather from the dark clouds I saw to the west.

A house stood on a rise a short distance away, unfinished looking and plain, but still a house. It was so slight that I wasn't sure it would stand, but it was better than a tent. All my years on the Kansas plains had taught me to appreciate any sort of a house that would not blow down, as opposed to the flapping of a tent in a storm.

By the time Autie came back to me, I was torn between coveting the house and worrying about him. "Autie! You don't look well," I said with real concern, for he had developed dark circles under his eyes and begun to cough.

"Several of the men have come down with something," he said, "but I'll be fine. I have to help them finish this."

"I'm going to take the puppies to that house," I said, rising from the trunk on which I sat.

Autie's eye followed the nod of my head. "Libbie, you cannot. We don't know who owns that."

"I can tell no one lives there," I said firmly, "and I'm going to spend the night there. I expect you to join me."

He laughed aloud, then made a mock salute. "Yes, ma'am, I'll be there."

The house was of two stories, which I could hardly fathom on the frontier, but it was indeed unfinished—no plaster on the walls to weatherproof it and keep out the winds. There was no stove, and we would have to bring water from a distance. But we were in a house.

We had brought Mary, the new cook, with us, and she helped me settle our belongings and drape blankets from the beams of the upper story to separate sleeping areas. Then she bundled up, for by now it was quite cold, and trudged to town with a basket on her arm, returning with a small stock of provisions and word that water and wood were being brought by some of the enlisted men. By then I had the puppies and their mother snuggled on a blanket, and more heavy blankets wrapped around the canaries to protect them.

"It be snowing, Miss Libbie," Mary said.

Snowing in April? Impossible, I wanted to say. But going to the door I saw snow so fine and dense that it made sight impossible.

By the time Autie returned, he was a sick man. Autie, who never gave in to illness, collapsed on the sleeping pallet I'd fixed upstairs. Quietly, so as not to alarm him, I found a soldier and sent him for the doctor, who came hurriedly—he had, he explained, many, many patients that day—and gave me strong medicine to give Autie every hour. He was to remain abed no matter what.

"What" turned out to be a Dakota blizzard. By midafternoon it was dark as night, and snow—fine, powdery white snow—drifted in around the windows, under the eaves, anywhere there was a crack. I had the suffocating feeling that we were trapped, with a white blanket settling over us, and it gave me comfort to know that the camp, full of soldiers, was within yards of our small shelter.

A knock on the door announced the adjutant, who had come for orders. From his bed Autie said weakly, "Break camp. The horses might not survive this storm. Have the soldiers take them into town and beg hospitality from the citizens. Use every house, barn, and cow shed you can. Take those new puppies with you, and see that they are kept warm."

"Yes, sir," he said, saluting smartly, and was gone, but not before I issued my own order to send the doctor again, for Autie seemed to grow weaker and weaker, and I more frantic each moment.

Within minutes we heard horses' hooves outside as the soldiers followed Autie's instructions. And then we were truly alone in that sea of white. Mary and I retired for the night, there being nothing else to do in the cold. I was wrapped in blankets three deep, but still my fingers were so numbed with cold that I feared I would drop Autie's medicine each time I gave it to him. The doctor did not return, and I can't say I was surprised, but I remembered the serious expression on his face when he commanded me to give the medicine every hour. Without it I was sure Autie would perish.

"Miss Libbie? Did you hear that?"

"That thud?" I whispered back. "Yes, Mary, I did. We must see what it is."

Together we flew downstairs toward the front door, where there was loud, desperate pounding. When we halloed, shouts came back to tell us there were soldiers outside. "A couple of us are in bad shape, ma'am," came one voice. "Open the door."

"I can't. It's . . . it's frozen shut." Even as I spoke, Mary and I pried and pulled with all our might. "We've taken down the bar. See if you can push."

Between our feeble efforts and the desperation of the men, we exerted enough force that the door opened with a suddenness that sent eight soldiers falling into the room. They had become lost in the snow and had seen the faint lamp Mary had left in the window. Two were badly frozen, suffering greatly, and we had no way of warming them.

"The carpets, Miss Libbie," Mary said suddenly. "They'se stacked over in that corner."

I had forgotten that the carpets were with our belongings destined for the garrison. We unwrapped the great squares and rolled the poor men into them. Still, they needed some kind of liquor to warm their insides, and much as I blessed Autie for being a teetotaler, I longed for whiskey. Never again, I swore, would I keep house without it.

"Mary, bring me the alcohol that lights the spirit lamps."

"Miss Libbie, if you use that, we can't make no coffee for ourselves."

"Bring it to me, Mary," I said levelly, wondering all the while if it were the kind of alcohol that would blind men. But the groans of these men convinced me I had to take the chance. They coughed and sputtered on the fiery liquid, but the two in such bad shape gradually revived somewhat, though their frozen feet were swollen and extremely painful. Those two men groaned softly throughout the night.

There was no sleep that night, what with running back and forth from Autie to the soldiers. Morning found us surrounded on three sides by drifts as high as a wall, and Autie still too weak to rise. There was little food—the soldiers had

some hardtack, and we had the remains of Mary's basket of
provisions—but Autie was too ill and I too anxious to eat.
The day dragged on—Mary sank into a corner, exhausted,
and I missed the sound of her voice, even raised in complaint. If I rubbed my finger on the window glass and melted
a spot, I could see drifts to the second story, though the wind
had swept a clear place in front of the door.

That night a drove of mules rushed up to the sheltered
side of the house. Their brays had a sound of terror as they
pushed, kicked, and crowded themselves against the frail
wooden structure. Then, as suddenly as they had come, they
rushed away. But throughout the night we heard the occasional neigh of a horse, almost human in its appeal for help,
or a lost dog lifting a howl of distress right under our window. Once the sound at the door was so human that we
opened it, only to see the strange wild eyes of a horse—those
eyes haunted me ever after. We did try to entice the dog
inside, but he disappeared into the night, with me wailing all
the while that he would surely die.

When the night was nearly over, I flew from my bed in
horror at a new and terrifying sound. A drove of hogs,
squealing and grunting, were pushing against the house and
battering at the door. By the time I was again down the
stairs, Mary at my heels, two soldiers were braced against the
door to hold it shut against the determined hogs.

"We'll take turns, ma'am," puffed one soldier. Worried
that their strength would give out before the hogs became
discouraged, I fled back upstairs. Hogs, I reasoned, could not
climb stairs. Exhausted, I fell into a restless sleep, burdened
with bad dreams, until, more pleasantly, I dreamt I smelled
bacon.

"Miss Libbie, you got to eat." There stood Mary with a
tray holding steaming coffee, along with some small bits of
steak and potatoes.

"Mary," I asked, shaking the cobwebs from my brain,
"how did you . . . ?"

"Well," she said reluctantly, "I had some candles . . .
from the train . . . and I figured I could cut them up and

burn them in bits, close together, to get enough flame to cook a bit."

She had stolen candles from the train, in other words, and was now reluctantly admitting to thievery. After hugging her, I ate with relish, and even Autie was able to eat enough to revive.

"Hush, old lady, you'll scare Mary," he said good-naturedly, as I wailed about our situation. "Someone will come help us directly," he assured me.

"Fine for you to say," I said angrily, "when you've lain abed these two nights, and I've been the one alone and terrified."

"How could you be alone with eight soldiers downstairs?" he asked, the twinkle back in his eyes.

Wounded that Autie would not commend my bravery and understand my fears, I curled up in a ball, my back to him in the bed. Autie simply reached over and tousled my hair, and then fell into the most peaceful sleep he'd had in two days.

Help came, of course, as Autie predicted. The officers of the Seventh, new to the Dakotas, were ignorant about the way to survive such weather, but some of the townspeople from Yankton gave them a cutter and led them out to the house.

Soldiers love a good story, and after they investigated the few men who had remained in camp, they came back with stories of men frozen to death and newborn babes come to enough of the laundresses that we could have peopled a children's home. Finally the stories reduced to one infant, born in a tent, apparently healthy in spite of his traumatic arrival, and several men who had suffered badly, but none frozen. The puppies, however, did die, and Autie mourned them as most men might a child.

A day later we were settled in Yankton, with the officers and their families ensconced in the hotel. The townspeople, as though to make up for our rude reception, determined to give us a ball, and we ladies burrowed in trunks for those bits of finery we had not supposed we'd need. Fashions change so rapidly that we found after a few months in the field we were quite out of style, while the officers in their uniforms always looked dashing and never out-of-date. The ball was festive, with even the governor on hand to welcome the Seventh to the Dakotas. Afterward our finery was again buried in the trunk.

But the gaiety went on those spring days in Yankton. Autie ordered a review of the troops in honor of the governor, and the entire unit paraded before him, who sat, mounted, beside the guest of honor. When the part came where the officers leave their companies and ride abreast to salute the commanding officer, I thought Autie would burst with pride. I knew he had a hard time remaining motionless on his horse. Ah, Autie, it may well have been your finest hour—mounted on a fine Kentucky horse, in command of an impressive body of men, the world at your feet.

One day we were invited to lunch aboard the steamer that had been retained to take the regiment's property up the Missouri to Bismarck. Afterward the owner of the steamer gallantly offered to drive me out to camp, and though I longed to ride with Autie, I was forced to accept the offer most graciously. Within minutes I regretted it. Autie, restless as always, rode on ahead, and the carriage began to sway from side to side, barely skirting deep gullies. My host was, I discovered, overcome with hospitality.

"Do you like life on the river?" I asked, trying vainly to talk intelligently and not notice the driver's vagaries, while my eyes were frantically searching the road for the next danger.

"Love it, love it," he said expansively. "Though the missus, she don't take to it. Stays in Yankton most the time."

More power to the missus, I thought. "Autie," I cried, far too loudly, when he rode near, "look how fast we go!" I tried to laugh, passing it off as a joke that only Autie would take seriously.

"So you do!" he answered heartily, and rode on, to my total dismay.

When we got to the cabin, all my nightmares came true. Mary had spread the wash out on the line, and horse and driver soon wound us hopelessly in the line and two weeks' worth of washing. The desperate horse—her name was Polly, as I learned from the shouts of her owner—tried to kick her way through packing boxes and woodpiles, and who knows what would have happened next if Autie hadn't finally ridden to my rescue.

"Why didn't you stop him before that?" I stormed once we were inside our house.

"The horse was reliable. I'm told it often had to make its way from place to place . . . ah . . . unguided by human hands, we might say. Oh, Libbie, you should have seen the look on your face." Unable to control himself, he doubled with laughter.

"Reliable! Not around laundry, it's not. And the look was fright!" Then I could not resist and collapsed in laughter with him. The two of us hooted so loudly that Mary finally climbed the stairs to inquire if we were ill.

The next day my escort arrived with a peace offering—a picnic hamper of ham sandwiches and salads and small pies. "My wife tells me I was in no condition to deliver a temperance lecture," he said, hanging his head.

The Seventh faced a march of five hundred miles. Maggie Calhoun and I were to be allowed to march with them, while the other women, from officers' wives to laundresses, rode on the steamer. After my carriage ride, I much preferred the march.

But as we rode out, fear settled over me, as suffocating as that blanket of white snow had been. I rode silently, lecturing myself as best I could, but doom had taken hold of me.

"Old lady, what ails you?" Autie asked.

"A strange feeling, Autie. I . . . we're headed into unknown territory, Indian territory. . . ."

"Look behind you," he commanded.

I turned in my saddle to see stretched for miles beyond me the horses and men and supply wagons of the Seventh Cavalry. Behind us, they twisted around bends in the road, forming a huge snake.

"How," Autie demanded, "can you be frightened with all these men to protect you?"

"It is not myself I'm frightened for, Autie," I whispered so softly, he barely heard. But he need not hear, for it was a litany he knew by heart.

"Custer's Luck, old lady, don't ever forget about Custer's Luck." He rode merrily along.

Ever since I'd first been allowed on a march, I'd determined to be a good sport. So soon I forced myself out of the doldrums and into high spirits. I could not help remembering that awful march across Texas, now six years behind me. How much I had learned about being an army wife and a good sport in six years. They had been hard lessons, but I was a seasoned trooper.

We rose at four each morning, taking only a hurried breakfast in the dining tent by the light of a tallow candle while soldiers waited to take the tent down the minute we ventured outside. Mary would begin to rattle the kettles as she packed, hinting that we should hurry. Within minutes of gulping down our meal, such as it was, the tent was packed, and "Boots and Saddles" sounded.

The column always halted once during the day to water the horses, and we used the time to take what lunch we could—a hard biscuit for some, perhaps a sandwich for others. When a stream was narrow, and the hundreds of horses had to be ranged along its banks to be watered, there was time for a nap. Both Autie and I could throw ourselves into the deepest sleep within minutes of hitting the ground, though I learned to appropriate the space under the wagon for its shade. I always had to dislodge the dogs before I could nap—invariably they crowded around Autie, paws resting on his chest and legs, but it never bothered him.

The troops were as efficient at setting up camp in the evening as they were relentless in tearing it down the next morning, and before my very eyes a tent city appeared each night. Tents were pitched in two long lines, facing each other, with the wagons at either end. Large ropes were stretched down this "street" to hold the horses. Since our tent was a bit apart, at one end of the street, I never tired of watching the camp. Maggie, Jimmi, Autie, and I would sit under the tent fly—Maggie and I usually having needlework or a book in our hands, for we believed that idle hands were the devil's work—and watch the scene.

A delicate blue line of smoke rose from the camp fire where the soldiers' supper was being cooked. Varying shades of rose and pink tinted an almost perfect sky, and the clear air brought familiar sounds—the bugler practicing calls, the click of the currycomb, the whistle of a happy trooper, even, occasionally, the irrepressible music of the accordion. Dogs bayed, and mules brayed, and it was all a symphony to Autie's ears. This was his world, his home.

We suffered through one more storm that spring, when the weather changed suddenly, and we found ourselves starting our march on a dull, gray morning that was stinging cold. Autie wrapped me in fur and wool until I was a shapeless mass, but still my fingers numbed with the cold until I simply had to give my horse his head. We rode like automatons, making slight progress, and finally camped by an ice-covered stream.

All the horrors of Kansas came back to me as the wind twisted and tore the canvas when the men tried to pitch tents. Tying and pinning the opening was of no avail, for the wind twisted off the tapes and flung far and wide the brass pins I had bought for that purpose. No camp fire would burn, and our Sibley stove—a cone of sheet iron, open at the top and bottom, with a pipe fit to the top—had been left behind. I fell into an unmistakable fit of the sulks, and then was in the valley of humiliation the next morning for remorse at my bad behavior. The cold of Dakota overcame me on that one day, but it was the last time I succumbed to it.

Autie and I loved to ride apart from the column in the late afternoon, just before we halted. The dogs—twelve in number now, mostly staghounds and foxhounds—accompanied us, leaping and racing about the horses. One day, when Tom was with us, two of the hounds started a deer, and Autie bounded after them. Tom and I rode leisurely along, wandering through the cottonwood trees that fringed the Missouri for miles at a stretch.

"Libbie, be very quiet," Tom said of a sudden to me, and I became perfectly cold and numb with fear.

Before us was a group of young Indian warriors, seated on the ground. I was in double danger—death or capture by the Indians, or a bullet from Tom. In recent days we had seen stakes in the ground with red flannel attached to them —"warnings to frighten us from comin' any farther," our guide explained—and though I knew Indians this side of the river were supposed to be peaceful, there was no convincing me at that moment. Indians were Indians to me.

At their first sight of us, the Indians snatched up their guns and leapt upon their ponies, prepared for attack. If time could have been measured by sensations, a century passed in those few seconds.

Tom rode forward and spoke to them coolly, though I could not understand what he said. Then, "Libbie, ride forward."

To avoid showing fear when every nerve is strung to the utmost, and your heart leaps into your throat, requires superhuman effort. I managed to move my horse and avoid screaming. Slowly and deliberately Tom and I rode through the mounted Indians and on toward the column. When we reached it and hands were lifted to help me down, I fainted dead away, something I've never done before or since.

"Libbie, you know the rule about mounting the horse that threw you," Autie teased next morning. "We'll ride off again today."

"Autie, I . . ."

"You what, old lady?"

There was nothing for it. That afternoon I rode behind Autie through the roughest country we'd yet seen. The horses had a knack for squeezing through trees, but forgetting to leave space for the riders on their backs, and I was several times lifted up by the resisting branches. Sometimes we ascended such steep cliffs that I abandoned the reins and wound my hands in the horse's mane to keep from sliding off. The sheer adventure of it made me forget about Indians and my previous fright. At last, my habit torn and my hands scratched, we came to a lovely bit of road. Sunshine flickered down through the branches of the trees and covered the short grass with checkered light and shade.

"I've some biscuits in the leather pocket of my saddle," Autie said, and I replied happily, "Oh good, a picnic."

Having eaten, we treated ourselves to a gallop over a stretch of smooth grass. Laughing with Autie and exhilarating in the fast ride, I never noticed my surroundings, until I saw that we were almost upon an Indian village. The column was Lord-knows-how-many miles from us, and we were alone, in a land where Indians were not noted for their hospitality.

Two old women peered out of a tent, making guttural growls and noises at us. An old man stared, his glance as malevolent as any I've ever felt. An occasional child peeked out from behind a tent, eyes dark with anger and hatred. But we did not see nearly the number of people we might have expected for the size of the village . . . and there were no warriors.

"Ride slowly, Libbie," Autie said softly. He rode as though he had not a care in the world, even slackening his pace to demonstrate that he felt perfectly at home. Autie from time to time raised his hand in the universal salute of peace, and I followed his model, though with an admittedly shaking hand. Autie later declared that I bowed as though before angry gods, nearly braining myself on the pommel— an accusation I vehemently denied. Still, if politeness would help . . .

Those few moments seemed a second century, after the one I'd lived through just the day before, but at last we saw why the village was so empty—the top of a nearby bluff was lined with bodies as the Indians, hidden from view to the front, looked off at a faint cloud of dust in the distance.

"It's the Seventh," Autie said quickly.

Next day Autie said, "I guess you'll stay behind today, old lady," as he started off on his afternoon ride.

"No, Autie," I replied. "It's worse to be left behind. I'll go with you." But there was never a day without a new terror —from rattlesnakes to sunstroke, which once overcame me to the point of dizziness. Yet I was driven by a determination to be with Autie, as though I knew I had not much longer to marvel at his energy and strength.

My reaction to him at night in the privacy of our tent was much the same, a kind of desperate passion as though at my back I heard time's winged chariot drawing near.

"Libbie, Libbie," he marveled one night after we'd spent ourselves in passion, "what has brought this change about in you? A year ago . . . two years . . . you would not sleep with me, and now you wear an old man out." He chuckled with obvious delight.

"Must be the Dakota weather," I answered lightly.

"Then we shall live in Dakota the rest of our lives," he said jokingly.

The day came at last when we reached Fort Rice and were ferried across the Missouri, still muddy and full of sandbars, in a rickety old boat. There we hoped for a bath . . . and found ourselves bathing in liquid mud. We learned to settle the water with alum and even to endure the taste of it, but our accommodation was for nothing. The regiment was to go out to guard the engineers of the Northern Pacific Railroad while they surveyed the route from Bismarck to the Yellowstone River. The ladies were to be left behind.

"Autie," I fumed, "I will not go back to Monroe. The last summer I was there, no one even knew that there was a campaign. 'Oh, is Armstrong on a march?' they'd ask, 'and what's the purpose of this one?' They think with the Civil War over, there's no need for soldiers. I need to be with army people."

"There's no place for you to stay at Rice," he said placatingly. "And you'd be miserable."

"I would *not* be miserable, and don't tell me that. I know there are no tents . . . but there are vacant rooms in the bachelor quarters."

"Old lady," he hooted, "surely you're not thinking of taking a room in the most awful of men's boardinghouses known in the West!"

"I might," I said loftily. "Your letters would reach me so much sooner."

"Well, your fellow boarders would never tolerate it, not for one night. There's nothing for it, Libbie. You'll have to go to Monroe . . . but you'll have Maggie with you."

And so began the summer of my discontent.

The days in Monroe dragged by, punctuated only by the mail. Maggie stayed with me in the house on Monroe Street, rather than returning to the Custer family farm, and I was grateful for her company. We two lived a Spartan existence, taking our meals in the kitchen and otherwise confining ourselves to the parlor and bedroom. The highlight of our day was the walk down Monroe Street to pick up the mail, and woe be the day on which we did not each get a letter.

Autie, as was always his habit, wrote frequently . . . about Indian skirmishes, his new hobby of taxidermy—I shuddered at the thought of a parlor full of stuffed animals— and about the series of articles he'd written, which had been well received—and well paid for—by *Galaxy Magazine*.

My letters in return overflowed, for it always seemed I had so much to tell him, in spite of my dull existence. "The *Galaxy* articles have been such a clever, lucky hit. . . . I am determined now that the public not lose sight of you. Take lots of notes of everything that happens. . . . Do not, dear Autie, ever go out with less than twenty-five men, for the Indians know you are abroad and are closely following you."

"Are you, old lady, presuming to tell me how to conduct a march?" he wrote back in mock anger, but I replied that I was sure he needed my advice, even from this long distance.

On a more serious note I once wrote of my pride in him. "Just think how quickly glory and honor have come to you, Autie. Most men are in the waning sun and yellow leaf before they have half your reputation. It adds a great charm for us to have our youth to enjoy these honors." But as I wrote, the grim thought struck me that Autie had fame and glory as a young man because he would not live long enough to enjoy it as an old man. I ripped the letter to shreds.

"Guess who I met today?" I wrote in mid-July. "John Rauch . . . the lawyer who once courted me. Oh, Autie, he would make an excellent husband . . . but what a monotonous and commonplace life I would have led!" I could not believe that I could ever have looked at another man, when I had Autie's love. In my bliss I forgot James Coker . . . and erased from my mind Tom Custer's devotion. I was firmly wedded to Autie, spiritually and physically.

With lively correspondence flying between the Dakotas and Michigan, the summer soon enough passed. In October Autie was to stop off in Toledo for a reunion of the Army of the Tennessee and then come to Monroe to collect me. Maggie would go with us back to the Dakotas.

But I could not wait another moment. I determined to take the train to Toledo.

"Libbie," Maggie protested, "you cannot just go to Toledo alone."

"Of course I can, Maggie," I said, fixing my bonnet. "Autie will be delighted."

"I wish Jimmi had come home with him," was all she could answer.

In Toledo, having arrived in advance of Autie, I went window-shopping, always looking for a way to update my pitiful wardrobe. As I stood looking at the grand clothes, I felt sure people were pointing at me, whispering to themselves, "Poor dear, why do you suppose her clothes, though of good quality, are so out-of-date?" I longed to shout back, "Because I've been with the Seventh Cavalry in the Dakotas! I am Mrs. George Armstrong Custer." Those who saw a dowdy but demure young matron peering into the windows would never have guessed the depth of my feelings.

One traveling dress of rust sateen with black cisele velvet trim particularly intrigued me. As I stood looking at it, I suddenly felt myself grabbed about the waist. Horror-struck, for a moment I forgot where I was and thought only of Indian attacks. But then, before fright could force me to embarrass myself, I heard the familiar, "Old lady! What are you doing here?"

Laughing and crying at once, I turned to Autie. His face

was sunburned to a ruddy red, though mottled pink where he'd shaved off his summer beard, and his hair was cut short again, but the blue eyes were as intense as ever . . . and they looked deep into my own.

"Oh, Autie, I came to surprise you. I couldn't wait. . . ."

"Nor could I," he laughed, "and I must have known you'd be here, for I've taken unbearable joking for insisting on shaving on a train tearing along at forty miles an hour. Everyone thought I must be meeting my sweetheart."

"And?"

"And I am meeting her," he said, wrapping me in a passionate embrace with little regard for the citizens who had to walk around us on the sidewalk.

We had a brief interlude in Monroe, and then it was off to the Dakotas again. Autie, as always, found it extremely difficult to part from his mother—I never saw him lose control of himself except when it was time to tell that frail woman good-bye. Then he would follow her about for hours, whispering words of comfort to her, sitting silently beside her. Mother Custer, having been an invalid for many years, always thought that each visit with Autie would be her last, and her efforts to be brave were heartrending. Never did she guess that she would outlive her darling boy.

At last we were in the carriage and on our way, Autie riding tight-lipped beside me while I, having learned painfully before, said nothing. To have reached for his hand in a comforting gesture, as I longed to do, would only throw him further into the depths of despair. We were on the train and well away from Monroe before he even favored me with a smile, and at that it was grim.

But nothing could quiet my happy heart. Autie and I were on our way back to the frontier and the Seventh. We were going home. The summer of my discontent faded rapidly from my mind in the face of the joys of being with Autie again. Perhaps, I remember thinking, the reason we were apart so often was so we could enjoy reunions.

Rebecca Richmond had declined to go with us this time, her heart having been captured by a civilian, of all things.

"Rebecca," I asked indignantly, "when you've met so many officers, how could you fall in love outside the army?"

"It was easy, Libbie," she said frankly. "I had your example before me."

"My example!" I was indignant. "There was never a woman more happily married than I."

"Perhaps," she mused, "but you live in constant terror of your husband's death, and even when he is not in peril, you live through long separations from him. I want a husband I can enjoy."

I turned away, struck by the truth of her words but unwilling even to think of trading my life for a so-called normal marriage. No, what Autie and I had was infinitely better, even if we had it only by fits and starts and always under a cloud of fear.

Rebecca Atwood's parents had consented to let her journey to Fort Lincoln with us, for I could not conceive of returning to those officers without a young woman to grace their winter evenings. No, I assured them, I will not let her marry in haste on the frontier without your consent and presence; yes, I will see that she is warm in the winter, protected from mosquitoes in the summer, and safe always from Indian attacks.

"Libbie," she giggled on the train westward, "how did you bear all that questioning by my parents?"

"By remembering my own parents," I answered, realizing that my very understanding marked me as of a different generation than the bright young thing next to me.

"I'm so excited, I can hardly sit still," Rebecca said with a nervous giggle, and I knew she would be a hit at the fort. I had done one more thing to take care of my soldiers.

Chapter Seventeen

 OUR TRAIN WENT AS FAR AS BISMARCK, WHERE AN alarming crowd was waiting to return with it to St. Paul. They were gamblers and murderers and other lawless citizens whose outrageous way of life had led the citizens to oust them. These shouting, cursing people were desperate to leave the territory on the last train of the season. Autie spirited us out the back side of the car, and we departed quietly for the post, though Rebecca's eyes were wide with mingled horror and amusement.

"The frontier," I said airily, and she rewarded me with a bright smile indicating that she was ready for any amusement.

The next amusement was not so funny. The Missouri River was frozen solid enough to bear our weight partway across, but then came a torrent of rushing water, which we would have to cross in a boat. Several soldiers rowed, while Autie sat boldly in the front of the craft, watching everything, and another soldier used a long, iron-pointed pole to keep the huge cakes of ice from capsizing our frail craft. Rebecca and I huddled in the bottom of the boat, refusing to raise our eyes even for a second, sure that any moment an ice floe would send our little boat spiraling down the river.

"Old lady, you're giving Rebecca the wrong impression of your character," Autie crowed cheerfully from his position on high, where he looked, for all the world, like king of the river. He was enjoying himself immensely.

"I never promised to make her brave," I quaked from the bottom of the boat.

"No," Rebecca said, "but you promised me adventure, and this is surely an adventure." She was not nearly as alarmed as I, and I envied her youth and its eternal optimism.

"Old lady, you've been through much worse than this," Autie said, a faint tone of reprimand tinging his teasing. "Remember the floods in Kansas when I wasn't even there to protect you."

"And are you protecting me now?" I managed to ask icily.

At last we were on firm ground again. Clinging to Autie's arm, I said, "Here I will live and die. I'll never cross that river again." But I knew somehow it was a hollow boast.

"Autie! Libbie! Over here!" Tom stood by a carriage, waving frantically, and we all piled in for the ride to the fort. Autie and Tom chatted incessantly during that brief ride, bringing each other up-to-date on happenings at the fort and at their family home in Monroe. I was so distracted listening to them that I scarcely paid attention as we reached the fort.

In the dim light, though, I could see an entire army fort, where before I'd left a barren plain with only a few buildings. "What's that?" I asked. "Surely it's new."

"That it is," Autie said, turning to smile mysteriously at me.

As we drew closer, a band broke into the strains of "Home, Sweet Home," followed by Autie's song, "Garryowen." Then we stopped before the brightly lit building—a two-story house with a large, inviting veranda. Autie had told me that we had a new house in the center of Officers' Row, but he had led me to believe that I would return to a cold and empty dwelling, waiting for me to bring to it the warmth of a home.

Instead, I saw a house where every room glowed. The lamps were lit, fires were in each fireplace, and the rooms were full of people. The entire cavalry post had turned out to greet us, and as we clambered down from the ambulance, the veranda filled with cheering couples.

"Autie?" I turned toward him, overcome with the emotion of the moment.

"They've come to welcome you home, my darling girl," he whispered tenderly in my ear. "Here, I've never carried you into a proper home before."

And with my protests echoing in his ears, Autie hoisted me into his arms and carried me over the threshold, to the cheers of the gathered crowd. He deposited me with such an earnest kiss as to earn another round of cheers.

Mary had prepared tables of food, and it was the most festive evening I remember of all my years on the frontier. Well after midnight the last visitor straggled out the door, and I leaned against Autie in happy exhaustion.

"Don't be too tired," he said lightly. "I want to make love to you in our new house."

"Autie! Rebecca will hear you. She's too young to know about such things."

"Bother!" He rubbed his chin against my forehead, his hands insistently pressing my body against his so that I could feel his need of me . . . and my own need rose in response.

"Rebecca?" I managed to call weakly. "Autie is very tired. Let me get you settled before we retire for the night." I saw her into her room, fussed over her a moment, checked the bedside water pitcher and towels, every nerve in me straining to rush to Autie.

"Libbie," she said sweetly, "Autie's waiting for you. Go on. I'll be fine."

With a kiss to her forehead, I left her and fled to Autie. When I would have rushed out of my clothes and thrown them aside, Autie deliberately slowed the process, unbuttoning one button at a time until I was nearly wild with wanting. His kisses—on my cheek, my neck, my breast—were like small flames, and clumsily I tried to return them. But he was, this night, the more controlled, and I was left to follow, almost helpless, where he led. When at last we came together, it was like a fiery explosion, need and pleasure and happiness and caring for him all wrapped into one big inferno.

"Autie," I whispered once I recovered my breath, "can't we live here forever?"

"No, old lady, we probably can't. But I will preserve this moment forever in my mind . . . and would preserve it for all time if I could."

I stifled a sob. Autie would never be content to make love to me, to be the consummate husband. He needed his wars . . . and his victories. In the battle that sometimes raged between us, this evening had been one of his victories . . . and I had willingly been conquered.

"Autie, wake up! I hear something." I poked at him as hard as I dared.

Stirring lazily, he mumbled, "You always hear things, Libbie. We are in a house . . . there are no rattlesnakes, no storm will blow the tent down. Go to sleep."

"Autie, something is roaring in the chimney."

Instantly alert, he sat straight up in bed, then flew, stark naked, out of the bed and into the hall.

"Autie, your nightdress!"

"Bother my nightdress! Bring it to me quickly!"

I did as he bid, and he struggled into the large unwieldy garment, while running up the stairs at the same time.

"This bedroom's on fire," he shouted from the room directly above that where we slept. "Bring me some water! And wake Rebecca!"

Rebecca had no need of wakening, for she came quickly to the head of the stairs to inquire about the racket. Laboring with a pail of water—much of which I sloshed on the stairs—I shouted for her to don a wrapper and get downstairs immediately.

As I went back for the second pail of water, I was stopped in my tracks by a loud explosion, and my brain reeled from fright. Autie had been killed—I was convinced of it. "Autie!"

"I'm all right, Libbie."

My relief was so great that I nearly sank down on the floor and forgot all other effort. But Autie, now clad in his nightshirt and nothing else, came flying down the stairs and out the door, crying over his shoulder, "Go to Maggie and Jimmi. I'll alert the sentinel."

Upstairs the roaring was louder than ever, and now we heard the cracking of beams as they split under the heat. It took no more urging for Rebecca and me to fly out the door. Just as we did, there was a report that sounded like a whole unit of artillery soldiers firing at once, or so I thought. I realized later that what I heard was the roof blowing off the house.

The sentinel fired his carbine in alarm, and in an incredibly short time men were swarming about the house. Autie had gone back to get his vest, with his watch and purse, and had buttoned this over his nightdress, so that he made a strange sight as he gave orders to the soldiers, as cool as if he'd been in the midst of a battle. They worked feverishly to remove our belongings, for there was not an engine nor enough water to battle the blaze, and all we could hope was to rescue but a few things.

The house burned very quickly. Fortunately, it was a still night, with no wind to carry the flames. Otherwise the whole garrison might have burned. It seemed that the chimney had been defective all along, and that gas from the petroleum paper, inserted between the plastering and the outer walls to keep out the cold, had exploded, creating the noise that I thought killed Autie.

Next morning I stared at a sorry collection of torn, broken, and scorched effects. Most of my clothes were gone, and I lost silver and linen, along with what laces and finery I had. But what troubled me most was the loss of my collection of clippings about Autie . . . and of the wig I'd had made from his curls when he cut them after the war.

Rebecca fared even more poorly, for every stitch of her clothing was gone, along with her purse, which carried the goods to replace the lost clothing. Next day she sat before us in borrowed clothes at least three times too large, when a clothes basket was delivered to the door with a note begging her to consider herself "the daughter of the regiment." The basket contained much of what she needed immediately, and later the wives of the Seventh came with needles and thimbles, and the scissors flew as they outfitted us both.

We had lived in our new house just under a month when it burned. We managed to find squatters' quarters on the post, while our house was being rebuilt.

The new house stood on the same spot as the old, in the midst of the seven frame houses of Officers' Row, which edged the parade ground on the west. Facing the line from the east were the barracks for enlisted men, with attached kitchens and mess halls. On the north and south of the rectangle that made up the fort were the commissary and quartermaster storehouses, adjutant's office, guardhouse, and hospital. The entire fort sat in a broad, level plain between the river and the slopes and rose to the tableland on the west; on the brow of the hills to the north were the buildings of the infantrymen.

There were about forty of us—officers and their wives—at Lincoln that winter, and we stuck to each other like glue. It was another winter of hunting and dancing, though Autie and I had fewer personal demons to keep at bay. And though he was always ready for a hunt, Autie danced less.

"My writing, Libbie," he would explain, closeting himself in his study, a room in which he delighted. Having at last a study all his own, he had decorated it with furniture pillaged from other rooms in the house and with an array of stuffed trophies—a buffalo he'd shot in Dakota, meek jack rabbits on the mantel, a black-tailed deer, and several antelope. Next to these trophies were photographs of the men Autie admired—General McClellan, Little Phil Sheridan, and the actor Lawrence Barrett, who had become his great, good friend. My picture, in my bridal dress, hung over the desk.

Galaxy Magazine was collecting his articles, intending to publish them in a volume entitled *My Life on the Plains,* and Autie rewrote—polishing, he called it—and rewrote until I was sure his hand would be numb. During the day I was to be at his side constantly; sometimes he wrote, other times he read to me from biographies of Napoleon, who fascinated him, or a life of Daniel Webster that he particularly liked.

Autie could not endure for me to be gone during the day, and I remember once when I went to visit with some of the wives, gathered over a quilt. An orderly soon appeared.

"The general," he said with a glint in his eyes, "sends his compliments and wants to know when he shall send the trunks."

The women all thought it terribly amusing, and I pretended to join the hilarity as I excused myself to return to my master. But I was seething, the kind of anger that rises up and then dissipates almost as quickly. I held on to it until I confronted Autie.

"That was rude," I said staunchly.

"But honest," he answered, completely unrepentant. "I do not like to have you gone."

I could have argued with him, protested my right to a visit with the ladies, but it would only have put a barrier, however small, between us, and I was driven these days by a need to be in harmony with Autie.

"You're hopeless," I said, going to him with open arms.

"I would stop writing if you'd accompany me to the bedroom," he murmured.

"Autie, not in the middle of the day, with the orderly right outside the door! Go back to your writing."

There were some among the group to whom I did not take easily. Two or three officers resented Autie because he was younger than they and had jumped over them in rank; others had been reprimanded by him and clung to their resentment.

"I shall not welcome Colonel Benteen into my house," I said defiantly. "He has been too critical of you."

"If you wish to please me?" he asked.

"Oh, all right, Autie, but I shan't be cordial."

And then, late at night, Autie would do his imitation of my greeting to Benteen or another dishonored guest—a coldly formal shake of the hand, a distant greeting, a demeanor so uppity that his act collapsed me into giggles . . . and made me promise to do better.

In the evenings Autie excused me to be hostess. He believed that as post commander he should keep his house open to the garrison at all times—but he also believed that I should entertain while he hid in his study. I would slip away as I could for a little visit with him, perhaps even a waltz to the strains that floated from a nearby room where others danced. But he made only rare and brief appearances in the parlor. The fact that he was being rude never occurred to Autie, and I lacked the nerve to tell him. Instead, I made bright little jokes to our company about his isolation and even, once, laughed about being married to a monk.

"Tom tells me you compared me to a monk," he said icily when we retired that night. "I should think you know better than that." His lovemaking was rough and demanding that night, as though he were both punishing me and proving that he was far from any monastery.

Spring is tardy in the North. Flowers bloom in Michigan long before they appear in the Dakotas, and I used to watch for the first blade of grass, the first bunch of flowers—a kind of blue anemone. But that spring of 1874 I had to wait for soldiers to bring me flowers.

"You must not go beyond the garrison limits," Autie said sternly. "I've posted station pickets on the high ground at the rear of the post. There are Indians all around."

"Oh, but Autie, to be confined . . . I want to ride, to see the prairie turn green."

"You shall ride with me," he said, "on the other side of the river."

The east bank was considered the safe shore, and the first mild day Autie proved good to his word and took me riding there. Making our way through the underbrush, we startled a magnificent black-tailed deer, which leapt straight into the air, his superb head turned searchingly toward us, and then bounded away, hardly seeming to touch the earth. Unable to resist the temptation, we followed, although we were without either dogs or guns.

"Libbie, stop!" Autie commanded after we'd gone but a little distance. "We cannot go farther."

"Autie," I protested, "this is the safe side of the river." I, who was afraid of everything, saw no reason for fear.

"It's not been four days since a patrol found the body of a white man staked out on the ground . . . tortured," he said grimly. "Right along here."

"Autie!" I held my ears, as though afraid Autie would reveal the details of the poor man's death, details I never, ever wanted to hear. "Take me home," I said quickly.

After that I never asked to walk beyond the pickets. We took our air by dawdling on the veranda, where we had a fine view of the valley and the mules, who nibbled at its sprouting grass.

"Indians! Help! Indians!" The shouts came to us distantly one early morning. Soon a guard, who'd been working prisoners just outside the post, came riding on the double, perilously seated on an unsaddled mule. With blanched face and protruding eyeballs, he called out that the Indians were running off the herd.

"Sound 'Boots and Saddles,'" Autie said to his orderly, "and keep it up until I tell you to stop." By then a cloud of dust could be seen rising through a gap in the bluffs.

With the sound of the first notes, the porches of the company quarters and the parade ground were alive with men. Without asking a question, they rushed to the stables, threw saddles on their horses, and rode to the parade grounds. Some were in jackets, others in flannel shirtsleeves, many hatless—they were a motley-looking crowd. But once they learned the cause of the alarm, they demanded immediate action.

Autie detailed one officer to stay with the garrison, kissed me quickly and cautioned me not to leave the post, and flung himself into the saddle, leading the command toward that cloud of dust. In twenty minutes from the first alarm, the garrison was emptied.

"Libbie," Rebecca said tentatively, "they've all gone. We're . . . we're alone."

"Of course not, dear," I said complacently. "The soldiers on garrison duty are here."

"Libbie, look about you." Her eyes were wide with fright, and she was paler than usual.

I had been so busy watching the exodus that I'd not paid attention to anything else. Now as I turned my head from side to side, surveying the post from one end to the other, I saw nary a soldier. "They've gone," I repeated wonderingly. Then, seeing Rebecca about to faint, I added, "It's perfectly all right, dear. They won't go more than a mile or so after those mules."

I would never have told that child what I knew about Indians—that they rarely attacked a post, but an unprotected post would be more temptation than they could resist, that they may even have driven the mules off as a trick to empty the garrison of its men and officers, that they could attack, burn the buildings, capture the women, that . . . my mind reeled with the possibilities, all of them dire. At least this time there was no James Coker nor Tom Custer charged with putting a bullet in my brain. It was cold comfort.

"Come, ladies," I said, mustering all my brave and cheerful tones, "we'll wait at our house for their return. They'll be along directly."

A group of nervous women followed me, though not one gave voice to the fear that lurked in all of us. We sat on the veranda, making idiotic small talk, our eyes glued to the bluffs.

"What did you say?" . . . "I'm sorry, I missed that. . . ." The conversation was fragmented, disjointed by our lack of attention.

Rebecca grabbed my hand so hard, I feared for a moment that she had broken it. "Autie's guns," she said. "Shouldn't you get them?"

In spite of my terror, I nearly laughed aloud. "What for?" I asked. "I know nothing about them."

Annie Yates, wife of Captain George Yates, surprised us all by producing a tiny Remington pistol. "I'll teach you to load it," she offered, holding the pistol nervously away from her.

I hardly thought one tiny handgun would do any good, but I praised Annie for her thoughtfulness.

The one officer who was left visited the pickets, making sure of their arms, and then came to reassure us. It was an impossible task, and I know he longed to give it up. We asked twenty times when the command would return—how could he know?—and how far they'd gone, and what Indians had attacked, and on and on with such aimless questions as only terrified women can devise.

Late in the afternoon a cloud of dust appeared over the bluffs, and we longed to run to the crest to see what was coming. "We must not," I said firmly, holding Maggie Calhoun by the arm, for I feared she would run off, her promise to stay within the garrison totally forgotten.

At length the mule herd returned, driven by a few soldiers. Our disappointment was obvious. The rest of the command, we were told, was pursuing the Indians. Dinner was a disaster—no one could eat, though Mary coaxed us with her best efforts—and the evening promised to set in long and anxious.

Suddenly the notes of "Garryowen" broke the evening silence, and as we rushed outside, we saw the men returning from an entirely different direction than that which had taken them away in the morning. It was a joyous reunion. Though the separation had not been long, it was intense.

They had captured no Indians, for the quarry had dismounted and hidden in the underbrush. Suffering from lack of food and water, with fagged horses, the command returned home rather than continue the chase. Next day men limped about the post, and when they sat, it was with the groans of old men, for they had not ridden during the winter, and a sudden ride of so many miles had bruised their bones . . . and their pride.

■   ■   ■

Spring may have finally brought the green shoots of new grass, but just as surely it brought the summer campaign. I remember once seeing a new, tender, green blade and crushing it under my heel, because it was a harbinger of a long and lonely summer for me. Autie never talked of official policy to me, so what I knew about forthcoming expeditions—and the policy behind them—came from post rumor, which was never lacking.

Sheridan was convinced that the army needed a post in the Black Hills, land that had been granted to the Sioux as part of their reservation in the treaty of 1868. Sheridan meant this post to discourage the Sioux from raiding to the east and south. What Autie didn't tell me—and I learned by rumor—was that the expedition was also to search for gold. For years gossip had placed large gold deposits in the Black Hills, and now the American imagination saw that sacred Sioux territory as the last great mining frontier of the West. I saw it as an abyss that could swallow Autie.

"I hear you've ordered an ambulance outfitted," I said one day as I sat by his side in his study.

"Oh, Libbie," he said quickly, "don't misunderstand. It's not for you and Mary. Why, you two couldn't get along in such cramped quarters. . . . I'd have to separate the two of you three times a day." But he was grinning as he said it, and I knew the ambulance was for me.

"The ginnel knows me and Miss Libbie could keep house in a flour barrel," Mary said, when I told her of his ploy.

I was relieved, for somehow I felt that as long as I went with Autie, he would be safe. It was an old, familiar feeling now, that need to be close enough to Autie to extend my protection over him. Sometimes I thought it pretentious of me . . . but not enough that I could banish the conviction.

"Libbie," he said, approaching me very solemnly one day at dinner, "the scouts have decreed that it will be a much more dangerous summer than we anticipated. You will remain behind."

"And Mary?" I asked, catching my breath with disappointment and hoping the tremor in my voice didn't show.

"Mary will go. I need a cook."

"That's not fair!" I flared.

"I am neither married to Mary nor in love with her," he said firmly, closing the subject.

Autie never realized that no terror on the march could equal, for me, the terror of being left behind with my imagination.

The Black Hills expedition marched out of Fort Lincoln on July 2, 1874. Autie had the band play "The Girl I Left Behind Me," and the women left behind watched as the Seventh left for the summer. Then we settled down to waiting.

It was a long summer, and the most remarkable thing about it was the mosquitoes. The short northern summer can boast hideously hot days, and we would walk out in the evening, seeking a cool breeze, only to be attacked by mosquitoes far worse than any I'd known in the South. We wore scarves over our heads, whisked handkerchiefs before our faces, and beat the air with fans. Yet if we were still for a moment, swarms of the wretched insects attacked instantly, so that constant motion was required. Still we longed to sit on the veranda, and someone discovered that wrapping one's ankles in newspapers and drawing the stockings over was effective protection; then we tucked our skirts closely around us and fixed ourselves in chairs from which we dared not move. We were a sight, though fortunately there were none of our men there to laugh at us.

I measured the summer by trips to Bismarck, which necessitated crossing the Missouri. With Autie by my side, I'd crossed reluctantly, but alone, or in the company of women and orderlies, I found the river increasingly terrifying. The current was so swift and the water so muddy that even the strongest swimmer could hardly save himself if he fell in. Several soldiers had drowned, trying to cross in frail skiffs to the drinking houses on the safe side. Every time I crossed, I imagined I saw the upturned faces of those men in the water, though I wouldn't in truth have known any of them. My fear was, I suspect, a reflection of my terror for Autie, but it was nonetheless real to me, and I hated those trips. I would rather have run out of staples and sewing supplies. And yet I found it impossible to remain behind when the others went shopping for diversion.

Autie wrote only four times during the whole long summer, letters full of the charm of the country that had never before, he told me, been seen by white men. It was a summertime frolic for Autie—except for the killing of his first grizzly, it was unremarkable. They encountered no Indians . . . and they found little gold. On August 30 they marched back into Fort Lincoln.

"Libbie, aren't you coming to watch them march in?" Rebecca, dressed in a fine new sprigged muslin, stared at me, aghast.

"I can't," I said, tears streaming down my face, even while I laughed with excitement. "I can't . . . let Autie see me crying." I was so overjoyed at his return that no power on earth could have dammed the tears that flowed down my cheeks. And if I went out now, all the world would see my swollen eyes.

But then Autie rode by our house, and I was out the door and down the steps before I even realized it. I only came to my senses when I heard a great cheer from the men, and I realized that they were cheering because I was in Autie's arms, pulled up onto his horse and locked in his powerful, welcoming embrace. Such displays are not common in the cavalry.

When I gained control, I looked at the men. They were sunburned, their hair faded, their clothes so patched that the original blue was scarcely visible. Their boots were out at the toes, and their clothing beyond repair. The instruments of the band were tarnished and jammed, but they could still play "Garryowen," the tune to which the regiment always returned. The Seventh was home . . . and from the clouds and gloom of the summer days, I walked again into the broad sunshine that my husband's blithe spirit made.

In September we left for Monroe, but we were back by late November. And Autie's spirits were raised to new heights by the news that his book, *My Life on the Plains*, drawn from the *Galaxy* articles, was now available in one volume of 256 pages.

We settled down for another winter at Fort Lincoln. Autie had surprised us all by renting a piano from St. Paul. When we returned to our house, it stood in the parlor.

"Maggie, play 'Jacob's Ladder,' " Jimmi cried, and we all joined in the singing. Then it was "Oh, Susanna!" and "Sweet Betsy from Pike" and, on Sundays, "A Mighty Fortress Is Our God" and "Fairest Lord Jesus," the only church service we had. At Christmas poor Maggie nearly wore her fingers to the bone, playing the traditional carols over and over, while we all sang, some of us off-key but all of us with enthusiasm. But beyond the piano the winter passed much as the previous one—long and dull for the officers, but filled for Autie and me with our delight in each other.

"Libbie, come sit by my side! I want to write!"

Chapter Eighteen

"IF I WERE AN INDIAN," AUTIE WROTE IN *MY LIFE on the Plains*, "I often think I would greatly prefer to cast my lot among those of my people adhered to the free open plains rather than submit to the confined limits of the reservation, there to be the recipient of the blessed benefits of civilization, with its vices thrown in without stint or measure."

Autie, who spent much of his career shepherding Indians onto the reservations!

"I'm an expert, Libbie," he crowed, "an expert on Indian affairs. Here, it says so in *The New York Times*." He waved the newspaper before my nose.

"Autie, I can't see these stitches," I said, brushing it away. "I know you're an expert. You know more about the Indian than anyone in the cavalry."

"You're right," he said smugly, beginning to pace about the small study. "I know him for what he is . . . a savage, more cruel than any wild beast of the desert."

"But the Ree scouts . . . ," I protested.

"They are my friends, and so are others. . . ."

Monahsetah? I wanted to ask, but I kept my counsel.

"But they are basically wild animals. It is our duty to civilize them."

"Yes, Autie," I murmured. Privately, my terror of Indians was so great that I saw no hope for civilizing them.

"It's almost time to march. . . ." he said restlessly, still pacing. "The Seventh is ready. I suspect we'll go back to the Black Hills."

Summer was nearly upon us again, and another campaign was inevitable. Autie could hardly wait, but I was filled with dread.

Disappointment lay in wait for Autie. Sheridan sent four hundred soldiers from Fort Laramie, under the command of Colonel Richard I. Dodge, into the Black Hills. Autie and the Seventh were left behind.

"There'll be an expedition to the Yellowstone," he told me confidently, after the announcement of Dodge's departure, "and I'd rather take the Seventh there."

Again I waited, heart in my mouth. But Sheridan sent infantry troops north on a steamboat, and Autie missed another chance for a victory. He and the Seventh were stuck at Lincoln, and the summer stretched before them long and hot, filled with endless drills and exercises designed to do little more than avert the inevitable boredom.

"Politics!" he stormed. "That's all it is, politics! Well, I can play their game as well as the next fellow."

And so Autie embarked on his brief career in the arena of national politics. Relieved of the terror of a summer expedition, I greeted this new development joyously, though it wasn't long before Autie's political games made me as apprehensive as his military campaigns.

Autie entered the political arena as a columnist, publishing his opinions under a nom de plume. Bits of gossip— President Grant wanted a third term, administration officials were upset by Democratic victories in Ohio and Indiana,

Sherman and Sheridan might be angling for presidential nominations—began to appear in the *World*. Oh, they were anonymous, all right, but to my eye there was no hiding where they came from. The familiarity with the military was an obvious finger, pointing right at Autie.

"Autie, I don't think it's wise for a lieutenant colonel to trifle with the commander in chief," I said boldly one day.

"Libbie," he replied in his coldest tone, "you stick to your embroidery. I shall run my affairs."

They're my affairs, too! I wanted to shout, but I bit my tongue . . . and worried all the more.

"Libbie!" he called, rushing in one day with the mail in his hand. "The *Herald* has launched an exposé of corruption at forts and trading posts on the upper Missouri. By God, it's about time! I'll feed them material. Ralph Meeker's the reporter behind it. You remember him?"

"Autie, shhh!" I cautioned, raising a finger to my lips as though I were dealing with a child. "You never can tell who'll hear you. And, no, I don't remember any Ralph Meeker."

"Bother! He visited once . . . oh, maybe at Hays. I don't know. But, Libbie, this may make my fortune! This may really do it, little girl!" He swung me off my feet and into a wild twirl around the parlor.

I failed to see how an investigation of corruption could make Autie's fortune. We all knew that the sutlers paid a high price—a bribe?—for the exclusive right to sell goods at any given post. And that sutlers' privileges were given out as political plums. But Autie had stayed blessedly free of such enterprise . . . though I'm sure he would have been tempted, had the opportunity arisen.

Twirling about there in the air, held in those strong arms that I adored, I wondered how many times I'd heard that before. This would make our fortune . . . or that . . . or a mining scheme . . . and then his articles . . . and now, I knew not what. Spying? Telling tales on the government he served? Autie was like a child, off in one direction, then another, with nary a thought behind or ahead but for the moment.

Dumping me unceremoniously, he went to his study,

where he filled pages and pages of paper with his bold, flowing handwriting. Late that night he said, "I must post this to
Ralph Meeker."

Several weeks later Tom lounged on the veranda reading
the *Herald*. "Seen this, Autie?" he asked, waving a page of
the paper. "Says here this reporter's uncovered fraud at the
forts . . . seems someone sells sutlers the right to operate
and makes them pay dearly. Now there's a business we
should have thought of, big brother!"

"Let me see," Autie said calmly, though I could tell that
he was in a pitch of excitement at seeing his news reach the
paper. He read the article slowly, thoroughly, and then said
calmly to Tom, "Hardly the business for the Custer boys,
Tom. Too risky . . . and dishonest besides."

Late that night I caught him rereading the article, as
intently as he had the first time. "I'll show them," he crowed.
"They'll see who knows what about frontier posts . . . and
then, bigod, they'll have to send me on the next expedition."

"Autie," I said wearily, "it's late, and I'm tired. Let's
worry about politics tomorrow."

But Autie was a driven man, and that night he made love
to me brutally, as though I were one of his political enemies.
It occurred to me that a summer campaign might have been
a blessing.

Meeker's articles continued from July through October,
when Autie announced that he had applied for leave and we
were traveling east.

"I'll take you to New York, old lady," he said, "if you can
find yourself the proper clothes."

"Autie, I can't find the clothes until we're in New York
. . . and then we can't afford to buy them!"

He laughed heartily. "Only temporary, only temporary.
I'll have to wear my old ulster . . . only car drivers wear
them now, they're so out of fashion."

I flung calico wrappers and wool riding suits together on
the bed, pulled out a velvet-trimmed princess sheath now ten
years out of date and a silk taffeta such as I was sure no one

in the East wore anymore, but I didn't care. We were going to New York. My heart fairly sang with the refrain.

That night Autie fell quickly asleep, but I, high on anticipation, was restless, even turning occasionally, which I always tried to avoid for fear of disturbing the little rest that Autie took.

He reached a long arm across my chest, pinning me to the mattress. "Are you a whirling dervish?"

"I'm sorry. I can't sleep. I . . . I'm so looking forward . . ."

"To getting away from Fort Lincoln? I thought you liked your life here."

"I do . . . but, oh, Autie, I can't explain. I'm just glad we're going east." I could not tell him of my fears and premonitions, of the certainty I had felt that I would one day cross the Missouri, headed east, leaving him behind, and of my now-bright hope that this trip east would change fate.

Pushing his hand aside, I turned toward him, pulling his head onto my breast and hearing him moan in anticipation as he moved his mouth along my body. Then we were lost to all but each other. Later, lying next to him while he slept again and I still lay wide-eyed, I thought myself the most fortunate woman in the universe. And I resolved to banish my foolish fears.

After a brief stop in Monroe—we went to see Autie's parents, but visits with them were so emotional as to be draining, and we stayed only a day—we were on to New York. Autie found a boardinghouse across from the Hotel Brunswick, and we settled in for a winter of gaiety. Each day was filled with receptions, dinners, dancing, and theater, and I met fascinating people—among them, Lawrence Barrett, the actor whom Autie had become friends with on his previous trips to New York, trips where I'd been left behind at Lincoln.

"Mrs. Custer," Barrett said, bending low over my hand, "I've enjoyed many a visit with your husband and always heard his glowing pride in you, but never, until now, could I truly appreciate his good fortune."

I blushed and smiled. I had been too long among men who gave freely of their love and support but were short on outright compliments, and I was unsure of my response. "It is my good fortune to be Autie's wife," I said.

"Yes, I suppose that's true, too. He is a remarkable man." And then I blushed all the more to hear someone praise Autie as I thought he deserved. Barrett was then performing in *Julius Caesar*, which Autie watched night after night with intent interest. The play, he told me, had much to say to anyone who would presume to lead other men.

This time, in New York, Autie was a celebrity as much for his book, *My Life on the Plains*, as for his hero's status. Sherman had said it was the best thing ever written about the plains, and a lyceum bureau asked him to prepare a series of lectures.

"Two hundred dollars a night, Libbie! We'll move to a hotel, one with some style, and you shall have new clothes . . . think what this will mean to our income!" Autie was exuberant and I thought this had more possibilities than most of his schemes.

"When will you start?" I guess I anticipated a speech—and two hundred dollars—the very next night.

"Oh, not until spring," he replied casually. "I have to have time to prepare. I won't be one of these off-the-cuff speakers with nothing to say. I have too much to tell people about Indians and the plains . . . and . . ."

His voice trailed off, but I mentally finished the sentence, "and about the follies of our government and our President." Perhaps it was better that Autie not make our fortune on the lecture circuit.

In February our money ran out, and we returned to Fort Lincoln. Autie never mentioned the lyceum circuit again.

When we reached St. Paul, we learned that the trains would not run again until April, because the winter was unusually severe.

"I'll see about that," Autie said self-confidently, and dis-appeared only to return within an hour and announce that a special train would be sent through for us. "The railroad is mindful of the protection I gave them when they were build-ing the track," he said, thoroughly convinced that the effort of a special train was nothing less than his due.

Not wanting to spend two months in St. Paul, I accepted this latest benefit of being married to Autie without a qualm.

The train had three enormous engines with two snow-plows, freight cars for baggage and coal, several cattle cars, passenger cars taking miners to the Black Hills—as long as the train was going anyway, I guess the railroad decided to turn it to a profit—and an eating house built on a flat car. Autie and I traveled in the paymaster's car, with a kitchen and private sitting room. We were well fed and comfortable, though the car was always cold in spite of a little stove.

The train seemed to fly along the tracks, until we came to a drift. The train would stop violently, then jerk forward a bit, only to stop again so hard that sometimes dishes crashed to the table. The crew would shovel until the track was clear, and we would proceed. Finally one day we came to such a sudden and abrupt halt that our belongings fairly flew about the car.

"Autie?" I asked tremulously.

"I'll see what it is," he said, welcoming a chance to be part of whatever was going on. In seconds he was bundled and out of the car, while I sat for what seemed long hours waiting word. The train did not move an inch.

"It's a wall of ice, Libbie, a solid wall," Autie exclaimed, slapping his hands together to warm them. His face was bright red, and crystals of ice glistened in his mustache, but his eyes shone with delight. If Autie couldn't fight Indians, he'd settle for a wall of ice.

"Snowplows are stuck in it now, and it's too much for hand shoveling. This is the end of the line, Libbie."

While Autie grinned at his doomsday pronouncement, my mind whirled with dread possibilities, most of which cen-tered on a trainload of people frozen to death.

As night fell, Autie began to pace restlessly from our car

to the passenger cars and back. At last he said, "Those officers in the coach have no place to sleep, poor fellows."

I had known Autie long enough. "You want to invite them to share our car," I said. There was no question in my voice.

"Exactly. I shall give them your compliments and your invitation."

And that's just what he did. Protesting would have done me no good, so I silenced my misgivings and crawled, at Autie's suggestion, to the far corner of the large bed he made by putting two folding beds together. Then, with the lights out and my head burrowed in the pillows, our guests filed in, blankets in hand. They slept on bedrolls on the floor, two small berths on the side of the car, and several—I knew not how many—in the very bed with Autie and me. Their snoring kept me awake hours on end, and as the days and nights wore on, my patience grew thinner and thinner. Autie considered it all a lark and never thought of any other reaction on my part.

The snow started with small flakes and soon fell steadily and thickly, and the wind whistled around the car, sometimes in gusts that rocked it ominously. Outside the windows nothing was to be seen but an endless white landscape. I noticed, without commenting on it, that Autie began to hoard the wood, letting the fire die down a little more each night. And there was no mistaking that our meals were less plentiful. Convinced that we would die in that spot, I tried to console myself that at least Indians would not get Autie.

Finally even Autie could not hide his concern. "I shall see if anyone aboard this train understands telegraphy," he announced, after discovering a tiny battery and a pocket relay in a cupboard in our car. He set forth among the other cars and soon returned with a man who knew enough to cut the main wires and fasten the pocket relay to the cut ends. In no time we were in contact both with the Fargo station and our friends at Lincoln.

"What about the old lady?" Tom asked. "Is she with you? I'll come get you both."

"No," I ordered, usurping Autie's authority. "It's too dangerous, Tom."

Of course, he came after us anyway, arriving with a whoop and a yell, his arms full of wraps and mufflers sent for us from the post. The drifts were too deep for him to drive the sleigh near the train, so Autie carried me to it and dumped me unceremoniously in the straw, along with the three hounds we had with us. We left amid cheers from those staying behind; they knew we would send help immediately.

We plunged into one deep white abyss after another, pushing through the drifts toward Lincoln. Snow fell continuously, and I feared at any moment it would turn to the driving, blinding whirl of a Dakota blizzard, forcing even the horses to stop in their tracks. When at long last we saw Lincoln and the lights of our own home, I could not speak for relief. A fire blazed in the fireplace, and friends greeted us with warmed cider. I was never so glad to be home.

The train, its passengers rescued, remained in that very spot until spring melted the wall of ice.

Within days Autie was summoned back to Washington in a political complexity too tangled for me to understand at the time. Representative Clymer, chair of the House committee on expenditures of the War Department, summoned Autie to testify about the illegal sale of post traderships. Vocal as he had been, at least in print, about the dishonesty of this practice, Autie had only suspicions, not facts. Clymer was wasting his time and Autie's. With difficulty I refrained from reminding him that his anonymity had been pretty thin.

But the whole thing ran deeper than corruption on the posts. Clymer's real purpose was to embarrass President Grant and reveal the vast frauds of the Republican party, thereby increasing the chances of a Democratic candidate for president. And Autie, of course, was a known supporter of the Democratic party, a political leaning inherited from his father—who was outspoken on the subject—and strengthened by our experiences in the South after the war.

Autie had made no secret of his criticism of Reconstruction policies.

Autie testified—hearsay testimony—but was detained in Washington for possible further testimony. While he was twiddling his thumbs in Washington—and looking for a new scheme—Sitting Bull left the reservation and refused orders to return. A summer expedition against the Sioux was inevitable, and the Seventh began preparing, even without Autie. Once again I saw and heard the signs of cavalry troops preparing for an expedition. The pace of life at Lincoln quickened as the men got their horses and equipment ready. Autie was missing it all, one of the times he liked best.

With each passing day Autie seemed less likely to return to Fort Lincoln in time to march with the Seventh. In his letters he tried to be cheerful, but his desperation was evident: "I worry constantly about my men," he wrote early in April. "I should be drilling them for the summer campaign. It will be a major one." Later that month he seemed sure that he would be returning almost any day. "I cannot see that they will have need of me beyond tomorrow." But tomorrows came and went, and by the first of May, he wrote, "I fear delay will make me miss the summer march. You could come east if that happened, which would be pleasant, but I cannot bear another summer away from my men. I *must* lead the march."

Autie cooled his heels in Senate antechambers and White House waiting rooms. Grant, offended that Autie seemed to be testifying for those sniffing out political scandal, refused to see him, and Autie's pleas to Sheridan were received sympathetically but with no results. Little Phil's hands were tied, and Autie was in the capital until the Senate released him.

"Autie'll be here in time, you can count on that, old lady," Tom said, swaggering across the veranda. "He's not gonna miss this action. We're gonna show that old Sitting Bull he's got no choice about reservation life."

"Hush, Tom," Maggie said softly, reaching for my hand. "The Seventh will march . . . and Autie will be here if he possibly can. But have a thought for those of us left behind."

"La," I said, forcing a light tone into my voice, "he's a typical bachelor and doesn't know to think about the women."

Indignant, Tom whirled on me. "I think about you both all the time, and you know it!"

I was taken aback by the force of his reply. "Of course you do, Tom . . . we're just all tense."

"It's because Autie's not here," Tom muttered. "The men are really up in arms. How can they keep him in Washington when no one else can lead the Seventh? Wouldn't surprise me if the men mutinied."

Deep down I knew there was no way that Autie would miss the march. He would by hook or crook arrive in time— it was another of my premonitions, as strong as the one that saw me crossing the Missouri alone. I wanted to pray that the Senate or the President or someone might detain him in Washington past the mid-May marching date, but that struck me as an unworthy use of prayer. And if my prayer had been answered? What would Autie have done for another long summer?

On May 1 Autie was released to return to Lincoln. He tried once more to see the President as a courtesy before he left the city but was not granted an audience and left immediately for Monroe. A telegram awaiting him there ordered him back to Washington to see the President—Grant, who had refused him an audience! Telegrams flew between Autie, Phil Sheridan, and General Sherman until at last Autie was allowed to proceed to Lincoln but was ordered *not* to accompany the expedition. Grant was extracting his revenge for Autie's Democratic sympathies and his participation, even against his will, in the Senate investigation. Had I been in Washington, I think I might have stormed the White House to protest this unfair treatment.

The news that Grant would not let Autie accompany the expedition filtered back to the post, where men gathered in knots to mutter and grumble. Maggie and I sat on the veranda, our nerves drawn tight by the tension around us. The very evening air seemed to crackle with anger.

"They won't stand for this," Tom said, having made a tour of the post. "The men need Autie."

Trembling, I asked, "Will you go without Autie?"

"If I'm ordered, I suppose," he answered, "but the very heart will be gone out of the campaign."

"A doomed campaign?" I asked.

"Don't even say that, old lady," Tom said fiercely. "Autie will be here, and we'll be victorious."

I knew better.

I had two days with Autie between his arrival from Washington and his departure for the Little Bighorn.

He returned to Lincoln on May 14. A series of appeals from both Autie and General Terry had succeeded to the extent that Autie was to march with the Seventh, but he was to take his orders from General Alfred Terry, who was in charge of the three-pronged Yellowstone expedition.

Colonel John Gibbon had marched from Fort Ellis on March 30, headed for the Little Bighorn. General George Crook left Fort Fetterman on May 29. Autie was to leave Fort Lincoln on May 16 with 600 men. Among them would be Captain Frederick Benteen, with a battalion of 125 men, and Major Marcus Reno, with 112 men—both officers had been critical of Autie, though I had always thought they were jealous of his successes. They would also be the ones who failed to support him in battle when he needed them, but that is an old story, known to all who study history.

"A toast," Jimmi Calhoun shouted, raising a glass high. "A toast to General George Amstrong Custer, the best damned Indian fighter in the cavalry!"

"Hear! Hear!" came the chorus around the table. I looked at these familiar and loved faces—Jimmi and Maggie sitting close together and holding hands under the table, Tom, looking flushed and triumphant, Autie's youngest brother, Bos, filled with excitement at the prospect of his first campaign, and young Autie, the son of Autie's sister, who had come to Lincoln because his uncle had promised to let him join the campaign.

"No fighting," he'd warned, "but plenty of excitement." When Emma asked if it was safe for her sixteen-year-old son to march on the campaign, Autie had expansively assured her that he himself would guarantee the boy's safety. "Besides," he added with a scoff, "half the Union army was younger than that during the war. You've got to let him grow up, Emma."

Now as Mary served our meal of beef with potatoes and turnips, great hunks of bread, and a pudding made with wild plums, Tom raised his glass for a second toast.

"To Autie," he said solemnly, "with our pledge to be beside him throughout the campaign."

"Hear, hear!" came the echo, as Jimmi, Bos, and young Autie took up the pledge.

I nearly had to leave the room and just barely managed to stave off tears by biting my lip so hard that it brought blood.

"Libbie? You are more solemn than usual. Surely you're not worried about this campaign?" Autie was at an emotional peak, so filled with anticipation that he could not bear my silence.

"I'm always worried about campaigns, Autie," I said softly.

"Custer's Luck, Libbie. Never forget that. Custer's Luck will bring us through."

I stared at him, aware that he really believed in his luck, believed that he, beyond other men, was favored by the gods, protected by them. There was nothing I could say or do. "Of course, Autie. I know."

In those two days Autie reminded me of the young Civil War general I'd married. We were together every minute, roaming the limits of the post on foot, Autie talking in bold, expansive terms of the future while I collected wildflowers and savored each moment of the present. Once we spread a blanket on the crest of the slope behind the post, and Autie napped briefly while I fanned away a stray fly or two and watched him intently. Another time we rode beyond the sentinels on horseback.

"You're not alarmed to be off the post?" he asked solicitously.

"No, Autie. I'm with you. You know, Custer's Luck."

Autie beamed and spurred his horse ahead, shouting a challenge to me, which I readily answered. For just a moment there, riding hell-bent for nowhere across the Nebraska plains, we were free and safe and I was young and happy. But too soon Autie reined in, laughing. "You're still the best horsewoman I know, Libbie. Once we show old Sitting Bull, I'll send for you and we'll have a grand summer, riding across new lands we've never seen."

"It sounds wonderful, Autie." Did my voice sound wooden only to my own ears, or did Autie hear it?

For two evenings officers and their families gathered on our veranda. There was among the men an almost feverish excitement, not only because they were going after Sitting Bull but because they had, they thought, triumphed through Autie's return. They boasted and laughed and joked like schoolboys going off on a canoe trip up the Hudson.

By contrast the women were quiet, already summoning an inner strength to see them through the days ahead. We would waste no energy with laughter, saw nothing to laugh about, and yet were constrained to match the men's moods. The result was a false gaiety that too often verged on tears. Maggie Calhoun once fled the scene, but it was only minutes before Jimmi detached himself unobtrusively from the men and followed her. Autie was so much the center of attention that I doubted he would notice if I fled, and yet I saw him, from time to time, look directly at me, his blue eyes piercing through my soul.

"Libbie is tired," he announced the second night. At a signal the crowd departed, all for their own quarters . . . and their own farewells.

We were new lovers again, exploring each other's bodies, slowly letting our desire build to a pitch, then resting, playing, caressing, only to rise again to new heights. By dawn we had not yet slept, and I felt drained, yet temporarily shed of my fears.

"Libbie, Libbie," he said softly, "you are more than I ever deserved or hoped for. I have always loved you, but never more than at this moment."

"And I you, Autie," I said, and meant it.

Maggie and I were to join the column for the first day's march, and on May 16 we rode through the fort at the head of the troops, Autie and Jimmi just in front of us. Behind us stretched the pack mules, the cavalry, artillery, and infantry, an endless line of wagons, the Indian scouts, and the men and women who cooked and cared for the troops. There were, so Autie boasted happily, about twelve hundred men and seventeen hundred animals. It would, I thought, take all day to get the column out of the post.

We passed through the Indian quarters, where the squaws and old men sang in that minor key that has always followed warriors off to battle, an eerie sound to my ears, especially accompanied by the monotonous tone of the drums that the scouts themselves beat as they marched. Then came Laundress Row, where wives and children of the enlisted men lined the road—women with tears streaming down their faces wailed out farewells and held forth tiny youngsters for one last glimpse. A group of children, unnoticed in the melee, had formed a column of their own. With handkerchiefs tied to sticks for flags and old tin pans for drums, they marched back and forth in imitation of their fathers. Then we moved on toward the garrison, where the officers' wives stood, sad-faced yet courageous, smiling bravely. When the band struck up "The Girl I Left Behind," it nearly undid all of us.

We had broken camp before the sun was up, and a mist enveloped everything. By the time we passed through the officers' quarters and out toward the plains, the sun began to break the mist. But the mist clinging to the earth created a frightening mirage that took up about half the line of cavalry, so that for some little distance they seemed to march equally between the earth and the sky. Two officers' wives, unable to restrain themselves, burst into loud wails on seeing this. At the head of the column, I was unaware of the eerie sight, but later when it was described to me, I shuddered.

Autie was at his best, riding back to chat with his men, then dashing to the front of the column again. "Do you see how they look, Libbie? Fine men, brave and brawny. This shall be a campaign to put all others to shame!"

Turning in his saddle to survey the men behind him, he said, "See, Libbie, how the sun catches the steel of their arms and turns it to flashes of light?" And at every turn in the road, he urged me to look back and admire the men of the Seventh. I did so, obediently, hiding the great lump in my throat and murmuring appropriate appreciations for the wonder of Autie's army.

We camped by a small stream that night, just a few miles beyond the post. Autie ordered the men paid, so that they could settle their debts with the sutler, and he ordered one round of whiskey for each man. Our tent was apart from the others, and we sat alone, watching the evening creep across the sky. Many times we had sat together under a tent flap, usually accompanied by Tom and other officers. Tonight they had left us alone.

"I'll send for you," Autie repeated. "Soon as it's safe, when we've reached the Yellowstone. It's magnificent country."

"I'll be waiting," I assured him.

We were not lovers that night. Autie held me in his arms, stroking my hair, as I sobbed gently against his breast. I had tried so hard, so long, and now, at the last hour, I could no longer hold back my fear and my grief.

"Libbie, why do you cry?"

"Oh, Autie, it's just my usual summer-campaign fears," I lied. "I'll be fine once you're gone."

"Trying to get rid of me?" he asked with a forced chuckle.

"No, never," I answered intently.

"Remember Custer's Luck," he said, and later that next

day we parted on that note, repeating the words to each other.

I can see him yet to this day, his hand raised as he signaled his men into the march, his eyes directed toward me, his lips forming those damned words about luck.

The rest of May and most of June dragged at Fort Lincoln. I was not the only wife more fearful than usual, though we each played games to hide our fear from the others. We made quilts, sewed shirts for our men even while thinking it useless, played with the children, reminisced about our lives back home, and made bold plans for the future—and we cried ourselves to sleep alone each night.

Three letters came from Autie during that time, each strong with optimism. "We expect no more than five hundred hostiles," he wrote in the first letter, "and we shall easily convince them of the error of their ways." The second lamented that it was "well into June, and we have seen no sign yet. The scouts say Sitting Bull will camp on the Little Bighorn." The third letter brought alarm, reporting that General Crook had met a large force of Sioux, undiscovered by his scouts, on the Rosebud River and had retreated in defeat. "We shall set things right with the Sioux," Autie wrote in his bold, flourishing hand. And then there were no more letters.

"Sing us a hymn, Maggie," I said one Sunday, trying desperately to lift the gloom that had settled over us. Some six or seven women were gathered in my parlor, each more grief-stricken than the next. Maggie, who played the piano better than I, would raise us out of our sadness, I thought.

She played "Nearer My God to Thee," followed by "Just As I Am Without One Plea," and a string of other familiar hymns. We sang and we prayed, but with little hope.

By the first of July the Indians on the post were whispering among themselves. "They talk of a great battle," Mary reported to me.

Maggie and I sat in my parlor for three days, every now and then going to the window to stare out, as though by looking, we could change things. The Indian police, lounging in front of the sutler's, did not look as chastened as I thought they should if the battle had gone to the soldiers, but neither did they look victorious. Looking for signs, I decided, was a futile and exhausting exercise.

"Libbie? What will you do . . . ?"

"If they don't come back?" I asked. "Don't even think that, Maggie," I said, denying that the thought had been in my own mind for months. "They *will* come back!"

"Libbie," she said steadily, "you know that's not true."

"I have to believe in Custer's Luck," I told her fiercely.

"Sometimes I think Calhoun's luck would have been better if he'd not linked up with Autie," she said softly. "But I guess we can't untangle that web of what should have been and what is."

"Jimmi was glad to serve with Autie . . . and fortunate, too," I said sharply. "He *is* your brother," I reminded her.

"And a great war hero," she said wearily. "I know, I know."

The whistle of the *Far West* sounded late on the evening of July 5, as she approached the landing at Bismarck. The women gathered at my house to wring their hands and wait.

"Surely they could send a messenger," said one.

"What could they be doing all this time at Bismarck?" asked another.

"Hush, sisters," Maggie said. "We shall hear soon enough." And she led us in prayer, though the voices that responded to hers were weak and faint.

I served tea and biscuits, which went untouched, and even thought of borrowing a bit of spirits from one of the wives who, I knew, kept such.

No one even tried to sew, all warnings about the devil and idle hands seeming too far behind us now, and few attempted conversation. We sat, in silence, watching the tall-case clock tick toward midnight and chime away the quarter hours.

"I must take the children home," Annie Yates said distractedly, even though her children slept peacefully enough

on my bed. "It is near midnight, and we must all try to
sleep."

Murmurs of agreement went around the room, and one
by one the women left me, always with a hug and a sob, until
Maggie and I were alone.

"Libbie? Shall I stay?"

"Oh, yes, Maggie. Let us be together."

And so, at three in the morning, we were still dressed,
lying wide-eyed and tense, when the knock came at the door.

"Mrs. Custer? I'm Captain William McCaskey of the
Twentieth Infantry. This is Post Surgeon Dr. Middleton and
Lieutenant Gurley. I'm afraid . . . we have some bad news
for you."

Behind me I heard Maggie gasp, but to my surprise my
own tone remained fairly steady as I said, "I've been expecting you. Please come in."

Lieutenant Gurley put an arm around Maggie, who
seemed about to faint, and I gestured toward a chair for the
others. The news was, of course, worse than we could ever
have expected. I had imagined, even prepared myself, for
Autie's death . . . but to lose everyone!

"Mr. Calhoun?" Maggie whispered, and collapsed in
tears when McCaskey said, "There were no survivors. They
were all killed."

"Tom Custer?" I asked, unable to believe his words.

A grim shake of the head.

"And Bos? And young Autie Reed? He was just a boy."

"They were all killed, Mrs. Custer," McCaskey repeated
gently.

"Poor Father Custer," I moaned. "All his boys, in one
blow." Then I turned to hug Maggie, for she had lost not
only her husband but all her brothers.

"Mrs. Custer? Will you come with me? I have other
wives to call upon."

"Of course," I said, numbly reaching for a wrap. Autie
would expect no less of me, and I would go to each of these
new widows, console them, hug them, and pray for them to
be brave. But inside, one thought raced through my mind: I
want to die *soon* to join Autie!

Lieutenant Gurley stayed behind with Maggie, who was too distraught to be left alone. But as we walked down the veranda steps, she came to the door and cried pitifully, "Did Jimmi send me a message?"

McCaskey turned toward her, his face solemn, his voice gentle. "They left no messages, ma'am."

Epilogue

> *Grow old along with me!*
> *The best is yet to be,*
> *The last of life, for which the first was made*
>
> —*Robert Browning,*
> *"Rabbi Ben Ezra"*

THE WORDS MOCK ME. I NEVER REALLY HAD A VISION OF GROWING old alongside Autie. Oh, when I was young, I thought nothing could part us. But I remember the time he watched an old lady on the streets of New York and then teasingly wondered aloud how I would look when I was old. When I turned the question on him, he replied that he would never grow old. It came to be something we both believed.

It has been fifty-six years since the battle—the Custer massacre some called it at first, though I was never sure if it was because Autie was massacred or because they were assigning him the blame for it. In these long years I've seen

Autie's reputation come and go, sometimes a hero, sometimes a spoiled, petulant, self-centered glory-seeker. And I've never said what I know to be true—that he was all those things.

Oh, at first everybody blamed Autie for that tragic day at the Little Bighorn. Crook and Terry got together and accused him of disobeying orders, attacking in a foolhardy manner, rushing in where he should have been cautious and studied. He was, they said, desperate to wipe out the humiliation President Grant had dealt him. But Autie was never humiliated by Grant's strange treatment that last spring in Washington; he was only puzzled. Crook and Terry were desperate not to be blamed, and Autie, being dead and silent, was an easy scapegoat. It made me furious, for they knew as well as I that whatever else Autie was, he was a great cavalryman and a great leader of men. After Bighorn there was no one left who knew how to fight the Indians.

The people knew, people who loved Autie and saw him as a hero. They raised money for his family, they put up statues in his honor and painted thousands of pictures of the battle—most of them atrocities—and they showered me with love, for the sake of the man I'd been married to. Autie had captured their imaginations in the Civil War, and he stayed larger than life in the public eye. Newspapermen loved to write about him, and magazine editors loved to use his own writing. In death Autie went from fame to legend . . . and I saw to it that the legend lived.

My life's work has been to defend and glorify Autie, and I admit that I have written of only one side of him and of our marriage. The dark side of Autie remains my secret, while the larger-than-life Autie has always been my subject.

Why did Autie die? In all that I've written and said, I have held my opinion. But I believe he died because Custer's Luck ran out . . . and because Benteen and Reno failed him, though they, too, were quick to accuse the dead. And because no one—not Crook, not Terry, not even Little Phil Sheridan—listened to Autie when he explained how desperate the Sioux were. Yes, I blame Autie's death on all those others . . . but I know that Autie was sometimes foolhardy and that he trusted too much in his luck . . . and that he never intended to grow old.

What, I have wondered, would my life have been like if Autie and I had grown old together? In a strange way, independence has forced me to grow. I went as a girl from my father's house to Autie's arms, never knowing I could take care of myself. Now I've had fifty-six years to take care of myself, and I've done things that I never would have done if I'd spent my life as Autie's wife. I've become a person in my own right, proud of my accomplishments and the recognition I've earned.

I never knew I could write, though I was always Autie's sounding board. Once General Sherman told Autie that he wrote so well, many people believed I did his writing for him and let Autie take the credit. Autie responded, "Then I should get credit for my selection of a wife." In truth, Autie's writing lacked discipline, as he filled page after page with his rapid handwriting. My writing is slow, careful, and deliberate. But I would never have written three books had Autie lived.

Who knows? There might have been other Monah-setahs. Autie and I might easily have lost the magic between us, even come to hate each other, for when love so strong sours, it can be nothing less intense than hate. Sometimes, secretly, I have thought it fitting and right that Autie died young, even though I have railed against his fate . . . and mine.

Many asked why I did not marry again. The truth is that I met no one I wanted to marry. I would rather have been married to Autie for twelve years than to most ordinary men for six times twelve years. But I would not trade my own life of late for those twelve years. I would not, could not, go back to being the person I was. I have come too far, grown too much, to let myself ever again be swept from a horse's back, or be called "old lady," or be fooled by an Indian woman with a red-haired baby.

But oh, how I have wished all these years for the joy of life with Autie.

About the Author

JUDY ALTER is director of Texas Christian University Press and a former president of the Western Writers of America. She has written novels, juvenile fiction, short stories, and articles. In 1984 her book *Luke and the Van Zandt County War* was named best juvenile novel of the year by the Texas Institute of Letters. In 1988 she received a Spur Award from the Western Writers of America for her novel *Mattie,* and in 1992 a Western Heritage Award from the National Cowboy Hall of Fame for her short story, "Fool Girl." Judy Alter lives and works in Fort Worth, Texas.

In her next novel, award-winning author Judy Alter brings another of the great women of the American west vividly to life in . . .

Strong, impulsive, and as daring as any man in her day, Jessie Benton was her father's daughter, and never so much as when she defied him. At seventeen, against Senator Thomas Hart Benton's express wishes, she eloped with the handsome young explorer John Charles Frémont, leaving behind the whirlwind of Washington society and politics she learned to love at the Senator's knee. Awaiting Jessie was a life unimagined, a boundless adventure that would take her from fever-ridden Panama to the San Francisco gold rush, and from the salons of European royalty to the wilds of the Arizona desert. *Jessie* is a story that thrills the imagination and tugs at the heartstrings, the unforgettable tale of a courageous woman caught between two men who would alter the course of American history—but only with her help.

Here is a sneak preview of *Jessie*, on sale in May 1995, wherever Bantam Books are sold.

That fall Father began to talk excitedly of the explorations of Joseph Nicolas Nicollet, a French explorer who had surveyed the upper Mississippi and then the upper Missouri and who was now preparing a huge map of his findings.

"The high plains are grasslands, not that Great American Desert the army keeps reporting. Nicollet has a bright young assistant—chap named Frémont—and I've been talking to him. He's as excited about all this as I am. We're going to get that expedition together, one way or another."

A flash of jealousy went through me. I wanted Father to talk to me, not some young man with a French name. "It sounds exciting, Father," was all I said.

Liza, being in her last year of formal schooling, was allowed to spend more weekends at home than I—the irony was not lost on me that she, who loved the school, was there less often than I, who loathed it—but from both her and Father, on his regular visits to me at school, I began to hear more about this Frémont person. He apparently had become a frequent visitor at our home, and Liza was quite taken with him.

I met him only once that fall, when Father brought him to a school concert where Liza was playing. Father introduced him with some pride as "that young explorer I told you about. He's going to map the road to Oregon."

John Charles Frémont had two things in common with the awful Count Bodisco. He was short and he was older, though not by as many as forty years. In fact, he was eleven years older than I and not much taller. I thought him no more than sixty-four inches at best. But after that first moment I never again thought of John's height or lack of it, because he had a certain self-possession that made him loom as tall as Father in my mind. He was tanned, with the look of a man who shared Father's passion for the outdoors—he had, after all, recently returned from a topographical expedition to the West—and he had deep-blue eyes that seemed to look right through me when he took my hand and bowed gallantly over it.

"Jessie, I've been looking forward to meeting you. Your father speaks highly of your capabilities."

Blushing, I thanked him and told him that Father spoke equally highly of him.

"We must be wonderful people," he said, smiling.

I wish I could say that something about John Charles Frémont, some romantic instinct, struck me at that first meeting, that I was forever after in love with him—stories since have woven such a romantic web about our first meeting. But it is not the truth. I thought him charming—perhaps a bit too charming—and I thought him extremely patient to flatter Father so by coming to his daughter's musicale.

But what struck me most was that outdoors quality he possessed, the self-assurance of a man who enjoyed the outdoors and would never be confined in a parlor. I had grown up under the tutelage of a man who was convinced that the healthy outdoor life had saved him from the consumption that had killed his brothers, and I naturally looked askance at any man content to sit indoors.

And when Frémont spoke of the lands he had seen—surely just the edge of the American West—his eyes glowed with excitement. "We saw land no white man yet has seen," he told me with fire, "not even Lewis and Clark. And there is more, much more land to be discovered. *I* want to find it."

I was not my father's daughter for nothing. I admired the passion, the determination, though it was admittedly self-serving. John Charles Frémont, I sensed, did not necessarily want to discover the West for the good of the United States —he wanted it for his own greater glory, and all the better that it served his country. Who could blame him?

We sat through Liza's piano playing, technically proficient but spiritually lacking. I looked at Frémont from time to time to see if he noticed but could detect no sign. He was attentive and properly polite, his eyes intent, his body perfectly still, while I had a bad case of the fidgets.

The interminable musicale ended, and Father and Mr. Frémont stayed only long enough to be polite, flattering Liza about her performance. Then they were gone, and we were back in the schoolgirl routine.

I thought no more about the lieutenant. He went back to his maps, and I to my endurance of school. The Christmas holidays—and the end of the term—were fast approaching, and my whole attention was focused on persuading Father that I had had enough of school.

"Father, I've brought your coffee." It was early in the morning—before six A.M.—the hour when I knew Father began his day. For years, as a child, I'd met him in his library at that hour, and now I knew it was the time he would be most driven by sentiment, most susceptible to my pleas.

He was already at work at his desk, the early-morning dark broken by the light of the candelabrum he had invented —four spermaceti candles fixed in front of a large white blotting paper, which reflected their light. Father was so intent on what he was writing that I had to knock gently before he looked up.

"Jessie!" His face brightened with pleasure. "I do miss you when you're away. Pour me some of that fine coffee you're carrying."

It was coffee liberally dosed with chicory, a taste he'd long ago acquired from Mother. I poured it, still steaming, into a huge cup and handed it to him.

"You have not told me about your work for some time, Father," I said.

The smile on his face bespoke his pleasure in sharing his work with me, though the news was almost grim. "It's a trying time for this country, Jessie. The slavery issue has not been laid to rest"—South Carolina had threatened some nine years earlier to withdraw from the union if slavery was made an issue—"and I foresee it breaking this country apart."

"Missouri is a slave state," I murmured. "You could own slaves yourself, if you'd a mind."

"I've no mind for that," he said vehemently. "When we preach democracy, we must put it into action. No man should own another man."

Amen, I silently agreed.

"But we move ahead on other issues," he continued, "the things that Jackson and I worked for—education for everyone, the abolishment of the poll tax—all those things have come to pass. We will make this a country for all people, not just the rich."

"And the American West?" I asked. Unbidden, Lieutenant Frémont leaped into my mind, though neither Father nor I had mentioned him. Suddenly, though, I could see that handsome, rugged explorer's face before my eyes with such clarity that it startled me.

"We're still working on the next expedition," Father said. "Nicollet wants to lead it, though I'm not certain his health is good enough. You'll see Frémont again while you're home for the holidays. He is here often."

Of course, I recalled that both Father and Liza had mentioned that Frémont was often at the family dinner table. Liza's interest in him was, to say the least, far removed from Father's.

"I think," my plain sister had said hesitantly, "that he may be . . . well, you know. . . ."

"No, Liza, I don't know," I'd replied impatiently.

"Oh, Jessie!" she said in exasperation, and never did tell me what it was that I didn't know. I guessed, of course, that she hoped Lieutenant Frémont was interested in her. Even more, I supposed, she was most interested in him. Instinctively I knew that Liza was the wrong person for this explorer —she had not the sense of daring to match his. Besides, she was much taller than he.

When at last my opportunity came, I lived up to Father's critical assessment of me as Don Quixote. Rather than working tactfully toward the moment, I leaped in with both feet, unfortunately, in my mouth.

Father's reaction should have been no surprise to me. "Leave the school? Of course you can't. Liza will finish her work this spring, and that leaves you another year. Absolutely not!"

Desperately I said, "Father, didn't you tell me part of the reason I had to go off to school was so that I would not entertain . . . ah, unsuitable suitors? Like Harriet Wilson did."

"The Bodisco marriage," he said loftily, "is quite a satisfactory one, I understand. Both parties are happy, and there is a blessed event expected."

That bit of news shook me just a little, reviving my uncertainties about Harriet's marriage. Obviously, if a blessed event was expected, the marriage had been consummated. The thought gave me a momentary shudder.

"That is beside the point," I said. "If Count Bodisco had courted me, you'd have been livid with anger."

He nodded his head warily, knowing he could do nothing but agree with me and yet not sure what trap I was leading him into.

"The point is, Father, he did not court me. And no one else has. I will be perfectly safe . . . and virtuous . . . here at home with you and Mother. And I do not need the studies at Miss English's."

"And what," he asked, "makes you think you don't need them?"

"Well, I've been correcting the French teacher all fall—oh, don't worry, I've been tactful. And once when I asked about studying the things that are important today—the issues that absorb your attention, like slavery and westward expansion—I was told that it was more fitting for us to study the ancient Greeks and Romans. Fiddle!"

I'd been calculating when I pointed out that a classical education had little to do with what Father thought was important, and I saw him start a little when I said that, as though my arrow had hit home. I followed with the final barb.

"I'm tired of learning to pour tea. I've known how to do that since I can remember."

He smiled ruefully. "You can pour a fine cup of coffee, I'll speak to that."

Boldly, I pushed my case. "And you'll speak to my leaving school?"

He was not to be caught so easily. "No, miss, I will not. School is your mother's fondest wish for you, and her word is law with me."

"May I tell her you will accept if she will?"

"No," he said, his firmness returning, "you may not even go that far. Now, pick up that quill and let me dictate this speech to you. It goes better that way than if I try to write it myself." He shuffled the papers on his desk, as though frustrated by them, and I obediently took a sheet of foolscap and sat with my pen poised.

I had not given up hope.

Perhaps it was cheating, even outright dishonesty—the thought has long worried me since—but I caught Mother on a day when she felt too weak to argue, too weak for disagreement. Her state also made her sensible of the advantages of having me home to be Father's companion.

"If you are insistent," she said, waving a thin arm in the air as though disassociating herself from the question.

"May I tell Father that I have your permission?"

"Yes, yes, you may tell him. Jessie, what is to become of you?" Then she put a hand to her head and said faintly, "I'll worry about it later. Would you bring me some tea, please?"

"Of course, Mother." I nearly flew on wings to the kitchen to get the tea.

Within days notice was sent to Miss English that I would not be returning and that a family servant would call for my belongings.

"You got your way, didn't you?" Liza asked angrily.

"You don't have to go back either," I said, "but you want to."

"Yes," she said, "I do. And I'll make a better marriage than you because I've finished at Miss English's."

I wanted to laugh aloud and point out to her that marriage or the prospect of it had nothing to do with my leaving the school. But Liza never understood my relationship with Father, and it was too late to try to tell her.

Lieutenant Frémont was at our house two or three times during the holiday, and I had several conversations with him —conversations that I thought he deliberately sought.

"It is a pleasure to see you here, Jessie," he said, bowing once again over my hand in his courtly manner. "I'm told the house lacks a certain sparkle when you're not present."

I hoped my laugh did not sound as self-conscious as I felt when I said, "Nonsense. Father may sometimes lack for a hostess, but . . ."

"One who understands the issues of which we men talk," he said smoothly, his eyes never leaving mine.

My gaze locked into those eyes, and I replied, "I am as interested in the progress of this nation as my Father is . . . and as dedicated to certain causes."

"The exploration of the West?" Was he laughing at me?

"Yes, of course," I replied hastily.

"Jessie!" Father's voice boomed out. "Don't be monopolizing Mr. Frémont's time. There are several people here tonight I want him to meet."

Father had gathered six or eight politicians—most of them men of significant influence in the government—for an evening around the fireplace. We had given them a sumptuous meal—gallantine of turkey, creamed oysters on toast, lima beans, watermelon pickles (carried by coach all the way from Cherry Grove), and a whiskey bread pudding. Now they were enjoying after-dinner glasses of port, the entire company gathered around the fireplace in the upstairs parlor.

Lieutenant Frémont had stopped me in the hallway outside the parlor, and it was evident that we were having a conversation tête-à-tête rather than joining the group.

"I am sorry, Father," I said with all the brightness I could muster. "Lieutenant Frémont has been talking to me of exploration . . . a favorite subject of mine," I added with a droll note in my voice.

"Of course," Father boomed, though his voice, I thought, lacked its usual heartiness.

The conversation that evening was not on such earthshaking matters as slavery or westward expansion but revolved around the forthcoming inauguration of Mr. William Henry Harrison. "He is a farmer," said one, while another countered, "So have been many of our presidents. And this one has been in the Congress."

"And a governor and minister to . . . what country was that?"

The discussion of Mr. Harrison's qualifications rolled around my head, while I sat and—unobtrusively, I hoped—watched Lieutenant Frémont. Every few minutes I would catch him flashing me a look that hinted at some shared secret . . . and somehow that look went right to the bone.

"I see," Liza said indignantly as we prepared for sleep that night, "that you are much taken with John Frémont."

"I only talked to him briefly," I protested. "I don't know if I am taken with him or not. Are you?"

"Of course not," she said indignantly, flouncing away from me.

Ah, Liza, I thought, *you are, and you don't know what to do about it. And I don't know what to tell you.*

It was far easier for me to analyze Liza's reactions to the handsome explorer than my own. I found, after that fateful night, that his face appeared to me at odd hours during the day and, sometimes, during restless and wakeful nights. I was not certain why he intrigued me, except that somehow, deep down, I felt we shared a sense of mission—the mission of westward expansion that Father had given to me before I was old enough to realize it. *Destiny,* I thought, *has brought this man into my life.*

Destiny, of course, did not translate into love, and with the examples of my parents and Harriet Wilson Bodisco before me, I was very much concerned about love, trying to puzzle out for myself—with absolutely no confidants—what it was, how I would recognize it.

Meantime, I tried to remain calm and collected when the lieutenant was in the midst of our family circle, which he often was after Liza returned to school and I stayed behind. I succeeded in being poised about half the time, or so it seemed to me.

"Aren't you the calm one?" he said with a laugh one night, again catching me in the hallway outside the parlor. "What would you say if I told you I've determined to marry you?" Those blue eyes were fixed on mine with a penetration so strong as to be mesmerizing.

"I would say you are being impertinent," I replied, my light tone hiding the rapid beating of my heart. "Come, the others are waiting for us."

Our hallway conversations grew more frequent—always brief, usually light—except when he made comments about marrying me, which he did occasionally—and always deliberately. I began to anticipate them with pleasure, and I kept seeing his face before me at odd moments. I was glad Liza was away at school.

Of course, the night came when he kissed me. The party had preceded us upstairs, and as I turned to mount the stairs, he laid a restraining hand on my arm.

"Jessie? A moment, please."

"Yes?" That pounding heart again. I was sure the breast of my woolen shirtwaist must be vibrating strongly enough to betray me as I turned toward him.

"I must tell you," he said seriously, "that I am in love with you. My comment about marrying you . . . it was not frivolous. I . . . I knew from the first moment that you would be special in my life. You had . . . the effect of a rare picture, that quality of sense and feeling and beauty."

Too taken aback to say anything, I simply stared at him. And he, with no hesitation, moved his mouth toward mine. It was a gentle, sweet kiss, one full of promise but strangely lacking in passion, if I could even have recognized passion at that point in my life. Still, I felt a burning on my lips long after he had taken his away.

"We . . . we must join the others," I said, more flustered than I could ever recall being.

"Yes, of course," was his smooth reply. To my further discomfort he looked greatly amused.

If John's kiss was inevitable, so was Father's anger. The anti-John campaign, however, began slowly enough.

"Jessie," Father said one morning when I joined him early, as was once again my habit, "you've been showing partiality to Lieutenant Frémont lately. I . . . well, girl, I don't think it looks proper."

"There is nothing improper about it, Father. We are always with your guests."

"Yes, yes," he said as he fiddled uncomfortably with the inkwell on his desk, "but you are also too often off by yourselves. Even James Buchanan commented on it the other night."

"Mr. Buchanan," I said archly, "needs a wife to keep him from meddling in other people's affairs."

In most circumstances Father would have laughed at my boldness, but he was too distressed this time to see any humor. "That," he said, "is not the function of wives."

"What is?" I countered.

"Promoting their husbands' careers," he said, with no hesitation.

I wanted to ask how Mother rated, then, but kept my quiet instead. The conversation had wandered from Father's initial concern, and I was willing to let him lead it where he would. He led it right back to Lieutenant Frémont.

"I wish you to pay less attention to him. I do not want Lieutenant Frémont courting you."

"He isn't courting me!" I replied quickly, though I could feel a blush giving away my own suspicion that he was, indeed, courting. "Besides, you think he shows a great deal of promise. You're ready to turn the next major expedition over to him if Monsieur Nicollet is unable to lead it."

"Giving him an expedition and giving him my daughter are two different things," Father said dryly. "He is an army man, with no family background that we know of, no money to speak of, and very few prospects for the kind of future I expect for you."

Something inside me stiffened at Father's words. He didn't know it, but *mon père* had just strengthened the lieutenant's case.

Without waiting for me to reply, he said, "I never issue orders to you, Jessie, and I hesitate to do so now. But I wish you to pay less attention to Frémont. He'll still get his expedition."

"Of course, Father," I said, though my heart was rebellious. What, I wanted to ask, about the order to go to Miss English's? That question, however, was not politic and could well have landed me back at the dreaded seminary. I realized I must tread carefully.

I couldn't have avoided John Frémont if I had wanted to, although clearly I didn't want to. At Father's gatherings he continued to seek me out, showing a rare talent for finding me away from the crowd—lingering to give the maid a suggestion about brandies, pausing to check my hair in the mirror before following the crowd to the upstairs parlor. My attitude stiffened a little in spite of myself, because I knew Father was watching like a hawk.

Once when Father saw me talking to John, he beckoned across the room, motioning me toward him.

"Excuse me. My father apparently needs me," I said, leaving John with a studied look on his face, as though he were puzzling out the situation.

"Yes, Father?" I asked, my voice indicating, I hoped, that whatever the ostensible cause of the interruption, I knew what lay behind it.

"Your mother needs you, I think, Jessie. She's had a difficult day."

"Of course," I said obediently, and left for Mother's room, where I found her sitting in a chair knitting, looking stronger than she had for days.

"Father said you sent for me?"

A slightly puzzled look crossed her face, but then she quickly said, "Yes, dear, I did. I . . . well, I wanted some company."

Mother rarely chose my company. Liza's ways were more soothing to her, and she hated listening to my ideas on politics and government. Such subjects were, in her view, beyond a woman's interests, which should be bound by her family.

"Mother," I said directly, "you have guessed that Father sent me up here to keep me from conversing with Lieutenant Frémont."

Her look said plainly that I had hit upon the truth. "We . . . we don't feel he is an appropriate match for you," she said, her belief in her own conviction giving her strength.

"I wasn't marrying him, Mother. I was merely talking to him." To myself I added, *But I may very well marry him, whether you and Father like it or not.*

John was gone by the time I returned to the parlor.

The next day a messenger delivered a handwritten note:

Have I offended you or your family? I would like to talk to you privately. If possible, meet me in front of Nicollet's studio at four o'clock this afternoon.

With utmost respect,
John Charles Frémont

The very secrecy of it thrilled me to the core. I felt a woman, no longer a girl. Of course I would meet him, if I had to lie to Father and sneak away from Mother to do it.

He was pacing the street when I arrived, deliberately a little late. "I thought you might not come," he said anxiously. "Can we walk a bit?"

"Of course."

He tucked my hand into his arm possessively, and I lacked the strength or will to remove it. For some minutes we walked in silence, while I burned impatiently to know what he wanted to say. Occasionally, when I glanced at him, I saw a faraway look in his eyes, as though he were plotting his next expedition. In a way, he was.

"I have noticed a difference in your father," he said at length. "He still professes interest in our maps and another expedition, but he is . . . well . . . less cordial. Have I offended him?"

As was my way, I took the direct approach. "Yes," I said, "you and I both have. He thinks we are too interested in each other."

He shook his head sadly. "I suspected as much. If I have offended you, Jessie . . ."

I whirled to face him, standing still to stare at him. "Oh, no, John"—it was the first time I had used his given name to his face, though I'd repeated it a thousand times in my mind —"you have . . . you have made me happy."

His face split into a grin. "I am so glad," he said. "You see, from the first night—the musicale at that awful women's school—I was captivated by you. I want to marry you, Jessie Benton."

With the feeling that events were moving too fast and that I was being carried along on a tide, I was speechless. But I was also thrilled. He was everything I wanted in a husband, and the thought that he had chosen me seemed so good that I was afraid I might wake from a dream any minute.

For a long minute we stood thus on a Washington street, staring at each other while passersby detoured around us with tolerant smiles, and then John put his arms around me and kissed me soundly, not the soft and gentle kiss he had earlier stolen in the house on C Street, but a strong, possessive kiss that sent a flutter coursing through my belly.

It was, of course, a shameful public display, and I pulled quickly away—well, almost.

"I am sorry," he said at once. "I had no right."

"It is all right," I said, taking his arm again, "but we best continue to walk."

Before my very eyes his elation turned to gloom. "There is the matter of your father," he said. "He does not think I am worthy."

"No," I protested, "that's not it. I . . . I am not certain what the problem is, though Father might never approve of any man I wanted to marry." It was only a small lie, I told myself, since in a way Father really did not think him worthy, and yet I could not bear to say that to this man whom I now loved with all my heart.

"You will continue to be welcome at our home," I told him. "I know Father that well. We shall simply have to pay less attention to each other."

"That," he said, grinning again, "is exactly the opposite of my intentions."

"Perhaps," I said boldly, "we could meet like this from time to time."

"Perhaps we could," he said.

And we did. We began a clandestine romance that was conducted all spring on the streets of the capital city. My arm securely clutched in John's, I wandered up one muddy street and down another. Of course, we met people who knew us— mostly who knew me—and, of course, the word got back to Father. But not until after the funeral for President Harrison, which was an amazing and wonderful day for me.

Poor Mr. Harrison, whose wife never wanted him in the White House anyway, died less than a month after his inauguration in March of 1841. The funeral procession was scheduled for April 4, and since it would not be easily visible from our house, John arranged to have the Benton family observe it from Mr. Nicollet's studio, which overlooked Pennsylvania Avenue and the approach to the Capitol. It was, he explained to Father, a courtesy to Mother, so that she could see the procession without exerting herself. Father had no graceful choice but to accept the invitation with pleasure, although he himself was an official mourner and would not join us. However, my Grandmother McDowell, who was visiting from Cherry Grove, would be with us.

April 4 was a cold, gray day, but John had built a fire in the fireplace and filled the studio with pots of geraniums—in honor of my mother and grandmother, he told everyone. A serving table was laden with cakes and delicacies, and comfortable chairs were drawn up to the windows for the ladies to view. John himself wore his dress uniform, "in reverence to Mr. Harrison," he explained. The workroom—and the worker—had been truly transformed.

Dimly, from the outside, we could hear the dirge and the tramp of horses, but inside all was cheerful. When the fire was roaring and his guests were settled with cakes and ices and their attention riveted on the parade in front of them, John drew me around the drape that sectioned off a portion of the workroom.

"Jessie," he said urgently, "I can wait no longer. Will you promise to marry me?"

"Yes, John, I will." There was no hesitation in my answer, and it was followed by another of those kisses that left me breathless and stumbling for words. I know that when we returned to the group, my face shone as red as the cherry ice John served, but all eyes were out the window and no one noticed.

Thus a funeral turned out to be the happiest day of my life to date. It was followed by disaster.

Father had always been somewhat suspicious of the funeral party, as I called it in my mind, but his suspicion turned to certainty when someone—or maybe several people—told of seeing John and me together on the street, more than once. Father, however, was a clever politician. He said nothing to me, and I had no inkling of disaster until John sent me another note.

Dearest Jessie,
I have been ordered on an immediate expedition. I must see you at once. Would Mrs. Crittendon lend us her parlor?

With adoration,
John

Maria Crittendon, the wife of a lawyer with whom Father was associated, had intuitively known of the romance John and I shared, and she, instead of frowning, had given her blessing—secretly, of course. Once she had caught me in a private moment and whispered, "I believe in romance. If I can help, let me know."

Now she could indeed help, but would she? Was it too bold a deed to ask of her?

Not at all, the lady assured me, and it was arranged that John and I would meet there at four o'clock the next afternoon.

"Papa Joe Nicollet is frantic," John told me, clutching my hand in his as we sat on the horsehair sofa in the Crittendon parlor. "He says he cannot complete the maps without me, and it is folly to send me off on a trumped-up expedition."

"Trumped up?" I echoed.

"He and I both believe that your father prevailed upon the secretary of war to organize this expedition, not for the national good, but to get me away from you."

"Mr. Poinsett would do that?" I asked incredulously.

"He is your father's good friend," John said. "The expedition is an opportunity for me—the chance to lead an expedition myself—but it still rankles."

"I shall miss you," I began tentatively.

"You best." He laughed. "And I hope you will wait for me. The expedition is neither dangerous nor long. I shall be back in Washington in six months."

Six months! I felt faint, but John grabbed my arm strongly. "If we love each other . . ."

"Yes," I whispered, "I will wait with happiness. *Le bons temps viendra.*"

"Yes, my darling," he whispered into my hair, "the good times are coming."